THE MEN OF
HALFWAY HOUSE
Series

A HUNTED Man

JAIME REESE

Published by Romandeavor, Inc.

(Kindle edition) ISBN: 978-0-9914570-4-5
(ePUB edition) ISBN: 978-0-9914570-5-2
(Paperback edition) ISBN: 978-0-9914570-6-9

First Edition, April 2014
Printed in the United States of America

Edited by Jae Ashley
Cover art and formatting by Reese Dante
Licensed material is being used for illustrative purposes only and any person
depicted in the licensed material is a model.

Para Mami.

If you were with me today, you'd simply say…

"I knew you could do it."

I miss you.

Trademark Acknowledgement

The author acknowledges the following trademarks for company names and/or products mentioned in this work of fiction:

Ferrari: Ferrari S.p.A.

Google Maps: Google, Inc.

Marine Corps: US Marine Corps, a component of the US Department of the Navy

Oscar: Academy of Motion Picture Arts and Sciences

Starbucks: Starbucks Corporation

Universal Studios: Universal City Studios LLC

Walmart: Wal-Mart Stores, Inc.

YouTube: Google, Inc.

Hope.
You can fear her,
ignore her,
resent her,
but she will never abandon you
when you need her most.

Chapter ONE

Cameron Pierce didn't really know what to expect when the entire nightmare began days before his eighteenth birthday, but here he was, standing behind a large metal door waiting for it to open and grant his freedom. Nine years, eight months, two weeks, and five days of hell. Even though he had to stay in a designated halfway house for the next few months, at least he wouldn't have these bars or barbed wire fences to constantly remind him of his nightmare.

He fidgeted. In exchange for almost ten years of his life, the prison system gave him a hundred bucks for expenses during transfer, and a plain, standard-issue cardboard box containing his personal items—a watch, ten bucks, and a pack of gum. Everything broken or useless, which pretty much mirrored his existence. He ditched the box and everything else then pocketed the cash.

The gears of the large metal door ground as they inched open. Cameron shifted his weight from foot to foot, waiting for just enough space to squeeze through the door. He looked over to the guard and concluded he'd be better off attempting to walk out of this prison with a little dignity. At the pace these doors opened, he figured he'd age another decade in the process. He closed his eyes and counted, begging for a little patience to come his way. He finally heard the grinding stop and opened his eyes.

There, in the middle of the empty parking lot, Sam leaned against a car with crossed arms and a smile.

Cameron groaned as he finally exited the prison gates.

Mr. Samuel Issacs, rehabilitation officer, also secretly campaigned for sainthood every chance he had. His job was to help a group of assigned inmates rejoin the world with others but his *mission* was to mentor them. Sam wanted to talk, help, and offer support. Cam, on the other hand, knew better than to open his mouth, and he damn sure wasn't going to risk Sam becoming some form of collateral damage.

Cam had learned that lesson the hard way.

"Hey, Sam," he said once he arrived where Sam was parked.

"Hey, Cam. I thought I'd give you a ride to the halfway house instead of having you take the bus," he said as he opened the passenger side door of the car.

Cameron waited, not sure if sitting in a car for hours with Saint Sam was a good idea.

"C'mon, Cam. I can guarantee you the drive with me will be better than a busload of people coming back from Universal Studios with stinky feet and a crapload of gas."

Cameron groaned.

Sam laughed. "Besides, I already filled out the paperwork so you're stuck with me. Get in."

Cam didn't say a word. He climbed into the car, sat in the passenger seat, and then closed the car door.

"Buckle up, it's the law."

"Are you kidding me?"

"Nope, state of Florida, it's the law."

"Since when?"

"Just strap in so we can get out of here."

Cameron groaned again as he pulled the belt and clicked it in place. He hated the way it cut into his damn shoulder. Who knew what else had changed while he was in prison. Just another reminder of things he had missed. He shifted in his seat only to have his movement limited by the seat belt restraint.

Wonderful.

Here he was, finally out of prison, yet somehow still found a way to be constrained in a small enclosed area. Hell, this was even smaller than the six-by-eight cell he'd called home for almost a decade.

How ironic.

* * * *

"Wake up, sleepyhead."

"Are we there yet?" Cameron mumbled as he tried to rub the sleep out of his eyes.

Sam chuckled. "Nope. We should be there in a few hours," he responded before switching off the car. "We're just taking a break right now, stretch our legs and grab something to eat really quick."

Cameron turned his head side to side to try to stretch his neck a bit then exited the car.

"How long have we been on the road?"

"A few hours," Sam responded as he came around the car to his side. "C'mon, I'm hungry," he added as he started to walk toward the rest stop entrance.

Cameron followed at a slower pace, still trying to wake up as he stretched his arms. When he walked into the building, he stopped. His senses were assaulted by the sounds of pounding music, loud people bumping into him from all sides, coffee machines hissing, the mix of smells coming from the different food vendors, and the voice through the speaker informing someone their order was ready. He screwed his eyes shut and lowered his head. He tried counting, hoping to calm his breathing. Prison wasn't quiet but at least he knew what to expect.

"Cam, you all right?" Sam asked.

Cameron looked over to him and noticed the worry crease between his eyes. "Yeah, it's just culture shock, I guess. I could have used a warning."

"Sorry, I didn't realize there would be so many people here. It's probably from that tour bus out there." Sam offered a comforting hand on Cam's shoulder. "Let's start with some food," he said, guiding him to the least busy food store farthest away from the gift shops.

After placing their orders, they sat in a quiet booth by the window in the corner. Cameron looked around, observing every detail, comparing the current with what he knew a decade ago. They had TV in prison that allowed him to keep up with the national news. He knew cell phones were smaller and cars were bigger. He knew Obama was president and that people wore those flashing blue light things in their ear for their phones. What he had lost was the instinctive knowledge of the world that was closer to him. New sauce bottles, photos on the wall he hadn't seen, these damn sippy cup things for coffee everyone had in their hand.

A pair of college-aged girls passed by, one smiled at him as she slowed her pace. He casually looked away as if he hadn't noticed. No sense playing a game he had no interest in winning.

"That's gonna happen you know," Sam commented with a smirk.

"What?"

"Girls showing an interest. They don't bite," Sam teased. "Well, unless you want them to," he added with a chuckle.

Sam didn't know. He wasn't sure how Sam would react, so he thought it best to stay quiet. It wasn't as if he shouted his sexual orientation from the top of C Block. That would have definitely garnered some unwanted attention.

"What's with the look?"

"Huh?" he finally said as if he weren't following the conversation at all.

"You're a horrible liar, Cam."

Cameron cringed. Sam could smell bullshit a mile away. Always did. That was why Cam avoided conversations at all cost regarding anything he wanted to keep to himself.

"So why didn't you ever tell me you were gay?" Sam asked unexpectedly.

Cameron froze. He'd managed to keep that quiet for years, but Sam figured it out as soon as the opposite sex circled like a bird of prey. He didn't know what to say so he shrugged as he looked down and played with his napkin.

"It's fine, you know."

Cameron looked up. "It doesn't bother you?"

"Why would it?"

"I don't know. I just figured it might."

Sam laughed.

"What's so funny?"

"I guess I just forgot to tell you. I didn't think it would matter."

"What?" Cam asked. Suddenly, he was blindsided by a thought. "Are you gay, too?" he whispered.

Sam laughed even harder. "No, Cam. You know Em was the only one for me," he said with a wistful smile. He stood from the table when he heard their order number called out. "I'll be right back."

Cameron remembered one of his conversations with Sam. Em, *his* Emily. How could he have forgotten and asked Sam whether he was gay. This damn sensory overload was messing with his brain cells. *Shit.* He knew better. Sam had one love in his life, his wife Emily, who had died a few years ago after a long battle with cancer. He remembered Sam telling him he didn't think he would ever be able to survive something like that again. Sam confessed it was the inmates he was charged with, 'his boys' as he called them, who kept him going, gave him the family he'd wanted to share with Em for so long. Cam closed his eyes and shook his head. Sam was more of a dad to him than his own father had ever been. In fact, the shirt on his back was bought by Sam. Literally.

Sam returned with a tray of food.

"I'm sorry. I didn't mean to bring up Emily," Cam mumbled.

Sam tousled Cameron's hair in a paternal manner. "Any chance to think about her is a good one."

Cameron half smiled. Sam was so damn optimistic and sweet it made his teeth hurt. "I need some of your happy pills," he grumbled before taking a sip of soda.

Sam chuckled and bit into his burger.

"So what did you forget to tell me?" Cameron asked some time later.

Sam was finishing the last bite of his lunch when he finally said, "The halfway house you're going to."

"Yeah?" Cameron encouraged.

"It's run by Matt. Matthew Doner and his partner, Julian Capeletti."

Cameron looked at him suspiciously. "Partner as is business partner?" he asked.

"No, well, yeah, but as his 'partner' partner, too," he said, using air quotes.

Cameron knew he must have had a blank look on his face.

"Do you prefer the term *boyfriend* instead? 'Cause if you say that around Julian, he'd probably kick your ass," Sam said before finishing off his soda.

Cameron didn't know how to respond. It was a mix of not knowing what to say or do and the realization that he would be living under the same roof as a couple who wouldn't be bothered by him being gay.

"They're cool, you'll like them," Sam said as he placed his empty cup and items back on the tray. "That is, assuming you ignore the occasional puppy dog stares and suck face they sneak in when they think no one is looking."

Cameron's eyes widened. "You're kidding right?"

"Listen, they're great. Matt is very easy to talk to. Julian makes a strong first impression but he's a teddy bear. Just don't tell him I told you that," Sam warned. "I think you'll fit in perfectly."

Cameron finished his drink as he exited the booth while Sam dumped the trash in the bin and looked at his watch.

"C'mon, Cam. We need to make sure we don't hit traffic or we'll miss the deadline," Sam said, picking up the pace a bit.

Cameron knew better than to start things on a bad note. Even though Sam was taking him to the halfway house, it was still considered a prison transfer, a furlough, with a very strict timeframe to arrive at his destination. He damn sure didn't want to start raising any red flags this soon after his release. He picked up the pace and headed out to Sam's car, glad to escape the sensory chaos of the rest stop service plaza.

Chapter TWO

"They want to enter a plea."

Hunter Donovan, Assistant State Attorney, tore his focus away to look at his assistant. "Of course they do, because they don't stand a chance in hell," he responded in a level tone then turned his attention back to review the case file on his desk.

Hunter looked up again to see his assistant worrying his lip. "What is it?"

Jessie Vega fidgeted with the files in his hand. "They're outside."

"So, walk out there and tell them no."

"He brought a team this time. It's not just the one attorney anymore. They won't take no for an answer."

"Oh really?" Hunter said with a raised eyebrow. He loved a challenge. The staff endlessly teased him on the appropriateness of his name. When Hunter decided to take down someone in court, the defendant became his prey. He was proud of his win statistics, but more so for the legitimacy of them.

"Wait—" Jessie started when Hunter launched from his chair to the office door.

Hunter exited and looked over to his left to see a group of three sharply-dressed men with briefcases surrounding the accused. There was no way this thug was able to afford the obvious high-end team of attorneys. One of their designer suits could easily pay several months of mortgage payments for most people.

The man he assumed hired this crew was the leader of the rapidly growing drug problem in town. The only tie between the drug pusher in the midst of the suits to the newly self-appointed drug kingpin was a simple marking on the nickel bags on the street. The same emblem found on the supply when this idiot was busted trying to hire a hooker for the night while transporting the stash. For some reason, the drug king wanted to keep this moron around. He just hadn't been able to figure out why.

He put on his game face and walked over to the team of men. He stood directly in front of the thug while his eyes scanned the accompanying crew. After making eye contact with each of the attorneys, he looked to the accused, and said one word, "No," then turned to walk away.

"Mr. Donovan, we wish to make a plea," he heard someone say forcefully.

Hunter turned again to face them. "Do you *wish* to tell me who hired you?" When he didn't get a response, he said, "As I said, my answer is no."

"You are making a grave error, Mr. Donovan."

Hunter slowly took a deep breath and walked back to the attorney who spoke from the group. "Are you threatening me?"

"No, Mr. Donovan, of course not," the man returned with an equal stare.

"Sounded like a threat, and I'm certain the entire office will agree with me." Hunter knew he was playing with fire but he needed to say something that would draw the room's attention and shift the power from the team back to him.

As expected, he heard a hum of chatter from his staff quickly followed by complete silence.

The attorney looked away briefly. "I simply meant it would be to your benefit to listen to our request."

"The only benefit I care for is information. Is that what you have to offer?"

"May we speak in your office?"

"Answer my question."

"In your office," the man responded in a firmer tone.

"Answer. My. Question."

"I come to offer something of value," the attorney responded with a negotiating tone.

"To you."

"To many," the man quickly corrected with a smirk.

"My answer is still no. I'll see you in court," Hunter finished before turning to return to his office.

"Maybe," one of the men said with a wry laugh.

Hunter continued his trek to his office, his steps not faltering a beat. He had managed to hold off opposing counsel for three months. Now with just under two weeks before trial, they were still soliciting him to plea. He had high hopes to be able to rid the streets of this new drug crisis—even if it was only one pusher at a time. He assumed this meant no one on his side of the table had been bought out. *Yet.*

According to the docket, Judge Peter Gonzalez was assigned to the court date. Hunter's father and Peter served together when they were younger. Peter opted to follow the legal field while Hunter's father chose to pursue his love for teaching. They were all friends, but knew how to clearly separate work from personal. He and Peter shared the same sentiments regarding their hometown: they'd clean up the streets, one case at a time.

He sat at his desk and noticed his assistant still hovering.

"Was there something else?"

"Thank you," Jessie continued to fidget. "They wouldn't leave."

"How long were they out there?"

"About fifteen minutes."

Hunter smiled. "You got them to wait that long? I'm impressed."

Jessie beamed. "I tried."

"Are those for me?"

"Oh yes, sorry," he said, handing over the stack of red folders.

Hunter scowled. "Who sent them over?"

"Same messenger."

"Shit." They had already investigated the courier. Squeaky clean history and it was damn near impossible to get any information from the confidential messenger service that employed him. Hunter despised the mysterious 'watch list' as he called it. It seemed someone higher up thought it was a good idea to keep tabs on recently released ex-cons who were likely to be repeat offenders. *So much for prison reform.* Even though, statistically, the red files were freakishly accurate in their predictions, he hated not knowing where the hell they came from—especially considering the degree of detail included in each case. He found it unsettling. Regardless, he was compelled to review the files for the sake of knowing what the hell was going on.

Hunter sighed. It was going to take him hours to get through these new cases. In typical red file fashion, each folder was about two inches thick and overflowing with endless chronological case files, mug shots, reports, background checks, and more. Some even included daily logs of surveillance after an inmate's release from prison.

He looked at his watch. "Damn it."

"Is there a problem with one of the files?"

"I think I missed the cookie window."

Jessie looked at him with a contorted expression.

"Never mind. I'm taking an early lunch. I'll review some of the cases while I'm out," he said, taking the red files and storing them in his briefcase. "Make sure I don't have anything for this afternoon please. It's going to take me a while to go through these."

"You got it."

Hunter grabbed his case and exited the office at a brisk pace. He could stand up to a team of goons and fight an unknown kingpin to the very end, but there was no way he could miss Lucy's homemade cookies. He had to make it to the diner and hope there was still one left with his name on it.

A man had priorities. Everything else just had to wait.

* * * *

Sam pulled his car up to the front of a place that looked like a house sandwiched between large office buildings. He turned the car off and looked over to Cameron. "Ready?"

"Yeah," he said then shrugged before exiting the car. He looked up at the two story house and wondered why the hell someone would want to have a house in this location. It just looked…odd. Definitely unexpected and, ironically, very welcoming. Well, better than barbed wire and a huge metal gate.

He walked up the path to the house and assessed the garden, or lack thereof. The landscaping needed some major work. With a bit of flowers, mulch, and a few trees, it would look dramatically different.

Sam met him at the door with a file in hand. He knocked then rang the doorbell. *Jeez, he's pushy with everyone, it seems.*

A dark-haired man opened the door with a huge smile and a ready hug. "Hey, Sam."

"Hey, Matt," he said, finally releasing him. "This is Cameron."

"Hi," he said, extending his hand. "Welcome to Halfway House, I'm Matthew Doner. Come on in."

Cam entered the halfway house, prison, *whatever*, and looked around. It was definitely built with the welcoming feel of a home with a living room, kitchen, and a wooden stairwell leading to a second floor. This wasn't a prison, it didn't look like one, and it certainly didn't smell like one. Cam closed his eyes and was instantly flooded with memories of his childhood home. The good ones— when his mom would be there waiting for him when he'd get home from school. He shook his head to dispel the vivid memories.

"Are you driving back today or tomorrow?" Matthew asked Sam.

"I'm leaving as soon as I finish here. I've got a few early morning appointments tomorrow."

"Okay, so let's take care of the formalities first then I'll show you around. Okay?" Matthew asked Cam.

"Sure, whatever's fine." Honestly, Cam didn't care. He was so tired all he wanted to do was stretch out somewhere and sleep for a few hours. Sitting in that car for the long drive wore away at the little patience he had.

"Great, let's go to the kitchen and have some coffee while we do the paperwork." Matthew led them out of the hallway into another room.

Sam sat at the dining room table and Matthew began to prepare a pot of coffee. Cam looked around, the kitchen was very basic but nice-sized with all the necessities—enough for a few people to be in here at once and not worry about rubbing against each other.

"How many live here?" he asked, curiosity getting the better of him.

"You're our first guest," Matthew said with a flush of color to his cheeks and a hint of excitement in his eyes.

"You mean ex-con?"

"Cam," Sam scolded.

"Sam, it's fine," Matthew assured him.

Matthew cocked his head to the side, assessing Cam as he leaned against the kitchen counter. "Actually, you're the second ex-con in this house if you count me. I own this house with my partner, J. You'll meet him later. That makes three of us living here...for now. But you are a *guest* in our home. This is not a prison, and I hope you don't feel as if it is one."

He wasn't going to burst the man's bubble and remind him that this was just an extension of prison for now. "So you and...J?"

"Julian," both Sam and Matthew corrected in unison.

Cam raised his hands in surrender. "Fine, you and *Julian*."

"Yes." Matthew turned and grabbed a few mugs out of the cupboard. "How do you take yours?"

"Black is fine," Cam responded. He had become accustomed to crappy, bitter black coffee. Coffee in prison tasted horrible but it was always a reliable source of caffeine, warm, and strong as hell. Sugar and other sweets were just too scarce so he hadn't had much of a choice but to forgo his sweet tooth.

Matthew placed three mugs on the table and grabbed the folder on the counter before sitting. "Sorry about this, but I need to ask you a series of questions and go over a few forms with you. Let's start with a few basics. Can you please confirm your full name?"

"Cameron Michael Pierce."

"Do you prefer Cameron or Cam?"

"Either is fine." He waited as Matthew added some notes to the file. "Which do you prefer? Matthew or Matt?"

He smiled. "Either is fine."

"Date of birth?"

Cam responded to each of the questions. Yes, he was currently twenty-seven years old, and yes, he had a father and a sister. No, they didn't want to see him, and he definitely wasn't interested in seeing them.

"We need to get you on the *Code a Phone* program for the aftercare drug monitoring because of the charges on your record."

"That's fine," Cam said. Random drug tests and bed searches had become part of his life now even though he had never once touched an illegal substance regardless of what his record stated.

Matt gave him a piece of paper with two numbers. "Here's the phone number you need to call every day and give this five-digit PAX code. The automated system will tell you if you need to go in for testing that day. Can you sign here for me?" Matt handed him another document and a checklist confirming the bits of information they had discussed.

Cameron stared at the paper. He hadn't actually put his signature on anything since his incarceration. He was a grown man and didn't remember how to sign his name. He clenched his jaw and grabbed the pen. With a few angry strokes, he scribbled his first signature in almost a decade.

Sam signed the necessary forms to complete the transfer then said his good-byes with a promise to visit soon.

"Let me give you the tour."

Cam followed Matt out of the kitchen.

Matt showed him around to the living room, the back porch, and yard. Even though there was a paved parking area that could easily fit several cars, there was enough land in the yard to do something, anything with some color. This place was in serious need of landscaping all around. Cam's hands started to itch. It was driving him insane to see so much dirt. It was like a blank canvas waiting to be painted with splashes of reds and yellows.

"Something wrong?" Matt asked.

"Nothing," he responded before returning inside.

Matt led Cam up the stairs to a sitting area and a hallway of rooms. A huge window greeted them and lit the loft with natural lighting. Down the hall, Cam could see several rooms.

"This first one on the left is ours. If you need something…knock. We're still painting the other rooms but we've finished yours." Matt walked to the end of the hall.

The last room on the right was *his room*.

"Mine, as in, for now because no one else is here yet?" Cameron could contain his excitement at the prospect of having some privacy. He'd learned the hard way to hide his emotions in prison. Anything other than anger was beaten out of someone. Excitement, happiness, and hope were counterproductive in the sea of hate, fear, and desperation.

"Yours. We figured our *guests* would want their privacy," Matt responded with a smile as he opened the door with a sweeping motion and waited for Cam to enter.

The walls were colored in a pale blue-gray tone and the white ceiling looked even brighter as the afternoon sunlight peeked through the window. A large bed dominated the spacious room. Definitely not the thin pad and barely there pillow he was used to. This bed begged to be slept in. He could easily make out a thick mattress with at least four fluffy pillows under the dark blue comforter. Next to the heavenly bed was a table, small, but large enough for the lamp and alarm clock. At the foot of the bed, to his left, there was a dresser with drawers and the biggest television he had seen in a bedroom, ever. It was larger than the community TV in prison and certainly larger than the small portable thirteen inch he used to have in his room as a kid.

"You can actually walk in and take a look," Matt encouraged.

Had he been standing there without moving at all? Cam took a step forward and looked to his right and caught a glimpse of a white porcelain sink. He took a few more steps and saw a full bathroom with a shower. *His own bathroom?*

"Mine?" he hesitantly asked, looking over his shoulder, but not directly at Matt. He feared acknowledging this seed of hope that had been planted. His own room *and* his own bathroom? Cam's only private moments were in solitary confinement.

A flood of memories blindsided him. He didn't want to remember. He hated being alone, in that hell. He recalled how guards came for him when all was quiet and beat him until he was at the brink of death. The bone-numbing pain he suffered for days, bruised and swollen without medical care since the staff insisted he had done that to himself in hopes of seeking escape. Then, just as he'd begun to feel slightly better, he was transferred—by convenient accident—to the wrong cellblock for just enough time to garner another beating by death row inmates with nothing to lose, craving vengeance on anyone with a pulse. He had learned to fight back, but there was only so much one could do against a crew of many.

Was he really free of the hell that had tried to suffocate him for almost a third of his life? Was this really his bedroom and his bathroom in what could be the start of something new? Or was this a cruel daydream that would chip away at his defenses and bring him lower than he had been in some time?

He didn't dare hope this was real.

"Yours," Matt responded softly. "We know you were in for a while so we weren't sure if you had enough clothes."

Matt was talking but Cam had a difficult time hearing him over the buzz in his head. He wasn't sure what he expected in this new place, but he certainly didn't anticipate something so radically different. He expected a comparable illusion of a prison, bunk beds, shared bathrooms, everything similar minus the barbed wire and dressed guards. He didn't expect something that would grant the illusion that he had escaped the nightmare. Was he really free? He closed his eyes and tried to steady his heartbeat and channel his panic to clear the internal hum.

And why is this guy being so damn nice?

"They're from second-hand stores and a few things from Walmart. Nothing glamorous but Sam gave us your approximate sizes so we're hoping they fit," he said, pointing to the various shirts and jeans in the closet.

Clothes? In my closet? Breathe in, breathe out.

"We set you up with some towels and some basics in the bathroom. The only thing you don't have here is a phone, but we've got a few outlets if you want to charge your cell."

Silence.

"Cam?"

Fuck, I need to respond. What the hell was he talking about? Oh yeah. "I don't have a cell," Cam forced out.

"Well, we'll work on getting you one, even if it's just basic so you've got one."

"I don't need one." *Breathe in, breathe out.*

"Just in case there's someone you want to call."

"There's no one," he snapped. *Fucking breathe in, breathe out.*

Matt's scrutinizing gaze burned into him. Cam just looked down, his vision pegged to the floor. *Breathe in, breathe out.*

"I'll let you get settled in. Job placement, coordinating counseling, orientation, and all that can start tomorrow. Julian should be home any minute but you guys can meet at dinner around six. Do you have any questions?"

Cam shook his head.

"If you need anything, I'll be downstairs."

Cam nodded. *Breathe in, breathe out.*

Matt hesitated at the door. Cameron willed the dark-haired man to leave the room before he lost it.

When he heard the click of the door moments later, he reached out to grab the bathroom doorframe for support. He pressed his head against the cool wall. *Shit.* His heart was beating too damn fast and his head was pounding so hard it seemed as if it were going to explode. He tried to walk over to the sink, but his feet were heavy, as if he wore anvils for shoes. He splashed some cold water on his face, hoping it would snap him back to the here and now.

It wasn't working.

Breathe in, breathe out.

His hands began to shake and his legs became weak.

His room, *his* bathroom, *his* closet…

Focus. Breathe in, breathe out.

Cam looked over to the window and the rays of light shining through were like a beacon calling to him. No, this wasn't a dream, dammit. He was free. Free of the bars, the solitary confinement, and the torture. Cameron needed to convince himself *this* was real, that it wasn't hope bitch-slapping him and teasing him to the brink of insanity. He tried with every fiber of his being to walk to that window; he needed to see the sunlight for himself and feel the heat on his skin. Two steps and he was unsteady, dizziness set in and his vision faded to black before he fell.

"Cameron?"

In the middle of the darkness and the hum, he could have sworn he distinctly heard his name. He wasn't sure since he didn't recognize the voice, but whoever it was sounded pissed.

"Cameron. Wake the fuck up!" the insistent, growly voice demanded.

Cam tried, but his eyelids didn't want to cooperate. His chest hurt, breathing was just too damn difficult. He gasped for air. Something cold pressed against his face. With every ounce of energy he had left, he tried again. Finally, a sliver of light seeped into the blackness.

"That's it. Open your eyes. Wake the hell up or I'm going to beat the shit out of you."

This, he could deal with. How ironic. Someone being nice, not so much.

He pushed himself and was able to open his eyes a little more. Everything was a blur, indistinctive, all the colors faded into each other but one...green. He saw crystal clear green eyes staring back at him.

"What's going to settle you?"

He needed to know this was real—that he was outside of the prison—but how the hell could he communicate with this insistent, growly, son of a bitch with the death glare when he couldn't even take a breath? He could hear the pounding of his heart amplified in his ears. He was lifted, moved again then held still. He heard a noise then suddenly hot air blew across his face.

"Open your eyes."

Cameron was running on autopilot. He was good at following instructions, most of the time. He willed his eyes to open and immediately shut them again when a flood of bright lights left him blinded with flashes of sun spots in the darkness.

"Take a deep breath," the pain in the ass said again. Cameron's arms were yanked upward and held, forcing his airway to open and take a breath. He began to cough as the hot air filled his lungs.

"Now open your eyes, Cameron," the voice insisted.

Cam pushed himself again and opened his eyes slowly. He could see the shape of buildings, streets, and the bright blue sky filled with clouds. He opened his eyes more, and his vision cleared, bringing more details into focus. He could see the cars driving up and down the road, the trees lining the street. Once his breathing began to level, his arms were released. He looked over and saw the same pair of crystal green eyes staring at him.

"What did it?"

"What?" he asked weakly.

"What caused you to panic?"

Cameron winced. He'd always dealt with the panic attacks on his own. Sometimes they'd make breathing difficult, the bad ones would knock him out completely. The panic attacks started shortly after he went to prison. They didn't happen often, only when a tiny glimmer of hope dared to surface among his hell. Then that hope would be strangled by desperation and hatred of his reality and he'd be left gasping for air. *My problem.* He knew better than to think things would change while he was inside. He was the idiot who dared to want something more. No one cared in prison and certainly no one gave a moment's interest to try to find out why one of the inmates could barely breathe or move. He had always gotten through them on his own, dealt with it the best he could.

"I don't know what you're talking about," Cam said weakly, sitting on the edge of the bed.

"You're a horrible liar."

Cam looked up and saw the green-eyed guy staring intently at him as if waiting for a better response.

Cam shrugged. "I'm fine."

My problem and I'll deal with it on my own just as I have for so many years.

The man pursed his lips and arched an eyebrow. He extended his hand in greeting. "I'm Julian."

"I figured," he mumbled as he shook the offered hand. He glanced over to see Matt standing in the doorway with a concerned look on his face.

Julian turned to look over his shoulder. "He'll be fine," he said to Matt. "He just got out after ten years. He's entitled to a little freak-out."

Matt nodded and forced a smile, the worry still evident in his expression. "I need to finish some paperwork," he said before leaving the room.

"Thanks," Cam said quietly, pulling at a string on his jeans.

"No problem. So, what caused you to panic?"

Cam sighed and glared at the stubborn man who took a seat next to him on the bed.

Julian sat silently for several nerve-wracking minutes, waiting for a reply.

One thing Cam had learned while inside...shut the hell up and don't say a word.

Julian exhaled heavily after a few more minutes. "If you live under this roof, you're going to have to learn to talk," he said as he stood. "Talk, not yell. Understand?"

Cam looked up and nodded. He could follow instructions.

"We've got a counselor available if you prefer to talk to a pro. Otherwise, you're going to have to talk to Matt or me about whatever the hell is getting you worked up."

Cam nodded again.

"Silence is not an option. Talk, write it down, draw a picture, use sign language...I don't care. Pick one that works for you."

Cam stared back at Julian without a response.

"We're here to help you, Cam, whether you believe it or not. If you don't talk, you go back inside or to a different Community Corrections Center. We don't have as many rules as the other centers, but this is one rule we are strict on. Understand?"

Cam nodded and tried to swallow past the knot in his throat. *I'll do anything to not go back to prison.*

Julian walked to the door and turned before leaving. "One more thing. You ever scare Matt like this again—"

"I'll have to deal with you," Cam said. The message conveyed in that glare was loud and clear.

Cam knew a lot of guys in prison who could talk a good game and used empty threats to establish their ground or walked around as if they owned the cellblock. It was all a façade, just a strategic way to avoid getting confronted and appear as if they were more than they actually were. He'd seen enough of these guys to know who *the fakers* were. He looked at Julian. He was the quiet guy, the one you watched out for, the one who didn't bother to talk about it. Rather, they were more men of action than words. Tall, well over six feet, with a frame built from manual labor, his entire presence was just intimidating and exuded a *don't-fuck-with-me* attitude that made you stop and turn the other way, if you could.

Every ounce of common sense told him not to piss off the man staring back at him.

"Good. I'm glad you understand my language. So you don't have an excuse to avoid the talking requirement. Dinner's at six. Don't be late," he finished with a glare as he walked out of the room.

Cameron stood by the window again. He was finally *out*. He breathed in the hot afternoon Miami air, so different from that of prison. It was pure, raw city magnified by the heat and humidity—a far cry from the stale sweat and urine aroma he'd experienced serving his time. He reached out and let his hand extend past the window frame. No bars, no wire mesh on the glass. He flexed his fingers and watched the play of shadows against his palm.

Cam smiled. He was out of prison.

One step at a time.

He figured he'd start with a shower, in *his* bathroom. Then, check to see if any of the clothes fit, get settled in, and squeeze in a short nap before he fell over from exhaustion. He needed to set the alarm just in case he passed out.

Being late for dinner wasn't an option.

* * * *

Hunter finally managed to escape the building after the last 'do you have a second' hallway discussions with various coworkers.

He breathed a sigh of relief when he walked into his favorite diner at the end of the block. Not only did this little hideaway offer him a place to escape the constant office interruptions, but Lucy made the best damn homemade cookies in town. Once a day, and only a handful of batches. He hoped he hadn't missed his chance to satisfy his sweet tooth.

Lucy wasn't at the register. *Damn, that probably means she's gone for the day.* Bill, her husband of forty years, was manning the coffee and sandwich orders from the late lunch customers. Without asking, Bill mixed the right amount of sugar and cream into a cup of coffee before handing it to Hunter. He preferred the Starbucks down the street rather than Bill's bitter brew, but he couldn't put a price on the peace and quiet every day at this diner and the fact that they'd let him commandeer a corner when he needed an escape from the office. And the irresistible cookies probably laced with some controlled substance.

"Thanks, Bill," Hunter said. Like an addict looking for a cookie fix, he scanned the deli for Bill's wife. "Where's Lucy today?" he finally asked when he didn't see her.

"She'll be here in a moment, she's on the phone," Bill responded before returning to the sandwich orders.

Hunter patiently sipped his coffee as he waited. After a few moments, Lucy finally emerged from the back room and smiled broadly when she saw him.

"You're late," she playfully scolded.

If he was late, that meant he missed the cookies. *Damn.* "Tough morning," he finally said with a somber grin.

She looked at him and smiled. "Well, I've got something for you that might make it a better afternoon," she said, reaching under the counter for a bag.

Hunter peered into the bag and saw two large chocolate chip cookies. He immediately reached in and, within seconds, had a mouthful of cookie. "You're an angel."

Lucy shook her head. "You need to have something to eat aside from cookies. How about your turkey sandwich today?"

"I could live off your cookies."

"Don't let Bill hear you say that," she laughed as she rung up his order.

Hunter cautiously looked over to Bill. "It's one of the reasons I married her," Bill joked, then lovingly gazed at his wife before turning to make a fresh pot of coffee.

Hunter yearned to know what it was like to love someone for so long. Know their quirks, joke openly, then, with a simple look, convey a telepathic *I love you* that was unmistakably genuine.

"Are you okay?" Lucy asked with concern. "You seem a bit...off."

"Office, issues, drama. Do you mind if I camp out here for a while today," he asked hopefully.

Lucy patted his hand and nodded. "We've already told you a million times, you don't need to ask. Just make sure you eat before you lose track of time with your paperwork," she finished.

Hunter set up his workspace in the corner and settled in. He munched on his sandwich as the remaining cookie sat on the table, beckoning him. He really needed to do something about this bad habit. Thankfully, he took advantage of his gym membership several times a week to stay in shape.

With his sweet tooth finally satisfied, he tried to relax for a few minutes before diving into work. Bill neared his campout area in the corner to wipe the tables other patrons had used.

"Is Lucy okay? She looked a bit tired," Hunter asked. Bill and Lucy were great but they were along in their years and working the diner a full day was obviously wearing on them.

The older man shuffled the towel from one hand to the other then looked over his shoulder to the back area. "She's been tired a lot lately. She's a stubborn hen, always trying to do everything. I'm surprised she lets me make the coffee and sandwiches." Bill shrugged and continued to wipe down the remaining tables.

Hunter tried to focus on his case files rather than worry about the woman who reminded him so much of his mother. He remembered the times when he'd bake with his mom. The smell of freshly baked chocolate chip cookies would fill the air of their small home. Somehow, his mother always knew when he'd had a hard day at school. She'd stand in the doorway and watch as Hunter would step off the bus. As soon as he'd see her with her apron wrapped around her waist and the wooden spoon in hand, he knew she waited for him to start baking. He never seemed to run to the house fast enough on those days. It was their private time. While mixing the dough, they'd chat about school, the pop quiz that was too difficult, or the bully who'd tried to take Hunter's lunch money. Lucy reminded him of his mom, and her cookies filled the diner with the same aroma that brought back so many special memories for him.

He imagined his parents would be like Lucy and Bill if his mom were still alive. His father, still to this day, reminisced about the love of his life. Hunter was one of the lucky ones with parents who were always sneaking kisses and holding hands every chance they had. He grew up in a house surrounded by love and the happiness that love created. After his mom passed away, yes, there was sadness, but also an overwhelming amount of wonderful memories.

He was starting to lose hope that one day he would find that with someone. He had just had a birthday a few months ago and knew finding someone became more difficult with each passing year. He was now officially a forty-year-old lonely man. *Lovely.* He never thought he'd reach this age and still be alone, but he was also never one to settle for anything.

He tore himself from his melancholy thoughts and tried to focus on the case files. He had a good two hours before his assistant would call. He could get a lot done without the interruptions. He took a deep cleansing breath and channeled his focus on the report in hand.

* * * *

Buzz. Buzz. Buzz.

Cameron reached out and slapped the source of the annoying noise. He looked over and saw the time display, then reluctantly dragged himself out of bed still wearing the towel wrapped loosely around his waist from his shower earlier.

Brushing his teeth, he ran a hand through his hair and caught sight of the scar and ink slashes on his upper bicep. He hated it so much he deliberately tried to avoid mirrors and short sleeves. He didn't want the constant reminder of prison or the memory of being held down, gagged, and marked against his will. He turned away from the mirror, disgusted by his own reflection. He had killed a man and had accepted the fact that he was accountable for taking a life. But almost a decade of constant fear of stepping outside the boundaries, the beatings, the torture, the threats, it was all just too much. They would look for him once they found out he'd been released. It was inevitable. They had made that very clear to him while inside—that he would be watched and reminded of what he had done and how he needed to stay exactly where he was.

He tried to fight back the anger that threatened this potential new start in his life. He took a few deep breaths to calm his heartbeat and steady his shaky hands.

One day at a time.

When he managed to calm himself, he searched through the closet and found jeans that fit and a blue T-shirt with sleeves long enough to cover the scars. He brushed his hair and tried to look presentable.

He walked downstairs and heard voices coming from the kitchen. It sounded as if Matt and Julian were having a discussion about the finishing details on the house. The chatter halted when he entered the kitchen.

"Hey," he said, tugging his shirt sleeves down then crossing his arms.

Seeing Matt and Julian together was a case study in opposite attractions. Matt was welcoming and polite with a refined, clean-cut air about him that felt as if he had had people drive him around for the better part of his life. He was about Cam's height and lean with fair skin that set off his bright blue eyes and dark hair.

Julian had clear green eyes that offered up a glare that would make a grizzly cringe. He looked as if he didn't want to be bothered and opted for a shadow of hair on his head instead of any style. He appeared exotic with an all-over olive-bronze coloring to his skin Cam was certain people spent small fortunes to acquire.

Matt smiled. "We were just talking about a few details we wanted to do to the house. Would you care to chime in?" he asked expectantly.

Cam shook his head. He wasn't sure what they expected of him. In prison, opinions didn't matter. If one was needed it was given to you.

"Okay," Matt said quietly, deflated, then started to set the table for dinner.

Julian glared at Cameron.

Shit. "Um, like…what?" he tried to quickly correct.

Matt brightened. "Well, I'd love your thoughts on whether you felt this place was welcoming. First impressions are important. I want to make sure our guests feel as if they've arrived to a new home. That's how we see it. So it really matters to us what you think about the house, your room, things like that."

Julian half smiled as he looked at Matt. He might come across as tough but there was no doubt the man was insanely in love with his partner and tried to please him.

"Um, the room is nice."

"Great!" Matt launched into a discussion about the color scheme choices and asked whether he liked the tones in the room and his thoughts about any needed changes.

"The room doesn't need any changes. Um..." He hesitated and looked over at Julian for an indication to continue.

Julian quirked an eyebrow then slightly nodded.

"The house is very welcoming, but I think it would"—he thought for a moment as he chose his words—"look more inviting if you added some landscaping out front. And you've got so much space in the back, you could do the same there too."

Julian half smiled.

"J, can we do that?" Matt asked eagerly as he set the food on the table.

"Yeah. Cam, where should we add them and what did you have in mind?"

Cam shrugged. "Um, some flower beds out front would... uh...work."

Matt grabbed each dish and served the pasta.

Cam leaned over his plate and inhaled the delicious scent of the colorful dish before him.

"So when do you want to start?" Matt asked.

Cameron stopped spinning the pasta on his fork and looked up. He tried to contain the excitement starting to build. Between the possibility of doing some landscaping and having his first home-cooked meal in almost a decade, he had a hard time formulating coherent thoughts. "Uh, start? You want my help?"

Cam was not going to get excited. He scooped a spoonful of pasta in his mouth and closed his eyes as the burst of flavors exploded across his taste buds. "What is this?"

"You like it?" Matt asked.

Cameron had his mouth stuffed full of pasta so he simply nodded.

"Spaghetti Carbonara. It's one of J's favorites. Well, anything Italian is his favorite," he finished with a smirk and a sideways look to Julian.

"Do you cook?" Julian asked.

Cam swallowed the mouthful of pasta. He had cooked a few basic meals out of necessity before going in, but it had been far too long to remember the details. "Um, no, didn't cook while I was inside," he responded. Thankfully he didn't have kitchen duty with the bear named Gino or Tommy who had a penchant for pain. "But…um…I'd like to learn."

"Cool," Julian responded as he rubbed his hands together. "I'll be the guinea pig. I can eat pretty much anything."

"I can show you how to do some basics then just let your creativity go from there. J can show you some practical stuff," Matt interjected.

"Uh…like how to open a can and read a label," Julian said with a chuckle. "Oh yeah, and how to use a microwave!" he added with enthusiasm.

Matt softly caressed Julian's cheek. "You do make an awesome pizza."

Julian turned his face to kiss Matt's palm. He then looked to Cam and schooled his features. "So, about those flower beds. What did you have in mind?"

Cameron hesitantly suggested a few flowers and waited for Matt or Julian to cut him off. When they didn't interrupt, he found the words came easier. He mentioned the best location around the house to set up the flower beds to get the right amount of light during the day. He had learned all about flowers, plants, and proper soils as a child during his endless hours in the garden with his mother—it had been their private getaway.

He stopped talking and saw Julian jotting down notes while Matt appeared mesmerized, listening to him ramble about plants. "Um, sorry. You can pretty much set up the flower beds anywhere and get some plants or flowers that will work wherever they're needed," he finished with a shrug.

"J, did you get all that?" Matt craned his neck to see Julian's notes.

"Yup."

"Once you've got the job situation squared away, we'll see what times are best with your schedule and we'll make it work," Matt said.

"You want me to help?" Cam asked again.

"More like you're going to do it and we'll help. Matt does not have a green thumb, he's tried, and I wouldn't know the difference between a"—Julian looked at his notes—"Bougainvy and Lirop."

Cameron chuckled. "Bougainvillea and Liriope."

"See, there you go."

Having the chance to do all the landscaping needed from setting up the flower beds to picking out the plants was just too damn exciting. He wanted to jump at the chance but had learned years ago not to get too enthusiastic about things since they usually ended in some disappointment. "Yeah, okay."

Julian responded with a half smile.

Cameron nodded. Nope, he wasn't getting excited. Not even a little bit.

After dinner, apparently it was Matt's turn to do the dishes for the evening. Cam and Julian retreated to the living room area tasked with choosing something to watch on TV. Julian sat on the couch and grabbed the remote.

Cam stood silently and shoved his hands in his pockets. "Change," he finally said, shuffling his feet.

Julian looked up at him and set the remote back on the table.

"You wanted to know the trigger for the attacks."

"Then you're shit out of luck. Change is inevitable. Get used to it," Julian said.

"Gee, thanks." Cam looked away for a moment. "I'm not used to people being nice to me," he said uncomfortably. Maybe stroking the guy's ego about his partner would stop him from poking around in Cam's business. "Matt was…nice."

"That's his nature. You're going to have to get used to that if you're living here. Try again."

"You're a stubborn son of a bitch."

Julian half shrugged. "I've been called worse. Don't change the subject."

Cam exhaled dramatically. "The thought of going back to prison, back to *that* life."

Julian looked at him intently, encouraging him to continue.

"And that all this wasn't real somehow," he finished quietly. "Hard to explain."

"Try," Julian said, glaring.

Cam shrugged and looked away.

"Matt's always telling me to 'use my words'," Julian said, mimicking Matt's understanding tone. "It's not easy but talking does help."

Cam exhaled heavily then looked up, searching for the right words. Matt and Julian were so different from everyone else he'd met in the last few years. If Sam trusted them, then maybe they weren't like the others. "It's not easy being inside. Some guys are built for that shit but it's tough. I adjusted as best as I could and figured out early on what I needed to do to make it. Every now and then, I lose my focus and I think about the what-if."

"The what-if?"

Cam shook his head. "It's stupid. I know better, but sometimes I wonder what it would be like…"

"To have a normal life, a home, and someone to love who'd love you back regardless of all your fucked up shit," Julian finished his thought.

Cam looked over to him with newfound understanding. "Yeah."

"Then reality sets in and you freak out because you want it so much you can almost touch it but then realize it's either not real or it's slipping away," Julian added in a faraway voice.

Cam nodded.

"Understandable basis for a freak-out."

"You sound a little more insightful about this than the usual person," Cam observed.

Julian crossed his arms and leaned back in the couch. "This is about you not me. I take it that's why putting you by the window settled you. It let you know you weren't in prison anymore."

"I don't know. I guess it helped to know I wasn't back there," he said quietly. *In that hell.*

Julian nodded. "Duly noted. Aside from panic attacks, what else is there? Do you get angry?"

"What?"

"Pissed off, hatin' life, pitch a fit, shit like that. Do I need to worry we've got a hothead under our roof?"

Cam shook his head then shrugged. "I guess that's probably what most people would expect. Yeah, I get pissed, I'm human, but I try not to get lost in that shit. I've seen what hate does to a man." He shifted his weight from foot to foot and looked away. "I don't want to be *that* guy. I know my limits and I know my temper enough to control it most of the time. I have the occasional panic attack when I make the mistake of wishing for something more. It's more embarrassing than anything."

"It's not a mistake to dream or have hope," Julian said firmly.

"Well, that shit gets beaten out of you pretty quick inside."

Julian leaned forward, clasping his hands and resting his arms on his thighs. "There's nothing wrong with wanting for something then fighting like hell to get it or freaking out when you think it's going to be taken away."

"It's a weakness."

"It's called being human," Julian corrected.

Cam winced.

"You just need to ease back into things. Pace yourself. If you feel the need to punch something, it better not have a pulse. Understand?"

Cam nodded.

"When you sense yourself starting to get overwhelmed and need to talk, just call me."

"I don't have a phone."

"Matt will get you one."

"I don't need one."

"Matt wants to get you a phone, so you're getting a phone. It won't be fancy. I think one of the rules is that it can't have a camera. He'll know."

"But I don't—"

"Don't upset Matt," Julian said, punctuating his statement with another glare.

"Okay."

Lying in bed later that evening, Cam thought about Matt and Julian. Had he seen them apart, he never would have guessed they were a couple simply because they were so different in personalities and appearances. But after being in the same room with them for a short period of time, it was impossible to deny the sizzle in the air, the subtle touches, the casual glances—they just worked, like two jigsaw puzzle pieces that were meant to fit together perfectly.

Cameron yawned as sleep weighed his eyes.

He wondered what it would be like to be that attuned to another person. He didn't think he'd ever get a chance to connect with someone on that level considering his history, but it sure as hell didn't stop him from wanting it as he finally shut his eyes and let sleep take over.

Chapter THREE

Cameron shot upright in bed. His heart raced as he looked side to side. *It's just a dream.* He closed his eyes and tried to calm his breathing. He gripped the sheets then slowly opened his eyes again. Looking around at his new room, Cameron realized this part of the dream was actually real. He got out of bed and walked over to the window.

Before he was moved to the C Block, his first cell had a small slit of an opening along the top edge. It was too high in the cell and too narrow to actually enjoy a view past the metal bars and mesh but enough to allow small rays of light to cut through and form a mild honeycomb pattern along the wall against his cot. After his relocation to the C wing soon after the start of his term, windows were non-existent in cells. He was only allowed outside into the common areas on specific days, during certain times, typically in the middle of the afternoon when the heat was at its worst and the sun at its highest point; where a look up would leave one blinded for doing so. That was assuming, of course, he wasn't in solitary or some other conveniently scheduled punishment that conflicted with the scheduled days. After so many years unable to feel the heat of the sun against his skin, he had become pale and his hair darker than he ever remembered.

He recalled one of his meetings with Sam.

"What do you miss the most?" Sam had asked.

"Sunrises."

"Not family or friends?" Sam asked with a frown.

"Sunrises," Cam firmly restated.

His father and sister hadn't visited him in prison. He had accepted it.

Seeing the bright, beautiful sun on those few occasions, although blinding and painful at times, was a welcomed reprieve. Missing the view of the rising sun was unbearable.

The sunrise was a symbol of a new start. When they were taken away, so was his hope for a new beginning.

Cam placed his palm on the glass and felt the warmth of the outside. He closed his eyes and took a deep breath then rested his forehead to the window's edge before finally opening his eyes again.

Still in the early morning hours, he could see the beginnings of a sunrise casting a hint of light across the clouds. He stared out into the sky, waiting for the sun to make its appearance. He didn't care if the buildings were blocking most of his view; the sun would rise above them and color the sky in various shades of pink, yellow, and blue.

His first sunrise in almost a decade.

This was as close to free as he had been in so many years.

Lost in thought, Cameron didn't know how long he stood there with his memories, observing the wash of colors spread across the sky. After the sun completed its ascension, he remained there for some time, watching the start of the day, the people walking in the street, the cars driving by. So much activity, color, and beauty.

He smiled as he thought about dinner the night before and the effort Matt and Julian had made to welcome him. It was nice to be involved, matter to someone, finally have a normal conversation and contribute something to a productive discussion.

Shaking his head free of the spiraling thoughts, he concentrated on the here and now. He couldn't resist the thought of taking another shower.

As he stood under the showerhead and let the blissfully warm rain of water soak him, he lathered up with that citrus soap he was starting to love. He absently washed himself as his mind wandered to the same nightmare that haunted him—he was finally out of prison, but somehow they managed to find him and send him back *inside* as soon as they'd heard he was free.

It wasn't paranoia.

He had been watched, constantly. They had men inside, both inmates and guards, who kept him in check with subtle threats and unmistakable innuendo to ensure he kept to himself. He was always on alert, careful of what he said and to whom. He began a slow friendship with the first inmate he shared a room with. The need to interact with someone was just too tempting. As soon as the comfort level rose, Cameron was sent to isolation for no apparent reason. When he returned to his cell a week later, he was greeted by a different cellmate. He never heard from his friend again or saw him on the prison grounds.

When Sam insisted on pushing for an early release, Cameron knew it was pointless to resist Sam's perseverance. All Cam requested of him was to try to keep it quiet with as little interaction as possible with the required personnel. Sam was perplexed at first, but perceptive. Sam never questioned him further.

He toweled off and rummaged through the closet looking for something to wear. He found a pair of jeans that fit comfortably and a white shirt. Finally dressed, he made his way downstairs following the smell of brewing coffee.

"Good morning," Matt greeted him when he arrived to the kitchen. "Did you sleep well?"

Cam nodded as he accepted the cup of coffee. No need to mention the recurring nightmare.

"Have you thought about what you'd like to do yet?"

"Are you talking about a job for now or something deeper here?" Cam asked then kicked himself for sounding harsh.

Matt laughed. "I'm referring to a job. I want to know if you've got any particular interest in mind so I can check our list of business partners for a match."

"Oh. Honestly, I don't care. Any job would be fine. I don't mind what I do as long as I'm not the center of attention or wearing a chicken suit or something."

"You're going to wear a chicken suit?" Julian asked as he entered the kitchen.

Cameron glared at Julian and heard Matt snicker as he handed Julian a mug.

Julian grinned before sipping his coffee.

"Be nice, J."

Julian chuckled. "What about the diner? Bill called me last week to ask if we'd had our first guest arrive yet. I think he's really worried about Lucy," he finished quietly.

"Diner?" Cam asked.

Matt nodded. "Lucy and her husband, Bill, have a diner a few blocks down by the business district. It's a small shop but it's been there for quite some time. Sandwiches, coffee, baked goods, stuff like that," Matt replied.

"Best damn cookies I've ever had," Julian quickly added in between sips of his coffee. "She makes all the stuff right there at the diner."

"Is that something you'd be interested in?" Matt asked.

Cameron shrugged. It sounded low-key, quiet, and casual. "Sounds fine."

Julian pushed off from the counter. "I'll give her a call. Maybe she'll like you and won't make you wear the muffin suit during sales," he said before leaving the kitchen.

"Don't listen to him," Matt said, waving his hand in the air. "Did you get a chance to go through the paperwork and handbook? Do you have any questions?"

Cam was momentarily distracted, still hanging on Julian's last words. "No questions."

"Okay. Well, if anything comes up just ask. I know it's a lot to take in."

Cam nodded. *No kidding.*

Julian rejoined them a few moments later. "Lucy's cool with Cam working there and is anxious to meet him. Said anytime was good. I'm on my way to run a few errands. I can drop you guys off at the diner."

Matt looked over at Cam, waiting for an answer.

This is quick. Out one day, job the next. "Let me call that number first to see if I need to do a drug test today then I'm ready to go."

"Great, I'll get the forms while you make your call," Matt eagerly said.

"Hi, Lucy," Matt greeted the older woman.

"Hello, sweetheart," she responded with an embrace. "Where is your young man?" she asked Matt.

"He dropped us off and had to leave but asked me to beg you to save a cookie for him this afternoon," he said with a flush of color in his face.

Lucy smiled and patted his cheek. "You boys and your sweets." She laughed softly then looked over to Cameron.

Cam didn't know what to say or do so he did what he knew best...stand still and stay quiet while he observed his surroundings. The diner sat on the corner of the building, two sides framed with windows from top to bottom, which provided an easy view of the neighboring streets. He looked around and liked the cozy atmosphere. The place was welcoming but seemed more like a bakery than a diner. Absent was the traditional barstool counter area. Instead, the sitting area was off to the left side with a little over a dozen small tables to easily accommodate a respectable lunch-size crowd. To his right, a glass case with clear shelves of various cold salads and sandwich ingredients began on one corner and joined with a smaller glass display of baked goods before reaching the cash register at the center of the diner. Behind the register area, he could see an open doorway leading to a back room with a large wall oven and more shelving.

"You must be Cameron," Lucy said quietly.

He responded with a nod and half smile then looked down. "You can call me Cam. It's nice to meet you, Lucy."

"It's a pleasure to meet you as well. Would you be able to start today?" she asked.

"That would be fine," he responded. He would love to start immediately and find something to do to keep busy. Although he liked his new room, he was anxious to actually have a job and work—something he hadn't had a chance to do since he was a teenager.

"Great!" Matt enthusiastically remarked. "I've actually got the paperwork here."

After leaving the necessary forms, Matt left Cameron alone with Lucy. As usual, Cam fell silent.

"Why don't we start by showing you around," Lucy said, breaking into his thoughts. She carefully wrapped her arm around his and watched him, as if trying to gauge his reaction.

He looked at Lucy appraisingly. She had that maternal quality that felt as if she could hold you in an embrace and soothe all the wrongs in the world. He placed his large hand on her smaller one and smiled.

She returned the smile and guided him around the little diner. She led him toward the back area, and he saw several ovens, a countertop with various-sized mixing bowls and baking tools. Off to the side was a small desk area, which probably doubled as their office, in between stacks of boxes.

"This is my little piece of heaven," she said with a smile.

"You like to bake stuff?" he asked.

"I'm the baker and Bill is the sandwich guy," she said with a warm smile. The love for her husband was obvious in her wistful expression. She neared Cam and whispered, "It's why we call it a diner and not a bakery."

Cameron genuinely laughed.

"Bill has a bad back so I usually have the boxes of supplies stacked in the corners when they're delivered. He's stubborn, so he won't admit he can't do it."

"Got it."

She walked over to the far end of the room and began trying to push away a few boxes. Cam immediately jumped in and lifted the boxes out of the way. She opened the double door and revealed an empty storage closet.

"Um, why is the closet empty?" he asked. "Most of the stuff in these boxes can probably fit in there. That would help organize things and free up some space to sort out the front and this back room," he asked perplexed. Seemed logical as hell to him to actually *use* the storage closet.

She patted Cam on the shoulder. "Sweetheart, you're working with two very old people who can't lift more than a tray of baked goods."

Cam nodded. "I'll take care of it. How are you guys with reaching and steps?" he asked, remembering that his mom used to use a tiny step stool to reach the upper levels of their pantry.

"Reaching is fine, one or two steps would work as well."

"Got it," he said while his mind immediately started cataloging things he could do with the closet space.

"Bill should be here shortly. Let me get you an apron and go through the different items and prices. I've also got to show you how to work the machines and the register. We have tons to do. Come, come," she said excitedly.

"Um, Lucy, one question," Cam asked hesitantly.

"Yes," she asked.

"Uh, do I have to wear a muffin suit or something like that?"

Lucy scrunched her eyebrows. "Remind me to smack Julian when he comes by to pick you up later," she said as she walked away, shaking her head.

Chapter FOUR

"Hunter, I need you to take these additional cases," Chief Assistant State Attorney Melanie Richards said as she handed over the files.

Hunter took the four folders and looked up at his boss in disbelief. "When did these get in?" he asked.

"We're getting slammed. I don't know what the hell is going on out there," she said with a sigh. "I think it's that new guy running the streets," she finished as she took a seat on his couch and rubbed her temples.

"Even then, you've got to admit, this is a ton of cases coming in, Mel. What the hell?"

"No kidding. I think Mr. Mayor is trying to showcase reduced crime as a major political point on the election ticket so he's pushing the cops, the judges, everyone."

"He picked the worst year to do it. I've got a huge stack of cases on my desk."

Melanie turned her head to the side to stretch her neck. "Did you get any red ones yesterday?"

"Yeah. Six of them."

She sighed then relaxed immediately after Hunter heard the pop of her neck.

Six related to his cases, four to hers. He really wanted to know who was supplying the detailed information and how the hell they knew what he and Melanie were working on at any given time.

Mel stretched her arms across the back of the couch. "I want to know who the hell is sending them over."

Hunter exhaled heavily and nodded. "Hey, how was your date last night with Rick?"

"Are you kidding me? You're thinking of a piece of ass now in the middle of this shitstorm?"

Hunter laughed. "Like you're not. Besides, I live vicariously through your hot dates."

Melanie sighed. "I had to cancel again. I feel horrible."

"You better stop cancelling on him. Finding a guy who loves your grace with the English language isn't easy."

"Fuck you."

"Careful, you're giving me a hard-on."

Melanie snorted a laugh. "Why are you single?"

"'Cause you're straight and I'm not."

Melanie shook her head and smiled. "How's your dad doing?"

Hunter shifted in his seat. "He's fine. Stubborn as always but he's taking his meds and trying to eat right. I've got to sneak over there every now and then to throw out his stash of bacon."

"Don't give him such a hard time. He's trying," she said before standing.

"I know."

"I think he just wants you to come by more often. I wouldn't put it past him to keep a pack of bacon around just so you can find it. Gives you an excuse to come by, you know?"

Hunter rubbed his face. "I know, I know. I need to see him more often. He worries about me so I figured I'd spare him that extra bit of stress."

She patted him on the shoulder. "I've got court in ten. I'll see you later," she finished with a wave good-bye.

Hunter sat back in his chair and looked at the new stack then over to his existing pile. *Does it ever end?* He often sat late into the night, reviewing case files and planning his courtroom strategy for trial, or rehearsing his opening and closing statements. He told himself it was simply because he wanted perfection in the courtroom. At least that was his rationalization to justify the early morning and late hours in the offices.

In the end, Hunter fooled everyone but himself. He was committed to his job—that was indisputable. Ultimately, he just didn't want to go home to an empty house. His recent birthday, benchmarking a major milestone, didn't help. No significant relationship or anything he would consider even mildly short-term. He hadn't found someone who could put up with him or the job or anyone who inspired him to entertain the thought of a compromise. He pushed aside his somber thoughts just as he had done endless times before and focused on the new stack of cases on his desk.

* * * *

"So you have the prices for each of the menu items and know how we plan out the daily specials. Any questions?" Lucy eagerly asked.

"I think I've got everything. But what's up with that machine stashed back there in the corner?" Cameron asked, pointing to the stainless steel, double dispensing espresso machine strategically stored behind two boxes of supplies.

Lucy smiled. "Bill hates that thing, so he hides it behind the napkin boxes, thinking I won't see it."

"How can you miss it?" he commented with a laugh.

Lucy neared as if ready to share a big secret. "I think he's scared of it. He refuses to even discuss it. I think he bought it only because I nagged him about it. I thought it would make a great addition to our menu if we offered a few different options rather than the traditional American coffee. But he won't give in."

Cameron quirked an eyebrow. "I'll take care of it," he said with a pat on Lucy's hand.

Cameron straightened his apron and began collecting some of the supply boxes scattered along the shelves, then worked his way into the various cabinets—leaving the coffee machine area for last. He noticed Bill looking over his shoulder whenever he'd near the corner where the machine was hidden. He made several short trips to organize the supply boxes in one of the empty closets in back. Within five minutes, he'd already removed most of the boxes, giving the entire dining area a more organized appearance. He casually worked his way to the boxes of napkins and gave Lucy a smile.

"Hey, what's this?" he asked, looking over to Bill.

"What?" Bill asked with an *I-don't-know-what-you're-talking-about* expression.

Cam grinned. "This," he said, pointing at the machine.

"That thing?" Bill's face scrunched. "It's the devil incarnate."

Cameron laughed. "C'mon, it can't be that bad."

Bill looked at him incredulously. "If you can figure it out, then it's all yours."

"Huh?"

Bill wiped his hands on the towel tucked at his waist and walked over to Cam. "Lucy's got the cookies and baked stuff, I've got the sandwiches, so if you want to handle this"—Bill waved at the machine with a strained expression on his face—"then you can be the coffee guy."

Cameron was taken aback. To the average everyday person it may have sounded boring or menial. Not to Cam. The fact that he would actually be *the* coffee guy actually mattered. It meant he would be responsible for something, take ownership of tasks, and be part of their little duo, contributing something neither one of them took part in.

"Deal," he said enthusiastically.

"Great. Don't come crying later with steam burns. I'll just say I told ya so," Bill yelled over his shoulder as he walked to the back room.

"Don't mind him," Lucy said with a wave of disregard. "We've got all the supplies over in that cabinet and we've got some of those fancy oversized mugs that were supposed to be for this machine."

"Thank you," he said quietly. Sam had mentioned something called YouTube that might be helpful in getting up to speed with learning a few things. Maybe they'd have something on how to do the fancy coffees and work a machine like the steam-hissing demon Bill avoided. He knew better than to dive right in and guess his way through the steps, knowing Bill's sentiments about the machine.

"What the hell? We have a closet back here?" Bill shouted from the back room.

Cameron and Lucy laughed. He'd only been here for a few hours and was comfortable with them. He never let his guard down so easily but there was something parental about them he craved.

He spent the morning working the cash register when needed, moving all the boxes from the front to the back room and making sure the main dining area was spotless. He had called Julian and asked about installing a few shelves in the closet and getting a single or two-step step stool at the store for Lucy and Bill to help reach the upper shelves. Julian arrived less than an hour later and started installing the shelving in the closet. Cam hoped to have most of the boxes cleared out and packed away by the end of the day.

He was happy to be busy. He'd smile whenever he looked up and saw the sunlight stream in from the windows surrounding the diner and the people racing up and down the street. He was finally free.

* * * *

Hunter looked at his watch and decided to take a break from the mountain of casework. He stuffed a few files into his bag and headed out of his office. "Jess, I'm off to lunch," he said as he passed his assistant's desk.

He walked into his favorite diner and breathed a sigh of relief as he got a whiff of freshly baked cookies.

"Afternoon, Hunter. Turkey today?"

He nodded. "Thanks, Bill."

Something was different. Incredibly different than yesterday it seemed. He looked around casually and observed the changes.

"Don't take this the wrong way, but this is probably the cleanest I've ever seen this place. You got rid of the boxes and...wait a minute, is that an espresso machine back there?" Hunter said with a wicked grin.

Bill scowled. "Don't you start with me on that, too. We've got a coffee guy, you can hound him about it," he said then focused on finishing the sandwich.

"Coffee guy?" he asked with piqued interest.

"Yeah, he started today. He's out back with Lucy rearranging her workspace." Bill walked over to the register with the sandwich on a tray and filled a cup with coffee with the usual mix. "I know you hate this stuff."

Hunter feigned offense. "I don't hate your stuff."

Bill laughed. "I don't know how you do it in court because you're a horrible liar. I know you hate my coffee. It's the only explanation for someone having that much cream and sugar with a tiny splash of coffee in it."

Hunter squirmed. "I do love your sandwiches," he said as he bent to view the display of baked goods, hoping to hide his embarrassment in the process.

"Good save. Maybe our coffee guy can figure out how to make a coffee you like that is actually coffee and not some sugar lava. Hey, Cam," Bill yelled.

"Yeah, Bill."

Hunter closed his eyes as the smooth voice unexpectedly weakened him. He felt as if he'd just been punched in the gut...repeatedly, then kicked in the balls a few times for good measure. Those two simple words in that firm yet silky tone attacked every muscle in his body.

He opened his eyes and tried to calm his racing pulse. Thank God for the clear glass that allowed him to peer through and watch the casual gait of the man as he approached, then turned to face the older, obviously shorter man. Hunter was hypnotized, tracing the perfect curve of the ass in profile, showcased for him through the dessert display case. *How appropriate.* Hunter took a deep breath and slowly straightened from his bent position to meet the new hire.

He froze.

Hunter raked his gaze up the man's body, wishing the guy had worn a tighter shirt that would leave less to the imagination. He was young, a hair under six feet and lean with just the right amount of muscle. Hunter's vivid imagination ran wild as he scanned every inch of this man and his pale skin. He glanced upward to see the dark, sandy brown hair hang lazily over the man's eyes. Hunter's gaze halted once it was met with the brightest blue eyes he had ever seen staring back at him.

* * * *

Well, hello there. Now there's a treat.

Cam looked into piercing silver eyes that seemed to burrow through his soul.

Damn that's hot.

He hated being under scrutiny while in prison, but for some reason, the way this man looked at him unleashed a surge of desire he had difficulty reining in. And for once, he loved being the focus of that much intensity.

The guy was a wall of a man, well over six feet tall and broad shoulders to boot. Not beautiful or a pretty boy, but slightly older and ruggedly handsome like a refined tough guy who filled out the suit quite nicely without overdoing it. He was a contradiction. He looked polished in a finely tailored suit and his closely cropped dark hair. Yet, he exuded a vibe that he would clearly get down and dirty if needed to kick ass. He didn't look like he took shit from anyone. The entire package was just sexy as hell.

"Cam, this is Hunter. He's a regular here and will probably get one of those fancy coffees from that demonic machine. I'll get that," Bill added the last when he heard the phone ring.

They stood, immobile, staring at each other. Cam's heart pounded wildly in his chest. He'd learned how to switch off the feelings of desire, want, and any sort of sexual interest that would get someone in some serious trouble while *inside*. Somehow, all that self-control he had managed to master during the last ten years flew out the diner window when he set eyes on this man.

"Hi, Hunter," Lucy said, instantly breaking the trance between them.

"Hi, Lucy," the man responded in a raspy voice that sent another bolt of desire straight to Cam's groin, triggering a moan to escape.

Hunter's vision immediately snapped back to Cam, and his eye color changed from pale silver to a rich, molten gray.

"Cam, Bill is moving things in the closet you just organized. Would you mind stopping him before he messes it up?" she finished with a shy, pleading grin.

Cam half smiled to Lucy then nodded to Hunter. There was no way he could get a single word out of his mouth with the tightness in his chest and throat at the moment. He could barely walk a straight line with the raging hard-on in his pants. He retreated to the back thankful to have escaped any potential embarrassment.

After he recovered and managed to convince Bill to stay out of the storage closet to reorganize everything, he walked back out to the front.

Every hair on his body rose, his skin tingled. He was being watched.

His heart raced and his palms began to sweat.

He looked around frantically until his gaze froze on the silver stare intently focused on him. Hunter sat in a corner, papers scattered in front of him, sipping his coffee as he watched Cam. He couldn't look away. The hypnotic state was broken when Hunter flinched and set the coffee cup down on the table, staring at it with a sneer.

Cameron chuckled as he wrapped his apron on again and immediately welcomed the next customer waiting in line. After he finished with the patrons and their orders, he wiped down the counter. His gaze absently strayed to the man in the corner. Hunter was intently focused on the papers in front of him when his phone rang. He mouthed a few words before he ended the call then stood and started packing his things.

With a short wave good-bye and a quick stride, Hunter exited the diner.

Mr. Hot Guy was a regular, so he'd have eye candy to look at every day while he worked in the diner. The job was good before, and it was starting to get pretty damn amazing.

After spending endless afternoon hours at the diner reading the manual and testing each dial, handle, gauge, and spout, Cam was a little more comfortable at least knowing how each item worked on the machine. He'd figured out what to do to avoid a steam burn and how long the milk needed to steam to get to the right temperature. He had practiced and learned as much as he could until Julian arrived to pick him up. Now he just needed to learn how to actually put it all together to be able to handle working everything with the morning crowd.

"How was your first day," Matt asked as Cam walked in the door of the halfway house.

"Good but weird."

"Why weird?" Matt asked curiously.

Cam shrugged. "I'm not used to interacting with so many people. I tried, and I think I did okay, but it's just a bit...I don't know...weird."

He wasn't ready to openly admit he tried to gauge which people were harmless and which were ones he needed to be careful with. He found it a little easier to interact with women, but the male customers—they were different. He wasn't sure if what he said would be misunderstood or what was the appropriate way to act around them in that type of setting. He kept things as professional as he should be, but always on guard.

He was a little more relaxed around those customers Lucy and Bill declared as regulars, but the others, not so much. He couldn't ignore the feeling that, somehow, the ghosts from his past would find out he was free and try to get him back into prison.

Then there was Hunter. The man just threw him off balance. The way he looked, those eyes, that stare, the slight hint of cologne he wore, and the smooth, deep, *sexy-as-fuck* voice. *Shit.* Just the thought of everything made him light-headed with the blood shifting to other parts of his body.

"It's a big change. I'm sure you did fine," Matt assured him.

Cam remembered what he needed to do. "Do you have a computer I can use?"

Matt nodded. "Anything in particular you need?"

"Do you have that YouTube thing on there? Sam said it was a good place to learn how to do things. I'm going to be doing the non-traditional coffee stuff at the diner and I wanted to see how some other people do it before I start on this stuff tomorrow."

Matt beamed. "Sure, c'mon," he said as he excitedly guided Cam to his office. He sat Cam down at his desk and launched a browser.

"Thanks."

"Just enter whatever you want to search for and there's probably some video on it," he finished then exited.

Cameron searched through videos, watched several, and took notes on tips of things to absolutely avoid. "What...the...hell," he mumbled when he encountered a video on latte art. That elevated plain, boring coffee to something downright extraordinary. He watched video after video on various pouring techniques and designs. Hell, if he could learn how to do this, it would be like creating a piece of art with each coffee he poured.

First, the thought of being responsible for something on his own, and now, the chance to actually create something different. Prison didn't require him to lead, manage, think, decide, or create anything. His pulse began to race and his chest tightened. He looked to his right. He needed to see the sunlight seeping into the window.

It's not a dream. I'm free.

He closed his eyes and took a few deep breaths. He wanted to give this new start a chance. He wanted to know what it felt like to laugh openly, to try something new, to just be normal again...even if only for a short time.

He exhaled heavily. He was tired of letting these ghosts get the best of him. However short-lived this chance at freedom was, he was going to try to enjoy it. Savor it for the treat that it was. And if he was able to benefit from a little eye candy, then he would certainly take advantage of that as well.

Chapter FIVE

Hunter spent the next morning in court going through the motions, cross examining the last witness and finishing with his closing arguments. Even though he was focused on the case and sticking to the game plan, his mind wandered endlessly to the new hire at the diner. It had been too long since someone captivated his attention so intensely. Eight years in the Marines had honed his ability to judge both situations and people, assess quickly and act quicker—all that was useless when it came to this man. He couldn't figure him out and Hunter wasn't beyond admitting that the mystery was part of the appeal. He obviously wasn't shy since he didn't look away when Hunter caught himself staring, but he wasn't open and outgoing either.

He seemed reserved, yet semisocial. Cam was always quiet initially, then seemed to offer women ready smiles and conversation while avoiding interaction with the male customers. He hadn't said a word to Hunter on that first day. Other than the moan which had escaped, there was no indication he might like men. Hunter wasn't sure if the staring match was attraction or simply a standoff. He hated not knowing and despised not having control of the situation.

After finally wrapping up the case, he headed out of the courthouse and walked the block to the diner. He looked at his watch again. It was the first time he made his way to the diner without a thought of having one of Lucy's cookies. Instead, it was the haunting gaze of those soulful blue eyes that drove his steps down the pavement.

* * * *

Dammit. So fucking close.

Cameron stirred the coffee to erase the billionth mistake at his attempt to create a latte art design. He wasn't about to give up, he figured he'd try again on the next order. All morning he'd been working the espresso machine. He was proud of the fact that he was able to handle the machine without being subjected to any of the 'demonic steam' Bill swore would kill his motivation. He was thrilled customers were enthusiastic about having a choice between Bill's traditional American coffee and one of Cam's lattes. He was nowhere near close to earning bragging rights, but he was definitely smiling at the yums of approvals from each of the customers.

"Cam, we've got another order for a latte," Bill shouted over to him in the corner.

He steamed the milk in the metal jug until the right texture was achieved while he brewed the espresso shots. He poured the coffee in, angled the mug and started to pour the heated milk into the cup, kicking in a little bit of movement when it was halfway full to start creating the design. With the final tilt of the cup and top off of milk, he swooped a thinner stream down the middle in the opposite direction and successfully finished his first design.

I did it.

Cameron couldn't hide the smile that invaded his face. His first finished design and it was absolutely fucking perfect. The medium brown coffee drink surface had a gradient, from dark to white, forming the shape of a heart. He thought about adding a few dabs of chocolate syrup to accent the heart but decided against it, worried he'd just screw it up.

He took a deep breath to control his overexcited heartbeat. He couldn't remember the last time he had been so damn proud of himself. He walked slowly with the mug to avoid spills, happy as hell at having completed his first after so many attempts that morning. He gently placed the mug on the tray next to the register. He smiled, still admiring the perfect heart floating on the surface. He glanced up, his smile vanished, and he quickly looked away.

Mr. Regular had placed the order. *Shit.*

Seriously, what were the odds of that happening?

The irony was not lost on him.

"Oh my goodness, Cam. Is that a heart?" Lucy asked, clasping her hands together.

Cam nodded and hated the total awkwardness of the moment. His gaydar had been disconnected for the last decade, and he wasn't about to alienate the one guy he was actually interested in until he had a better handle on whether Mr. Regular was even gay. All he saw were questions in those silver eyes and the thought of getting his ass kicked for making an unwelcomed pass was not at the top of his list.

"Is this what you've been trying to do all morning?" Lucy asked.

"Yeah, um," Cam said, thinking quickly, "I thought it'd be nice to do this for that customer who was talking about her anniversary thing this morning?"

"Kathy, the one who's celebrating her first anniversary tomorrow?"

"Yeah, her."

"That's so thoughtful of you. I'm sure that would make her morning." Lucy excused herself when she heard the ding from the timer in the back room, and Bill went off to help a new customer with their sandwich order, leaving him alone with Hunter.

Hunter deflated. The questions no longer lingered in his gaze.

Cameron thought the best approach would be a professional one. "Can I help you with anything else, sir?"

Hunter's cheeks flushed with color.

Cameron cocked his head to the side, questioning. *Is the attraction mutual? Or is it something else that's embarrassing him?*

Hunter shook his head, avoiding eye contact. "I just need to pay."

Cam inhaled and let the smooth tone of Hunter's voice flow through his body. He rang up the items as Hunter withdrew his wallet from his back pocket.

"That will be six twenty-eight—"

Hunter placed the money on the countertop while Cameron casually observed each of his movements, however minimal.

"Sir," he added, remembering to keep it professional.

Hunter's cheeks flushed with color again.

Bingo. Cam didn't understand why that one word would trigger a heated flush of embarrassment in the man. Cam reassessed him. Hunter looked to be in his mid-thirties and obviously fit. The whole package was just enticing as hell and a few years didn't matter to Cam anyway.

Hunter took the tray and made his way to his corner of the diner.

Cameron watched him open his bag and take out some folders then remove the items from the tray and place them on the table. He ate his sandwich and just stared at the coffee mug. He'd take another bite and would turn the mug as if seeing it from a slightly different angle. He had already eaten half his sandwich, yet hadn't tasted his latte.

Cam wanted to grab the man and shove the coffee down his throat. Why the hell didn't he try it already? He couldn't hate the taste if he hadn't tried it. He took a deep breath to settle himself. For some reason, he just needed to know Hunter liked it, but all the man did was stare at the damn thing.

He couldn't take this anymore.

He took another deep breath then stormed to the back room where Lucy was cooling the cookies she had removed from the oven a few moments before.

"Are these ready yet?" he asked.

"Yes, they've already cooled for a bit," Lucy said.

"Thanks," he said, pulling one of the dry wax bakery tissues to grab one of the new flavored white chocolate chip cookies from the rack. He stomped out of the back room and into the dining area to Hunter's corner.

He sat there, sandwich finished, still staring at his damn coffee.

Cameron walked up to him and extended his hand that held the cookie. "You forgot your cookie," he added lamely.

Hunter looked at him, perplexed. "Thanks," he said as he reached for his wallet.

"On the house."

"Thanks," he said hesitantly as he took the offered cookie.

"Aren't you going to drink that?" Cam asked, pointing to the latte.

"I like the design," he said with a half smile. "I don't want to mess it up."

Cameron grabbed the spoon from the coffee dish and stirred the latte, erasing the heart design.

"Why'd you do that?" Hunter asked mournfully.

"Just drink your coffee," he mumbled.

Hunter cautiously raised the mug to his lips for a taste while maintaining eye contact with Cam. "It's really good," he said with a hesitant smile.

A wave of relief flooded Cam's senses with the approval. Watching Hunter take another sip of the coffee he'd mixed and his unmistakable expression of enjoyment was all Cam needed at that moment. He curtly nodded then retreated to the cash register. He withdrew money from his pocket to cover the cost of the cookie and added it to the register then tended to the new customer who had entered the diner.

Having a few minutes to think about what he had done made him realize how odd his actions were. He sighed. He hated prison, but at least there he knew what to do and exactly what was expected. Here, all bets were off. Cam wasn't sure how he was supposed to act with someone he was attracted to who might or might not be gay. It probably didn't matter anyway, he was certain Hunter thought he had a screw loose at this point based on how he had acted a few moments ago.

Cam had to find some way to make it up to him and regain possession of his sanity.

* * * *

Hunter didn't have a clue what the hell was going on. First, he thought the amazing heart design in the coffee might have been meant for him but Cam quickly pissed away that idea before it had a chance to take root. Apparently, it was meant for some other customer, a woman. *Great.* The first guy in a long time to light a fire inside him and he was straight. Hunter was bummed and wasn't going to lie to himself. He'd hopelessly stared at the damn design and all he thought about was how much time and practice it must have taken to do something like that. But what the hell did it matter, it was for someone else. He just couldn't bring himself to drink the coffee and make the heart disappear. How sappy was that?

He'd been so lost in thought he hadn't noticed Cam walk up to his table with the cookie. The man was actually talking to him rather than just taking an order or ringing up the bill. Hunter was stunned at how attractive this man was, in full view without the counter blocking an inch of real estate.

He almost kicked himself for vocalizing how he felt about the design. He did like it and was upset when Cam stirred it away. That quickly, the heart and whatever it may or may not have represented was gone.

Hunter finished his coffee and cookie and tried to wrap up the last of the case file he was working on. He looked at his watch and sighed, remembering his afternoon appointment. He glanced over and saw Cam walk to the corner where the coffee machine was stationed.

Hunter could talk his way out of just about any situation, but here he was, staring at a guy who drove him out of control and gave off all kinds of mixed signals. He took a deep breath then exhaled, not knowing what to do for the first time in his life. He wasn't the kind of guy to give up, especially when he wanted something so intensely.

His phone chirped on the table...a text message from Jessie reminding him of his appointment.

He packed up the files, dumped his garbage, and was on his way to exit the diner.

"Hunter, wait a second," he heard Cam say.

Damn, there was something about hearing Cam call his name that tightened his chest. He turned and saw Cam standing there holding a lidded plastic coffee cup.

"Yours was probably cold by the time you drank it so here's one to-go."

Hunter smiled. He didn't dare hope this meant anything more than someone just giving him a cup of coffee to-go.

"Thanks," he said, taking the cup.

"See you tomorrow," Cam said, then walked away without waiting for a response.

Hunter strolled the block to his office and thought about Cam. Those crystal blue eyes contrasted boldly against his dark, sandy brown hair and light skin. He wasn't thin, but for some reason, his jeans slung low on his hips and his shirts seemed a little looser than those worn by guys his age.

His age. Hunter didn't want to think about that.

He finally arrived at the office and dropped his bag on the couch. With a full schedule for the afternoon, he had to get his brain in gear.

He settled in his chair and popped the lid off the cup.

Hunter couldn't help the smile that formed on his face once he saw the heart design floating on the surface of the coffee.

Tomorrow couldn't come soon enough.

Chapter SIX

Cameron was on auto-pilot. Thankfully, he'd received endless latte orders to keep him busy, trying new designs and perfecting them. So far, he was able to complete heart and rosette patterns. He'd even found it was easy to mix them together for a Christmas tree-like design with a heart tree topper.

Bill or Lucy would inform him of a new order, he'd take a peek at the patron—girls got hearts, guys got the leafy rosette. No need to piss off some dude with a heart design. And the rude assholes, the ones who wouldn't have the courtesy to hang up their fucking phones when placing their orders with Bill or the ones who acted as if Lucy owed them something for coming in, fuck 'em, no design for them.

Pissed didn't begin to sum up how he felt.

Where the hell was Hunter, and why hadn't he come into the diner for the last few days? He'd been thinking endlessly about the man, and it was driving him to the brink of insanity. He could probably manage a day, maybe even two without seeing him. But he obviously couldn't seem to handle three days plus a weekend. He didn't even know if the man was gay. He was so frustrated he'd barely spoken a word since arriving at the diner. Lucy and Bill kept circling him to check up on him and that, too, was driving him crazy. They meant well, but the fucking hard-on in his pants wasn't letting him form a cordial sentence all damn day. Cam just needed to see Hunter. Maybe that would somehow settle him. He'd find some way to figure out if the man was gay or not. Maybe he'd just make a fucking latte penis in his coffee and see if that design perked his interest.

"Sweetie, you want to take a break?" Lucy asked carefully. "You've been working all day."

Cameron shook his head. He sure as hell didn't need a fifteen minute break of doing nothing other than thinking about those piercing silver eyes. *Fuck.*

"I'm going to be out back cooling the new batch. If you change your mind, just come get me, okay?"

Cam nodded and finished working the heart design for the thin blonde in the green business suit. Lucy delivered the coffee order to the customer before disappearing to the back.

Cameron closed his eyes and took a few deep breaths. He had survived the extra busy morning crowd and typical lunchtime rush without any issues or obstacles. If Hunter hadn't shown up by now, then he probably wasn't going to come in today, and he'd just have to deal with not seeing him for yet another day.

"Cam, register please," Bill called over from the sandwich station.

He took a deep cleansing breath. He had a job to do. It was no one's fault he was lusting for a guy who might or might not be gay. He started to walk over to the register and stopped.

Hunter.

There, standing at the register with his head down, talking on the phone, dressed to kill in a dark blue suit and blue-gray tie. Cam inhaled deeply and tried to calm his breathing. Damn, the man looked good.

"They panicked after yesterday's testimony and walked in today wanting to cut a deal. I'll finish up the paperwork when I get in," Cameron heard him say into the phone. "No, don't reschedule anything, I'll just use the time to prep for the other cases. I'll see you in a bit, if anything comes up, just text me."

Cam walked to the register as Hunter closed and pocketed his phone.

Hunter looked up and half smiled. "Hi."

Cameron was mesmerized by those silver eyes. The slight ease at seeing Hunter warred with the sexual tension at being near him.

Hunter arched an eyebrow.

Cam realized he hadn't responded. *Shit.* "How can I help you, sir?"

Color rushed to Hunter's face as he looked away. Damn, he liked knowing he could unsettle this man with a simple word.

"Turkey sandwich, cookie, and one of your lattes please," he mumbled.

"You a lawyer?" Cam asked.

"Yes," Hunter responded, making eye contact again.

Cam stood there and assessed him, uncertain if Hunter being an attorney should concern him. He didn't cause Cameron to put up his guard or get the vibe that Hunter could easily be bought or swayed by others.

"Does that bother you?"

"I'm trying to figure out if you're one of the good guys or bad guys," he said candidly.

"I promise I'm one of the good ones," Hunter said softly with a tired smile.

Cam nodded. One thing he had learned in the last ten years was to trust his gut. "Chocolate chip or macadamia?"

"Chocolate chip."

Cameron went to the back and returned with a chocolate chip cookie in a bag.

"Is Cam short for Cameron?"

"Yeah."

"Have you worked on any other designs today?"

"A leaf looking thing called a rosette. Are you gay?" Cameron froze the moment the question escaped his mouth. He was so preoccupied with the rapid-fire questions and answers he didn't realize the one question his brain kept asking should have remained quiet.

"Yes."

His heart pounded against his ribcage and his chest tightened. Now that the question was out of the way, he didn't know what to say or do.

"Is that a problem?" Hunter asked.

Cam shook his head. He rang up the rest of the order, gave Hunter his change, then went to his machine to prepare the coffee. He returned a few minutes later with a latte bearing a combo rosette heart design.

"Nice," Hunter said with a full grin.

"Are you going to drink it this time or stare at it?"

"You could take a break and join me to supervise."

Wait a minute. Is he flirting? Is Hunter flirting?

"Cam, take your break," Bill said with a smirk, clearly overhearing the exchange.

Cameron was dazed. He looked over to Bill then back to Hunter. He wanted to sit with him, hell, he wanted to pounce on the man and lick every inch of him. But what if he said the wrong thing or asked another question best left unasked?

Hunter's phone chirped. He reached into his jacket and read the display. He groaned. "I need to go to the office."

Cam nodded.

"How old are you, Cameron?"

Does that matter? What am I supposed to say? Crap. His brain was getting fried, and damn, he loved the way his name sounded in that *sexy-as-fuck* voice.

Hunter's phone chirped again.

"Damn it. I've got to go."

Cameron stuffed the sandwich Bill passed over to him into a bag then immediately grabbed the latte mug, emptied the coffee into a lidded cup, and handed it to Hunter.

"That's the second design you've erased," Hunter said with a wry grin.

His cell phone chirped again, and Cam could swear he heard Hunter growl. His rock hard dick was going to explode he was so turned on right now. "I'll make you two tomorrow. Now go before you scare the other customers."

Hunter looked at Cam with an odd expression then shook his head. "I'll see you tomorrow."

Cam nodded and watched Hunter as he turned to exit the diner. He knew his attempt at flirting had completely failed with his inappropriate questions and comments. Who was he kidding, he didn't know the first damn thing about how to flirt. He should have kept it professional.

Just before opening the door, Hunter turned and gave Cam one of his piercing glares. He then smiled and waved good-bye.

Cam returned the smile before Hunter turned away to leave.

Well, damn. Maybe this flirting thing wasn't so hard after all.

Chapter SEVEN

Hunter sat in his living room, staring at a case file, trying to make sense of an illogical situation. Preston had agreed to a lesser sentence with a simple condition to turn in a decent lead of a 'business associate'. Not even an hour after leaving the courtroom, his office had received notification the defendant was reneging on the deal and wanted to finish the trial. Hunter raced back to court. In the end, a deal for a three year term was declined in exchange for a twelve year prison sentence. *Fucking moron.* It didn't make any sense at all for someone who swore the drugs found in his possession were not his.

Hunter finished the last of the paperwork and stuffed the files back into his bag. He was too wired. He needed to let off some tension, or he was never going to get some sleep tonight. He quickly changed into his workout clothes and headed out to the gym.

While driving, his mind absently wandered to Cameron. Cam captivated him with his weary smile and mesmerizing blue eyes. He had been tense all damn day at the trial, bothered he would miss seeing him another day.

Why the hell hadn't Cameron answered the question about his age before the damn text messages kept interrupting? Maybe he wasn't as young as he looked. He could hope. For some reason, the thought of lusting after a guy almost twenty years younger than him seemed off.

Fucking midlife crisis.

He didn't feel his age. Cam calling him 'sir' just made the age difference more apparent. Maybe it was the whole, respecting elders and shit. He groaned. He hated being self-conscious, that trait wasn't part of his DNA.

He thought the interest was double-sided but then Cam became distant again when Hunter had asked him to join him for coffee. He sighed. Maybe it was best not to push. He could do that and maintain his sanity. Problem was, staying sane was not at the top of his list of priorities, seeing Cam and getting to know him was.

* * * *

"Hey, Dad?" Hunter asked as he closed the door behind him to his father's home. He put his keys and wallet on the table by the door before yelling again, "Dad, you home?"

"Where the hell else am I going to be at this time," his father responded, exiting the bedroom in his tank top and boxer shorts with his hair sticking up in all directions. "Be quiet or you'll wake the neighbors."

"It's only nine o'clock." Hunter chuckled and gave his dad a hug. "How ya doing?" he asked, assessing his father with an arched eyebrow.

"I'm fine," his father responded as he sat on the couch and motioned for Hunter to sit on the side chair. "Sit over there so you don't stink up my good couch."

Hunter laughed. "Sorry, Dad. I had to work off some stress at the gym." He took a seat and watched his dad position himself more comfortably. He noticed the thinner frame his father now bore and how his hair shone silver against the light. Regardless of his appearance, Thomas Donovan was fiercely independent and strong-willed.

"Stop looking at me like that. I'm not your courtroom prey."

He groaned and rubbed his face. "Sorry, Dad."

"What's wrong?" his father asked, obvious worry coloring his expression.

Hunter sighed. "Even when I don't want to, I think I give off that vibe."

"A case going badly?" he asked with concern. "You're married to that job. You need to go out, find yourself a nice young man, and settle down."

Hunter stared at his father in disbelief.

"Fine, then find yourself a guy and go fuck like bunnies."

"I'm *so* not having this conversation with you." Hunter got up from the couch and headed to the kitchen.

"You're not going to find any bacon in there," his father yelled from the other room.

Hunter shook his head and smiled as he raided the cupboard.

"Pantry, top shelf," his father said, leaning on the doorway. "Get enough for both of us."

Hunter looked over his shoulder and stared at his father as he walked over to sit in one of the seats at the kitchen table.

"And get some milk too while you're up."

Hunter grabbed the package of sugarless treats from the pantry then poured two glasses of milk. He slid one of the glasses over to his father and sat in the seat next to him.

"Wow, the whole package. That bad?"

"Dad, stop." He opened the container and dunked one of the wafers in the milk. "These things taste like shit."

"Suck it up. They're the only thing my stubborn son will let me sneak into this house."

Hunter glared.

His father watched him chew on the soggy treat.

"What!"

"What's his name?"

Hunter closed his eyes and heavily sighed while he finished chewing. The image of Cam immediately came to mind. Cam's bright blue eyes and the way he easily smiled with some of the customers at the diner. The way Cam's muscles flexed and his ass tightened slightly in his jeans when he moved boxes around. The smooth, firm timbre of his voice when he spoke, echoed in Hunter's head.

"What's his name?" his father asked again, jolting Hunter back to the conversation.

"Why do you assume there's someone?"

It was his father's turn to glare.

Hunter caved. "Cam. His name is Cameron. He works at the diner by the office," he finished before jabbing another wafer into his milk.

"Obviously, you like him. So what's the problem?"

"I don't know," he mumbled with a mouthful of moist treat. "I don't know what to say."

"That's a new one. Knowing you, you're probably doing that stare thing rather than talking to him."

Hunter shook his head as he chewed.

"You're a stubborn ass. You don't even know you're doing it. You're probably freaking him out."

"What the hell am I supposed to say, Dad? 'Hey, Cam, I like you—let's go fuck like bunnies?' You can't be serious."

Hunter almost spilled his milk when his father slapped him across the back of the head. "What the hell, Dad! Those were your words not mine," he said, rubbing the back of his head.

"I can't believe I'm having this conversation with you." His father pressed his palms to his eyes. "You obviously like him so damn much you don't know what to do. What are you worried about?"

Hunter shrugged. "He's younger than I am."

"Is he legal?"

Hunter pinched the bridge of his nose. "For fuck's sake, Dad. Really?"

His father laughed. "Son, it's not like you're my age. How *much* younger?"

"I don't know for sure. I asked him but I didn't get an answer."

"And?"

"And what?"

"I was fifteen years older than your mother, and I loved her more than I thought it was possible to love someone else, and she loved me the same. Age is bullshit. Ask him out."

"It's not that easy. Sometimes, I think he's flirting or something, but then I'm not sure. Maybe he's just being nice to me because I'm a customer. I don't know, Dad. I think he *sees* me as...old," Hunter mumbled the last part.

"Has he called you an old fart or something?"

Hunter just shook his head at the direction the conversation had taken. He couldn't believe he was sitting in his father's kitchen, having cardboard sugarless tasteless wafers with milk, talking about his love life or lack thereof.

"He calls me sir."

"So. Some people are into that stuff."

"Oh hell, Dad." Hunter got up from his seat to empty his glass in the sink.

"Stop it and listen," his father said in his tone of authority.

"If Cam were a girl, I could tell you what to look for—the hair flips, the giggles, and all that other flirty stuff your mom did, which I loved to let her think I didn't notice. But I don't know what it is you guys do. I do know one thing—I was terrified out of my mind to talk to your mother even though I knew, from that first instance, that she was the one for me. I'd sit in those damn uncomfortable church pews for hours just to watch her. When I finally got the nerve up to talk to her and ask her out, you know what she said?"

"No, you've never told me this story," Hunter said with a soft tone and wistful half smile.

"She said...'It took you this long to ask me out, how long is it going to take before you kiss me?'"

Hunter laughed. "What did you do?"

"I kissed her right then and there," his father said with a devilish grin.

His dad rose from his seat and walked over to Hunter. He cupped Hunter's face and looked at him for some time without saying a word.

"You're freaking me out," Hunter said after a few moments of silence.

"I want you to listen to me very carefully."

"Uh huh."

"I want you to be happy. I'm tired of seeing you overworking yourself—sacrificing your life and putting everyone else first. Something about this young man has you all screwed up in the head. That's not like you. The biggest mistake you can make is to ignore that. Just talk to him. Ask him out. Your persistence is one of your strongest character traits. If he says no, try again until you tire him out and he gives in."

"People have been known to get arrested for that," Hunter said. "Stalking, harassment, restraining orders—"

His father squeezed Hunter's face tighter and searched his expression. "I don't remember you ever getting like this about anyone."

"I haven't, that's why I'm so damn…" Hunter paused, searching for the right word. "Confused. Besides, it's way too soon for it to be anything that serious. It's only been a week."

"You're scared because you don't know what to do."

"I'm not scared."

"Of course you're not."

"Dad, reverse psychology won't work on me."

His father finally released Hunter's face. "I knew I loved your mom on that first day and married her a few months later. Same thing happened to your grandpa and his. It's part of our DNA."

"What are we? Werewolves?"

"I have heard you growl on an occasion or two."

Silence.

"You're not old, Son."

"I'm forty."

"That's not old, you stubborn mule," his father said, exasperated.

"I thought I was a werewolf," Hunter deadpanned.

His father paused and looked down, lost in thought for a moment then shook his head. "I'm glad you're here because I wanted to talk to you about something."

Hunter wasn't about to let his guard down. He had learned some tricks from his dad and knew a switch in conversation was a tactic to get his way.

"I'm seeing someone."

Um, that's unexpected. "Uh...what?"

"I'm seeing someone. She makes me smile," his father said with a grin. "We get along great, and we talk about all kinds of stuff and have a lot in common."

"Okay," he commented, not knowing what else to say.

"She's not your mom—no one ever will be. We just like each other's company and I've got a date this weekend with her. We're going to go watch a movie on Miracle Mile."

"Okay." Hunter thought about it. The thought of his father seeing someone else was surprising. He knew his mother wanted his dad to move on, she was very clear about that before she passed away so many years ago. His dad was the one who seemed resistant to taking the next step, said he could only ever love someone that much once in his life. Hunter wrapped his arms around his father and gave him a hug. "I'm happy for you, Dad."

"Me, too," his father said as he patted Hunter's back. "So if this old fart can get the nerve up to ask someone else out, so can you."

Fuck, I walked right into that one.

"Smooth, Dad."

His father laughed. "All kidding aside, just ask him. Otherwise, the what-ifs are going to drive you insane."

Hunter couldn't argue that point. "I'll figure something out."

"You always do," his dad responded in his proud-father tone.

"I've got to go." Hunter turned and gave his father another hug. "Thanks, Dad."

"I didn't do anything but give you a hard time," he said, squeezing Hunter tighter.

Hunter released his dad and looked at the man who always seemed to know exactly what Hunter needed to hear throughout his life, even if he didn't know it at the time. He pressed his forehead to his father's. "I'll see you soon. Have fun on your date."

Hunter waved good-bye to his dad. He drove off and wondered how the hell he was going to focus on getting some sleep when all he could think about was seeing Cam the next day. He wasn't sure how he was going to do it, but he had to get his brain in gear and focus on his cases. Even if the only thing on his mind had the most alluring blue eyes he'd ever seen.

Chapter EIGHT

Hunter wasn't stalking...much. He also wasn't kidding himself as to the reason why he was sitting at the diner so early in the morning. He just wanted to see Cameron, hear his voice, see his smile, anything...something.

He had arrived at the office early, hoping to catch up with a few case files only to receive notice Preston had been found dead in the holding cell. How he had managed to get a sharp object and slit his throat was under investigation, and the FBI wanted to immediately review Preston's case, in detail. Another day gone to hell, but there was no way he was going off to meet with the feds unless he got a chance to see Cam before the weekend.

As luck would have it, Cam started later today. Hunter looked at his watch for the billionth time. He had stretched this as much as he could and only had a few minutes before he needed to leave and hoped like hell Cam arrived before then.

He looked at his watch again. *Damn.* Resigned, he stood and walked over to the counter just as Bill finished up with a customer.

"Um, Bill?"

"Yeah."

"Can you tell Cam—"

Tell Cam what, exactly? That he waited for over thirty minutes like a psychotic stalker because he wanted, no, *needed* to see him? "Uh, can you just tell him—"

"Why don't you tell him yourself," Bill said with a chin up gesture toward the door.

Hunter turned, and there was Cam, walking along the sidewalk toward the front door. When he entered, the surprised expression was quickly replaced by a scowl.

"You're early today," Cam said once he walked up to Hunter.

"Yeah, something came up and I'll probably be away all day. So, I…uh…wanted to come by before disappearing all day."

"Oh," Cam said and fidgeted.

"How old are you?"

"That's the second time you've asked me that," Cam said with a half smile. "Does it matter?"

Yes, no, Hunter wasn't sure anymore.

"Sir?"

Hunter's cheeks heated. He looked up and saw Cameron with a broad grin on his face. "You do that on purpose, don't you?"

"Gets you every time," Cam said with the first full smile directed at Hunter.

Hunter stifled a laugh and stared at Cam, both men with silly grins on their faces. He couldn't believe how much a smile brightened this man's entire face.

"I'm twenty-seven," Cam finally answered.

Hunter nodded and breathed a sigh of relief. "I thought you were younger."

"I get that a lot."

"I just had a birthday. I'm, um…forty."

"Is that supposed to bother me," Cam asked, still smiling. "Sir?"

Hunter chuckled with a grin still plastered on his face.

"If it makes you feel better, I'll be a whopping twenty-eight soon."

Hunter shook his head. He had the sneaking suspicion Cam was going to give him a shitload of grief about the age gap. But if it really didn't bother him, then Hunter would welcome the teasing if they got to spend more time together.

"I know you need to leave, but can you wait two minutes?"

Hunter nodded then Cam walked off and, in a few quick strides, made it behind the counter to the corner where the coffee machine resided.

He looked over to Bill who was wiping down the sandwich area with a knowing grin. Hunter didn't care if he'd heard. He finally broke through the awkwardness with Cam and was pretty damn proud of making some form of progress.

Cam returned with a lidded coffee cup in hand. "I figured you were going to have a long day and you could use one of these. No design today because you're supposed to drink it not stare at it."

Hunter reached for the cup. Their fingers grazed as they held the hot drink. Their gazes fixated on one another and both took a slow, labored intake of breath. Hunter's pulse began to race, his heart fluttered frantically. He wondered if Cam had also felt a jolt pass through his body when they'd touched. He cautiously raised his index finger and brushed Cameron's digits, still gripping the cup. Cam gasped, maintaining eye contact. His eyes looked dazed, darkening to a beautiful shade of sapphire with each stroke of Hunter's finger. Cameron swayed slightly. Hunter withdrew the cup from his grip and broke the trance.

Cam steadied himself and blinked rapidly until he focused again on Hunter. "You were leaving," he said, his hoarse voice barely audible.

Hunter nodded. He fought to control a base desire in his body to grab Cam and take him over the countertop. "Monday," was all he trusted himself to say. Saying 'have a nice weekend' or 'see you on Monday' would have expelled more energy than he could spare.

A customer entered the diner, immediately followed by another.

"Monday," Cameron whispered. "Sir."

Hunter shook his head, smiled, then turned to exit. Before walking out, he looked over his shoulder to see Cam still standing in the middle of the diner with a smirk on his face.

Waiting to see Cam again…Hunter knew he was in for the longest weekend of his life.

* * * *

FBI agent, Connor Ellis, shook his head in disbelief. "So you expect me to believe Preston gave up a deal of three years for a twelve year term then decided to kill himself? What…out of regret for making a mistake or something?"

Hunter leaned back in his chair. "I don't expect you to believe any of this. You think this makes sense to me?"

Connor exhaled heavily. "We've got to be missing something. Let's go over it again."

"We've been over it four times already. There's nothing on these damn papers that's going to make it any clearer. He was busted with drugs on him, which he claimed were not his. Insisted he was set up, but who the hell was going to believe a guy with a drug record the length of my arm. He agrees to take the deal in exchange for some intel, but then changes his mind, and the next day he goes back to trial, which ends exactly the way it was going to end. Now, if you want to figure out what's going on, you need to look at what's not on paper."

"What do you mean?"

"C'mon, Connor. I'm sure you can see there's got to be something else going on here."

"I go by the evidence. I don't go by gut."

"I've known you for years, have you really lost the ability to see through bullshit?"

Connor ran his hands through his hair. "Okay, let's go over what's not on paper."

"I think something else is going on but I'm not entirely sure yet. I just know something is off with this case."

"Stop being so cryptic. Just tell me what you're thinking," Connor said.

Hunter wasn't about to reveal that Preston's name had appeared on his desk in a red file exactly one week before the arrest. He still didn't know the source or purpose of the files but knew the information in Preston's file did not add up to the series of events in the last few days.

"I know he was scared shitless in court. The guy was completely freaking out and kept telling his attorney he wanted to deal. He freaked out so badly they ceased jury selection and that's when we started negotiations."

"So what changed his mind?"

"That's the answer we need to figure out. The next day in court, he was a different person. The panic wasn't there anymore. He was too calm, disconnected."

"So you think someone got to him?"

Hunter steepled his fingers and tapped the tips on his chin. "I don't know for sure, but I can't help thinking, yeah, someone got to him. But the question is why and what the hell convinced him to give away a chance at freedom to do it."

"Okay, let's go back to the drugs on him. The ones he claims weren't his. Are they related to this new drug guy on the streets?"

"I don't know for sure. The heavy guy on the streets right now marks his bags. They all bear a logo and the ones he had in his possession did not."

"The star logo?" Connor asked.

"Yeah," Hunter said as he reached for a sheet of the notebook paper and withdrew the pen from his jacket inside pocket. He sketched the logo he had memorized after seeing it on so many crime scene images. A five-pointed star with four rotated "L" shapes around it. As if the star was on top of a rectangle. "This one."

"So the drugs that were planted were not from this drug guy."

Hunter looked over thoughtfully. "Or maybe they are but they just hadn't had a chance to print the star on them yet."

"Maybe he wanted to sell the drugs, get a cut, create some competition. Some competitors would hurt business and boost sales for the Star Man."

"Fuck, man, don't give this guy a nickname," Hunter said, rubbing his eyes in frustration.

"It's not me, everyone on this case is calling him that. It just hasn't hit the press."

"I don't think the guy is eliminating competition."

"Why not?"

"Preston wasn't pushing."

"Everyone always says 'it wasn't mine'," Connor said with air quotes.

"No, I mean he worked on cleaning up his act. He was clean when he got out and stayed that way for the whole month of his probation. He was focused on being there for his family. That's why this doesn't make any sense."

Hunter had a wealth of information available to him on Preston courtesy of the red file. He had detailed transcripts from Preston's interviews and evaluations, knew Preston was determined to stay out of trouble because of the three-year-old daughter he'd only been able to see grow via visits on occasional weekends while inside. He wanted to be a good father and made every effort available to him to reform his ways. Throwing all that away was a complete contradiction to everything he had worked on in the last few years.

"A lot of things don't make sense here. I don't even know how the hell he got the sharp wedge of plastic to slit his throat," Connor said, rubbing his eyes.

"Have you gotten the forensics report back yet?" Hunter asked.

"No, they're still working on the autopsy. I'm hoping it'll be ready later on today."

"Do you have the pics?"

Connor nodded and reached over to the file on the edge of the table. "Here you go, we've got a blood splatter guy working with forensics to rebuild the scene. He bled out like crazy."

Hunter looked at the images, each one filled with a disturbing amount of blood covering every inch of skin. The gash at his neck, a deep, straight cut just above his Adam's apple left no room for survival.

"He didn't do this to himself," Hunter said absently, still reviewing the crime scene photograph.

"How do you know that for sure?"

"Look at the cut." Hunter turned the image so Connor could look at the photo.

"Yeah, it's a straight cut of the jugular. What are you seeing?"

"It's a clean straight line, no hesitation. It starts behind his right ear, cuts across his neck and stops just past his Adam's apple."

"Hunter, it was a cut with an obvious decision made. That's why it's a clean line."

"But he didn't do that, he couldn't have. Preston was right-handed. The natural thing would be for a right-handed person to start the cut under the left ear," Hunter explained, while holding the pen up to his neck to demonstrate, "not under his right. That would be unnatural."

"How do you know he's right-handed?"

"I noticed when he was signing the paperwork for the deal before he withdrew it."

Connor squinted his eyes and rubbed his temples. "So now we've got a homicide here."

"Something else is going on, I don't know what, but if he didn't slit his own neck, then obviously someone with access did."

A pregnant silence filled the room.

They stared at each other. Implying there was someone on the force who was dirty never worked out well. "Let's keep this between us for now. I want to see what the coroner's report reads on this, and I'm going to interview the staff members present that night. If something is going on, then I think we need to tread carefully here."

"Glad to see you took off the bullshit blocking sunglasses."

Connor shook his head. "This just went from bad to worse. I think I liked it better when I didn't see through the bullshit."

"Somehow, I get the feeling that's what someone else was hoping for as well. We've been at this for a while and there's not much else I can do here," he finished before standing.

"Thanks, man," Connor said, still sitting, frustrated, with his hand in his hair.

"Good luck. If you need me, you know where to find me," Hunter said before exiting the office.

Hunter had no idea who was involved or the reasons why, but it undoubtedly crossed both sides of the law.

Connor was right, this had just gone from bad to worse.

NINE

Mondays suck.

Hunter looked forward to Monday for one reason and one reason alone: to see Cam again. It certainly wasn't to race to the office for an impromptu meeting. He looked at his watch as he waited for the elevator doors to open. He squeezed through the opening as soon as he heard the ding and headed straight for the conference room where Mel was gathered with her assistant, the other assistant state attorneys from the office, and Jessie. He knew something was wrong the moment he saw Mel pacing the room.

Mel looked up when he entered. "I'm glad you made it," she said and exhaled.

"I've got court in less than an hour...I can't stay. What happened?"

"We received a notice this morning. Judge Peter Gonzalez was dismissed," she said.

Hunter stilled. "What do you mean 'dismissed'?"

"The notice from the court said he was charged with tampering with evidence and all his cases are under review."

"Mel, I know Peter. This is bullshit."

"I know. I wanted to make sure you knew first thing. We're all sorting our cases to make sure all the Ts are crossed and Is dotted."

Hunter pinched the bridge of his nose. "Jessie, please pull all the cases where Peter's assigned so we can go over them when I get back today."

"No problem," Jessie said. "I already started gathering the files when I heard the news."

Hunter looked at his watch. "I've got to go. We'll talk more about this later. I should be able to wrap things up by lunchtime."

Mel nodded as he raced out of the office. Maybe he'd be able to get more information at the courthouse. News of this type spread like wildfire through the grapevine. Right now, he needed to channel his focus on the hearing. He hated Monday trials. Everyone was pissed and things moved too slowly. He certainly wasn't expecting news like this to jump-start his day.

* * * *

Hunter exited the elevator to his office floor and loosened his tie. A simple one hour slam dunk hearing had extended to four hours of sidebar disputes and bullshit delays.

Mondays suck.

"Sir?" Jessie said, looking up at him with a strained expression.

Hunter felt a prickling in the back of his neck. "What happened? Are you okay?"

"It's Mel. She got a call about two hours ago and she—"

"Sons of bitches!" Mel yelled as she exited the elevator.

She spotted Hunter and bee-lined over to him.

"What the hell?" Hunter said. Mel didn't do hysterics.

He followed her into his office and saw her throw her bag on his couch.

"I'm sorry, Hunter. I'm so damn sorry," she said and slumped on the couch. She rested her head in her hands and mumbled.

Hunter knelt before her and pulled her hands away. "What happened?"

Mel sighed. "A call came in about the Carlos Ortega case while you were in court."

"And?"

"It was one of Peter's cases. Kevin Mackler, the replacement judge, demanded the preliminary hearing happen immediately to start clearing out the docket. I tried calling you but it went right to voice mail."

"My phone was off. The hearing took longer than expected."

Mel roughly pulled her hair away from her face. "I didn't have a choice. I had to step in."

Hunter nodded. As supervising counsel of the department, Mel was usually called to fill in when another assistant state attorney wasn't available. "What happened?"

"I'm still trying to figure it out. It was horrible. The attorneys were bastards. Three sons of bitches. I wasn't familiar enough with the case and—"

Hunter held Mel's hand to stop her rambling. "Mel, what happened?"

Mel stopped talking and stared at him incredulously. "They threw out the case, Hunter."

"Why?"

"Fuck if I know. It all happened too fast, and I was having a hard time focusing on anything other than the mess that started early this morning—"

Hunter squeezed Mel's hands to still her. He was just as angry but it wasn't going to resolve the situation. "We'll wait for the minutes of the hearing to come in. Once we have the written ruling, we'll review it and refile."

"You know how the system is. That could take weeks."

"I know, but we've got enough to keep us busy here with our regular cases especially now with Peter getting dismissed. Ortega isn't going anywhere. If he was released, they'll figure we won't pursue it further, and he'll continue doing what he's doing."

Mel exhaled and lowered her head. "I'm sorry."

"Stop it."

Mel looked up at Hunter who still knelt on the floor in front of her. "You should get up. Anyone who looks through your open door is going to think you're proposing."

Hunter chuckled and stood. He could feel the pulse of a headache begin to form.

Mel stood and reached out to squeeze his arm. "You look exhausted."

"It's been a crappy day. I'm going to take a quick break and grab something to eat."

Mel nodded. "Don't take too long. We need to go over a few cases. I'm not getting blindsided like this again." She turned and walked out of Hunter's office.

He looked over his shoulder at the blazing Miami sun filtering through his window. He imagined Cam's face, those eyes, and that smile. His simmering anger slowly dissipated. He couldn't resolve anything in this state of mind.

All he wanted—needed—was to see Cam.

* * * *

Cam gave up on waiting for Hunter to show up at the diner. If Hunter hadn't arrived by now, he just wasn't coming in. He grunted as he lifted the heavy box of supplies and placed it in the storage area. He wiped the sweat from his brow and thought it was rather poetic. Just when he'd decided to finally start this week on a different note, bite the bullet and try to make a move, to do something, anything, Hunter didn't make an appearance at the diner.

Just my fucking luck.

Thoughts of this man consumed him—the way he watched him with that piercing stare, the hesitant smile, soothing voice, large hands, and filled out suit. He liked Hunter, more than he had ever liked another man.

"Hunter," Cam chuckled. "I'd be his prey any day."

He shook his head and huffed a laugh. He liked the way Hunter stared at him. Cam had observed the guy enough to know he didn't look at anyone else in that diner the way he looked at him. Even if Cameron didn't see him when he walked in, he had a heightened awareness of Hunter. He was compelled to seek him out. Looking around, searching, he'd find Hunter…watching him. Cam was flattered he seemed interested. A flush of color tinted the man's face whenever Cam caught him staring.

Cam tried to control his desire for Hunter. For almost a decade, he'd managed to repress any sexual urges out of sheer survival while in prison, but Hunter set him off balance and his intense gaze ignited a raw lust he had never experienced. His vivid imagination kept him aroused for the better part of the day and most of the night. He needed to do something because an accidental touch of the man's skin just wasn't enough.

"Why don't you take your break now, Cam," Lucy said as she walked into the back room.

Cam finished straightening the stack of boxes when he looked over. "I'm almost finished, I can take it a bit later."

"Hunter's at his corner," Lucy said with a devilish grin.

A tingling sensation traveled through Cam's body. "When did he get here?" he asked in a hushed tone.

"A few minutes ago. He just walked in, waved, and sat in the corner. He's too quiet. Maybe you should go take your break?"

Cam looked at her and chuckled. He enjoyed how Lucy teased him with little encouragements like this. Between Matt, Julian, Lucy, and Bill, they had all managed to make him comfortable and accepted in his new surroundings. Something he was easily getting accustomed to since his release. Lucy had quickly picked up on the attraction and couldn't resist her desire to play Cupid and nudge Cam every chance she had. She insisted Hunter was a good man who needed someone like Cameron who always seemed to make him smile.

"What if it's not mutual," he'd tease her just to get a rise out of her.

She'd immediately stop whatever she was doing and plant her hands on her waist. "I'm old, not blind, young man."

He shook his head and chuckled at the memory as Lucy continued to rummage through the drawers. "What are you looking for?" he asked.

"There's a lightbulb that's out in the eating area. Maybe you could go change that," she said.

He pointed to the drawer on the far left of the room and watched her race over and pull out the box of bulbs.

Lucy handed him the bulb with a simple command, "Go."

"Which light is it?"

"Above table four."

Cam arched an eyebrow. Table four was directly in front of Hunter's usual corner. "How convenient."

"Funny, I thought the same thing. Now go," she said, shooing him away.

Cam grabbed the ladder from the storage closet and made his way to the front sitting area. Hunter's demeanor was different. He sat with his elbow on the table and his head in his hands. He looked upset, defeated—definitely not the way he normally looked. Seeing Hunter like this, Cam needed to distract him, anything to remove this out of character somberness.

As if sensing Cam's presence, Hunter lowered his hands from his face and looked up. He stared at Cameron as he walked toward the sitting area. His expression softened. His eyebrows changed from bunched to relaxed and his eyes were no longer squinted. Slowly, one side of his mouth began to form a smile. Cameron did a mental fist bump.

"Hi," Cam said, trying for casual. No sense in giving the guy a hard time today with the 'sir' thing since he already looked as if someone had kicked him in the balls.

"Hi," Hunter responded with a full smile.

"Don't mind me, I just need to change the bulb." Cam moved some of the tables out of the way and made space for the ladder.

Cam didn't need to look at Hunter to know he was being intently watched. He could feel Hunter's gaze ghosting over his skin with each of his movements. He reached over to unscrew the light fixture and heard a groan escape from Hunter's corner. Cam casually glanced over his shoulder and saw Hunter staring at his body. Cam smiled. If it took giving a little bit of a show for Hunter to come in for the kill of his prey, then so be it.

He was game.

* * * *

For God's sake, there was no way in hell he could control this raging hard-on in his pants. Hunter didn't have the strength to tear his eyes away from the sliver of skin peeking out from under Cam's shirt. With each additional stretch of his arm, his shirt would rise and fall—hiding then revealing just a tiny bit more. Hunter couldn't look away and risk missing even a millimeter of skin.

Hide, reveal, hide, reveal.

Fuck.

He could tell Cam's abs were tight and sculpted, his waist narrower than the jeans he wore. One of those quick shifts revealed a slim line of hair traveling downward. God, he wanted to explore, lick, and taste every inch of him. Hunter groaned again.

Cam stepped down the ladder and smiled.

Is he smiling because he knows I was watching? Hunter's face heated.

Cam walked over to Hunter's table. "I thought you weren't coming by today. It's later than your usual time."

Hunter cocked his head to the side. Cam looked different today, more relaxed, casual—and thankfully, had dropped the 'sir' when he spoke.

"Work sorta caught up with me."

"Just coffee today?"

"Yeah, I was too late for Lucy's cookies," he said with a shrug.

"You should eat something."

"I will if you join me." Hunter's throat tightened as he let the invitation escape. Better to throw it out there before he had a chance to think about what he was actually saying.

"Give me a minute." Cam walked into the back room. He exited within seconds, the ladder replaced, with a bag and two drinks. He walked toward the sandwich station where Bill was wiping down the bins.

He watched Cam wash and dry his hands then grab the items to start assembling a sandwich. Bill and Cam chatted while they worked, an occasional laugh escaping the conversation. Hunter closed his eyes and let the sound of Cam's laughter filter through his system. Everything this man did excited each of his senses. He pulled out the chair when he saw Cam amble over to the table with his hands full.

"Thanks," Cam said. He sat and set the bag and bottle of soda to one side, gave Hunter a bottled water, then split the sandwich in half. "Only water for you until you eat something," he said in a playfully chastising tone.

Hunter smiled when Cam handed him the half sandwich. "Thank you," he said before taking a bite. It was nice to have someone make sure he ate a meal.

Hunter was distracted, watching Cam, seeing how his throat worked with each pull of his drink. His took a deep breath, trying to dispel the visuals his mind conjured. Cam looked over at him from the corner of his eye as he tipped up his soda to take a drink.

"You like watching me," Cam said matter-of-factly as he put down the bottle.

"You're easy on the eyes."

Cam chuckled. "You need to get your eyes checked."

He looked at Cameron and couldn't resist reaching out to wipe away the little bit of sauce at the side of his mouth.

Cam jerked to the side and looked at Hunter's slightly smeared thumb. He looked back to Hunter, hesitated for a moment, then slowly licked the sauce off. He then pulled Hunter's thumb into his mouth with his tongue.

A tidal wave of lust traveled Hunter's body in an instant. His heart began to brutally pound against his chest and his almost hard-on was now in full force and painful as hell. He focused so intently on trying to control the rhythm of his breathing he couldn't remember to finish chewing the bit of sandwich in his mouth.

"Mmm...that's the best part," Cam said once he released Hunter's thumb.

Cameron's eyes darkened and a wicked grin slowly spread across his face.

"Swallow," Cam commanded.

Shit, that brings on an entirely different visual. Hunter had a hard time connecting thoughts with actions. Cam pointed at Hunter who still had a mouthful of turkey sandwich stuffed in one of his cheeks. Finally snapping back to reality, he quickly finished and carefully swallowed the food, trying to avoid choking. He chased it with several gulps of water, hoping to cool off the rising heat in his body. Hunter tried to regain control of himself as the desire thrummed through his veins. He looked at Cameron as he reached into the bag and pulled out a single chocolate chip cookie.

"I saved one for you when I noticed you were late."

"We share," Hunter said in a gravelly voice, trying to stave off the need coursing through his body.

Cam casually glanced over at the empty counter area where Bill had left only moments ago.

They were somewhat alone now and mildly sheltered from view in that corner. Well after the lunchtime rush, there were no other patrons in the diner and the exterior streets had only a handful of pedestrians racing to cross the street.

Cam broke off a tiny piece of cookie for himself and finished eating before he offered a much larger piece to Hunter.

Rather than take the piece from Cam's hand, Hunter slowly leaned over and took the offering into his mouth, never breaking eye contact. He swiped his tongue along Cam's finger, savoring the way his skin tasted. Cameron let out a moan as a slight shiver visibly traveled his body. Cam intently watched Hunter suck his fingers clean of any melted chocolate. Hunter withdrew and slowly chewed the piece of cookie, waiting for Cam's reaction.

Cam's chest heaved slightly. His bright blue eyes changed to a deeper shade and his pupils began to dilate. He continued to stare at Hunter's mouth, apparently captivated, until Hunter finished chewing then swallowed.

Cam seemed to be in a trance when he slowly inched closer to Hunter, parted his lips as if anticipating a kiss, then hesitated.

Hunter leaned forward and quickly grabbed Cam's face with both hands then closed the distance with contrasting gentleness, cautiously observing Cam's reaction. Cam reached up when Hunter was only inches away. Hunter instantly halted before closing in. The tips of Cam's fingers slowly outlined his features, down the side of his face, then along his jawline before Cam withdrew his hand and hesitantly looked at Hunter with a worried expression.

"Don't stop," Hunter whispered before he closed his eyes and tried to control the surge of desire Cam's gentle, tentative touch ignited within. Hunter patiently waited and held Cam's face, reluctant to let him retreat. He gasped when Cam's fingers returned to his face, ghosting over his cheek, his eyes, and the slope of his nose. His entire body shivered with the current generated from the barely there touch tracing his features then moving down his neck. Hunter parted his lips when Cam's touch circled his mouth. His breathing became labored in anticipation of the kiss. He opened his eyes and saw Cam's vision following the same path as his exploratory fingers. The subtle yet teasing touch drove him mad. He resisted the urge to pull Cam in and cease the exploration, worried Cam would withdraw completely.

Cam finally stopped the gentle torture and met Hunter's fierce gaze. The reverent look in those crystal blue eyes staring back at him caused a moan to escape Hunter. He cautiously pulled Cam closer, breathing him in slowly as if his inhale of breath were a rope pulling Cam closer.

Their lips finally met.

Hunter slowly ran his tongue along Cam's soft lips, unable to resist the opportunity to taste the man who invaded every waking thought since they'd met. He tasted chocolate and a hint of spice from the sauce mixed in with an enticing unique flavor that was obviously Cam. He slowed when he sensed Cameron's hesitation but refused to release him. Within seconds, Hunter felt the subtle tug behind his neck and the whisper of air across his face as Cam inhaled deeply before responding in kind. Hunter's heart slammed against his chest and a rush of desire coursed through his body when Cam became aggressive, pulling him closer, demanding more.

Every thought left Hunter's mind and only Cam existed, the taste of him, the scrape of his stubble against Hunter's flesh. Hunter became dizzy with desire and overwhelmed by the need for the heat of Cam's body pressed against his own. His hand followed the curve of Cameron's spine until it reached the small of his back. He greedily pulled Cam closer, yanking him roughly off his seat and onto Hunter's thigh. Hunter groaned into the kiss and his heart raced with excitement when Cameron's hardness pressed against him.

Hunter's pulse escalated further. His body craved more, to claim and possess. He lifted the back of Cam's T-shirt and splayed his hand along Cam's strong, narrow back, absorbing the fireball of heat emitted from Cam's body. Their tongues battled for dominance. The small flicker of passion ignited into an inferno of desire that consumed Hunter. The kiss became more heated and urgent, absent of any hesitation. He tightened his arm around Cam's back while the other firmly gripped the back of his head, forbidding Cam's escape. Cam wrapped both arms around Hunter and forcefully pulled him closer, deepening the kiss.

Cam separated from the kiss with a gasp moments later, his chest heaving. His Adam's apple bobbed as he desperately sought some air. Hunter was bereft with the separation. He leaned in and kissed the base of Cam's neck and worked his way up, kissing, sucking, biting—trying to tame the desperation to own this man in his arms. Hunter rubbed his cheek against the side of Cam's face like an animal trying to mark his mate. The scrape of Cam's stubble left his skin growingly sensitive to each additional graze. A strangled growl escaped him as he fought to control this desperate need to possess. He touched, licked, and smelled every millimeter of skin he could reach. He heard a moan escape Cam's throat when he inhaled Cam's scent at the crook of his neck—the scent amplified by Cam's body heat invaded and drugged his senses, spurring him on just as much as the sounds Cam's made with each touch.

Hunter ran his tongue hesitantly up Cam's neck, tasting the salt from the beads of sweat bursting from every one of Cam's pores. Wanting more, he kissed and bit Cameron's jawline until Cam hissed. When their eyes met, Cam's pupils were so dilated there was no visible blue in his eyes. His lips were kiss-swollen and richer in color. His breathing labored and his cheeks were flushed. Cam looked debauched and incredibly alluring.

Cam's gaze traveled to Hunter's lips, and before Hunter could react, Cam plundered his mouth again and grabbed at his clothes with more fervor, his arms, anything he could grasp while Hunter did the same. Desperation surged in response to Cam's aggression. He gripped the back of Cam's head and held him in place as he feasted on him like the last meal of a death row inmate. Stubble scraped, fingers dug into skin, and both struggled to pull closer. Everything else was irrelevant—the age gap, anyone watching, or whatever anyone said. Every fiber of his being craved this man with pure need. Only Cam's heat, taste, and smell flowing through Hunter's senses could satisfy the desire coursing through his veins. He couldn't remember ever wanting anyone or anything more in his life.

The sound of the vibrating phone across the table broke into their haze of lust. They parted slowly. Their heavy breathing mingled as they each glanced toward the register area, thankfully, still absent of the owners. Looking at the surrounding glass exterior, only a handful of pedestrians raced by, oblivious to them and their closeness.

Hunter sighed and looked over to the insistent phone. Cam tried to free himself from the embrace but Hunter held him tight around the waist.

He wasn't ready to let go.

Cam hesitantly rested his forehead on Hunter's shoulder and took a few more deep breaths. Hunter reached for his phone with his other hand, looked at the display, then pressed the button to ignore the call. After returning the phone to the table, he wrapped his other arm around Cam and just held him close. Hunter relished Cam in his arms, the way Cam's body flawlessly fit against his own. He thought he heard Cam sigh before hesitantly resting his cheek against Hunter's shoulder. Hunter closed his eyes and pulled Cam closer—reveling in the warmth and weight of his body, and the intoxicating scent that soothed the desperation within.

It was shockingly perfect.

After a few moments, Cam raised his head to look at him. Hunter unwillingly released one hand from the embrace and softly brushed Cam's cheek with his knuckles. "You have no idea what you do to me," he whispered softly.

"Then you should have kissed me sooner." Cameron shyly smiled and bit his kiss-swollen lower lip.

Hunter moaned. He leaned in and delivered a soft, slow, tender kiss. Cam's tentative, shaky fingers combed through Hunter's hair. Hunter ran his hand down to Cam's lower back and traced random patterns on Cam's skin, hoping to soothe the new hesitation in Cam's touch. He brushed Cam's cheek with his other hand and slowly wrapped his fingers behind Cam's neck while his thumb continued to stroke Cam's skin. The raging hunger and desperation was replaced with a welcomed tenderness. The pace was slow, exploratory rather than demanding, but Hunter's heart still punched feverishly against his chest. Nothing existed in time and space but this man and this tender, leisurely discovery of taste and touch, the soft brush of lips and gentle graze of fingers against his skin. Hunter's body shuddered. He held back a strangled moan that threatened to escape with each subtle gesture. This was more than a lust-filled kiss or the passion of a new partner. It was rooted in something much deeper, more connected, purer. A shiver traveled his body at the thought. It was too right, too perfect.

They reluctantly parted when Hunter's phone rang again.

"You should get that," Cam said in a hoarse voice. "And I need to get back to work before I get fired for mauling the customers." Cam withdrew from Hunter's arms with a grin.

The annoying phone stopped ringing.

Cam stood and adjusted himself with a wince. If he was anywhere near as turned on as Hunter at that moment, he could probably smash a brick wall with his hard-on.

"See you tomorrow?" Cam asked as he combed his hair with his fingers.

"You can bet I'll be here," Hunter replied with a teasing grin.

Hunter's eyes were drawn to the casual sway of Cam's hips as he walked away.

Cam turned and walked backward as he spoke. "Don't get here so late."

"I think I prefer late if I get to have lunch with you like this again."

Cam laughed and shook his head then turned to walk into the back room with a wave good-bye.

The sound of Cam's laughter was a song he could easily commit to memory. Hunter took a deep breath and tried to calm his racing heart. He hadn't kissed someone like that since he was a teenager with raging hormones.

Maybe Mondays aren't so bad after all.

The phone rang again and he knew he could no longer ignore Melanie's call.

"Hi, Mel," he finally said when he answered.

"Get your ass back here, please. We've got a stack of stuff to go through."

"I'll be there in a few. Bye."

He ended the call and returned the phone to its place on the table. He wasn't ready to leave just yet. He didn't even want to move and risk wiping away any memory of his kiss with Cam. He smugly smiled. Cameron had gotten just as worked up as he had.

Reluctantly, he rose from his seat and finished straightening out his suit. Bill walked toward the register from the back room and looked over to Hunter with a smirk. He was busted and he was damn sure not going to be embarrassed about it. Cam was going to be his. Period. One time wasn't enough.

He grabbed his briefcase and headed for the door. "See you tomorrow, Bill," he said over his shoulder with an extra perk in his step.

"Bet I will," was the last thing he heard Bill say before the man burst into laughter as Hunter exited the diner.

Chapter TEN

Cameron worked the morning rush with smooth, practiced movements. He couldn't stop thinking about Hunter and their kiss. Not only was it incredible to inspire that much desire in someone, but it was that last, completely unexpected, tender kiss that seemed to leave the greatest impression. He inhaled a shaky breath.

He hadn't realized how much he liked being kissed.

He reminisced about the way Hunter touched him and the way he let Cam touch *him*.

Cam hadn't known that type of attention, for someone to want to hold him so closely and not want to let go. Sure, he had kissed some guys as a teen and even had a boyfriend, but it was different. Based on his experience, having sex didn't necessarily include affection of any kind. It was sex, plain and simple, a discovery of bodies and sometimes awkward and usually too fast. His one boyfriend had never held his hand and rarely found the occasion to kiss. And he sure as hell never wanted to hold Cam or touch him unless he was getting off in the process.

Everything about Hunter was different. The way he smiled, the way his eyes danced with mischief. Most importantly, in Hunter's arms, the world could crumble around him, and somehow, Cam knew he would be safe.

It felt perfect.

It felt right.

Cameron closed his eyes and took a deep breath before tending to the next customer. It was dangerous to hope for anything, pointless to want something that would be taken away quicker than it had arrived. He could have easily misunderstood the signals.

He took another deep breath. No sense in hoping for something that wasn't there. He really liked Hunter, more than he cared to admit to himself, but he figured there was no way someone like Hunter would feel the same. Sex, sure—why not. He was human, very male, and had a libido that was bitching about being on hold for a decade. He wasn't bold enough to think it was mutual, but something in him continued to fight his resistance and demanded he dare hope for more.

It felt perfect.

Cameron looked up and his chest tightened when Hunter entered the diner. A grin spread across his face.

"Good morning, sir," Cameron said when it was Hunter's turn at the register. "How may I help you today?"

Hunter's smile grew and spanned the entire width of his face.

"Good morning. When do you take your break?" Hunter asked quietly.

"When the morning rush is over, in about ten minutes. You're really early today," Cam said in a hushed tone. He looked over to the other customers rattling off their breakfast sandwich orders to Bill.

"I couldn't stay away," Hunter said, leaning over the counter. "I've got a few minutes before I need to head back to the office. I'll just have a coffee and wait, if that's okay."

Cam eagerly nodded and swore his heart actually skipped a few beats. His body hummed. Hunter excited him and injected life into his dormant desire. He prepared Hunter's latte, told him he'd be with him in a few minutes, then began to complete the morning rush orders in record time. Finished sooner than expected, Bill left for the store to get some lunch supplies, and Lucy went to the back to start her lunchtime baking. Cam grabbed a bottled water, took off his apron, and sauntered over to where Hunter waited patiently in the corner.

He couldn't stay away.

Cam tried to control the hope that started to bloom.

He pulled out the chair and sat next to Hunter. Before he had a chance to settle in his seat, Hunter pulled the chair closer to him, dragging Cam along with it. Their knees bumped and an instant rush of excitement coursed through Cam's body from the accidental contact. He inched closer to Hunter, needing more. He reached under the table and tentatively placed the tips of his fingers on Hunter's knee, hoping Hunter wouldn't reject his touch. He needed the contact, to know that he was really sitting close to this man.

He took a slow, deep breath when he felt the fabric of Hunter's pants brush his trembling fingertips. It had been too long since he'd shared any level of intimacy with someone. His heart began to beat faster at the thought that a thin shred of material was the only barrier between his fingertips and Hunter's skin.

Hunter immediately covered Cam's hand with his own, laced their fingers, and positioned their hands so it rested firmly on the center of Hunter's thigh.

"Don't ever hesitate when you want to touch me," he whispered in Cam's ear.

The puffs of Hunter's breath against his skin made him gasp just as much as the words. Cam closed his eyes and tried to settle his breathing. His heart raced with excitement and his arousal pressed painfully against his zipper. He needed to keep himself in check, control this intense level of want that threatened to take over. Want for Hunter, closeness, affection, for everything and anything he cared to offer him.

It felt perfect.

Hunter placed a soft kiss on Cam's neck then nuzzled the sensitive skin below his ear.

Something in Cam shifted at that subtle gesture. The desire, the need, and even worse, the hope that Hunter wanted more contact with him kicked up his heartbeat and a stab of pain speared his lungs.

"Cam?"

Just breathe, count, something to fucking calm down. His chest tightened and breathing became more difficult. A tingling sensation rose within and spread across his limbs.

"Cam, open your eyes and look at me," Hunter said gently, with a soft, yet firm, tone.

Cam opened his eyes and through the haze of want coursing through his body for this man and impending fear of losing control, his vision focused on the piercing silver eyes staring back at him.

"Match my breathing," Hunter coaxed, the authority in his tone replaced with concern.

Cam tried to focus, he looked at Hunter's lips to detect the intake of breath but hell, looking at those full, kissable lips was a huge mistake. His lungs constricted, robbing him of precious oxygen.

"Hunter," he barely managed to say between gasps, squeezing Hunter's hand tighter as the little oxygen that managed to enter his airway pierced his lungs like blades of ice.

He couldn't breathe.

He screwed his eyes shut, trying to push past the pain in his chest. Dizziness set in and his body started going numb.

A firm hand gripped his neck then pulled him forward. "Listen to my voice, and do what I say." Whispered only for him to hear, Hunter's voice brooked no argument.

Cam tried to focus on the soothing tone and the sounds of his words as they filtered through his body.

"Take a deep breath, hold it."

He inhaled shaky gasps of air then fought the pain in his chest as he held his breath.

"Now exhale."

Cameron did as commanded.

"Again," Hunter ordered. "Take a deep breath."

After a few breaths, Cam began to feel his legs and arms again as a prickling sensation traveled along his body. He could feel Hunter still firmly holding his hand under the table while the grip behind his neck remained steady. Each breath came more natural now, easier, more manageable. He opened his eyes and saw the stunning silver eyes that dominated his thoughts filled with concern.

"Okay?" Hunter asked, releasing the hold on his neck and shifting his hand to the side of Cam's face to stroke his cheek.

He nodded. "Sorry," he said, his voice shaking.

"Panic attack?" Hunter asked.

Cameron lowered his head. Something as basic as holding hands and getting this close to Hunter freaked him out, even after practically attacking the man the day before when they kissed.

He knew the trigger.

Hope.

Sitting with Hunter for more than a heated spur of the moment kiss meant a glimmer of a chance for greater intimacy, and he couldn't restrain the instinctive desire his body craved for affection.

"How did you know?" Cam asked.

"I have a Marine buddy who had a few episodes when he lost his parents and almost lost his brother in a car accident a few years ago. It was a tough time for him with everything going on. What triggered it for you?"

"You," Cam said before thinking of his words. Holding hands had never been his thing, then inside, he'd become accustomed to being guarded, keeping his distance from others out of sheer survival. He certainly wasn't used to someone *wanting* to touch him this way. "I'm not used to this," he said, tightening their clasped hands under the table.

"Good."

Cam looked up, perplexed. "Good I freaked out?"

"Good you're not used to guys coming in here and being like this with you during your breaks."

"Oh. Yeah, um…it's been a while."

"Me, too. I seem to lose myself in my work and tend to forgo a personal life," Hunter said, refusing to release Cam's hand.

"Good," Cam snapped with an unexpected stab of jealously.

Hunter smiled. "I suggest we do this more often."

"More often?" he asked, still trying to keep his heart rate in check and his breathing level.

"I can't have you freaking out whenever I get close to you, so how about I start coming to the diner twice a day. You know, to get you into the habit of seeing me more often," Hunter said with a teasing smile as he casually stroked Cam's hand with his thumb.

Cam pretended to consider the suggestion. "Only if it means more of this," he said, squeezing their entwined hands.

He didn't want to let go. Ironically, their joined hands had caused him to panic, but now the comfort seemed to soothe him back to his normal self.

"Deal."

"Why stop at twice? Just move into this corner so I've got you here all day."

Hunter laughed. The sound echoed through Cameron's body like a soothing balm.

Cam looked over to the counter and saw Lucy preparing her display for the lunchtime baked goods. She casually glanced over at them, smiled, then quickly looked away before walking back to tend to her cookies.

"I think Lucy likes you."

Hunter chuckled. "I think Lucy likes *us*."

Cameron smiled. He dared to stroke Hunter's thigh with his thumb.

Hunter reached over and delivered a chaste kiss on Cam's cheek. "I've got to go back to the office. I'll be back a little after the lunchtime rush."

Cam reluctantly nodded, not really wanting to let Hunter leave. They were sitting alone in the dining area, with the aroma of Lucy's baking filling the air. Cam inched forward and risked a quick kiss.

Hunter placed his hand on Cam's neck, holding him in place. He gently sucked on Cam's lower lip then slowly swiped his tongue to soothe the sting. Hunter moaned when Cam opened his mouth wanting more. Finally releasing their held hands, Cam gasped when Hunter's fingers brushed against his skin at the base of his spine, tracing a slow, circular pattern—damn, he liked that.

"It's just me," Hunter mumbled between kisses, probably trying to avoid another freak out.

They kissed slowly, tasting, exploring each other. Cam pulled away, trying to catch his breath. "I don't want to stop but—"

"Neither do I, but we need to." Hunter rested his forehead against Cam's. "You're driving me crazy."

"You're driving me to have panic attacks so I think we're even."

Hunter smiled and gave Cam a quick kiss before standing. "I'll be back later. Want to have lunch?"

"I can talk to Lucy and Bill about having lunch in the back instead of out here."

"You don't want to go out somewhere else?" Hunter asked, brows furrowed.

Cam shook his head. He wasn't sure if leaving the diner would be an issue with Matt so he preferred to avoid a problem and stay. He figured a half truth was better than a lie.

"I'd prefer to stay here just in case Lucy or Bill needs me for something that can't wait."

Hunter smiled. "You're amazing, you know that?"

Cam shrugged.

"I've gotta go."

"You keep saying that." Cam smiled.

"Stop looking at me like that and maybe I can get my brain to focus on walking."

Cam chuckled. "Maybe I should hold you down and prevent you from leaving."

"Fuck," Hunter groaned. "I'll be back later."

Cam tracked Hunter as he walked out the diner and down the street until he could no longer distinguish his figure in the crowd.

He sighed.

He'd kept his distance from others as a necessity for survival, but the need to be close to Hunter consumed him. He'd never felt wanted like this by anyone.

As much as it scared him to discover this, the thought of losing it terrified him. He closed his eyes and exhaled a shaky breath. Cam knew it was a matter of time before he'd no longer be able to be with

Hunter. It was inevitable. Once Hunter found out the truth, Cam figured he would keep his distance. If that didn't push him away, he knew those who wanted to keep him in prison would.

It was the same endgame regardless—him alone, just as he had been these past ten years.

He'd deal with it when that time came. Until then, he'd cherish every second he could steal with Hunter before losing him.

* * * *

Hunter returned that day for lunch as promised then made it a point to go by the diner at least twice a day—for mid-morning coffee and a late lunch break—the rest of the week. He had joked with Cam about more frequent visits and it seemed Cam had relayed the joke to Lucy.

Lucy saw him arrive that afternoon and did as she had done each instance since—she walked around the counter, hooked her arm in his and led him to the back room.

"Sit," she said and handed him a cookie.

He tightened his lips, trying to hold the smile. "Yes, ma'am."

He turned as she walked out only to see Bill guiding Cam into the back room, with his hand at the back of Cam's neck. Hunter couldn't contain the smile anymore.

"Keep him busy so he stops cleaning my diner," was all Bill would say before leaving them alone.

He loved seeing their tag team efforts in pushing them together; they had no shame in hiding their intentions. Come to think of it, the only thing they hadn't done was shove them into the storage closet and throw away the key.

With every visit, Hunter would sit with Cam and they'd have lunch or just sip a coffee while talking. Cam chatted endlessly about anything botanical. He'd smile wistfully when he'd mention his time in the garden with his mom as a child. Cam's mother had passed away when he was young, a subject Cam avoided.

"When your mom died, how did you handle it?" Cam had asked him softly.

"It was tough but my dad and I had a ton of great memories with her," Hunter had responded. Cam would then switch gears and steer the conversation elsewhere. Hunter recognized the pain in Cam's expression, so he knew not to push the topic further than he was willing to reveal on his own.

Somehow, being with Cam, Hunter was able to escape all the drama surrounding his work and recent issues with his cases. Ironically, he was sharper, more focused, and able to block everything else out when around him.

"How the hell is that possible," Cam had asked when he mentioned this. "I can't focus worth a shit when you're around me."

Hunter shrugged. "I don't know, maybe it's just that when I'm with you I can't think of anywhere else I want to be."

Cam raised an eyebrow. "I wouldn't have pegged you for a sappy guy."

"If you'd like, I can keep my distance, avoid the touching, kisses, and all that other sappy stuff." Hunter smiled. He took Cam's hand, raised it to his lips, then kissed his palm.

"I didn't say I couldn't tolerate some sap," Cam said with a scowl, pulling his hand from Hunter's grip.

"Tolerate?"

"Yeah, it's a sacrifice, you know, but I'll put up with it."

Hunter chuckled as Cam leaned into his shoulder.

"I can see you absolutely hate enduring it."

"Yeah, it totally sucks. But I'll deal with it," Cam finished, nuzzling the crook of Hunter's neck.

"Funny, I wouldn't have pegged you for a sappy guy," Hunter reciprocated the tease.

"Yeah, well, I'm not. And if I happen to have any sort of sweet shit on me, it's all your fault."

"I'll take the blame for this any day," Hunter said, wrapping his arm around Cameron's shoulder and pulling him into an embrace. "Do you have any plans this weekend?"

Cam positioned himself more comfortably in Hunter's arms before responding. "Yeah, I'm working on some landscaping stuff where I'm staying."

"I'd love to see it."

Cam fidgeted. "Um, I'm not finished with it yet so it's just dirt and stuff dug up. It'll take a while to get to the point where it looks nice," he mumbled. Cam fell silent and tightened his hold on Hunter.

Cam's muscles were tense. Hunter sighed and pulled Cam closer into the embrace, hoping Cam wouldn't distance himself as he often did. He'd eventually earn Cam's trust with time. In the meantime, he relied on unspoken cues and learning his tells. Hunter didn't mind the challenge.

"Then when you finish," Hunter said.

Hunter nuzzled closer into the warmth of Cam pressed against him. He had an uncontrollable base need to feel the heat of Cam's skin, hear the timbre in his voice, see that soulful blue gaze stare back at him—just as much as he needed the air that filled his lungs. He wanted to be alone with Cam, but it seemed Cam was most comfortable within the confines of the diner. He'd deal with it if he had to.

Cam looked up from within the embrace and slowly sucked in his lower lip as his vision shifted to Hunter's mouth.

Hunter had learned this tell in Cam. Cam would endlessly joke and tease, but a serious verbal declaration of what he felt or wanted was something Hunter imagined wouldn't come easily…if at all. Hunter knew the request for a kiss would never come, but the desire in his eyes was unmistakable.

He cupped Cam's face and delivered a slow, lazy kiss—the ones that seemed to elicit the most sounds of approval from Cam.

The sounds that sent shivers throughout Hunter's body.

He didn't dare ask Cam how he felt.

Hunter just hoped Cam felt the same.

Chapter ELEVEN

The sweat trickled down the side of Cam's face and neck. He scooped up the dirt with his hands and worked it around the flower bed full of impatiens he'd planted. He sifted the soil then sprinkled in a little slow-release fertilizer near the roots. He smiled as he worked, using the trowel to open the hole for each new colorful addition.

He couldn't believe it when Julian had surprised him with flower beds at the front and back areas of the house, exactly as he had described, even more shocked to see Matt with a shovel in his hand helping Julian dig a hole. They listened to him, allowed him to manage the project and direct them on what he needed them to do. He mattered for the first time in too long.

"Hey, Cam," Matt said, poking his head out the front door.

Cam looked up and squinted to block out the sun. "Hey."

"Can you take a break for a bit?"

Cam's chest immediately tightened. *Shit. Did I do something wrong?* He silently followed Matt into the kitchen and washed his hands while he watched Matt grab two glasses and fill them with cold lemonade.

Matt gestured for Cam to sit then grabbed the file at the end of the counter.

Cam sat and just looked at the manila folder with his name written on a tab. He exhaled heavily. He couldn't stop his leg's rhythmic jumping up and down.

Matt cleared his throat then smiled. "I just wanted to sit with you and go over a few things."

"Is something wrong?" he asked.

"Not at all. I just thought that since you've been working for two weeks, we'd sit and have a bit of a benchmark at this point. Just so we can see if there's anything we need to work on."

"Okay," he said hesitantly, stretching out each syllable, looking at the file Matt held.

"I had a chat with Lucy and Bill and both are extremely happy with your work. They think you're easy to work with, a quick learner, and have a wonderful way with the customers. They're very pleased to have you there and raved about their trust in having you long term if you'd like."

Cam breathed a sigh of relief.

"You've also passed the random tests you've been called to take and you've been doing some beautiful work here with the landscaping."

Cam quirked a smile. He hadn't heard this much praise in such a long time he wasn't sure how he was supposed to react. It was silly at how pleased he was with himself that someone who was probably only a few years older than him was complimenting him on his work. He wasn't sure what he was supposed to say so he simply said, "Thanks."

"If you want to read my notes, you can. I have an open policy when it comes to the content of your files."

Cam nodded. This wasn't so bad after all.

"That covers the formalities. Is there anything you want to talk about or any questions you have now that you've had a chance to settle in for a bit?" Matt asked as he closed the file and waited for Cam to speak.

Questions. He had only one and it related to the subject that dominated his thoughts. Hunter. He was a little hesitant about the fact that Hunter was a lawyer, but wasn't that the same as others condemning him because he was an ex-con with a record?

He was tired of sharing him with the other patrons in the diner. He was thankful Hunter hadn't pushed to be outside the diner, but there was only so much mauling he could do there before it started to just get too weird, regardless of whether Lucy and Bill pushed them together every chance they got.

"What's the policy on staying out late and weekend stuff outside of here?"

Matt straightened. "Have you met someone?"

Cam's face heated. "There's a guy."

"Oh?" Matt teased. "Did you meet him at the diner?"

"I met him at the drug place," Cam deadpanned.

Matt blinked, with a blank expression on his face.

"That was a joke," Cam said with a wicked smile. "Yeah, at the diner. He's a regular."

Matt's cheeks reddened. "Sorry. J says I'm a little slow on the uptake sometimes. So you like him?"

Cam nodded.

"Has he asked you out?"

Cam shook his head. "I kinda change the direction of the conversation when I sense he's heading that way. We've been hanging out at the diner during my breaks. I just want to know the rules on this. I don't know. It might not go anywhere but—"

"You want it to."

"You weren't slow on the uptake there," he finished with a grin.

Matt chuckled. "Does he know about you, about your record?"

"I met him the first day at the diner so it's been about two weeks. There's no way I'm going to spill my life story so soon. Besides, it's probably not that serious anyway." He added the last part, reluctantly. Cam needed to tell Hunter the truth, which would probably lead to Hunter walking away and any potential—whatever it was between them—would go away. He couldn't imagine a lawyer wanting to hook up with an ex-con, regardless of how much of a 'good guy' Hunter claimed to be.

"Not your life story, but this is important. It's a big deal and it's not good to keep it a secret."

"I'm not keeping it a secret, I'm just not wearing a fucking T-shirt that reads 'I'm an ex-con'," he snapped. He rose from his seat to wash his glass in the sink. He battled with himself. It was probably best to keep his distance and not get involved with someone but he couldn't stay away from Hunter. It didn't matter if they spoke or just sat there drinking their coffee while they stared each other down until one of them laughed.

Cam liked everything about Hunter and enjoyed just being near him, touching him, kissing him in that lazy way. He wanted more kisses and everything else that came along with the deal. He wanted to know what it was like to be on the receiving end of that much desire. Having one boyfriend as a teenager and kissing a few others hadn't prepared him for a man like Hunter. He suspected Hunter avoided those types of kisses when they were together for the same reason he tried to not think about it. If they kissed like that again, chances were they wouldn't want to stop. And even though Lucy and Bill encouraged them together every chance they had, they wouldn't appreciate the peep show in their diner.

"Okay. Well, according to the rules, you need to have continuous employment for fifteen days before you can be considered for the next stage so you're just about there. Three weeks after your arrival here, you can request a pass for late nights or weekends."

"So I've got about a week then." He returned to his seat at the table.

"Well, you could swing it without a pass but your curfew here would be nine pm," Matt smiled.

"Wonderful. It'll make him feel like he's dating a teenager with a fucking chaperone. Yeah, that'll get him excited."

"That was a joke, I assume."

"Your uptake's getting better."

Matt smiled.

They were silent for a few moments, Matt drinking his lemonade and Cam tugging at a loose string on his jeans.

"What happened, Cam?"

"I was working on the landscaping and you wanted to do the benchmark thing."

Matt glared at Cam. "I meant what happened with you. I've read your background, you were at the top of your class and taking advanced placement courses. So that tells me you were working your way to a higher education. But here you are now and..." Matt's voice transitioned from exasperation to defeat. "You didn't even finish high school."

Cam's body stiffened. He didn't want to talk about what happened and he certainly didn't want to relive that day. He just wanted to move on.

"If it was self-defense why did you let them accuse you of all these other charges?"

"What are you talking about?" Cam asked, immediately on alert. There was nothing in his file about self-defense. "I killed a man."

"Cam, I know what happened. I know you went to that house to save your sister from her boyfriend. You arrived there and then it got ugly. What happened was an accident."

Cam closed his eyes and took a deep breath. He didn't want to talk about this...any of it. He didn't want to relive that day. All he did while in solitary confinement was relive that damn day. Over and over again. He didn't want to go there...couldn't go there. He hated what he had done and how stupid he was to not have seen it coming.

"Cam?" Matt prompted after an extended silence.

"Drop it," Cameron demanded.

"No. You make it sound as if you're a killer and you're not. If you were, you would have had every intention of killing that man when you walked into that house. And you didn't. That's why they couldn't add a murder one or two charge on to this ridiculous list of charges."

"Doesn't change the fact that I killed a man."

"The intent is everything, Cam. You didn't have malice. It was an accident. That's why it's manslaughter and not murder."

Cam leaned over the table and jabbed his finger in the air toward Matt. "Look, I'll suck it up and do what needs to get done. Take the fucking drug tests and do the damn check-ins, but that's it. I'm not talking about what happened. It's done, it's over."

"But Cam—"

"No!" he yelled as he abruptly stood, tipping the chair back with such force it crashed to the floor.

Recognizing the limits of his temper, he needed to leave the kitchen...now. He raced out and headed upstairs, taking two steps at a time until he reached his room and slammed the door shut. He paced the room like a caged animal needing to burn off some of the heightened energy that thrummed through his body. He was spinning like a top, and it was only a matter of time before he fell over.

Fuck. Why the hell does Matt have to push, why can't he leave it alone?

He crossed his arms and squeezed himself tightly, trying to hold in the rage that threatened to spill. His body twitched and his steps faltered. He increased his pacing, hoping to outrun the need to explode. His heart slammed against his chest and his pulse raced. His entire torso shook as he gasped for air.

No, no, no.

He stood in the doorway of his bathroom, attempting to ground himself with the doorframe pressed against his back. He grabbed the sides of his head, fisting his hair in his hands.

The pounding in his head wouldn't stop.

The blinding anger left him powerless.

He looked at the doorframe.

Bam. Bam. Bam.

His chest heaved with each rapid, clipped breath, but somehow, the new pain in his hand slowed him down and gradually replaced the rage. He paced the room again, the anger boiling within heated his skin. After the last ten years, he should have known better than to open himself up to someone or hope things would change.

He cradled his hand, the sting of pain enough to break through his anger. He walked into the bathroom, shaking his hand, trying to bring some movement back into his numb fingers. He glanced up and saw his reflection, catching sight of the misshaped scar and ink on his bicep. His legs weakened. He hated himself, hated what had happened, and hated that making any sort of connection with others would endanger them. The thought crippled him and brought him to his knees.

He didn't want to be alone anymore.

His body shook uncontrollably. He tried to brace himself against the bathroom cabinet before he lost himself completely. His bloody knuckles had smeared the pristine white surface. Wasn't that always the case with him, he'd come in and ruined something that was perfectly fine without him? He inhaled a choppy breath as he looked around. He crawled over to the wall and yanked at the roll of toilet paper with his shaky hands then tried to wipe the cabinet door clean. The white became pink as the blood continued to smear. He looked over his shoulder and saw a trail of blood smudges from his hand along the tile.

"Shit," he said with a tremble in his voice. He sat cross-legged on the bathroom floor and leaned over, cradling his hurt hand while he rhythmically rocked back and forth. He closed his eyes and forced himself to take a breath, hold for two seconds, then exhale. He thought of Hunter and his soothing voice, those silver eyes.

Oh God.

Please, please, please.

He repeatedly inhaled and exhaled with thoughts of Hunter mixed in until he felt the ripples of anger dissipate. The tightness in his chest began to loosen.

"Cameron?"

He looked up to find Julian standing in the doorway of the bathroom with Matt directly behind him.

"Sorry," Cam said brokenly, looking over to Matt. Guilt sliced through him at the expression on their faces. "I'm sorry."

"I shouldn't have pushed, Cam, I'm the one who's sorry."

"What the fuck did you do?" Julian asked, using his chin to point to the blood-smeared cabinet.

Matt pushed Julian aside and knelt on the floor next to Cam. He extended Cam's hand and moved each finger. "It's not broken."

"What did you hit?"

"C'mon we need to get some ice on this," Matt said, pulling Cam to stand.

"What. Did. You. Hit?"

"Doorframe," Cam mumbled. "I didn't want to fuck up your wall."

Julian nodded. "Good call."

Chapter TWELVE

"You know what I don't get," Melanie said before plopping herself on Hunter's office couch.

"How it's possible anyone gets any work done with constant interruptions?" Hunter teased with a wry grin.

"Fuck you, I'm being serious."

Hunter put his pen down and crossed his arms, giving Mel his undivided attention.

Melanie rolled her eyes dramatically. "You can be such an ass sometimes. I'm talking about Gonzalez. The man went AWOL. I've contacted everyone I know and no one's got a clue where he is or where he'd go. It's like he vanished into thin air. They just can't find him."

"Who's 'they'?"

"We've got the tri-county area with BOLOs out on him. I just found out that the day they went to his house to break the news to him, he was already gone."

Hunter sat upright in his chair. "Wait a minute, he didn't get the news he was being dismissed?"

"No. They went to tell him they were going to investigate him and he never answered the door. That's the weird part."

Hunter rubbed his chin as he thought of the different scenarios of what could have happened. "It sounds like something must have happened to him."

"I agree. A judge finally granted a warrant to get into the house and that's when they discovered he wasn't there and hadn't been there for a few days."

"That's not like him."

"Yeah, something's not right here. Let's just hope he turns up. He's got a lot of explaining to do," Mel finished before standing.

"Leaving so soon?" Hunter leaned back in his chair with his hands behind his head. "You interrupted my work, you might as well hang out."

Melanie rolled her eyes again. "What the hell has gotten into you? You're..." She repeatedly snapped her fingers searching for the right word.

"What?" Hunter chuckled.

She pointed at him quickly when the word finally hit her. "Happy. That's it!"

"Wow, you had to search your vocabulary for a safe word, didn't you?"

Hunter shook his head and chuckled. Mel was a force. If he hadn't seen her in trial with his very own eyes, he wouldn't believe how fierce she was in the courtroom—and curse word free. But damn did she let loose once she was out of that courthouse.

Mel smirked. "I was trying to be nice, you shithead," she said, walking away. She spun back around. "Oh yeah, almost forgot why I in-ter-rupt-ed."

"Oh, you had a reason?"

"We've got a meeting at two today."

"Who with and what about?" Hunter asked.

"Mayor, chief of police, they're all coming over to bake brownies. Fuck if I know what they want."

"You have a lovely handle of the English language. You kiss your boyfriend with that mouth?"

"Yeah, and he loves it," she said, sticking her tongue out and licking her upper lip seductively before waving good-bye. "See you then."

He grabbed his cell phone and speed-dialed a call. He had to find Peter.

"Hey, Dad," he said once his father answered.

"Hi, Son."

"How was your date?"

"How was yours?" his father countered.

"Dad, stop." A smile spread across his face. "I just wanted to ask if you've heard from your fishing buddy," he asked, not wanting to use Peter's name and risk anyone hearing.

"Nope, but I do know someone who has."

Hunter straightened. "Dad, are you home?"

"Nope, grocery shopping, and before you ask, no, I'm not buying bacon."

Hunter chuckled. "I'll come by the house so we can talk more. Will you be home soon?"

"I should be home in about an hour. Are you okay?" he asked with obvious concern in his voice.

"I'm fine. I'll see you in a little bit," he said before ending the call. He was not going to start a conversation about what he needed over the phone. His dad could go off on another tangent and who knew where it would lead.

Hunter looked at his watch and knew he had a few minutes to spare before the meeting. There was no way in hell he was disappearing for a few days without seeing Cam.

* * * *

"Are you sure you're okay?" Bill asked for the hundredth time.

"I'm fine," Cameron said, switching hands to hold the milk pot. His scraped knuckles and swollen hand made it too difficult to grab the small handle to pour the steamed milk.

"We can stop selling the fancy coffees until your hand heals."

Cam smiled tiredly. "You don't need to do that. It just takes me a little longer than usual to do a couple of the things, but it's fine. I just feel bad I can't do the designs like this."

"Are you sure you're okay?" he asked again.

Cameron hated the worry he saw in Bill's expression. Thankfully, Lucy hadn't come into the diner yet. He couldn't handle worrying the both of them. He had been a complete idiot last night. His pained hand just served as a constant reminder of how his past seemed to always come back to haunt him. He wasn't sure why he thought this time would be different.

"I'm fine," he repeated and continued to work slowly to finish the morning rush orders. Between the coffee orders and simultaneously working the register with Bill, the exhaustion weighed on him as if he had worked a double shift. His pained hand was a bit swollen and the over-the-counter pain pills hadn't kicked in yet.

"Go ahead and take a break. Get some ice on that thing," Bill said as he took the last latte coffee order then handed him a towel with some ice cubes inside.

"Thanks," he said before going to the back room.

He sat at the table, icing his hand. *Fucking moron.* He should have known better than to get too comfortable in this new life. It was damn near impossible for someone to not ask questions. Why couldn't he just lock everything up in a closet and throw away the key? Move on, start new. He shifted the ice on his hand and hissed as the edge of the ice hit his raw skin.

"Hey, Cam," Hunter said, poking his head in the back room.

Startled, Cam stood and turned, keeping his hurt hand behind him, resting on the chair's backrest. He couldn't help smiling at the sight of the more casual version of Hunter. "Hi."

He stood, arms crossed without his suit jacket, only wearing the vest with tie and shirt sleeves rolled up past his elbows. Cam's body immediately took notice of the muscled arms and shirt-hugged biceps.

"Bill said you were back here, I've only got a few minutes."

"You look good."

"Thanks," Hunter responded with a grin. "I'm leaving town for a couple of days. I left the office for a few minutes because I wanted to stop by and see you before leaving."

They stood, looking at each other, neither one making the first move.

Cam cocked his head. "What are you thinking?" he asked after a few moments of silence.

Hunter laughed uneasily.

"What?" Cam insisted.

"I seriously don't know how I'm going to be away from you for a few days," he said with a look of need in his eyes.

Cam gave him a teasing smirk. "I'm sure you've got a vivid imagination. I bet you'll come up with something."

"That's the problem."

Cam reached out to place his good hand on Hunter's chest. Hunter stepped forward into the touch, closing the distance between them. He wrapped his arms around Cam and pulled him closer. Cam brought his arms up and circled Hunter's shoulders. One of Hunter's hands held the back of Cam's head while the other tentatively landed at the base of his spine. Cam's pulse raced as Hunter pulled him closer. He felt a kiss at the side of his neck, then another just below his ear, and another along his jawline. His rising hard-on was now in full force. He groaned. Cam angled his head, granting better access, hoping and praying Hunter would continue. Damn, it felt good to be worshipped.

Hunter finally reached his face, softly kissed his cheek, then stopped.

Cam opened his eyes, dazed and drunk with desire. The need in Hunter's gaze forced Cam to yank Hunter closer for a kiss. Hunter pulled him by the waist with one hand and angled his head with the other, demanding more. Cam moaned as Hunter licked his lips, begging for access. Their tongues dueled. Cam pushed up against him, craving friction. He shook with need when an equal hardness pressed against him. Hunter withdrew, slowly peppering kisses along Cam's face.

Hunter took a deep breath and exhaled slowly, then rested his forehead against Cam's.

"You stopped," Cam said breathlessly.

"I don't want to scare Bill or the customers."

Cam stroked the back of Hunter's neck.

"I don't think it's a secret how much I want you," Hunter whispered, his lips ghosting over Cam's.

Cam weakly smiled. It took too much effort to regain control of his body. His heart beat brutally against his chest, drugged with the heat of Hunter's body and the full lips brushing against his own. "It's mutual," he said, barely audible, before he realized the words had escaped.

Hunter inched back slightly, breaking the spell. "By the way," he began before reaching around behind his own neck and gently grasping Cam's hurt hand by the wrist. He looked at the swollen knuckles then looked up at Cam. "I won't ask what happened, because, if you want me to know, you'll tell me. But I do need to know if you're okay."

Cam looked away. "Yeah," he responded weakly after a few moments of silence. His throat tightened with emotion. Usually, people cared about 'what' he had done and never cared about how he felt or if he was okay.

"Good." He grabbed Cam's chin and turned his head to brush a quick, gentle kiss on his lips. "Go out with me."

"What? Like a date?"

"Yeah, a date. An actual date outside of the diner. We can do anything you want. I don't care as long as it's just the two of us."

Cam froze. All the blood drained from his face. Matt was right. He needed to tell Hunter the truth. It was only fair to be completely honest and let Hunter decide if he wanted to pursue this further. But his fear of losing the one person who gave him some peace and made him want to dream for something more prevailed. "I thought you were leaving for a few days?"

"Yeah, but when I get back."

"Oh," he said.

"You don't want to go out with me?" Hunter asked with a frown.

"I do...soon," he finished lamely.

"Can I call you while I'm away?" Hunter asked cautiously, confusion coloring his expression.

Cam quickly recalled the rules on phone calls. Thankfully, Matt's rules were lax on times and length. "Sure."

"What's your number?" Hunter asked expectantly.

Shit, what *was* his number? Heck if he knew. Why the hell would he call himself?

"Do you have your cell?"

Cam had left the cell phone back in his room, hoping to avoid any comfort calls from Matt about his run-in with the doorframe. "Not with me."

Hunter checked his pockets and frowned. "Shit, I raced out of the office to come over here and I left my wallet." He grabbed the pen off the wall clipboard next to the phone and tore off a sheet of notepaper.

"Call me and leave a voice mail with your number or text it to me. I'll call you after I finish for the day when you're off work. It might be a little late."

Cam nodded. He could deal with hearing that *sexy-as-fuck* voice echoing in his ear.

"I've got to go. I've got a meeting before I leave."

Hunter pulled Cam into another embrace and nuzzled Cam.

"You need to stop doing that if you plan on making it out of here," Cam teased. He didn't really want Hunter to let go.

"I'll see you soon," Hunter said, stepping back, cupping Cam's face then placing a soft kiss on his lips. When Cam opened his eyes, the desire in the silver gaze made him groan.

"You're killin' me," Cam said, forcing himself to look away. His body screamed for Hunter's heat.

"I'll be back soon," Hunter said before finally leaving.

Cam leaned against the wall and closed his eyes. He could still feel Hunter's hands on him, the taste of his kiss.

Bill poked his head into the back room. "Are you okay?" he asked for the billionth time today.

Cam looked over to him and simply nodded, knowing words were just not possible at that moment.

He was more than just *okay*. He couldn't remember the last time he'd felt this good.

Chapter THIRTEEN

Hunter raced back to the office, hoping to make it in time for the meeting. He exited the elevator on his office floor and Melanie immediately flagged him over to the conference room. The typical staff members were in attendance in addition to the mayor, Frank Weston, his assistant, Lydia, and the chief of police, Harold Kramer.

"I want to know what the hell is going on! How close are we to catching this son of a bitch?" the mayor thundered.

"My team caught a critical player and you guys failed to make it stick," Chief Kramer mumbled.

"Don't go there, Harry. You know that was out of our hands and the judge threw out the case," Melanie defended.

"That's a crock of shit," he huffed.

Hunter sat back and observed the childish back and forth yelling. He hated wasting time and this meeting was headed nowhere. It was just a bitching session. The mayor was pissed his numbers were slipping. An election was coming up and he needed a big selling point—capturing the drug dealer affecting the city would definitely add a feather to his cap and secure a win.

"Where the hell is Gonzalez?" the mayor asked. "He was dismissed, not exiled. He needs to get back here. I don't give a shit where he is. Find him!" the mayor yelled.

In the absence of capturing a drug dealer, it seemed nailing a dirty judge was second best. Hunter was glad Peter was in hiding.

"I'm the chief of police, not a private investigator. I'm too busy trying to clean up these streets and bust guys for you, just so the two of you," he said, waving his hand over to Mel and Hunter, "can fuck things up and set him free. I'm not going to spend my time chasing after a dirty judge who's AWOL. Go to hell."

"Guys, we're not going to resolve anything like this. Let's figure something out so we can wrap up these cases. Any suggestions?" Melanie asked.

Silence.

"I want this done. The election is in two months, and I want arrests and convictions. This won't look good for me at poll time."

"I know, Frank," Mel said.

"This reflects on you as well, Mel, so get on it," he said as he stood. "I'm tired of wasting my time here." He signaled to his assistant to follow him as he left the room. The chief of police and the remaining attendees exited, leaving Melanie and Hunter alone in the room.

"Sorry about that," Mel said with a furrowed brow.

"About what? The mayor wanting to get reelected and the chief pissed they threw out the case. Hell, I'm pissed about that too."

Mel relaxed in her seat. "I know, but I don't want them to make you look bad. You've been working your ass off lately more than ever on these cases."

"I'm a big boy, I can handle it."

Mel snorted a laugh. "Yeah, big boy," she drawled, kicking his chair playfully.

Hunter chuckled. "Hey, I've got to leave town for a couple of days. Is that okay?"

"Is something wrong?" she asked with concern.

He hated lying to Mel, but he needed to find Peter without further delay. "Everything's fine. I just need to go check out some places for my dad. He's too stubborn to be on his own. It shouldn't be more than a few days."

"Any pending case stuff I need to pick up?"

"Nope. All the depositions are done or scheduled, two of the court dates got cancelled because they accepted the pleas and Jessie is up to date on any of the files I've got in the queue. I have a few case files I need to review but I'll take those with me. If anything comes up, just call me."

"No problem. Keep me posted, okay?"

"I'm going to leave in a few to beat the traffic."

Melanie nodded then rose from her seat. "Pick up a hitchhiker along the way and explore some reckless abandonment." She quickly ducked out of the conference room to avoid the pen that flew across the room aimed at her.

Hunter shook his head and laughed. He left the conference room and walked back to his office. He pulled out his briefcase and removed the files he didn't need then sorted through his planner to confirm nothing would be left pending.

"Hey, boss," Jessie said, entering the office.

"Hey. I'm going out of town for a couple of days. If you need to reach me, just give me a call or text me."

Jessie nodded then walked a few steps closer to Hunter.

Hunter peered up from his briefcase just as Jessie looked over his shoulder.

"What's going on?" Hunter asked, narrowing his eyes.

"I had a package dropped off on my desk before your meeting started. I opened it and there was this inside with your name on it," he said, handing over an envelope.

Hunter looked at the white envelope with a blue stripe along the return address area. The envelope was blank other than a single word, *Hunter*, printed on a stick-on label in the front.

Hunter stared at the file as if it were a snake that would snap out and bite. He looked up and saw Melanie's assistant approaching the door. He quickly grabbed the envelope and stuffed it into his briefcase.

"Excuse me, Mel wanted me to grab the deposition transcriptions before you left."

Jessie shuffled her out of the office. "I've got them at my desk."

"Jessie, call me if anything comes up," he said with a firm gaze, hoping to telepath his hidden concern.

"No problem, boss," Jessie said with a nod.

Hunter had to get the hell out of the office and go see his dad. He finished packing a few files into his case then darted out.

"Dad?" Hunter asked as he entered his father's home.

"What's going on?" His father stood in the living room with his arms crossed.

"Turns out Peter disappeared before anyone notified him of his dismissal. Honestly, I thought he was AWOL, trying to clear his name."

His father sighed and shook his head. "Well, this puts a whole different spin on things."

"I know. They've searched the obvious contacts and places. You said you know someone who's heard from him?"

Thomas rubbed his chin. "Karyna. She called me yesterday, and I barely understood what she was saying. It's as if she was talking in code or something. I assumed it was some new lingo or something you younger kids do. Now it makes sense. She must have reached out because of Peter but didn't want to mention him by name."

"No one would think to look for her to find him. I guess she figured hearing from her would jog your memory and you'd make the connection."

"Probably. Now, go talk to her. And be ready, I'm guessing she'll probably try to jump you."

"Dad," Hunter chastised. "Don't go there please."

"Son, I know you don't play for that team," his father smiled. "She always did seem to find an excuse to come over and fish with us when she knew you'd be there to bait her hooks and help her throw her lines."

"Dad, can we please get back on target here. This is important."

"I know, I know. By the way, how's your young man doing?" his father asked, waggling his eyebrows.

Hunter groaned. His father and his tangents were going to stress him out. "Dad, please."

"Okay, okay."

"I'm assuming she told you how to get a hold of her?"

"Yup," his father said, walking over to his phone directory. He scribbled some information on a piece of paper and walked back over to Hunter. "Here you go."

Hunter looked at the scrap and saw a phone number and address. "Thanks," he said, shoving the paper into his pocket.

"You leaving now?" his father asked.

"Yeah and you can't tell anyone where I'm going. Got it?"

His father nodded. "What excuse did you give for leaving?"

"I told them I had to look into something for you. Um, I kinda mentioned I was looking at retirement places."

"Great. Blame it on the old fart who needs looking after," his father grumbled.

Hunter laughed. "Thanks, Dad. I gotta go," he said.

"Be careful, Son. Please. If someone's done this to Pete—"

"I know, Dad. That's why I've got to find him."

He pulled his father into an embrace.

His father tightened his hold. "Don't think I haven't noticed how you're avoiding the subject."

Hunter released his dad and glared at him. "Yes, I saw him earlier, and yes, I asked him out. Happy?"

"What did he say?"

"He said 'soon', I guess that's better than a no," he added before laughing.

"Yes, that's better than a no," his father said then patted him on the shoulder. "You're smiling with your eyes, you know? That tells me you're happy."

Hunter grinned as thoughts of Cameron flooded his mind. The way he smelled, his taste, the soft yet strong lips when they kissed, the way Cam's body fit perfectly against his. He wanted to believe he was slowly breaking down Cam's iron walls.

"Yeah, Dad. I'm happy," he said wistfully. "I've gotta go. I'll see you soon," he said before waving bye.

Chapter FOURTEEN

Cameron called Matt before he left the diner. Rather than ask Julian to pick him up, he decided to walk the few blocks to get back to the halfway house. He didn't want to be a bother—he knew Julian was planning something for Matt's birthday today but didn't have a clue what it was.

The swelling in his hand had lessened and thoughts of Hunter and a future date lingered in his mind. Where would they go, what would they do? He wanted to enjoy the peacefulness he always felt when they were together. The worries that riddled his mind would vanish, and the fear of trying to fit in, blend, survive, everything just righted itself with Hunter.

He took the steps up to the house and heard a familiar voice. He walked in and saw Sam talking with Matt.

"Hey, there!" Sam said before grabbing Cam into a hug.

"What are you doing here?" Cam asked Sam and looked over to Matt.

"He escorted over two guys to our house," Matt responded proudly. "J's showing them around. They're getting the green rooms," Matt said with a nod and a smile.

Cam chuckled. Matt and his fricken color-themed rooms. Cam didn't care about the colors—he just cared that the green rooms were the farthest away from his.

"Oh, there he is," he heard Julian say as he walked down the stairs. "This is Cameron." He gestured toward him.

Cam nodded in acknowledgement.

"This is Cole," Julian said, pointing to the guy wearing a knit beanie, then he turned to the tall guy with the serious expression. "And this is Luke."

Cameron extended his hand in greeting. Cole gripped Cameron's hand enthusiastically. He was constantly shifting from one foot to the other, unable to stand still. He was a ball of energy, with a devilish grin and a mischievous glint in his mismatched eyes. He wore a beanie low over his forehead and thick black hair peeked out along the back. He was about a head shorter than Cam and stocky, couldn't have been much taller than five-eight, give or take an inch.

"Dude, this place is awesome!" Cole said with a huge grin and a wealth of enthusiasm.

"Yeah," Cam answered. He turned to Luke who stood silently, observing. "Nice to meet you."

Luke firmly shook his hand then made eye contact. A clear *you-leave-me-alone-and-we'll-be-fine* vibe screamed from his gaze.

"Ignore Luke's tough guy act. You should have heard him with his girlfriend on the phone."

"I'm going to beat you in your sleep if you don't shut up," Luke said with a sideways glare targeted at Cole.

"Cam, keep everyone busy here for two minutes," Julian said to Cam in a whisper.

Cam simply nodded. He wasn't sure how he was supposed to entertain anyone or keep them busy.

He noticed Matt's curiosity piqued and the man looked ready to follow Julian into the kitchen. "I wouldn't do that," Cam said.

Matt looked over and bit his lip. "What the hell is he doing?"

Cam shrugged. He did know it was Matt's birthday but he couldn't even acknowledge that without risking a chance at Matt figuring anything out.

"So how long have you been here?" beanie guy asked.

"Couple of weeks," Cam responded.

"What did you do?"

"What did *you* do?" Cameron asked.

"I boost exotics and sleepers," Cole said with a grin.

"Boosted, Cole. Past tense. The goal is to not do that anymore," Matt corrected.

Cole guffawed. "Dude, if a Ferrari pranced in front of me, I can't promise I'd have that much self-control."

"Then we'll have to work on that," Matt said with a smile. Matt had a distant look on his face then tugged the back of his hair. "What are sleepers?"

Cole moaned. "They're the powerful sexy ones no one pays attention to. But I do."

Cam chuckled and took pity on Matt. "They're cars that don't look fancy on the outside but have a lot of power under the hood. Think of it as high performance in disguise."

"Oh, I get it," Matt said shyly.

"Dude, you're totally giving me a hard-on right now," Cole said to Cam.

"Keep it in your pants, Boost Boy," Cam said as Julian walked out of the kitchen and glanced over to Sam moments later.

As if on cue, Sam started herding the new arrivals to the kitchen. "I'm starving. Matt you got anything we can nibble on? We didn't get a chance to grab anything on the way here."

Matt fidgeted. "Um, we might have something...I think." He looked around and saw Julian lingering then looked back over at Cam. Matt raised an eyebrow then stood in front of Julian, arms crossed. Julian half smiled, grabbed him, and pulled him into the kitchen.

Cam followed the others into the kitchen. On the table was a birthday cake with a single candle and two wrapped gifts, one noticeably larger than the other. Everyone applauded and Matt's face immediately flushed when everyone broke out in unison to sing him "Happy Birthday". Even Luke looked as if he was mumbling the words. Julian wrapped his arms around Matt from behind and rested his chin on Matt's shoulder as he sang. Cam had never seen Julian with such a huge smile on his face. He transformed into a different person right before Cam's eyes.

Matt blew out the candle and everyone chanted to open the gifts. Julian handed the large box over to Matt. When he unwrapped the gift, he gasped, then immediately looked up to see a smiling Julian staring back at him. Matt pulled out a beautifully carved, square wooden sign that read 'Halfway House'. Along the edges were additional carvings.

Matt looked up at Julian with such emotion even Cam's chest began to hurt. "J—" was all he was able to say before Julian rushed to his side and resumed his position behind Matt, arms wrapped around his waist and chin resting on his shoulder.

"You guys really called this place 'Halfway House'? Um, you never actually gave it a name?" the beanie guy asked.

Julian gave him one of his six-foot-under glares. "You got a problem with that?"

Cole raised his hands in surrender. "Nah, man. But you gotta admit. It's weird as shit that you didn't actually give it a real name."

"That *is* a name," Julian snarled.

"Uh, yeah. If you say so," Cole said.

Matt wistfully spoke as he grazed his fingers over each of the names carved into the edges. "There were so many people who played a part in this house, whether they knew it or not. Both in the original idea that inspired this house, and in every detail since. It began as a tribute to a friend of mine, but it developed into so much more. Coming up with a name that would represent them all and what they meant to the both of us was impossible."

"Oh," Cole said, shuffling his feet. "Sorry."

Cam neared the sign to get a better view. He could read a few names, all hand-carved and slightly burnt in the recessed carvings. Liam, Eleanor, Marie, even Sam's name was etched into the wood.

Matt turned in Julian's arms and muttered a barely audible "I love you" to which Julian immediately whispered a response in his ear.

Cameron closed his eyes. It felt voyeuristic to be in the same room at that moment to witness so much tangible affection. He'd never openly admit it, but he was both jealous for not having someone who openly cared that much for him, and angry that his circumstances would probably never allow it.

"Open the other one," Sam encouraged.

Matt separated from the embrace with a shimmer in his eyes and a huge grin on his face. He reached for the next box.

"Um, maybe you should wait to open that one," Julian said in an odd tone.

Sam laughed. "Now you have to open it here and now."

Matt immediately ripped open the box as Sam and Julian snapped quick comebacks at each other.

Matt held a picture frame in his hands encasing a cut out newspaper clipping. Even though it had been flattened in the frame, it was obvious the ad had been folded at one time. The top of the frame had a decorated heading that read 'Boner looking for a handyman.'

Cole snorted a laugh. "What the hell is that?"

Julian tried to hide his smile.

Sam looked over to the picture frame. "Is that the ad we ran?"

Matt nodded and casually sniffled then looked over to Julian. He placed a hand on his waist in a poor attempt to seem hostile as a wicked grin spread across his face. "That's Doner, D-O-N-E-R."

Julian burst into laughter.

"But that says Boner?" Cole said, confused.

"Long story, Cole. But I think someone's going to get one hell of a beating tonight about it," Sam teased.

Cole looked over to Matt and Julian then back to Sam. "I know I'm not the brightest bulb in the shop, but I, uh, kinda think that was the plan."

"Happy birthday, Matt," Cam said before removing himself from the conversation and racing upstairs.

He closed the door then reached for the cell phone on the nightstand. He pulled the folded paper from his pocket and spread his hands over it gently to smooth it out.

Hunter.

He took a few breaths and debated whether he should call now or wait. Cam didn't want to call and interrupt him at work and he wasn't sure what exactly to say. He figured he'd try sending the phone number via a text message. He touched a few menus but couldn't figure out how to send the message. *Fricken technology changes.* He grumbled then dialed the number scribbled on the paper before he could change his mind.

After two rings, voice mail answered the call. Cameron sighed when the sound of Hunter's voice echoed through the line. He closed his eyes and enjoyed the dip in his voice as he asked the listener to leave a message.

The beep of the recording jolted him back to the moment. "Um, hey, it's me. Cam. Shit I didn't write my number down but I guess you can get it from that caller ID thing you have or something. I guess I'll talk to you later. Bye." He pressed the button to end the call. Cam closed his eyes and sighed. He hoped he didn't come across like the fool he thought he sounded like in that message.

A knock at the door interrupted his thoughts.

"Cam?"

"Hey, Sam," he said as he opened the door.

"How are you doing?" he asked, entering the room. "Adjusting well? Matt says you're working at a nearby diner."

"Yeah, I'm settling in okay, I think." He shrugged.

Sam looked at him, assessing in his usual I-know-more-than-you're-telling-me sorta way. "So I heard you got pissed off yesterday. Want to tell me what that was about?"

Cameron inhaled as panic started to set in. *Shit, if Matt filed a report about him losing his temper—*

"Hey, don't freak out, Matt's fine. He just wanted to make sure you were okay and he didn't want to push you. He mentioned it today when I came over for the transfer is all."

Cam exhaled with relief. "I fucked up. I got pissed off when Matt started asking questions and I sorta…yeah…took it out on that." He gestured to the bathroom doorframe which had a few new dents along the edge.

"You all right?" Sam asked with concern, reaching for Cam's bruised hand.

"I'm better. I just…I don't know," he said, looking up at Sam. "I just don't want to go back there and I want to forget all of it and try to move on. It just feels like I can't sometimes." His body slumped.

"Hey, don't start that," Sam said before throwing an arm over Cam's shoulders. "It's just going to take a while to adjust. You've got a job, soon you'll be out of here and you'll meet someone and things will start looking and feeling different with time. You'll see," he said encouragingly, patting Cam's back.

"I met someone."

"Yeah?" Sam asked with a smirk. "At the diner?"

Cam nodded eagerly. "He's different."

"How so?"

"I feel safe when I'm with him," he said without hesitation.

Sam smiled. "It's about time someone made you feel safe." He pulled Cam into a hug.

No more questions, no interrogations, no reprimands or what-ifs. Sam just knew when not to push and when to listen.

They separated when Cam's phone chirped. He looked at it and saw a notification displayed on the screen. *What the hell do I do with this now?*

His face heated. "Um, I think I got a text. Can you show me how to work this…thing?" He waved the phone in his hand in frustration.

"It's easy. You're going to be texting like a mad man soon." Sam took the phone and walked Cam through the menu options.

Got your message :) Bad reception here. I'll call you as soon as I get to the hotel. –H

A smile spread across Cam's face, imagining Hunter's voice.

Sam bumped his shoulder. "I think he's got it as bad as you do."

Cameron beamed. "Quick, show me how to reply to this thing before he realizes how crazy he is and changes his mind," he said with a laugh.

* * * *

Hunter drove up to the small house by the lake and parked his car off to the side. His phone chirped. He smiled when he read Cam's response.

You better. —Cam

He closed his eyes and held the phone to the side of his face as he imagined Cam's teasing tone and laugh. He hadn't lied to his father when he said he was happy. He was. Happier than he'd ever been and there was only one reason.

Cam.

He looked up when he heard a dog bark. An older version of a childhood friend exited the front door of the small house. He emerged from the car and the small woman immediately raced toward him. Hunter laughed when she jumped up and wrapped her arms around his neck.

"He told me you'd come but I didn't believe him," she whispered in his ear.

Hunter released her. "Who told you I'd come to see you?"

"Tio Pedro." She always called Peter—or Pedro as his Latin counterparts referred to him—her uncle, even after he no longer dated her mother.

"When did you last talk to him?"

She grabbed Hunter's hand and led him inside her home. "C'mon," she said.

"Karyna, what's going on?"

"I don't know, but he doesn't want anyone to know where he is. He only wanted you to know."

"How did he know I'd come to see you?"

She laughed. "He said you would eventually end up here or your dad would lead you here. But he also knew no one would guess to come see me when looking for him."

"He has a point."

"He usually does. When I didn't hear from you right away, I called your dad. I thought hearing my voice might jog his memory."

"It did," Hunter said with a smile.

"It's been so long…stay for dinner."

They chatted over an early evening meal. The conversation seemed to steer in the direction of childhood memories where they recalled their summers together and Karyna's poor actress portrayal of a girl who couldn't fish.

She sighed. "Why did you have to be gay?" She leaned her head over on the couch as they continued to chat after they ate.

Hunter chuckled.

"You know, you're the only boy I ever had a crush on?"

"Um, sorry."

"Don't be. You always told me you liked guys but I just assumed that was your way of turning me down nicely. I figured if I couldn't have you then no other girl should either so I accepted it."

"Psycho much?"

She launched at him and punched him in the shoulder before pulling him into a hug. "I did miss you."

"Sorry I haven't stayed in touch."

They separated and she looked at him with scrunched eyebrows. "Tio said you work too much."

"He's right. But I'm trying to slow things down a bit. I'm kinda getting tired of it," he said, casually picking at a loose thread on the couch's armrest. "So you know where he is?"

"Yes, but you're going to have to drive for a while to get there. You'll need a map and GPS."

He wrote the coordinates she provided on a scrap of paper and the general driving directions for the route.

"That bad?"

"He thinks so."

Hunter arrived at a hotel between Karyna's house and Peter's location a few hours later. He was too tired to drive the extra eight hours to get to where his family friend hid. He dropped his duffle bag on the table and put his briefcase on the chair. He grabbed his cell phone and noticed the battery was low. He dialed his father's number as he pulled the charger from the bag.

"Hi, Son. How's it going?"

"Good, Dad. Sorry if I woke you."

"It's okay. You know I don't keep the same hours when I know you're away. So how did it go?"

"I visited the first place today. It was nice, like family." Hunter's paranoia didn't allow him to casually chat about something like this over the phone. He knew his father would pick up the critical details, regardless of how obscure he was in the conversation. Too much fiction and too many real life cases left enough of an impression to ignore a little protection where family was concerned.

"I figured it would. I've heard great things about that one."

Hunter smiled. His father may be getting up in his years but he was still more perceptive than most.

"Are you checking out the second place, too?"

"Yeah, it's next on my list but I'm taking a break in between the drive."

"Got it," his father responded. "Get your rest and make sure you keep an eye out for the ladies. I want to make sure I've got some options."

Hunter rubbed his face. Even with an undercover conversation, his dad still managed to plant visuals or tease him to the point of discomfort. "Dad, I gotta go. My battery's dying and I want to jump in the shower before crashing."

His father laughed, knowing he'd hit his mark. "Good night, Son. Be safe on the road."

"Will do. And you behave yourself." He disconnected the call before his father had a chance to respond with another quick comeback.

He plugged his phone into the charger then made his way to the shower. He undressed and stepped into the hot spray, closing his eyes as the water eased the tension from his muscles. He grabbed the soap and opted for a quick shower in hopes of calling Cam before it was too late in the evening.

With nothing more than a towel wrapped around his waist, he reached for his phone with the charge cable still connected and dialed the number he'd been thinking about endlessly for the last few hours.

"Hi," Cam answered on the second ring.

"Hi," Hunter responded with a smile. He lay back in bed and rested his head on his arm. "Did I call you at a bad time or is this okay? I know it's kinda late."

Hunter heard Cam's muffled laugh through the phone. "I was starting to think you forgot about me and wouldn't call."

"Not possible." After a few moments of silence, Hunter asked, "How's your hand?"

"Better. Swelling's gone down. It'll probably be fine tomorrow. So are you like on vacation or something?" Cam asked.

"Not really. Running an errand."

"Oh, okay."

More silence.

Hunter waited.

"Um, what do you want to talk about? Is this one of those what-are-you-wearing sorta calls?" Cam asked, chuckling.

Hunter laughed. "I'd much rather touch you than talk about it. I really don't care what we talk about. I just want to hear your voice."

"Perv."

Hunter snorted a laugh. "Yeah, 'cause you're a saint. Tell me something about you."

"Uh, what do you want to know?"

"Tell me about your day at the diner or something about you, your childhood. I don't know."

"Oh, okay. That's easy."

Cam spoke endlessly about his mom, their yard projects, and even mentioned the botanical contest they had entered. They placed fifth in the contest but Cam didn't care—he told the story as if they had won the grand prize and his mother was the queen of the garden.

Hunter reminisced about his mom as well and their private baking times in their small home. He laughed as he told Cam about the endless fishing trips with his father and so many of the odd events that would happen when they'd take out the boat or go on the bridge. The conversation easily transitioned into their teenage and school years. Cam excelled in the sciences while Hunter stood out in math and sports. He avoided the subject of school otherwise and segued into talking about their first kisses and how awkward they were.

When they talked about fathers near the end of their telephone conversation, Cam's tone changed.

"My father didn't like the idea of his son being gay." The hurt in Cam's voice was obvious.

Hunter knew when not to push. "Any brothers or sisters?"

Cam hesitated. "Sister. I haven't spoken to her in ten years."

Hunter sensed this was a sensitive subject. He treaded carefully. "Your decision or hers?"

Cameron paused. "Hers," he said quietly. "What about you, any brothers or sisters?"

"Nope. I'm an only child. My parents' pride and joy," Hunter joked.

"I bet."

Hunter looked over at the clock on the nightstand. He couldn't believe he'd spent over two hours on the phone with Cam. It was so easy to just sit back and talk to him, to get to know him. He was tired but he didn't want to hang up the phone.

"I'm glad you called."

Cam chucked. "You called me."

"I meant before. To give me your number."

"Will you be back soon?"

"I plan to. Hopefully in a couple of days." Hunter sighed.

"Good."

"Miss you."

"You need to get your ass back here," Cam teased.

"I promise."

"You better."

"Night, Cam."

"Night," Cam started then hesitated. The line was silent for a few moments.

"Cam?"

"Um, call me tomorrow, okay?"

"Promise."

"Night," he said before the line disconnected.

Hunter closed his eyes and replayed the sound of Cam's voice in his head. A smile was plastered on his face as sleep finally took over.

Chapter FIFTEEN

Cam heard an insistent noise that interfered with the dream of Hunter pulling him closer into another heated kiss. He opened his eyes and realized his phone was vibrating across the nightstand. He reached for it and read the display—*Hot Guy calling*.

"Hi," he answered, his voice still thick with sleep.

"Don't tell me I called you on your day off."

"Nah. I was still in bed."

"I thought you started at eight."

Cam looked over at the clock display that read seven. "I still have time. Are you on the road already?"

"Yeah, I thought I'd get a head start and a few hours driving time in before the traffic got too bad. I wanted to call you before you got in to work just in case I couldn't get to the phone until late."

Cam got out of bed and made his way to the closet to pick out his clothes. He continued the conversation as he started to remove his sleep pants and dress for his day.

"What are you doing?" Hunter laughed.

"Getting dressed for work. Why?"

"You're huffing and puffing. It's kinda hot."

Cam groaned. "Don't get me started unless you want me to jump the first guy I see this morning."

"Not funny."

"Don't tease me. You know I've already got a hard-on with your name on it so don't make this harder on me."

"Harder?" Hunter chuckled.

Cam groaned. "You're evil, you know that?"

"So are we going out when I get back?"

"I hope so." Cam paused. He needed to talk to Hunter before things moved along further. After last night's call, he undoubtedly wanted more but it wasn't fair to expect anything if he wasn't honest with Hunter about his past. "But, um, we need to talk before we do."

"We're talking now," Hunter said in a questioning tone.

"Yeah, but…um…not over the phone. It's too easy for me to just hang up and it's important."

"Is this the kind of conversation where you tell me you're straight, secretly married, and have three kids?"

"I'm gay, not married, and no kids. It's important. I'll probably chicken out midway if I tell you over the phone. So when we see each other, okay?"

"Cam?"

"Yeah?"

"Are you breaking up with me?"

Cam nervously chuckled as he heard the hesitation in Hunter's voice. "I didn't realize we were like boyfriend and um…boyfriend."

"I assume you don't usually go around and make out with people at the diner on breaks. At least, I hope not. I figured we were something more."

"I hope so, but I…I just need to talk to you, okay. Please, Hunter. Don't push me on this right now."

"So it's serious then?" Hunter asked curiously.

Cam hesitated. The emotions clogged his throat and tried to prevent him from speaking further. "Yeah," he croaked. He was on the brink of panicking. He cleared his throat and tried to regain his composure. "I've got to finish getting ready for work. I'll see you soon?"

"You bet," Hunter responded. "Cam?"

"Yeah?"

"I'm not going anywhere."

"I hope not," he faintly responded, almost in a whisper, before ending the call.

He stood, light-headed, half dressed in the room. He clutched the phone to his chest when his knees buckled. He wrapped his arms around his legs and lay on the floor with his eyes screwed shut as he rocked back and forth.

He hoped and prayed he would be granted some mercy and allowed this one little piece of heaven with the piercing silver eyes that made him feel wanted and safe.

* * * *

Hunter finally arrived at the coordinates Karyna provided. The place would be damn near impossible to find without the map and GPS. He couldn't recall how many turns he made at non-existent streets. Just behind the brush of trees, Hunter saw a tiny house with a dirt driveway. He drove up the narrow path and parked his car next to the dark, nondescript compact. Before he had a chance to exit his vehicle, Peter stood in the doorway of the small shack with a smile.

"Took you long enough," he announced as Hunter walked the path and closed the remaining distance between them.

Hunter greeted him with a hug and pat on the back. "What the hell happened to you?"

"C'mon in. I'll tell you what I know." He guided Hunter inside.

"Thanks." Hunter took the offered glass of lemonade.

Peter sat in the chair opposite Hunter and leaned forward. "What did they tell you guys?"

"That you were dismissed for tampering with evidence. They're investigating all your cases."

"Assholes," Peter scoffed.

"I know it's bullshit, but what the hell happened?"

"They tried to buy me off, when I refused, I started getting phone calls and messages."

"What kind of phone calls and messages?"

"The typical 'stay away', 'back off or else' bullshit. It was entirely too dramatic for me so I didn't pay it much attention."

"What changed?"

"I got a folder via courier. Nothing fancy about it at first glance, just a red file with a note on it."

"Red?"

Peter nodded. "In it were photos of me...like surveillance shots, and my schedule, hell, there were even pictures of me having dinner at the restaurant with a friend. I felt so damn uncomfortable. I'm usually aware of being watched because there's always some guy out there who's pissed off I put them away. But this was different. It was too personal. Then I found some documents in the folder. *Fake* documents, stuff I hadn't signed or written, with my name and forged signature on them."

Hunter stood from his seat and walked over to his briefcase. He pulled out one of the red files. "Did it look like this?" he handed over the red folder.

Peter took the file and thumbed through the endless mix of images, reports, details, and more. He glanced up with a questioning expression. "Exactly like this. Where did you get this?"

"They mysteriously appear at the office. Some for me, some for Mel, but they always seem to be related to the cases we are working at the time. The guys fit perfectly with each case and arrest at just the right time."

"I can tell you, I didn't do shit wrong, and if that's what these files mean, then something's going on."

"What did the note say...the one with the folder."

"One word. *Run.*"

"No shit," Hunter said, sitting back in the chair again. He closed his eyes and leaned his head back. His mind raced, trying to recall all the cases and convictions since the red files started several months before. Hunter shot upright. "Wait a minute."

"What?"

"What if the folders aren't for the guilty ones but the scapegoats?"

"Scapegoats?"

"Yeah," he said, grabbing another red file from his case. "This guy, for example, is the perfect target for a case we're working on now. I mean fucking perfect. No question. When I got this file a few days ago, it was almost too easy. That's why I didn't push it. Then I get a text from my assistant today, letting me know the guy was arrested last night—with the drugs *on* him. He says they're not his but no one's buying his story. Easy case, slam dunk, he's going back in for violating his parole."

"Is it the same drug case that was scheduled for our hearing?"

"No, the drugs that were found on him didn't have the emblem logo thing on it. In fact, most of the slam dunk cases are those that don't relate to the new guy on the streets."

"It's too easy."

"Exactly," Hunter said. "And to be honest with you, seeing that you were the subject of a red file tells me they aren't the guilty people."

Peter sighed. "You know I didn't do any of that tampering with evidence thing they're accusing me of, right?"

Hunter looked over at Peter with a glare. "I know you well enough to know it's all bullshit. Your morals border on those of a priest."

"Thanks. It's nice to know someone's not questioning me. They ruined me, you know, and right before I could retire." Peter sounded defeated.

"Not if we can figure out this shit and who's sending these files. They've got too much info in them. Confidential stuff no one should be able to easily access, surveillance logs, data not included in the original case reports. So it's got to be a higher up. The question is, who's trying to give us the heads up about the scapegoats and why?"

"Maybe someone who wants to help put this guy away or help break down whatever the hell is going on that is causing all this to happen. I don't know." Peter straightened in his seat and leaned forward. "I just know that when I got that red file, I bailed. There was no way in hell I was going to hang around and wait with a bull's-eye on my head for these bastards to come get me. I smelled the bullshit a mile away and knew that once I saw one of the doctored documents in the file, I was done. So I had to leave."

"Running makes you look guilty."

"Well. Them not being able to find me makes it look like I disappeared, right? Not as if I'm avoiding some arrest."

Hunter laughed. "Good point. I know you've got everyone wondering what the hell happened to you. The only thing people are saying is that you've gone MIA. That's it. It's as if you've disappeared off the face of the earth. I think people are more concerned about your disappearance than your guilt right now."

"Exactly what I needed to happen. If it looked like I was running or hiding, then it would be a simple case closed situation of evasion. This way, people are wondering what happened and where the hell I am. Maybe that'll lead them to look into things a bit more and question what's going on."

Hunter laughed. "You're so dramatic."

"Fuck you."

"Can I have your autograph? I think you're going to win an Oscar here."

"Shut up." Peter laughed and shoved Hunter. They chatted for a bit and caught up on family and some of the latest court and case issues they'd encountered.

"I've got to go. I've got a long drive back, and I'm going to need daylight to get out of this area." Truth be told, he was anxious to get back and find out what Cameron wanted to talk about.

"Be careful out there. You don't know who's involved or who you can trust."

"Yeah. Speaking of which—if I do need to go to someone, which judge do you think would be the go-to guy."

Peter responded without hesitation. "Dylan Stanford. He's a no nonsense ass, but he's not one to be bought."

Hunter laughed. "Yeah, he's an ass."

"Watch your back, Hunter, and trust your instincts."

"Take care of yourself. I'll get a message to you somehow when it's safe to come back."

"You got it."

Hunter left Peter's hideaway. He tried to think of any prior interactions with others that may have been questionable, but nothing stood out.

"Shit," Hunter muttered in frustration. He wanted to finish these cases, catch this kingpin who was ruining the streets, review all the red files again with a new perspective, and finally talk to Cameron about his mysterious in-person conversation. He didn't have answers for any of this, and he just wanted to get back home.

Hunter fished his phone from his pocket after driving through several towns only to notice his phone was still searching for a signal.

"Dammit." He wanted to talk to Cam before it got too late but his phone just wasn't cooperating. He set his phone to charge and continued to drive. After reaching a rest stop, he checked again and hoped that one bar of service was enough to make a call. After two failed attempts at connecting, the call finally went through.

"Hi there," Cam answered.

"Hey. How are you?" Hunter asked, closing his eyes as Cam's voice filtered through his system.

"Good."

"You sound off, you okay?" Hunter asked.

"Yeah."

Hunter knew Cam well enough to know he wasn't *okay* regardless of what he said. "Is this about that talk you want to have when I'm back?"

Cam grumbled. "How was your day?"

"Long. Too much driving and headaches. But I'm heading back already."

"Yeah?"

"I'm hoping to be there probably tomorrow if all goes as planned."

Silence.

"Cam?"

"Yeah?"

"It doesn't matter, whatever it is you want to talk about, I already told you, I'm not going anywhere, so stop stressing okay?"

More annoying silence.

"Besides…you owe me a date," Hunter added with a smile.

"If you still want me after our talk, then I'll go on as many dates with you as you want."

Hunter held the phone closer to his ear, wishing it was Cam instead. He hated the worry he heard in Cam's voice. "Promise?"

"I swear."

"You do realize you're driving me nuts not telling me what you want to talk about."

"Then fucking stop pushing!"

Hunter closed his eyes. He shouldn't have forced it.

"I'm sorry," Cam quickly added then exhaled deeply. "I figured if I told you I wanted to talk, then you'd push me until we spoke…but I thought you'd at least wait until you got back. Not telling you is like lying and I don't want to lie to you. Fuck man, I suck at this."

Cam might be getting worked up over something that wasn't so bad. Whatever it was, it was important to Cam to get this off his chest. "Thank you."

"For driving you nuts or for biting your head off?" Cam laughed nervously.

"For not wanting to lie to me," Hunter said earnestly. "Lets me know you care."

"Don't get sappy on me."

"I'll call you when I get back in town."

"Okay."

"See you soon," Hunter finished before disconnecting the call.

Whatever Cam had to tell him was obviously wearing away at him. Hunter needed to get his ass back and get rid of this wedge that had worked itself between them. He wished Cam would realize that whatever he had to say just didn't matter. If there was a problem, they'd talk through it, work on it, whatever. He wasn't the type to give up so easily on something, or someone, he wanted so much. He just wished Cam would believe him.

Chapter SIXTEEN

Hunter finally checked into a hotel in the middle of the night at some point between Peter's hideaway and home. After taking a quick shower, he sat on the edge of the bed and stared at his briefcase. Grumbling, he decided to bite the bullet and scan a few of the files before he passed out.

He walked over to his bag, took out the folders and sorted them as he usually did. He realized he'd forgotten about the last minute envelope that arrived during his meeting. He placed it on the table away from the others and stared at it for entirely too long, waiting for something to spring free of the seal.

"Fuck it," he said out loud. He undid the metal clasp and pulled out a single, thin, red folder.

"Fuuuck," he groaned and rubbed his face. Even though most of the face in the mug shot was covered with tousled hair, the piercing blue eyes were unmistakably those of the man who had stolen his heart.

Hunter ran his finger along the image. Those blue eyes held anger and unmistakable pain. His face showed the beginnings of some serious bruising.

What happened to you?

He closed the file again and read the name label, "Pierce, C." A few simple letters on a label, yet they held a wealth of emotion for him. He debated reading the file, wondered if this was what Cam wanted to talk to him about when he returned. He tapped the closed file with his fingers. *Is this considered an invasion of privacy?* His desire to protect Cam overruled. He opened the folder and began to read.

He re-read it, repeatedly. He couldn't find the congruency between the man on paper and the man he had come to know.

"This doesn't make any sense," Hunter mumbled to himself. The charges read like a hodgepodge of items, nothing logical based on the report of what had happened and the evidence in the photos.

Cameron had responded to his sister's call for help. The end result was the death of the sister's boyfriend by a single gunshot to the chest. Cameron was charged with voluntary manslaughter and sentenced to ten years.

Hunter pulled out some of the other documents in the folder and found one of the court transcripts. There had been an attempt to charge Cam with possession of the firearm used, even though it belonged to the family of the sister's boyfriend. Luckily the judge found that illogical and threw out the charge.

Hunter lowered his head and exhaled heavily. A firearm charge would have forced a mandatory minimum of twenty-five years.

Something wasn't right. The bruising on Cam's face, the gun not belonging to him, any lawyer with a fraction of skill could have easily attributed the death to self-defense.

Cam was charged with weapons possession because he had a "blade-like object" in his back pocket that day as well as a long list of charges including petty theft, violent personal crimes, and a drug charge. Hunter looked at the evidence photos. A fucking two dollar pocket knife key chain.

"Shit." Hunter exhaled and rubbed his temples. The headache pulsing behind his eyelids tried to push forward.

He continued to read the additional pages of transcripts, noticing some of the pages were redacted while others were highlighted. Hunter stretched his neck from side to side. None of the dots were connecting in this case, and he couldn't understand how a call to come to a sister's aid could end in a ridiculous checklist of charges and a ten year prison term.

He read the pages, then read them again, flipping each sheet of paper sharply as he yanked the next page. He stepped away from the table and began to pace the room.

Cam was guarded, but he wasn't the kind of guy who would do everything reported in that case file. Hell, he was probably wary of people because of all this and who knows what he'd had to go through during the last ten years.

Hunter sat back in the chair and ran his fingers through his hair.

"Shit!" he yelled and threw the file across the room, sending the papers flying through the air.

He leaned forward and lowered his head onto his crossed arms. He thought of Cam, the smile that made his heart skip a beat, the laugh that made his chest tighten. The tension began to ease from his body. The frustration replaced by determination.

In a short amount of time, he'd gotten to know Cam. The person described on paper was not the man he'd come to love.

He wouldn't deny it to himself. Cam had stolen his heart from the start.

He stood and began collecting the scattered sheets of paper. He sat and willed himself to focus on solving the puzzle he had been handed. No statement from his sister had been taken that day. He searched the additional memos, and after a few torturous minutes of his heartbeat echoing in his ears, he found the sister's boyfriend's name, Bradley Mackler.

"Son of a bitch," he said under his breath.

He pulled out his laptop and launched a browser search window to confirm.

Buried within a news archive dated the same as Cam's report, he found a headline.

Bradley Mackler, son of Judge Kevin Mackler, killed by an intruder.

"An intruder?" he said to himself.

He searched for information on the home where Cam and his sister had been, the homeowner's last name on record was not Mackler. He returned to the redacted documents. Most of the information was blacked out, but there, on a document citing a specific Florida statute protecting information from public record, was the same address listed on Cam's crime report with "K. Mackler" several paragraphs below. The house was titled under an alias for Mackler. Even Hunter kept his home address confidential on the county records to protect against retaliation from someone unhappy with a verdict.

There was something missing, and it was obviously a critical piece to the puzzle. He looked at the picture of Cam. There was so much anger and pain in those eyes. He needed to find out why someone was now targeting him. He knew Cam was wary of new people, so that added another element to the puzzle.

He remembered their conversation the other night. *His sister.* She hadn't spoken to him in about ten years. *Her decision.* He opened the file again and searched for any information on her. After a few minutes, there, in an obscure sticky note was Cam's sister's current married name and address.

With renewed vigor, he stuffed the files back into his briefcase then grabbed some clothes from his duffle and quickly dressed. He knew there was no way in hell he'd get any sleep and figured he owed Cam's sister a visit since she was only a few hours away. He checked out of the hotel and raced over to his car.

He was going to get to the bottom of this and save the one man who had managed to awaken hope for something more and the desire to fight for it.

Hunter shielded his tired eyes when the sun rose behind the small suburban home. The lack of sleep had zapped his energy and had him running on pure determination and several cups of rest stop coffee. The crappy coffee in lieu of his latte was just another reminder of how much he missed Cam.

He finally exited his vehicle and stretched before making his way to the front door. After the second round of door knocks, a young woman answered—with striking blue eyes just like Cam's.

"Can I help you?" she asked through the narrow opening of the door.

"Are you Jasmine Brooke, formerly Jasmine Pierce," Hunter asked in a soft, gentle tone, hoping to counteract his ragged appearance.

"Who are you?"

"I need to ask you about that day ten years ago."

Jasmine straightened. "I don't want to talk about that." She pushed the door closed.

Hunter stopped the door with his shoe. "Please. Cam might be in trouble and I need to know what happened." Screw the soft tone, he needed answers.

She paused. "Have you seen him?"

"Yes. If you have a few minutes, I need to talk to you."

She worried her bottom lip and gripped the door tightly. "Give me a minute. Come around back and we'll talk outside." This time, Hunter let the door close.

Hunter walked around to the back porch and slowly paced the walkway. Jasmine reappeared within minutes with a man by her side. "This is my husband. I only have a few minutes."

He extended his hand in greeting. "This shouldn't take long."

Her husband shook his hand then retreated to one of the seats on the porch.

Hunter was too tired for a cordial exchange, and he was on a tight time table. "Can you tell me what happened that day?"

Jasmine twisted her hands together then sat in one of the rocking chairs. "I don't know where to start."

"How about we start from the moment you called Cameron."

Jasmine took a deep breath. "I had gone out with my boyfriend on a date, and he said he needed to go by his house because he had forgotten something."

"Your boyfriend, what was his name?" Hunter knew from the red file pages, but not the official report.

"Brad."

"Bradley Mackler?"

"Yes," she said as she tucked a few strands of hair behind her ear. "We went to his place and...um...he was very aggressive with me. I freaked out, he was my first boyfriend and it was our third date. He kept pushing and I kept resisting. I finally got away from him and locked myself in the closet in his house. I called Cam from there and asked him to come get me."

Jasmine wrung her shaky hands.

"What happened when Cam arrived?"

"Brad had managed to break into the closet. I was fighting him off in the living room when Cam showed up. I guess he pushed open the front door because he was there with us seconds later. He pulled Brad off me and was getting ready to punch Brad but he stopped when he saw him. They started arguing."

Hunter cocked his head. "They argued?"

Jasmine twisted the edge of her shirt. "I didn't know." She looked up at Hunter with pleading eyes. "I didn't know Brad was Cam's boyfriend."

Hunter closed his eyes and shook his head. "Wait. Cam's boyfriend?"

"Brad had been dating Cam for months but I didn't know. I swear it! I knew Cam was gay, but I didn't know he and Brad were together. I didn't know," she added weakly as tears began to spill.

"What happened next?"

"It got really ugly. They were punching and yelling at each other. Then Brad grabbed me by the arm and Cam lost it. I broke free of his hold but he kept punching and yelling at Cam. Brad was so much bigger and he wouldn't stop. He just kept hitting him over and over again." She rocked herself in the chair with her head in her hands.

"Brad was yelling louder with each punch. I saw Brad pull out a gun and Cam fought harder, trying to keep the gun away."

She became very quiet and distant.

"I didn't know Brad had a gun with him. Brad pointed the gun at Cam's face and they fought for the gun. A shot went off. That's when Brad stopped fighting back."

"So it was just one shot?"

Jasmine nodded. "It was horrible, there was blood everywhere. I was so stupid." Tears rolled down her cheeks.

"You didn't know they were dating and you didn't know Brad had a gun."

"No, not that."

"What?" *For fuck's sake, there's more?*

"I was mad at Cam. I was a stupid kid who was pissed that her brother had stolen her boyfriend and I said things to him I can't take back." She looked at him pleadingly. "I told him how much I hated him and how I didn't want to see him again."

Hunter closed his eyes and exhaled. Cameron had been the big brother, and she had turned him away when he probably needed her most. "He must have known you were upset at the time."

"I kept telling him the same thing over and over that day. I didn't realize how hurtful that was until a few years later. All I kept hearing was Brad telling Cam how he had only hooked up with me because of his father and how the only reason he could stand *me* was because I had Cam's eyes," she mumbled.

"You two do have the same eyes."

She nodded. "I wonder how he's doing, if he's okay, if he hates me. I hated myself so much for the things I said to him. He was alone in there and it was my fault," she finished on a sob.

"What about your father?"

Jasmine looked up at him. "I never saw him again. He showed up that day after I called him and told him what happened. He left after they took Cam. I was all by myself there. The police took me home. My father never came back and I didn't know what was going on with Cam. The next day, there was a knock at the door. That's when two cops told me my dad had disappeared and my brother was arrested. Since we didn't have any other family, I was put in a foster home until I was eighteen."

"You were fifteen at the time. Why didn't you go see him after you were eighteen?"

"I tried to visit him once, a few years ago, after I finally got the nerve up to face him. I didn't think he'd want to see me again. So I didn't push. And I know it would have been too hard to see him like that. I was so stupid. I was so consumed with the thought of Brad cheating on *me* with Cam that I didn't realize it was the other way around. That Cam had walked in on *his* sister and cheating boyfriend."

Hunter had heard enough. He clenched his jaw repeatedly. Why hadn't she tried harder all these years to offer Cam any sort of support in what was probably the worst set of years of his life?

"I need to go."

She stood quickly. "When you see Cam, please tell him I want to apologize…that I want to see him if…if he'd let me," she finished quietly. "I can't make up for what I said or those lost years. I don't expect him to forgive me. But I need him to know that I *am* sorry for the things I said and for how much I hurt him."

"They never took your statement. Would you be available to come down to Miami if needed?"

"Absolutely."

Hunter nodded. "I'm going to hold you to that," he said sternly.

He thanked them for their time and headed back to his car.

With this last minute detour, home was now a day's drive. He sighed. He couldn't do that trip even if he wanted to in his current state. Instead, he drove to a nearby hotel just outside of town.

Later that night as the fatigue seeped into his soul, Hunter knew one thing with the greatest of certainty.

If someone was going to try to take Cam away from Hunter, then they damn sure had one hell of a fight coming.

Chapter
SEVENTEEN

Hunter sat in his car at eight in the morning the next day and battled with himself on how best to approach Cameron with what he had learned. He needed to understand. Cameron was guarded and it was obvious he had a little bit of a temper simmering just beneath the surface—but he wasn't the criminal his case made him out to be.

He ran his hands through his hair. He was exhausted, mentally and physically. He hadn't been able to get more than a few hours' sleep in the hotel.

He drummed his thumbs on the steering wheel. He'd played this out a thousand different ways but nothing sounded right. He pushed his head back against the head rest.

"Damn it," he muttered. There was no perfect way to talk about this.

"Fuck it." He straightened and switched off the engine of his car. He looked over to the diner and saw three men dressed in suits at the counter. Hunter stiffened. He didn't need to distinguish their faces to know they were the same three men, the attorneys, who had accompanied Carlos Ortega during his case.

Hunter intently watched as they spoke with Lucy. His heart pounded madly in his chest watching each shake of Lucy's head in response. Moments later, Bill joined her, with crossed arms. The three men left the diner, said a few words to each other, then went their separate ways.

He rubbed the back of his neck then looked at his watch. He needed to know if Cameron was okay and what had happened, but the three men would recognize him immediately. He patiently waited to allow a few more minutes until they were farther away.

He finally exited his car and sprinted to the empty diner.

"Lucy, is Cam here?" he asked, trying to hide the desperation in his voice.

Lucy looked at him with concern. "Come," she said, taking him to the back room.

Cameron wasn't there.

"Hunter, what's going on? You look ragged. What is it?" she asked, wringing her hands.

"Were those men here looking for Cam?"

She remained silent and fidgeted.

"Lucy, please. I need to see Cameron."

"Hunter, what the hell is going on?" Bill asked, joining them in the back room.

"I'm going to find out. But I need to know where Cam is and I need to know if those three men were looking for him," he said firmly.

"They said they were attorneys," Bill responded.

"I want to protect him, too. But I need you to tell me where he is." Hunter knew time was of the essence. All the red file cases had each closed within a week of their arrival to his office. Cam's clock was ticking and he wasn't about to let these three assholes get to him first.

He started to pace, his stomach twisted. He could hop over to his office, log into his computer, and pull the file up in the system, but that would flag an inquiry he was not ready to discuss. He stopped and focused his glare at Lucy.

"They already know where he works, it's a matter of time before they find out where he lives, if they don't already know."

Lucy gasped and covered her mouth. She looked over to Bill, pleading with her eyes.

Bill nodded to her, and she immediately reached for the phone and dialed a number.

"Matt, hello, it's Lucy. I have someone here who needs to speak with Cam… Something's wrong, Matt—"

Hunter stopped her before she said too much. Maybe it was his paranoia, but he'd discovered too many dirty dealings lately and knew these three men were involved somehow.

"Wait a second," she said before handing the phone over.

Hunter took the offered phone. "Hello?" he said.

"I need to know who you are and what this is in regards to."

"I need you to let Lucy know it's okay to give me the address. I'm not discussing this over the phone," he finished before handing the phone back to Lucy.

"Hello," she said. "Yes, I know him, and so does Cam." She watched Hunter as she chose her words.

She hung up the phone and tore a sheet off the notebook hanging on the wall. She scribbled a quick note and handed him the piece of paper. Her eyes held tears that were ready to spill. "Please, Hunter. Cameron may have done something before, but—"

"Lucy, I've gotten to know Cam. I'm not judging him by his case file but I do need to find out what's going on."

Hunter looked at the address on the paper. He could easily be there within minutes.

"Hunter, watch yourself. Those men were obviously bad news," Bill said.

Hunter quickly nodded and exited the diner. He raced to his car and drove to the address only blocks away, double checking his rearview mirror every other second. He arrived at the address and confirmed the location. A small building, made out to look like a house, in the middle of the business district. It was two stories with a traditional front house-like entrance. Beautifully colored landscaping welcomed its visitors, and a wood carved sign hung above the door that read, Halfway House. Refusing to leave his car out front, advertising his arrival to passers-by, he drove around to the rear. He easily found the only house-like building with a driveway. He parked next to the dark truck and remained sitting in his car for a moment, staring at the back door leading into the house.

He tightly gripped the steering wheel, closed his eyes, and took a deep breath.

Hunter didn't know what to expect or what exactly was going on. But there was one thing he knew—there was no way he was abandoning Cameron. He'd do anything for Cam if the situation called for it, regardless of the repercussions.

He exhaled and opened his eyes, surprised by how easy it was for him to decide his fate. It had taken him a lifetime to find someone who made him feel the way Cam did, and he was not about to give up on him.

Hunter exited the car and reached the back porch with two quick steps.

The door opened and he was greeted by the extended hand of a dark-haired man. "Hello, we spoke on the phone, I'm Matthew Doner. I own Halfway House and I need to know what's going on."

Hunter shook his hand. "Can we talk inside?"

Matt drew him into a large living room type area where another man waited with arms crossed leaning against the wall.

"The only reason you're here right now is because Lucy trusts you and there was a sense of urgency. So who are you and why do you need to speak to Cam?"

Obviously the man against the wall wasn't leaving. He pushed off from his resting spot and extended his hand in greeting while assessing Hunter. "Julian Capeletti."

"Hunter Donovan, I'm an assistant state attorney. I need—"

Matt immediately interrupted, raising both hands. "Wait a minute. Is this official? If so, then you need—"

"I *need* to speak to Cam," Hunter said in a firm tone.

Julian stepped in between them. "I don't give a rat's ass *who* you are. Don't use that fucking tone in this house."

Hunter blew out a deep breath and ran his fingers through his hair. "Please, I need to speak to Cameron."

"Then I suggest you put in a formal request. I'm sure you're well-versed in the required protocols," Matt said authoritatively.

Hunter took a step into their personal space. "There's no time for that—"

Julian grabbed Hunter by the jacket and began to push him toward the back door. "I fucking warned you."

Hunter resisted and Julian became more forceful.

"Stop," Cameron said, appearing in the room. "Please."

Pain sliced through Hunter's chest when he heard the words Cameron choked through. Julian released him and looked over to Cam as if waiting for the next command.

All Hunter could focus on was Cam's steady gaze filled with immeasurable sadness and his bobbing Adam's apple. He stepped forward to go to Cam only to be stopped by Julian. Rather than attempt to fight the single track mind of the house bodyguard, he looked over to Cam.

"Can we talk? Please, Cam?"

"You don't have to," Matt said to him.

"It's fine," Cam said, looking away. "Just say what you came here to say."

It was crushing Hunter to see Cam like this. He pushed past Julian with renewed force and reached Cameron in three strides to scoop him up in an embrace.

"I told you I wasn't going away," he whispered in Cam's ear.

Cameron's arms tightened around his neck and slid upward to grip Hunter's hair so tight he thought Cam's hands would withdraw with chunks of hair in them.

"I was going to tell you, I swear," Cam said, his voice trembling.

"I know," Hunter said, reaching under Cam's shirt to his lower back. He exhaled a shaky breath once he made contact with the heat of Cam's skin.

Cameron finally loosened his hold and Hunter set his feet back on the floor. Cam backed away slowly, lowered his head and hid his face. "I didn't want to lie to you," he mumbled.

"I know," Hunter said, dipping his head, seeking Cam's gaze. He reached out, pushed the hair away from Cam's face, then gently placed his hand on Cameron's cheek, drawing his face up to make eye contact.

They were joined by yet another man.

"Dude, whose sexy lady is that in the backyard?" the man with a beanie anxiously asked when he appeared in the room.

"I thought you came alone." Matt immediately raced to the back window. "I don't see a woman."

Julian shook his head and rubbed his shaved head. "Cole, not the time or place. Matt, he's referring to the car."

"Hunter, this is Cole," Cam said.

"Oh, so you're *the* guy," said the man with the beanie and enthusiastic handshake.

Cameron clasped Hunter's other hand and led him to the kitchen, leaving the three men in his wake.

He was in for a serious discussion with Cam, but all he could think about was how he was willingly being led by a man who thought he was *the* guy.

* * * *

They arrived at the kitchen and each took a seat.

"State Attorney's office? That's a hell of a lot more than just being a lawyer. How did you find out? Did you run a background check on me or something?"

Hunter gave Cam an incredulous stare. "No, I never would have thought to," he said.

Cam exhaled and slumped in his seat. "Thank you for trusting me enough to say something like that."

"It's the truth," Hunter said, reaching out to him.

Cam withdrew his hand from Hunter's hold and placed his hands in his lap.

"You don't believe me?" Hunter asked, flinching.

Cam wrung his hands under the table. No one had willing stood by his side for so long he was reluctant to believe anything would change, especially not with the one person who mattered most to him.

"Cam, please talk to me."

"Are you telling me you're okay being with a murderer?" Cam said sharply.

"You're not a murderer."

"I killed a man!"

"It was self-defense."

Cam vehemently shook his head. He had relived that day repeatedly, every movement, word, and action. He had been filled with more hate than he had ever known in his life at finding the man he cared about with his own sister. There was murder in every punch he threw when he thought of his boyfriend being a cheater and rapist. When the gun went off, Cam had never openly admitted to anyone the sense of relief at knowing Brad couldn't hurt anyone else again. Anyone could call it self-defense, but in his mind, he knew he was glad Brad was dead.

Cam crossed his arms and turned away. "You can call it whatever you want, but the truth is I killed a man that day."

"You were protecting yourself, that's self-defense. It's not me calling it whatever I want, he came at you with a gun and the intent to kill. The gun accidentally went off. It could have been you or him. I, for one, am thankful it was him."

Cameron looked at Hunter, his eyes widening. "The only reason you're saying that is because you don't know the whole story. If you did, *you* wouldn't be here with me right now."

Hunter stood. "I know more than you think I do and I'm still standing here."

Cameron quickly stood and invaded Hunter's space. "Brad, the guy I killed, was *my* boyfriend! Someone who I thought cared about me! Someone who'd take me to his place and fuck me every chance he had for months but kept me hidden away like some dirty little secret. Then he goes off and starts dating my sister because I wasn't enough for him. No, I don't think you'd still be standing here if you had known all that. So go! Now that you know…leave!" He finished, shoving Hunter away from him. Hunter's nearness wreaked havoc on Cam's system. He needed Hunter to leave now before he had a chance to see him fall apart.

Hunter straightened. His expression hardened. Cameron thought his words had finally pushed him away.

"I did know Brad was your boyfriend."

Cam looked away and tried to focus on a spot on the floor. He was light-headed and completely dazed. This wasn't how it had played out in his mind. None of this was. Anyone would run at the first chance they had. Who the hell would want to be with a man who had admitted to killing his boyfriend?

"You're supposed to leave," he said weakly.

"Supposed to?" Hunter asked softly.

"Everyone always leaves."

Hunter stepped closer and reached for Cam. He ran his fingers through Cam's hair then rested his hand against his neck. "I already told you, I'm not going away."

Cameron closed his eyes and leaned into Hunter's hand, desperate for his touch. He wanted to reach out and wrap his arms around him, but didn't want to push his luck and risk breaking the weak tether that held them together.

Hunter's other hand cradled and lifted Cam's face to force eye contact. "I promise I won't go away. But there's a lot I don't understand and I need you to fill in the gaps."

Cam's heart pounded violently in his chest. He had to look away. He didn't dare think what he saw in those piercing silver eyes was love. He wanted to believe, to trust, but he had been burned too badly before.

Hunter may be current with many things, but part of his appeal was classical, chivalrous—when a man's word was as golden as a handshake to close a deal.

"Promise?" he asked quietly, still turned away. He couldn't bear watching the shift in Hunter's expression when he realized Cam had called his bluff.

"I promise. I swear, cross my heart and—"

"Stop!" Cam said, his throat tight with emotion. A childhood phrase, but he couldn't bear the thought of Hunter finishing the words.

Hunter held Cam's face and their eyes met. "I promise you, Cameron Pierce, I'm not leaving. So please, help me understand what happened."

Cameron was on the brink of being overwhelmed by the emotion screaming from Hunter's expression. He had to close his eyes and take a deep breath to calm his racing pulse.

He nodded.

Hunter sighed. "Thank you," he said before softly brushing his lips against Cam's.

Cam's lips trembled as he hesitated to return the kiss. There were too many emotions battling within him.

Hunter pulled away and stroked his cheek. "Sit, let's talk."

They returned to their seats at the kitchen table, facing each other.

"Let's start with the charges. They don't make sense," Hunter commented, perplexed.

Cameron took a deep breath and shoved his hands between his legs to stop the shaking. "I didn't know about all the charges at the time."

"They didn't bring you in to talk about it with you?"

Cam shook his head. "They took me to the police station, and I sat in a room for what felt like hours, in a chair, cuffed. I remember freaking out every time I looked down and saw all the blood on my shirt."

Cameron paused. His throat was dry and his chest hurt as he relived that day. He looked down and could picture the light blue shirt he had worn and the large blood stain covering his chest.

"An interrogation room?"

Cam looked up. Hunter's question jolted him back to the present. "Yeah, I guess. It was a small room with a table and two chairs. Not like the fancy ones you see on the TV shows. I remember staring at the paint peeling in one of the corners."

"You said you sat there for a few hours. Didn't someone come talk to you?"

Cam shook his head. "They came in a while later, but they didn't want to talk. They just took me to a holding cell."

"Did you talk to a lawyer?"

Cam shook his head again. "It was a couple of weeks before my eighteenth birthday so I was still a minor. Supposedly, my father was the one handling everything with the cops and the lawyers. When he showed up that day at the house, he told me it wouldn't be so bad because I was a minor, so it would be juvenile detention center stuff."

"So no one actually sat with you to detail what you were accused of?" Hunter asked, obvious frustration in his tone.

"No. When *I* asked, they told me my father had taken care of everything."

Hunter ran his hands through his hair.

"I'm sorry," Cam said, rubbing his chest to ease the tightness. "I was stupid."

"No, you were a kid and you were freaked out and trusted your father. What happened when they took you to the holding cell?"

"Nothing. I sat there for two days. Two fucking days with the blood still on my shirt." Cameron closed his eyes and tried to take a deep breath. He gasped when Hunter's hand landed behind his neck and applied gentle pressure.

"Breathe, Cam."

Cameron tried to focus on the soothing tones of Hunter's voice and the rhythmic sensation of the fingers pressing into his neck.

"They took me from the holding cell straight to juvie. I figured I had just killed someone and I had to serve some time for what I had done. But I knew something wasn't right. I resisted, I tried to ask questions, but no one was talking to me."

"What happened when you got to juvie?" Hunter asked, still massaging Cam's neck.

"When they checked me in, that's when someone finally told me what I was charged with. They read off the offenses like a fucking grocery list." Cameron rested his elbows on the table and buried his face in his hands. "I was so fucking stupid. I can't believe I actually trusted my father and thought he would take care of anything."

"What did your father say when you spoke to him about it?"

Cameron lowered his hands and looked to Hunter. "I never saw my father again after the day of the shooting."

Hunter exhaled heavily and lowered his head.

"I'm sorry," Cam said hesitantly, reaching out to Hunter.

Hunter grabbed his hand and kissed his palm. "You went through hell, your father failed you, the system failed you, and you're apologizing to me? For what?"

"You can break your promise and leave. I'd understand," Cam finished quietly.

"I don't break my promises, and I'm not leaving. What happened after you got checked into juvie?"

Cameron sighed. "I got a visit from my lawyer."

"The one your father hired?"

"Yeah. He went through the charges with me. I argued with him but he said there was nothing *I* could do until I was eighteen. I didn't even get a fucking chance to say anything. I never got a trial or hearing or anything at all where I could say anything to anyone. I was told that my father had 'taken care of everything'," he said with air quotes.

"I saw the list of charges in your file. It's—"

"Bullshit. That's what it is. Fucking. Bullshit. I was charged for possession of a weapon. It was a fucking key chain nail clipper with one of those barely-pinky-size dull ass blades that pull out of the side with the little scissors. I've even got a drug charge. I've never touched any type of drug, ever. For fuck's sake," he finished, burying his head in his hands again.

"What did you do after that?"

Cam straightened again and exhaled heavily. "The only thing I could do. I tried to get another lawyer and file an appeal. *'Sorry, I was an idiot kid and my father was an asshole'* wasn't enough of an excuse to get it off my record."

"I assume you couldn't get an appeal."

"Lawyers refused to speak to me because I was a minor. They all required a parent or guardian. They couldn't find my father, so I was stuck in juvie."

"Then what happened?"

Cameron wrung his hands in his lap. "On my birthday, they came and took me to another prison. I was surrounded by murderers and rapists. I was so freaked out," he finished sadly. His body began to shake again. He took a deep breath. He remembered what happened too vividly, how he felt, what he saw, everything.

Hunter's rhythmic massage resumed on his neck.

"What happened after you got to the prison?"

Cam closed his eyes for a moment, the tension easing with each gentle press of muscle. "I got a visit from a guy."

"Who?"

"I don't know. I think it might have been Brad's dad because he looked like him. He said 'it wasn't supposed to turn out like this but it ended up working out for him anyway'."

"What else did he say?"

"That was it. He walked in, said that, then walked out. He didn't even introduce himself."

"Are you sure that's what he said?"

"I'm positive. I played it over in my head thousands of times, trying to figure it out."

Hunter took his phone out of his pocket and began tinkering with the buttons.

"Am I boring you?"

"Smart-ass," Hunter said, intently focused on his phone.

"What are you doing?" Cam asked, craning his neck to look at the screen.

Hunter's eyebrows were scrunched as he continued to press and swipe his finger until he turned the phone over to show Cam the display. "Is this the guy who came to see you that day?"

Cameron would know that face anywhere.

"Yeah. He's a little older there, but that's him. Who is he?"

"Judge Kevin Mackler. Brad's father."

Cameron's thoughts wandered. He'd tried to decipher the riddle for so long, he'd thought of every possible scenario, and always seemed to come up empty as to what it meant.

"Earth to Cam?" Hunter said, waving his hand in front of Cam. "Where did you go?"

"Sorry," he said, getting up from the seat. He walked over to the refrigerator and grabbed a bottle of water. He leaned back against the counter, took a sip, and realized he never got an answer to his initial question. "So how did you find out about me?"

"Long story."

"Seems we're in a storytelling mood. So talk."

Hunter told him about the red files and how they began to anonymously make appearances in his office several months before, all related to current cases. He explained how each subject of a red file was found guilty of a crime and sent back to prison usually within a week of having received the files.

"Interesting story but what does that have to do with me?" Cam asked.

Hunter rose from his seat and stood a few steps before Cam. "I received a red file on you a few days ago. This morning I go to the diner to talk to you and there were three guys looking for you."

Cameron paled. The energy drained from his body as he slumped back against the sink. *The nightmare...they're coming for me.* A tingling sensation began in his legs then traveled up his body, out to his arms. He swayed. His body slipped down against the counter until he hit the floor.

I can't go back there!

The panicked voice in his head screamed repeatedly as his heart raced.

"Cam?" He faintly heard his name.

I can't go back there! I can't go back there!

He could hear his heartbeat pounding in his ears, muffling out everything but the echoing screams in his head, begging for freedom.

"Cam!" He heard his name again, more forceful. It had the same tones as that soothing voice he loved to hear.

I can't go back there! I can't go back there!

The voices continued to scream.

* * * *

"Cam, answer me!"

Hunter's heart pounded so hard he thought it would rip through his chest. He'd seen Cam panic once before but nothing like this. His entire face went blank, and the life had vanished from his eyes in a split second.

"Cameron!" he yelled again, more panicked.

Hunter pulled Cam's limp body against his chest and brushed the hair off his paled face.

Julian raced into the kitchen and found Hunter crouched on the floor holding a lifeless Cam in his arms.

"Get him outside. Now," Julian commanded.

Without question, Hunter lifted Cam and raced to the back, out to the patio where he had originally entered.

"Cam, c'mon. Answer me. Open your eyes. Breathe. Do something," Hunter yelled, desperation eating away at him as he cradled Cam in his arms.

"Cameron! Wake the fuck up already," Julian yelled as he patted a wet towel on Cam's face.

Hunter finally breathed a sigh of relief when Cameron shifted and opened his eyes a few moments later. He crushed his body against Cam's, needing to have him closer, to know he was still with him. He looked over to Julian and silently thanked him.

"It helps when he knows he's not inside," Julian said, folding away the towel. "The fucker already gave us a scare like this."

Cam's arms slowly wound around Hunter's neck.

"Don't ever scare me like that again," Hunter said with fire in his voice.

"I can't go back there," Cam whispered in a broken voice. He gripped Hunter's shirt tightly and pressed against him. "Please," he said as his body began to shake.

Hunter held him tighter, hoping to gift him with some of his strength and resolve. "I won't let that happen."

He wasn't sure if he could keep that promise, but knew he couldn't stand the thought of Cam not being by his side.

"Dude, you went like catatonic and shit. That was freaky as hell."

"Fuck you, Cole," Cam said in a muffled, weak voice, still hanging on to Hunter.

"Cole," Julian warned and finally stood.

"Let's give them some privacy," Matt said.

"But I wanna know what happened with the guys at the diner."

Cam sighed. "How much did you guys hear?"

Cole quirked eyebrow. "You're telling a story with a nosy audience in the next room. I'm guessing, we could have probably heard you if you'd farted."

"Cole!" yelled Julian.

"Shit," Cole mumbled before racing back into the house and running upstairs.

Hunter was thankful Julian bolted after Cole and Matt trailed along, finally giving them a few moments alone.

"Why does the beanie guy drive Julian crazy like that?" Hunter said.

Cameron positioned himself more comfortably in Hunter's arms. "Julian reminds him of his big brother."

"Does Julian know that?"

"I don't think so."

"Maybe beanie guy should tell him so he doesn't wake up one day missing a limb."

Cam chuckled.

"Feeling better?" Hunter whispered in Cam's ear.

Cameron nodded and looked up at Hunter. "Seems I tend to panic when I think I'm going back. I'm sorry," he said.

Hunter separated from the embrace. "For freaking out at the thought of going back to the hell you were in for almost a decade? I think most people would freak out by that."

"No. For making you give a shit."

Hunter half smiled and cupped Cam's face. "I more than give a shit. I'm—"

"Don't."

"Don't what?"

"Just don't. Please. Whatever you were going to say, just don't. Not now."

Hunter looked at Cam and saw fear in his eyes. He wasn't sure if it was the torment of possibly going back to prison, or the panic of exploring something more between them. He couldn't imagine what Cam had gone through all those years, what had happened to him in prison, or how alone he must have felt. He still had so many questions.

"How about we make a deal?" Hunter said.

"A deal?"

Hunter stroked Cameron's cheeks with his thumbs. "I'll wait to tell you how I feel until you're ready to hear it. But whenever you tell me you're ready, you're stuck with me. I don't come with a return policy. So you need to be sure you want me for the long haul. Deal?"

"What if I'm never ready to hear it?"

"I'm a patient man."

Cameron softly laughed. "No, you're not," he said with a half smile.

"I am if it means I get you."

"You still want me, after everything?" Cameron asked in disbelief.

"Yes." Hunter closed the distance between them to press his lips against Cam's. Cameron wrapped his arms around Hunter's shoulders and pulled him closer to deepen the kiss. Hunter tightened his hold, hoping to convey the unspoken words of affection.

After a few moments, Cam slowly withdrew and looked at Hunter with renewed determination. "Deal."

A smile tugged at the sides of Hunter's mouth when he saw a tiny spark of hope in Cam's eyes break through the despair he knew battled within.

"So no return policy?"

"Nope."

"What about exchanges?"

Hunter chuckled, relieved Cam felt good enough to tease him. He nuzzled Cam then kissed him below the ear.

"Tell me, what do I need to do now?" Cam asked, his voice slowly returning to its normal strength.

"Well, first we need to get off this porch floor because my back is killing me."

"Your back hurts…sir?"

Hunter's cheeks heated. He looked at Cam and had never been more thankful to see the mischief in his expression.

Cam laughed as he slowly stood, Hunter immediately followed. In an instant, he was pressed up against Cameron. He snaked his arms around Cam's waist and pressed a tender kiss on his lips then grabbed his hand and pulled him back inside the house.

"I need to find out why you're being targeted."

"They wanted to keep me in prison, that was obvious by the things that happened in the past few years. I'm out so I guess they want to put me back in there."

"But there has to be a reason. There's more to it than that and that's what I need to know."

"Why do you think there's more, because of the red file thing?"

Hunter nodded. "There's got to be something linking you to one of my cases."

"How the hell can I be tied to anything? You know where I've been for the last few years." Cam sighed.

"I need to get a better handle on what's going on. It's the only way I'll be able to know what I need to do next to prevent something from happening."

"Okay. What do you need from me?"

"I need to interrogate the hell out of you to find out where the damn connection is."

"If that's what it takes to keep me out of there, fine. Let's just do it and get it over with."

"Cam?" Matt asked, coming into the living room. "We should probably get Sam in on this. Maybe he can help as well?"

Is there no fucking privacy in this house?

Cam deeply exhaled then nodded.

"I'll give him a call," Matt said, grabbing the phone.

"Who's Sam?" Hunter asked, trying to control the stab of jealousy threatening to unsettle him.

"He's my rehabilitation counselor. He's also a friend," Cam added as he reached for Hunter's hand.

"Fine," Hunter grumbled.

Julian and Cole walked into the living room. Cole looked at Cam and Hunter then smiled. He opened his mouth to say something when Julian quickly smacked the back of Cole's head.

"Ow, dude, why'd you do that?"

Julian shot an icy glare in Cole's direction that made him cringe. "That was for whatever the hell you were about to say. You need a fucking social filter for that mouth and brain of yours."

Cole rubbed the back of his beanie and went to the kitchen.

"I've got to take Cam in for his test. Is that going to be a problem?" Julian asked Hunter.

"Test?" Hunter asked.

Cam exhaled. "Stupid fucking drug test thing. I called this morning and I need to go in. That's why I wasn't at the diner for the early shift."

"Are you going with him?" Hunter asked Julian.

Julian nodded.

"Sam's on his way. He'll be here within the hour," Matt said, joining the conversation.

"Okay, Julian, you go with Cam and please—"

"I'm not letting him out of my sight if someone's looking for him." Julian finished Hunter's thought with undeniable determination in his eyes.

"Thanks. Then get back here and we'll talk. That should give Sam enough time to get here and hopefully get you back at the diner before lunch."

"Should he be going in if people are looking for him?" Matt asked with obvious concern.

"If he skips work, it's got to be reported and it'll raise a flag in the system. We need to keep things as close to *normal* as possible right now."

Hunter turned to Cam. "You don't go anywhere unless you've got Julian or me with you. Clear?" Julian may have been an ass when Hunter first arrived to the house with his insistence on barricading him from Cam, but he was undoubtedly a worthy asset in a fight.

Cam nodded without hesitation.

"You guys go do your test. I need to swing by my house. I'll be back within an hour." He needed to shower, change, and see his father for a few minutes.

Hunter followed Julian and Cam out back.

He now traveled down a path where there was no turning back. He looked over at Cam and remembered how this man had finally given in and placed his fragile trust in him.

Hunter would not take that lightly.

Chapter
EIGHTEEN

Hunter stood in the living room of Halfway House with his boyfriend, listening to the events of that day when Cam took a life to protect his own. Over and over, every detail had been reviewed, every disgusting word that had been said, every punch that had been delivered, and still, there was no reason why Cameron had been targeted. The judge, Brad's father, had something to do with this, and Hunter needed to find that missing piece of the puzzle. He wasn't going to stop until he found it.

"Okay, it can't be something from that day, so it has to be something from before. Tell us about Brad," Hunter prompted.

Cam began rambling about how he met Brad in school and how they kept different circles of friends. Brad was the stereotypical football player, loved by teammates and feared by the smart students he'd corner in between classes. Cam was the exception. Brad had turned on his charm, and Cam, happy to finally explore the chance of a relationship with a guy he liked, fell into the trap. Brad never told him how he felt unless he played a guilt trip to manipulate Cam into doing something or giving in to Brad's whim.

"I know what you're thinking," Cam broke into Hunter's thoughts. "I was a dumb kid, very naïve. I was just happy to finally be able to have a boyfriend and I didn't see how much of an asshole he was. I see that now, I didn't see it back then."

"Cam, no one's here to pass judgment. We're trying to figure this all out," Sam added with a comforting touch to Cam's shoulder.

Hunter glared. *Who the fuck is this man and why the hell does he feel the need to touch Cam or sit so fucking close to him.*

Julian chuckled. "Sammy's a saint-in-training. He's harmless," he said with a knowing look to Hunter.

He looked at Sam and didn't give a shit how harmless Julian thought this man could be. "Yeah, well, I can't think when you're sitting that close to Cam so do me a favor and go sit somewhere else." Hunter stared Sam down until he stood and took another seat.

Cam continued to revisit the details of his relationship with Brad. Every. Fucking. Stomach-turning. Detail. Hunter had no issue listening to a court case's gory, blow-by-blow account, but listening to the man he had fallen in love with talk about hope, a relationship, and a future was just too much—especially when Cam was hesitant to take those same steps with him.

"Okay, just stop," Hunter said as he sat on the couch next to Cam. He was frustrated and tired, both physically and mentally.

"Sorry," Cam said as he leaned into Hunter. "I know you must hate this."

Not caring about the audience, Hunter wrapped his arms around Cam and pulled him into an embrace. He needed to hold Cam, stake his claim, hide him in a padlocked safe on a deserted island to escape this chaos that was trying to break them apart. He pressed his nose to Cam's hair and inhaled the scent that always seemed to calm his senses. Hunter focused on the man in his arms—the way their bodies fit perfectly together, the soft, smooth feel of his hair.

Hunter began to relax, the tension leaving his body.

He stilled, blindsided by a thought as his mind cleared.

"Where would you go on these dates?" he asked as he slowly released Cam.

"His place," Cam responded a bit confused.

"He didn't live with his father? In the house where you went to your sister?" Matt asked.

"Not that I know of. I hadn't ever been to that house. That's why I didn't recognize the address when Jas called me."

"Where was *his* house?" Hunter asked.

"Down South. Pretty much away from just about everything," Cam added embarrassingly.

"Did you ever see or hear anything out of the ordinary?"

"No. We'd, um…be in the bedroom most of the time and then leave."

"No weekends or overnights?"

"Nope. I'd have to leave early enough to make the drive back to my place before my father got home. I didn't want Jas to be alone with him when he'd get out of work."

Hunter put his head down, trying to organize his thoughts.

"Wait a sec, there was a guy who came by one time. It was really quick and I didn't even catch the guy's name. When he saw me, Brad freaked out a bit and told me to go wait in the room."

Hunter's gaze snapped back to Cam. "Do you remember what he looked like?"

"Seriously? I might recognize him if I saw him again, but it was ten years ago, and I was more focused on Brad at the time than this guy who showed up. All I remember was that he was big and broad as hell."

"How long was he there that day?"

"Few minutes, that's why I didn't think much of it."

"Did Brad say anything about the guy or his visit?"

"No. Just told me the guy made some crack about Brad dating Ken."

"Ken?" Matt asked.

"Barbie and Ken. The guy. I guess the ass thought it was funny to call me Ken."

"Maybe he thought you were purty?" Cole chimed in after making an appearance.

"For fuck's sake, Cole. If you don't disappear, I'm going to beat the shit out of you," Julian said, exasperated as he roughly rubbed his eyes.

"I remember seeing something on the kitchen counter before I left," Cam commented.

"What was it?" Hunter asked.

Cam huffed. "It was a stupid sketch. Like a moron, I thought Brad had doodled something and I was praising his skills. He told me he hadn't done it, but it wasn't there when I arrived, so it must have been that guy. It's probably nothing but that's the only thing I remember from that guy being there."

"What was the sketch of?"

"A star and a square thing. I mean, it was seriously basic. Nothing fancy."

Hunter snatched one of the napkins from under the cup, took his pen from his suit pocket, and started to scribble on it. "Did it look like this?"

"Yeah," Cam responded, confused. "How the hell did you know that?"

"That's the link to my case." Hunter rubbed the back of his neck with his free hand. "Shit."

"How bad is this?" Sam asked.

"This is the logo that's appearing on tons of nickel bags flooding our streets. We've got zero leads on this new drug guy. We had one case against him and it was thrown out. I'm still waiting on the written ruling to find out what the hell happened. It would have tied the drugs with the logo to at least one dealer who was obviously an intermediary based on the amount of drugs we found on him. Other than that one case, we haven't had a single lead at all."

A pregnant silence filled the room.

Hunter looked over to Cam and saw him worrying his lower lip. He held up the napkin with the rough sketch. "If you saw this there, then this has been going on for a while and Brad may have had something to do with it. I'm going to assume his father does as well."

"Why do you think his father is involved?" Matt asked.

"Because he went to see Cam in prison, and he's also the judge who threw out my case."

"The judge can't be the only one involved," Sam interjected. "Cam's parole hearings were always delayed or cancelled. I was stonewalled when I started asking questions. I was told paperwork was missing, which I know I completed. It didn't take much to figure out whoever was throwing these roadblocks along the way wanted to keep him in there. I just didn't have a clue why. Getting his early release wasn't easy, but I found a few people in the system I knew and trusted. Aside from the bureaucratic hurdles I had to deal with, I know Cam had several experiences inside the prison as well. Cam?"

Cam sighed. He'd obviously lost his momentum when the connection was finally found. He talked about the times when he was threatened by guards who said they were watching him and the inmates who told him to keep to himself or they'd report back that he was talking too much.

Hunter could tell Cam was slowly breaking down. His voice no longer held the determination from the beginning of the conversation. He repeatedly ran his hands through his hair to hide the shaking as he recounted several incidents during his time inside. It was obvious there were both inmates and guards who were determined to keep him in check.

"Cam, tell him about the incident in the laundry room."

Cameron paused to regain his composure, he looked exhausted. He had his head down and took a few deep breaths. He appeared as if he was battling with something before he finally spoke. "I had laundry duty that day. The room is always supposed to be guarded, both to come in and to go out because it's too easy to transport stuff with the large bins they had. Anyway, a group of inmates gathered around me then jumped me and held me down. They grabbed me and threw me onto one the folding tables. One of the guys shoved a rag in my mouth to shut me up while the other guys pinned my arms and legs. Five of the guards disappeared, one stayed. He was the lookout."

Cameron closed his eyes and flexed his hands open, then closed. He took another deep breath. He held it for a moment then deeply exhaled before regaining his composure then continuing. "One of the guys had these needles and he started to work at my arm with them. It hurt so fucking bad, and I couldn't yell for help because of that shit in my mouth. I tried to fight them off and the guy got pissed because

I was moving so much even though the others held me down. He wouldn't stop digging into my arm with those needles. He said he was supposed to mark me for one of the guys on some trade."

Cam's contained fury shone in his eyes when he turned to Hunter and spoke in a level tone. "I'm no one's fucking bitch. I had my choices taken away, but I wasn't going to let them take that one from me." Cameron shook off the anger evident in his expression. "Shit like that happens after a while for some of the guys. They don't like loners in there."

He paused. He steeled himself and continued, "I fought as hard as I could and I finally got free. I still don't know how I managed to get past them and the guard out of that room. My arm was covered in blood. It burned so bad it felt like it was on fire. I just ran, I knew I had to get out of there," he added quietly.

"One of the nurses saw me and yelled at one of the guards down the hall to get me and let me through to her wing. He was one of the guards who had walked out. He tried to act as if he hadn't heard her but she kept yelling at him and threatened to report him. I think the only reason he finally gave in was because she was screaming so much and drew too much attention."

"I was in the medical wing for almost three weeks with rips in my skin and this massive infection from the needles they used on me," he finished, pulling up his sleeve, exposing the partial ink and slash scars that marked his arm. "I guess I'm lucky I didn't get any diseases," he finished with a shrug.

Hunter barely glanced at Cam's exposed bicep—he pulled Cameron into a tight embrace, hoping to soothe the unsteadiness he heard in his voice. Cam's body relaxed against him. His arms slowly wrapped around Hunter's neck then tightened. The heavy puffs of breath brushed against his ear as Cam tried to even out his breathing.

"You did nothing wrong," Hunter whispered in his ear. "Nothing."

Cam tightened his hold even more. "Then why did they do this to me," he whispered in a shaky breath so only Hunter could hear before releasing him. He retreated and straightened in his seat, took a deep breath, and placed his clasped hands on his lap.

They began to chat about other events during Cam's time. Sam recalled some of the instances where the early release process had been delayed and retold some of the stories Cam had previously confided. They began to make notes, trying to narrow down the list of the people involved.

Hunter looked over to Cam and noticed a subtle shift in the man. Something wasn't right. Cam stared off at nothing in particular, his eyes had a distant, empty look in them as if his mind had wandered elsewhere. Each new story revealed more of his time inside. He wasn't sure if Cam was distancing himself from reliving them or if he was growing uncomfortable with the revelations.

Cam yanked his sleeve down and muttered under his breath, "I'm tired of it…tired of seeing it every time I happen to cross a mirror."

Hunter inched closer, he could see Cam's nostrils flaring and his jaw muscles flexing. He tried to use a gentle tone to settle him. "We can go see a doctor and find out what can be done about it."

"Fuck it," Cameron spat before jumping off the couch and racing to the kitchen.

Hunter launched after him and arrived to the kitchen just in time to see Cam reaching up to his bicep with a scouring pad.

"Cam!" Hunter yelled to stop him as he tore the pad out of his hand and brutally grabbed Cam by the waist, pulling him flush against his body. He caged Cam in his arms, hoping to prevent the man from hurting himself. Cam's body shook convulsively and the loud, sharp intakes of breath through his nose echoed in Hunter's ear.

Cam violently tried to push out of the hold. "I can't!" he yelled, millimeters from Hunter's face then struggled further, trying to break free. His eyes were crazed and his entire body shuddered. "I can't fucking take this. I'm tired of it. I hate it. They fucking marked me. They. Fucking. Marked. Me!" He yelled so loudly the veins in his neck corded pushing his skin tautly at the sides, his face was flaming dark red, and he continued to fight for release of Hunter's hold.

In an instant, Cam's knees buckled and the dead weight of this near six foot man in Hunter's arms almost weakened him. He quickly shifted his position to hold up Cam before he fell to the floor. "I've got you. I'm not going anywhere."

"I can't do this anymore," Cam whispered in a hoarse, broken voice, his limbs hanging weakly like a lifeless doll.

Hunter lifted Cam onto the kitchen table and stepped in between Cam's legs where he sat. Now at eye level, he cupped Cameron's face, forcing him to look into Hunter's eyes. "You're stronger than you know. Don't you fucking dare give up now."

"You deserve better," Cam confessed, with the sound of defeat in his voice and the pain of ten years of torture evident in his eyes. He was slumped over, exhaustion permeated his body. Even sitting, he swayed slightly. "I'm not good for you, Hunter."

"You're right. You're not *good*. You're the best thing that's ever happened to me," he said firmly.

Cameron closed his eyes and pressed his forehead to Hunter's. "You're full of shit sometimes."

Hunter moved his hand down Cam's face until it rested on the side of his neck. He could feel Cam's racing pulse below his palm. He raised his lips to Cam's forehead and placed a gentle kiss. He couldn't imagine everything Cam had been through in the last decade of his life. He'd heard so many details in the last hour, but knew it was only a fraction of what Cam had suffered each day.

"Everything that has happened to you played a part in defining who you are today. You're strong and determined. You've been through hell and you're still standing, in spite of it all. You know how I feel—"

"Don't. We had a deal," Cam said as he wrapped his arms around Hunter's neck and his legs around his waist, pulling Hunter closer to him. "Please don't...not until I'm safe enough to hear it and tell you the same."

Hunter exhaled with relief as hope began to build within. Hearing Cam's unspoken declaration gave him renewed strength. He tightened his hold, pulling Cam even closer, their bodies fitting perfectly together. "Don't give up on me, okay?"

Cam didn't respond.

"You know, it's not easy finding someone who puts up with my staring and ogling, so you can't just walk out and leave me."

Cam chuckled weakly. "I like the way you ogle me. It's kinda hot."

"Don't give up, okay?" He softly grazed his knuckles down Cameron's cheek.

Cameron nodded slowly.

"Now we know why they're targeting you."

"Why?" Cam asked, perplexed.

"I'm guessing it's because you can connect the judge to the drugs. My instincts are telling me we need to check out that house. I'm willing to bet you weren't supposed to be there, and the fact that the guy showed up at the house, tells me it was a known place of contact."

"You think that's it?"

Hunter nodded. "Question is, do you remember where the house was? I know it was a long time ago."

"I remember how to get there and I can even give you the layout of the house if you need it," Cam responded confidently.

Hunter smiled. "That's my guy."

"By the way, I kinda like that." Cameron grinned.

"Good, get used to it." He effortlessly lifted Cameron off the kitchen table and set his feet back on the ground. He snaked his arm around Cam's waist to offer support.

"I like it when you manhandle me."

"If you want, I'll throw you over my shoulder and pound on my chest too," Hunter teased.

Cam quietly laughed. "Maybe I'll shock you one of these days and do that to you."

Hunter leaned in for a quick kiss and whispered in his ear, "I'm game for anything you want."

Cam groaned and rested his head on Hunter's shoulder.

"Now you need to get to work and try to act as if nothing is going on. Got it?"

Cameron nodded as Julian entered the kitchen with Matt and Sam following close behind. They each looked at Cam with concern, but to their credit, they didn't push the point.

"I called Lucy and asked if I could hang out at the diner today. After this morning's visit, she and Bill are on board with having me hover," Julian said.

"I'm going to contact an old Marine buddy of mine who's a detective. I think he can help us here. I'm not too sure who I can go to yet, but I know he's a safe bet. I'll stop by the diner later—"

"No," Cam interrupted. "We don't need to crowd Lucy and Bill, they'll just worry, and I don't want to freak them out more than they already are. Besides, Julian will be there."

"True," Julian added.

Hunter battled with himself. He didn't trust Cam's safety to anyone else but he couldn't hover all day. He turned Cam into his arms for a tight embrace.

"It'll be fine," Cam whispered in his ear.

Hunter released his hold and captured Cam's face. He stared into the blue eyes that had captivated him since that first day. His chest tightened at the fear that flashed in Cam's eyes. "You don't go anywhere without Julian. Okay?"

"Okay."

He pulled Cam into another hug. "Please," Hunter whispered in his ear. The fear of losing Cam grabbed at his heart and wouldn't let go.

When they separated, Cam's expression was different, pensive. He searched Hunter's face then smiled as he placed the palm of his hand on Hunter's cheek. "I promise."

"What do you need me to do?" Matt asked, obviously eager to help.

Hunter looked to Matt then back at Cam. "I need you to fill out whatever forms are required for a weekend pass. Cam's mine as of tomorrow evening," he finished with an unmistakable glare in Cameron's direction.

"No," Cam confidently responded.

Hunter raised an eyebrow, welcoming the challenge.

"You got it wrong. You're mine," Cam corrected with the wicked smile that always seemed to make Hunter's heart skip a beat.

Hunter smiled.

Cameron had no idea just how right he was.

Chapter NINETEEN

"Hey, you're back!" Melanie said as Hunter exited the elevator.

"Yeah, got back this morning so I figured I'd come in and catch up on things."

"You look like shit," she said, walking with him toward his office.

"It's nice to see you, too."

Mel rolled her eyes. "What I meant was, why didn't you just take today and tomorrow off so you could rest up. Seriously, you look like someone kicked your ass then turned around and kicked it again. Go home."

Hunter chuckled. "I don't have court dates so I'm just checking on cases and doing paperwork. I don't plan on human interaction so I'm good."

"Well, the mayor wanted to meet with you. Jessie is scheduling that for you. I think it's best to wait until next week when you don't have this *thing* going on." She circled a finger in the air, pointed at Hunter.

"What does he want?"

"Who the hell knows? Go hibernate in your office. I don't want you scaring the staff." She shoved him into his office and walked away.

Hunter dropped his bag on the chair. He casually stood behind his door to catch a glimpse of himself in the hanging mirror he kept for those mornings when he slept in the office. He rubbed his face when he saw his reflection. He wasn't a vain man, but even he knew when his appearance was too rough to bear. He looked as tired as he felt and his stubble was past shadow and pushing scruffy.

"Hey, boss," Jessie said, pushing the door open.

"Fuck." Hunter rubbed his face when the mirror hit him. He sure as hell didn't need to add a broken nose to the mix.

"Crap, I'm sorry! I didn't know you were behind the door."

"It's fine," he grumbled.

Jessie looked at him with narrowed eyes.

"Yeah, yeah, I know. I look like shit. I was in a rush to leave the house this morning and should have shaved. I'm just going to catch up on some paperwork." He walked around and sat in his chair.

"Well, I wrote an update for you on your cases when you told me you were on your way back." His assistant handed over a few files.

"Did we get anything new?"

"Nope. It's been...unusually quiet."

"Really?"

Jessie nodded. "The only thing that's come up is the mayor's meeting. I scheduled that out for you for next week. I wanted you to have a few days of peace before having it."

"Thanks."

"I'll let you hide out." Jessie closed the door behind him as he left the office.

Hunter stretched his arms and moved his head from side to side. He was so damn tired he wasn't sure if he'd make it the whole day. He took out his cell phone and dialed a number.

"Detective Calloway."

"Hey, Aidan, it's Hunter."

"To what do I owe this honor?"

Hunter laughed. "Smart-ass. I need your help with something."

"Go ahead."

"Would you be able to meet me tonight?"

"Yeah, just tell me when and where."

"I'll text you the address. It's close to my office."

"Let's make it around eight."

"Thanks. It'll be good to see you again."

"And you, Sergeant," Aidan said before disconnecting the call.

Hunter smiled as he leaned back in his chair again. There was a certain level of trust forged with his ex-Force Recon Marine group after being in the field, knee deep in enemy territory with no support other than the men on the team. They may have all gone their separate ways after serving, but his brothers in arms would be there for him if needed.

He just hoped his trust in Aidan would instill enough faith for Cam to trust him as well.

* * * *

Cameron worked on another latte art design as his thoughts wandered to Hunter and their first weekend together. He repeatedly shifted his weight from foot to foot, bouncing on the balls of his feet like Cole usually did when he was anxious. Hunter had become his rock. He had worked his way into Cam's life and refused to let go...more like he bulldozed his way in and pitched a tent. Friday afternoon seemed like it was taking forever.

Cam smiled as he heated the milk.

He was thankful Hunter was persistent. He would still be bottled up in his protective shell, locking away all emotions and hope if Hunter had given up. But here he was, smiling like a jackass, thinking about the man who made him dream bigger than he had ever thought possible. Even after knowing the truth about his past—and entirely too much detail regarding his time inside—Hunter still wanted to be with him.

No sense hiding the big goofy grin etched into his face.

"Cam, back room," Bill yelled from the sandwich station.

Shit. He wasn't sure what triggered Bill's command but he wasn't taking any chances. He switched off the machine, dropped off the coffee order with the customer at the register, and trotted to the back.

Hunter.

"I don't think Lucy would like you snooping around her cookie recipe." Cam crossed his arms and leaned against the doorway.

Hunter turned and a huge smile spread across his face. "Hey."

One simple word, but the way he said it drove Cam to launch himself forward into Hunter's arms.

Hunter immediately tightened his hold on Cam and buried his face in the crook of Cam's neck. "Mmm, I needed this."

A bolt of desire shot throughout Cam's body when Hunter's hand reached his lower back. He inched forward to press his body against Hunter's.

Hunter groaned and Cam instantly became rock hard.

"Fuuuck." Cam pushed up, needing more friction. He pulled Hunter down for a demanding kiss. His pulse raced when Hunter's taste flooded his senses.

Hunter separated from the kiss and nipped at Cam's chin, then swiped his lower lip before diving in again to explore Cam's mouth. He lowered his hands below Cam's ass and tugged him forward, pressing his arousal against Cam.

Cam's heart slammed against his chest.

Before he had a chance to deepen the kiss, Hunter pulled away a few inches.

Cam was bereft until Hunter cradled his face and placed a slow, gentle kiss on his lips.

Hunter pressed his forehead to Cam's and exhaled a shaky breath. "Not sure how Lucy or Bill would handle the sight of me pawing away at you by her cookies." He slowly pulled Cam by the waist and wrapped his arms around him in an embrace.

Cam chuckled. "I'm glad you're here."

They silently held each other, off in one of the corners of the back room. The body heat mixed with Hunter's unique scent was heavenly.

Cam's hand traveled to the arc of Hunter's back underneath his suit jacket while his other hand ran up the swell of his arm to the thickness of his neck.

Hunter moaned. "I love it when you touch me," he whispered in Cam's ear.

"Good, 'cause I like touching you," he said while his hands further explored the dips and swells of Hunter's arms and back.

"I'm not going to make it until Friday afternoon if you keep doing that," Hunter said hoarsely with a nervous laugh.

"Mmm. Go ahead, throw me on the cooling cookies and have your way with me," he said, resting his head on Hunter's shoulder.

"Sadist. Now I've got a visual that is going to drive me insane."

Cam smiled. "That should hold you over until Friday."

"That will *torture* me until Friday."

"Well, good thing it's just today and tomorrow."

Cam stepped back and looked up at Hunter, assessing him.

"Yeah, I know, I look like shit," Hunter grumbled.

"I was actually going to say you're kinda hot with the rough thing you've got going on." He ran his fingers down Hunter's stubble.

Hunter hissed and grabbed Cam's wrist to stop the contact. His eyes darkened to that shade of molten gray Cam loved so much. His glare filled with unmistakable want and need.

Cam groaned. "Don't look at me like that if you want me to stop," he said, turning away.

He could feel the heat emitted from Hunter's body as he neared to whisper in Cam's ear. "That's the problem. I don't want you to stop."

Cam moaned. His hard-on bordered on extreme pain and standing too close to the only man he wanted wasn't helping. Any attempt to keep his head straight was damn near impossible. He took a deep calming breath and one step away from Hunter, then another.

"You stay there," he said to Hunter in a warning tone.

Hunter chuckled, straightened, and clasped both hands behind his back in an *at ease* position. "Your wish is my command."

Command, commando. Damn it, I'm losing my mind. Cam stared, visuals of Hunter pulling down his zipper to reveal him going commando danced in his mind.

Hunter's devilish grin nearly set Cam off again. "Where did your mind go?"

Cam scowled. "Do you go commando?"

"Briefs."

"White?"

"They're black."

He slowly walked back to Hunter, intently looking at him. When he stood before him, he reached for the buckle of Hunter's pants. Hunter immediately grabbed his wrists to stop him.

"What are you doing? Absolutely not here."

"I want to see."

"No. Not here. I know Lucy and Bill are fine with us hanging out at the diner, but not for this."

"I just want to see," Cam persisted. "I do have some self-control."

Not really, but hey, I can bluff.

"Not 'til the weekend. It'll give you something to look forward to," Hunter said with a half smile.

"Fucking tease," Cam said with a glare.

Hunter chuckled. "I've got to go and your break's about over." He placed a chaste kiss on Cam's pursed lips before turning to leave the back room.

"Hey, Hunter," Cam said.

Hunter stopped and turned, arching an eyebrow, encouraging Cam to continue.

"Commando. Just in case you're wondering. The underwear they bought me never really fit."

Hunter inhaled sharply, closed his eyes, and turned his face up toward the ceiling. He exhaled deeply as he gripped the doorframe.

He held the position for a few seconds before opening his eyes and giving Cam a death glare. "That was cruel."

"Next time, let me look."

"Damn it," Hunter huffed under his breath.

Cam smiled wickedly as he adjusted himself.

Hunter shook his head. "You're frying my brain cells, I almost forgot. I spoke to my friend, Aidan, he can come by the house this evening."

For Cam, that was the equivalent of throwing a bucket of cold water on him then trapping his balls between two ice blocks. "What did you tell him?"

"Nothing yet. I figured we'd cover that when he comes over. He'll be there at eight."

Cam nodded. "Thanks."

"Cam, can I steal you for some help at the register?" Bill asked, poking his head into the back room.

"Sure."

Hunter walked back over to Cam and cradled his face, staring at him for a few seconds. His eyes sparkled with emotions Cam was too afraid to explore. He sighed when Hunter's thumbs softly stroked his cheeks.

"We'll get through this, so don't let it get to you. And as far as this weekend, yes, I'm as worked up as you are. So don't torture me anymore please."

Cam anchored his hands on Hunter's forearms and smiled. "Okay." He reached up and gave Hunter a chaste kiss.

"I'll see you tonight." Hunter gave him one last look, filled with need, before he turned and walked out of the back room.

Cameron couldn't take his eyes off Hunter as he walked away. He returned to the front to help Bill at the register. He rang up the order for the customer, still wearing that goofy grin from earlier in the day.

Cam sat in the living room of the halfway house opposite Hunter's Marine buddy. One thing was crystal clear. Aidan Calloway was completely different from the cops Cam had encountered during this whole mess. He obviously hated wasting his time. A quick introduction and immediate "What's going on?" question launched them into a discussion of the situation. Cam was instantly at ease and answering every question Aidan shot in his direction about the house and what he saw.

Aidan removed the items from the living room table and spread out a map of the tri-county area.

"Where?" Aidan prompted.

Cam stared blindly at the map for a moment. He closed his eyes and thought back to the many drives to the house in the middle of nowhere. His head spun with thoughts and emotions. Would this be over soon? Could this lead to something? What if he couldn't remember? His chest tightened and his heart raced. He opened his eyes and looked over to Hunter, standing only inches away.

"Just try to remember as best as you can," Hunter encouraged, closing the distance between them.

He glanced over to Aidan and back to Hunter. Both watched him intently. He noticed Aidan didn't seem to mind Hunter's proximity. As if reading his mind, Hunter placed his large hand against Cam's lower back and began to softly stroke him in that soothing circular motion. Cam looked over to Aidan who didn't even bat an eyelash with the gesture.

Cam focused on the map again and suddenly the path to the house stood out as if he'd highlighted the roads with a marker. He ran his fingers along the map, following the same path he'd taken to the house for months, almost ten years ago, until his finger finally reached the house's location.

"There."

Aidan and Hunter looked at the map more closely and nodded. Aidan then referred to his laptop for a closer view, trying to pinpoint the exact house. Cam guided him further on the screen using street level views on Google Maps. They finally found the house, tucked in the woods, hidden away from plain sight.

"What are our options?" Hunter asked.

"They never got a statement from Cameron back then so getting one now, out of the blue, might cause some waves. So that's not an option until we have something a little more solid. It's been ten years, so we need to check out the house before jumping to any conclusions. I can scope out the place for a bit, off record, to see if there's anything that merits pursuing." Aidan folded the map and stood with his hands on his waist. "If I see anything, I might be able to pull a warrant from a judge. But I'd need to have something concrete at that house before that can happen. And I need a judge who won't tip off Mackler."

"I've got a name for that. Dylan Stanford. Peter recommended him," Hunter added.

Aidan nodded. He held out his hand for Cam to shake. "Thank you," he said.

Cam's eyes widened as he extended his hand. "I should be thanking you."

Aidan shook his head. "You've finally given me a way to pay back Hunter. I've got quite a tab with him. I have some time tonight so I'll go check it out for a bit and keep you guys posted."

"Thanks," Hunter said to Aidan with a slap on his friend's back.

He hoped Aidan would find something at the house quickly so he could move on from this never-ending nightmare that haunted them.

Chapter TWENTY

Cam pressed his forehead against the cool glass of the passenger side window. He absently stared at the outside edge of the highway as it raced by in a blur, the road fading into the trees and neighboring cars in a mix of colors. The smooth, quiet rumble of the car's engine revving let him know Hunter was just as anxious to start the weekend as he was.

Hunter had picked him up after leaving his office, when the *weekend pass* time period started. After obsessing for far too long about having some alone time with Hunter, he was finally granted a weekend of heaven. But all he could feel was utter disappointment.

"You okay?" Hunter asked, breaking into Cam's thoughts.

"Huh?" Cam asked as he leaned back against the headrest and looked over to the man who had stood by him, without fail, during the past few days.

Hunter shifted his focus off the road for a moment to glance at Cam. He smiled as unmistakable affection with a hint of mischief glinted in his eyes. "I asked if you were okay?" He reached over and gripped Cam's neck.

"I'll be fine." Cam moaned and reveled in the rhythmic massage.

Hunter's brow furrowed with obvious concern, as he switched focus between watching the road and trying to decipher Cam's mood. "I know you'll be fine, but something's bothering you now. You look…disappointed. Do you want me to take you back to the halfway house?"

"No!" Cam immediately responded and straightened in the seat. "Hell, no!"

Hunter smiled then withdrew his hand from Cam's neck. He pulled off into the emergency lane and put the car in park. "I'm glad, but I know something's bothering you."

Cam sighed. He had not expected their first weekend together to start like this. He closed his eyes and took a deep breath. "I'm just pissed off. I was hoping…I thought…fuck!"

"We can do that later. Right now, I want to know what's bothering you," Hunter asked playfully with a raised eyebrow.

Cam couldn't help but chuckle. "You're worse than I am."

"Hey, you think I haven't been thinking about our weekend together for a while now? I don't want you to be pissed off. So just tell me what's eating away at you." He reached over to stroke Cam's cheek.

Cam leaned into the caress like a cat craving a scratch. "I just thought that by pointing out the house, something would have happened by now, you know? That this would be over or something," he finished with a deep exhale.

"I know." Hunter continued to stroke his cheek with his thumb. "It's only been a couple of days, and you can't wave a wand and have everything magically resolved in seconds. Aidan did say it seemed as if there was some activity at the house so promised to keep going by and checking up on it."

"I know," he said, his shoulders hunched. He was tired of worrying about everyone who managed to get close to him. Sometimes, all the attention was a bit overwhelming, but secretly, he craved the closeness he was deprived of for far too long. He had fallen victim to a false sense of security and had actually grown to care about Lucy, Bill, and overprotective Julian and Matt. Now, he bordered on panic at the thought of these people suddenly becoming collateral damage. He closed his eyes as he tried to control his racing heartbeat.

Hunter cupped Cam's face with both hands. "Cam, breathe."

Cam opened his eyes to see Hunter's fiercely steady gaze. That was all it took to wipe away his disappointment and focus on their weekend together.

"Fuck, you're hot when you look at me like that."

Hunter gave him a wicked smile.

Cam reached over to kiss that smile off his face but was stopped by the seat belt locking him in place. "Ugh, I hate these fucking things," he said, struggling while trying to loosen the strap that seemed to get tighter.

Hunter laughed. "Hold that thought," he said, turning back in his seat. He put the car in gear and eased into traffic again then casually placed his hand on Cam's thigh.

Cam focused on Hunter's large hand on him, the pressure of his grip, the heat of his touch through his jeans. All his thoughts evaporated, he couldn't even remember what they were just talking about. He closed his eyes, numb with the sudden flood of desire that coursed through his body.

He opened his eyes and looked over at Hunter. "How far are we?" His voice so hoarse he barely recognized himself.

Hunter's vision snapped to Cam with a glare of equal desire. "Don't do that to me. We're almost there."

Cam inched over toward him as much as his belt permitted, and leaned over to run his fingers though Hunter's hair, happy to finally figure out how to pull the belt without it locking. "How far are we?" he asked again, closer this time to Hunter's ear as he ran his finger under Hunter's shirt collar.

Hunter noticeably swallowed and withdrew his hand from Cam's thigh, then firmly grabbed the steering wheel with a white-knuckled grip.

Cam reached into Hunter's suit jacket and began to loosen Hunter's tie.

"What are you doing?"

"I thought it was obvious."

"Here?"

"I'm getting a head start. You've got way too much shit on."

"We're almost there."

"You keep saying that, I'm tired of waiting." He slid out Hunter's tie then slowly began to undo the top button of Hunter's shirt. He smiled when the car's engine revved. He reached into Hunter's shirt. Ripples of desire spread through his body with the touch of Hunter's heated skin and the wiry hair on his chest.

"Four minutes."

"That's a long time," he said, then began working the second button of Hunter's shirt.

"You're killin' me."

"Don't they call it *the little death*?"

"Three minutes."

"We're counting down now? Two buttons down, about four more to go."

Two more buttons and two minutes of additional torture later, Hunter slowed as he rounded the corner of the neighborhood of homes. Cam immediately straightened in his seat and was awestruck by each house they drove by. Hunter pulled into the driveway of a Spanish-style home surrounded by trees. The one-story was a bit smaller than the other insanely-sized multi-story Coral Gables homes on this block, but far more welcoming. The exterior was a pale mustard shade of stucco with a dark barrel tile roof that accentuated the earthy tones of the exterior. Minimal landscaping was needed with the huge black olive tree in the front and the mixed purple, red, and pink bougainvilleas surrounding the property. The open spaces, absent of fencing and with plenty of land between the neighbors, gave the illusion of openness with a touch of privacy.

"This is yours?" Cam asked, stunned.

"Yup, this is my house. I wanted something away from the craziness of the city. This came up as a steal some time ago so I bought it. It's very private, which is a major plus."

"It's just you here?"

"Yeah, just me. As an added perk, the neighbors use theirs as winter homes so there's no one else on this block for the better part of the year."

Cam frowned. He looked down at his frayed jeans and long-sleeved T-shirt and knew he was out of place.

"C'mon, grab your bag," Hunter said as he exited the car.

Hunter unlocked the front door and stepped aside so Cam could enter first.

"Wow." Cam walked inside and looked at the equally impressive interior. Impeccably clean, incredibly organized, and impossibly sterile. No pictures on the walls or tables, everything was a stark black, white, or steel...elegant and sleek, but cold and unwelcoming. A complete contradiction to the warm, welcoming exterior and the man Cam had come to know. He didn't belong in this house and for some reason, he didn't think Hunter belonged here either.

He opened his mouth to say something, but suddenly, Hunter was there, pushing him hard against the wall by the entrance. They kissed, the first real, private, passionate kiss where Cam wasn't worried about someone seeing or walking in on them. Hunter devoured Cam's mouth and held him still as he pushed Cam's shirt up and over his head. Untamed desire he had controlled for almost a decade instantly flooded his system. He stepped back just enough to let Hunter peel the shirt off him and immediately latched on to his mouth again with equal ferocity. Without breaking contact, he frantically finished undoing the buttons on Hunter's shirt.

Hunter's breath came fast and hard, his nostrils flaring like a bull. He broke the kiss to work his way down Cam's neck. "I want you so much."

Cam's heartbeat raced and his entire body began to shake with the need to feel the heat of Hunter's body. He pulled Hunter's shirt open and down his arms. Hunter deftly freed himself then pushed his body up against Cam to hold him steady against the wall.

Groin to groin, there was no denying the want between them. Cam grabbed Hunter by the hair and pulled him into another searing kiss.

Hunter groaned and grabbed Cam as he pushed against him in a slow sensuous movement. Cam let out a strangled moan when Hunter's hand pushed inside his jeans and closed around his shaft.

"Fuck." Cam gasped into Hunter's mouth then reached behind Hunter to grip his ass and pull him closer, needing more friction.

Hunter's solid, hard-muscled chest pressed against his was better than any fantasy he could have conjured up. He frantically reached past the curls of Hunter's treasure trail and tried to unzip his pants. Frustration bloomed as the desire that shook him prevented him from coordinating his movements. He wrapped his arm around Hunter's neck and held on when his legs began to give way with each stroke of Hunter's hand.

It had been too long, and now, there was just too much too soon and with entirely too much desire to extend this past a few quick thrusts. Cam was close and could tell from Hunter's short breaths that he wasn't far behind. Cam focused on the deep, slow rhythm Hunter had set—the grind of their bodies swaying together, Hunter's hands on him, pulling up and down Cam's shaft with deliciously mesmerizing pressure. His skin became hypersensitive to the brush of Hunter's stubble against his neck and his warm breath against his ear.

Everything faded to black. Nothing existed but this man, his presence, the way Hunter's body pressed against his, each groan and gasp he caused. He reveled in the utter desperation Hunter showed, taking what he needed as soon as they were alone. Hunter wanted *him* in spite of everything he knew about Cam. He could hear the catch in Hunter's breath, and that was all that was needed before he lost it hot and hard in Hunter's hold.

Cam finally settled his breathing and began to feel his legs again. Hunter's strong arms were still wrapped around him, holding him in place.

Hunter rested his forehead against Cam's after a few moments. "Fuck."

Cam jolted back to reality when he registered Hunter's tone. "Don't you fucking dare," he shouted in a throaty voice. The thought of Hunter rejecting him was like a flaming hot knife slicing through his chest. With renewed vigor, he desperately pulled himself out of Hunter's hold and pushed him away.

"Cam—"

"Do you regret what we just did?" he yelled, trying to ignore the pain that cracked his voice.

"No," Hunter thundered in response. "All I've been thinking about is you, being with you, wanting to touch you and feel you. You can't imagine how much I want you, but to grab you and rub off on you like a horny kid for your first time in ten years was not how I fucking pictured our first time would be!"

Hunter's loud, powerful voice resonated off the bare living room walls and echoed his anger. Cam stalked forward. Hunter stilled when he was a mere breath away, invading his personal space.

In a calm, level tone Cam said exactly what he thought in that moment, "Mr. Donovan, feel free to slam me up against a wall...anytime...anywhere...just make me one promise." He punctuated each word, intensely staring at Hunter, refusing to back away.

Hunter's breathless voice shook. "Anything."

"Don't ever stop wanting me enough to do so."

With enough power to rival Hunter's grip on him earlier, Cam grabbed Hunter and shoved *him* against the wall, pressed his body against Hunter's, held *him* prisoner between the wall and himself. He gripped Hunter's hair and delivered a no-holds-barred kiss with unmistakable desire. Hunter didn't protest being held by Cam. Instead, he simply moaned his approval into the kiss.

A devilish grin curled Hunter's kiss-swollen lips, when they separated. "I promise."

Cam kissed a path up Hunter's neck. "So, what else have you pictured us doing?"

Hunter moaned then pulled Cam into an embrace. "How about we move things into the bedroom and slow it down a bit?"

Cam pressed his cheek against the side of Hunter's face. He loved the heat of Hunter's body against his, the way he held him in his arms, the way his chest hair brushed against his skin, his scent. He was past the point of no return. He didn't care about location or pace, he just wanted Hunter, any way he could get him.

"Okay," he responded softly.

Hunter grabbed his hand and pulled him to follow down the hallway into the bedroom.

Cameron entered the room and was immediately taken aback by the high ceiling and open space. The room looked like a sparsely furnished, oversized, one bedroom apartment with four pieces of furniture. The large bed and small neighboring nightstand faced the door on the right-hand side of the room. A narrow, long window between the bed and the master bathroom on the right allowed for a clear view of the yard. The sofa shared the same wall to the left of the bed—both available sitting areas to view the large television mounted on the opposite wall. Even though both the bed and couch looked welcoming, Cam would bet the angled desk area off to the far corner of the room was the most used.

"This room is set up like what most studio apartments would look like. You know, you could hang out in your living room and make it look a little lived in," Cam said with a wry grin.

Hunter chuckled. "I've spent more time in this room than in any other part of the house."

"It's obvious the second you walk in. Why do I have a feeling you spend more time at that desk or sleeping on that couch than you do this huge bed," he said, looking over to Hunter.

Hunter wrapped his arms around Cameron from behind. "Because I think you know me pretty well by now."

Cam smiled as he leaned back into the embrace and rubbed Hunter's arms around his midsection.

"I'm going to jump into the shower really quick. Give me a few minutes," Hunter said, releasing him. "Make yourself at home."

"Huh? What?"

"I picked you up right out of work. I want to wash the office off before we get into bed and my suit pants are starting to stick to me. I'll be quick." He delivered a chaste kiss before heading into the bathroom.

Cameron heard the shower turn on. There was no way in hell he was going to waste even five minutes of their weekend away from Hunter. He stripped his jeans and took a deep breath before entering the bathroom.

Hunter was under the spray of water rinsing his hair as the steam rose and obstructed part of Cam's view. He opened the shower door and Hunter looked in his direction with eyes that immediately darkened with desire. Finally, in full view of Hunter's body, Cam's brain froze. His eyes took in the sight, staring at every curve and how the rivulets of water traveled along each arch and crevice of his muscles. The heat burned in Cam's blood and a jolt of lust shot straight to his core. His brain may have stopped processing, but his body was more than ready.

"Get in here," Hunter said in a raspy voice.

Hunter pulled Cam into the shower by the waist and closed the door. Cam was sandwiched between the cold, wet tile walls and Hunter's hot and ready body. The full skin on skin contact wasn't enough. He gripped Hunter's broad shoulders and pushed up against him, groin to groin.

"You feel so fucking good," Hunter growled before biting his ear then jawline.

A tingle began at the base of Cam's spine. No way was he going to lose it this quickly again without getting more of this man. He gripped Hunter's face and turned his head to expose the neck he desperately wanted to taste.

Hunter groaned and thrust forward in time with Cam's suction. His hold around Cam's waist tightened, his thrusts sped up.

Cameron stopped torturing Hunter's neck and released his shoulders, then, without hesitation, dropped to his knees on the shower floor and was at eye level with Hunter's full arousal. He grabbed Hunter's shaft with one hand and swallowed as much as he could.

"Shit," Hunter yelled. He reached out for support, one hand on the wall, the other rattled the shower door with the force of his push to steady himself.

Cam closed his eyes and reveled in the feel of Hunter heavy on his tongue. Each moan he pulled from Hunter drove him harder and deeper.

"Fu..." was all Hunter managed to say on an exhale before digging his fingers in Cam's wet hair, encouraging him to continue.

Desire chased up Cam's spine when he saw Hunter's intense, darkened gaze on him. Hunter's hand moved from Cam's hair, to below his jaw, nudging him to stop.

"Get up here," Hunter said in a raspy voice.

Cam dug his fingers in Hunter's hips and sealed his mouth on him, harder. Hunter's taste was addicting, and the feel of him filling Cam's mouth drove him to desperately need more.

Hunter pulled him up by the hair and pushed him against the wall for a soul-branding kiss. Cam moaned as he struggled to keep up with the full force of Hunter's invasion, consumed by the heated trail of Hunter touching and tasting his skin.

Cam eased back, needing to catch his breath. He gasped when he saw Hunter's silver, heated gaze filled with so much promise of passion. He tried to level his breathing as he watched the water travel through Hunter's hair, down his face. Hunter's long lashes were soaked, his kiss-swollen lips parted as he, too, tried to settle his breathing.

Cam's heart beat furiously against his chest. With renewed energy, he gripped Hunter's hair and pulled his head back and latched onto his neck again. He wanted to mark Hunter, claim him, let the world know this man was his and everyone needed to just…back…the…fuck…off.

He heard a sound then gasped when Hunter's finger entered him. He looked over his shoulder when he heard the sound again and saw Hunter squeeze out lube onto his fingers.

"Where did you get that from?" Cam asked breathlessly.

"I've been prepping for this weekend. I've got a bottle of lube in every corner of the house," he said with a wicked grin before snapping the cap shut and delivering another passionate kiss.

Their tongues fought for dominance while Hunter continued to explore and stretch inside Cam's body. His arms encircled Hunter's shoulders as his body swayed, demanding more friction from Hunter. "I'm done with the foreplay," Cam said between kisses. He was too close and didn't want to lose it in the shower. "Let's go to bed."

Hunter looked at him as he worked a third finger inside. He brushed his lips against Cam's. "It's been too long and I don't want to hurt you. So deal with it."

Cameron was quieted when Hunter sealed his mouth with another kiss. Cam madly rocked back and forth, needing friction against Hunter's hardness and his exploratory fingers. Desire ran hot through his veins, making him teeter on the edge of release.

"Shit," Hunter said when the water began to get cold. He withdrew his fingers gently then reached back and switched off the water.

"Bed," Cam said. He walked out of the shower on shaky legs and reached for the nearest towel. Hunter dried himself as he predatorily stared at every move Cam made.

Hunter discarded the towel and stalked over to him. Cam's heart pounded violently, watching the play of muscles move with each step. Hunter grabbed his hand and pulled him back into the bedroom.

Finally.

Cam stood frozen by the bed and blankly stared at the perfectly flattened sheets. Fear coursed through his veins, cooling the desire that had driven his actions only moments before.

Hunter stepped before him and cradled his face. "Talk to me. You're not panicking, but your mind is going a million miles a second."

Cam looked away. He wanted Hunter, the pressure and heat of their bodies pressed together; he just didn't want this to be an epic failure falling short of any expectations. He sure as hell wasn't a virgin but his experience was beyond lackluster.

"We'll go slow. Follow my lead. We'll stop if you want. Okay," Hunter said gently. He stroked Cam's cheeks then softly brushed his lips in a ghost of a caress.

Cameron looked at Hunter and wondered how the hell he always seemed to know exactly what Cam was thinking and how to say the right things to keep the panic at bay. He nodded. He stood still by the bed, waiting for some indication of what to do as his heart beat feverishly against his chest. He closed his eyes and tried to settle his breathing and focus on the present rather than his embarrassment. He sensed movement and opened his eyes to see Hunter kneeling before him.

"What are you doing?"

"This," Hunter said, then wrapped his lips around Cam's full erection.

Cam sharply inhaled through his nose and gripped Hunter's shoulders for support. The heat of Hunter's mouth on him, surrounding him, was surreal.

He wanted to remember every lick, pull, scrape, and suck. He reveled in the sounds of pleasure Hunter made. He swayed with each pull of Hunter's mouth and he gasped when Hunter's warm breath skated across his sensitive skin. Shocks of pleasure spread throughout his body, weakening his legs. It wasn't just the excitement of a new experience, it was Hunter, and his desire to give Cam pleasure. He was light-headed, dizzy with desire as he ran his shaky fingers in Hunter's damp hair, encouraging, not wanting this beautiful torture to end. He gripped Hunter's shoulder hard, digging his fingers deeper in response to the heat of Hunter's mouth as he took him again.

Cam blinked rapidly and stared blindly at the ceiling when everything abruptly stopped. He looked down and saw Hunter gazing up at him.

Hunter slowly stood. "You didn't like that?"

Cam nodded and looked away as a flush of heat spread across his face. He'd have to be dumber than a stump to not like what Hunter did. It was no wonder everyone wanted a blow job. Hell, he wanted another one right now.

"Cam?"

He glanced back at Hunter and noticed the concern etched in his expression. Hunter brushed his knuckles along Cam's cheek as he usually did when he hoped Cam would say something he was holding back. He didn't want to talk, he didn't want to have to admit that stepping into this bedroom made him realize that he didn't really have enough experience to back up all the buildup from weeks of teasing.

Cam sighed. "That was the first time anyone's ever wanted to do that to me," he quietly mumbled as his face heated again.

"I love the way you feel, the way you taste," Hunter said, ghosting kisses along his face. "We'll do it again later, if you let me."

Cam looked up and smiled broadly. *Hell yeah, times a million.*

Hunter brushed his lips slowly against Cam's then traced Cam's upper lip with his tongue. Cam moaned and ran his tongue alongside Hunter's. His chest tightened when he tasted himself on Hunter's tongue. *An intimate mark on my man.* He reached to pull Hunter closer, wanting to extend their unhurried, lazy exploration. Hunter's fingers traced his skin softly, a hint of a touch kindling every single inch of Cam on fire.

Finally they separated and he watched Hunter walk over to the side table and grab the lube and condoms from the drawer before tossing them onto the bed. Cam took that as his cue and jumped onto the bed in the position he knew—face down on his knees—as anticipation thrummed through his nervous, shaking body.

He just hoped Hunter was too anxious to notice.

* * * *

Hunter saw the tremble in Cam's hands as he positioned himself on the bed. He tried to hide it by burying his fists in the sheets, but the shaky breathing was a dead giveaway. Hunter controlled the anger that simmered directly beneath the surface. Cam's previous and only lover had been a selfish asshole. Regardless of whether Cam got off, his other lover had used him and hadn't taken the time to appreciate the gift of trust Cam so rarely gave.

He reached out and ran his hand along Cam's back. Cam exhaled loudly and arched into the caress as goose bumps bloomed across his body like a row of dominos falling. Hunter wanted to see Cam's face, to spot the cues he needed so he'd know when to stop or slow down, but knew better than to push him. He inched closer and pressed his chest against Cam's back, then ran his hands along Cam's side, tracing a finger slowly along each curve of lean muscle. Hunter exhaled a shaky breath as he cautiously explored with touch, hoping and needing to establish a connection that would break through Cam's iron wall. He placed a trail of kisses along Cam's body, fighting the curl of desire that twisted along his spine. Unable to resist the urge to be inside Cam, he grabbed a condom and lube to begin readying himself.

Cam inhaled deeply when Hunter rubbed against him. He pushed back and spoke in a menacing tone. "Hunter, I swear, if you start with the fingering shit again, I'm going to cut your balls off."

Hunter smiled and kissed Cam's back, enjoying the slight twitch against his lips. He positioned himself, keeping constant contact with Cam as if he were circling a wild horse that would unexpectedly buck.

Cam fisted his hands and lowered his head.

Hunter took a deep breath and slowly entered Cam's tight, welcoming body. He fought for control, overwhelmed by the feeling of finally being inside the man who had stolen his heart. He bowed his head, struggling to keep the emotions at bay as Cam's heat enveloped him.

Hunter bent over Cam's body and wrapped his arms around his waist, wanting to hold him even closer. He rested his head on Cam's shoulder as their breaths mingled, both unsteady, both emitting enough body heat to power a city. He patiently waited until the tension in Cam's muscles began to ease.

Cam moved lower, his backside still raised in offering. Hunter reached for Cam's hands and entwined their fingers, his arms protectively barricading Cam, resting his weight on Cam's body, pressing him into the mattress and pushing himself farther into the welcoming heat. Cam's body contoured against Hunter's, each curve corresponded perfectly to each dip. Cam looked over his shoulder, his mouth parted with an exhale, staring at Hunter with eyes that had darkened to a deep sapphire.

"Don't stop," he said breathlessly as he placed a kiss on Hunter's arm.

A surge of need traveled Hunter's body at the soft brush of Cam's lips. "Touch me," he whispered in Cam's ear, guiding his hand to Hunter's thigh. He tested a short thrust, pushing himself deeper into Cam. "Please."

Cam moaned and turned his head, seeking Hunter's lips for a kiss. Cam's demanding fingers dug deeply into Hunter's thigh and pulled him closer. Hunter groaned and began a slow, sensual rhythm, never breaking contact with Cam's lips. They shifted, gripped, and pulled tighter, both seeking to get closer, both demanding more as the sounds of need echoed in the otherwise silent room.

Cam broke the kiss, gasping for air. "Hunter."

The needy way Cam said his name and the sounds of pleasure he made triggered a surge of desire throughout Hunter's body. The want for this man and the desire to claim him was too strong. He needed to calm himself or this torturous pleasure would end too soon.

Hunter kissed a path from Cam's neck over to his bicep.

"What are you doing?"

"What does it look like I'm doing?" He kissed the raised skin that formed a misshapen set of markings on Cam's bicep.

"Don't, it's…it's ugly," Cam said with a shaky voice.

"Shhh." He peppered kisses down Cam's neck and shoulder. Hunter ran his tongue down Cam's bicep, tracing the partial ink design and each of the scars that marred his skin. When he reached back up to Cam's shoulder, his gaze was met with intense blue eyes filled with restrained emotion.

He placed a gentle kiss on Cam's trembling lips. "I want all of you, I don't care."

"It's ugly. I hate it," he finished quietly and turned away.

"Look at me."

Cam turned to meet Hunter's stare, his blue eyes brimming with sadness. There was nothing he wanted more at that very moment than to tell Cam how much he loved him, but that was something Cam wasn't ready to hear.

He brushed the hair out of Cam's face. "I like having a sexy boyfriend with a tattoo. It's kinda hot. You're such a badass," he teased, then nuzzled Cam's ear.

Cam chuckled. "You're fucking nuts," he whispered.

Hunter moaned as the rumble of laughter became a vise on his shaft. "Turn around."

"What?"

"Turn around," Hunter repeated in a hoarse voice as he slowly withdrew. He refused to have Cam's back to him any longer.

Cam looked confused but turned as requested, facing up on the bed. "You do realize I don't have girl parts, right?"

Hunter smiled. "Thank God for that," he said as he positioned himself between Cam's invitingly open legs.

Cam reached out to touch Hunter's abs when he neared. Hunter closed his eyes and sharply inhaled as Cam's finger's left a line of fire on his skin. He opened his eyes and his gaze locked with Cam's. Cam looked at him with a glint of mischief in his eyes, as though knowing exactly the effect he had on Hunter. Cam sucked in his lower lip, and Hunter groaned before bending to deliver another kiss. He pulled Cam closer, aligning himself without breaking contact. He finally separated from the kiss, staring intently at Cam, and moaned as he entered Cameron again in one swift movement.

Cam arched his body off the bed and instantly locked his legs around Hunter, pulling him closer and impaling himself. He dug his fingers in Hunter's thighs as his body writhed, lifting himself, drawing Hunter deeper.

Desire coiled in Hunter's body as the vise tightened around him and threatened to nudge him closer to that crest he wanted to avoid so soon. He began a slow, steady, disciplined rhythm. His body begged for friction but he forced his iron will to stave off the need that coursed through his veins. Everything was in slow motion, each pull and push, every breath and touch.

Their eyes locked. He inhaled sharply, fighting the swell of emotions trying to overtake him.

Their bodies moved in concert, tighter, faster, and harder as they neared the crescendo. Hunter's pulse raced and his heart pounded furiously against his chest with the heat of Cam's touch and the sweat-slicked glide of their bodies. Hunter's hips thrust on their own accord in a desperate urgency to own him.

"Oh fuck!" Cam yelled and bowed his body when Hunter obviously hit the mark he sought.

He ignored the sting of Cam's blunt nails digging deeper into his muscled back. Pure ecstasy infused his blood and drove him to piston uncontrollably into Cam with every ounce of power he had. Sweat trickled down his brow as he pushed himself harder. He reached for Cam's hard shaft. The instant touch yielded another yell as Cam arched hard and stilled before spilling his release into Hunter's hand.

The tight grip around Hunter pushed him off the edge. Tremors rippled throughout his body as he roared his climax. He collapsed onto his forearms and rolled to lie on his back next to Cam.

They worked to steady their breathing, their legs and arms spread wide.

A hand clumsily fell on Hunter's face a few moments later.

"Ow," he said conversationally. He looked over and saw Cam watching him with a huge, lazy grin. His eyes danced with wonder and mischief.

"I hope you're ready for round two, old man. 'Cause that was worth an encore," he said in a slurred voice as his fingers trailed a path along Hunter's face and neck.

Hunter lazily chuckled. "Give me a minute to recover, and I'll show you what this old man can do."

And he did.

Chapter
TWENTY-ONE

Cam opened his eyes and tried to shift in bed. He barely had enough energy to move let alone fight to be liberated. He looked down and saw Hunter's arm and leg spread across him.

His stomach fluttered. This was the first time he had ever slept in the same bed with another man.

Every muscle in his body hurt, he ached in places he didn't know could pain him. But he didn't care. Last night he had been worshipped, spoiled, and worn out. He looked over and saw Hunter still asleep, his head turned on the pillow, facing him. He could see the slight bruising on his neck.

His mark. *Fuck yeah. Mine.* He smiled smugly to himself.

"Good morning," Hunter mumbled into the pillow with his eyes still closed.

"I thought you were sleeping."

"I don't want to sleep when you're looking at me like that," his words muffled against the fabric.

Cameron chuckled. "How do you even know I'm looking at you if your eyes are shut?"

Hunter opened his eyes and looked at Cam. "I can feel you looking at me."

Cam had never been this connected to anyone. He reached out and stroked the arm that encased him.

"What time is it?" Hunter asked, not moving.

Cam craned his neck to see the clock on Hunter's side table. "It's almost nine."

Hunter closed his eyes. "We've got to get up."

"Why?"

"There's someplace I want to take you."

"Where?" Cam asked, sitting up when Hunter rose from bed.

"It's a surprise. I'll make us some breakfast before we leave." Hunter grabbed a pair of jeans from the drawer and dressed.

Hunter reached over to kiss Cam. Cam grabbed him by the waist of his pants before he had a chance to walk away. He smiled when he saw the number of bruises and scratches on Hunter's torso. He ran his fingers over each discoloration that would ultimately bloom in color. When he looked up, Hunter's molten silver glare was filled with unmistakable desire.

"Mine," Cam said possessively.

"Yours," Hunter responded with equal fire.

Cam rested his weight on his knees and pulled Hunter into a greedy kiss.

Hunter separated from the kiss with a groan. "Get dressed. I'm going to make breakfast so we can leave."

Cam scowled as Hunter left the bedroom. He could hear his steps travel through the house and reach the kitchen. He debated getting dressed but then heard the clanging of pans. Grumbling, he got out of bed and stretched.

Cam joined Hunter in the kitchen moments later. "Why is most of your house so….plain? It's almost as if you don't live here, other than your room."

Hunter poured juice into two glasses. "I hadn't noticed that really. I guess it's because it doesn't really feel like a home. Feels more like a house where I sleep. I'm usually up at the crack of dawn and can't wait to get out of bed and into the office."

"You didn't wake up early this morning."

Hunter walked over to Cam and pulled him close by the waistband of his pants then wrapped his arms around him. "No, not today."

Cam quirked an eyebrow. "Is this the part where you get sappy on me?"

Hunter sighed then pulled away from the embrace. "There's no one to welcome me when I get here from work. It's just a house."

Cam crossed his arms. "It's a nice house."

Hunter straightened to his full height and crossed his arms in the same manner, mirroring Cam's stance. He looked at Cam in that way he did that reached inside Cam's soul. "It's a house. Maybe if you were here with me, I'd see it more as a home."

Cameron continued to stare while the words sunk in and rattled his soul. With everything going on, Cam refused to hope for a future until his past was resolved. He wouldn't be able to survive if something happened to Hunter because of his ghosts.

Hunter reached out and placed his hand on Cam's cheek. "C'mon, let's eat so we can leave." He withdrew and turned to grab the dishes while Cam remained still, his body slowly becoming numb.

Cam didn't want Hunter to think he didn't care or that his words hadn't struck a nerve. He pushed a whisper of a voice past the lump in his throat.

"Hunter—"

Hunter immediately turned and, in two strides, grabbed Cam's face and delivered a kiss with unmistakable desire. Cam gripped Hunter's shoulders and returned the kiss with just as much passion, hoping to convey how much he wanted to be with him.

Cam tried to open himself, to allow the feelings behind the unspoken words to filter through his system, but he couldn't. He knew what it was like to hope and want for something then to have it all disappear. He wrapped his arms around Hunter and just held on.

Breakfast could wait.

"So where are we going?" Cam asked as they walked down the sidewalk of shops.

"You'll see."

They finally stopped in front of a small space with a window full of various types of color and black tribal-like designs covering his view of the inside. "A tattoo parlor?"

Hunter nodded. "If you don't want to do this, we can leave. I got a referral to this place and a specific artist. Aside from the traditional tattoo work, this person specializes in tattoos on and around scar tissue."

Cam was too busy looking at the interlocking designs on the window to focus on what Hunter was saying. He looked back at Hunter when he realized he had stopped talking.

"Sorry. What do you mean tattoo scars?"

Hunter shook his head. "Tattoos on and around scars. I figured they could look at your arm and work with the current ink you have there and maybe add to the design or create something else to cover some of the scars you hate. Change it up to something you choose. Never mind. It was just—"

Cam grabbed him by the hand and hauled him into the shop.

"Hi, can I help you?" a slim woman asked. Ink trailed down her neck and spanned across both arms all the way to her wrists. The design was so intricate and intertwined it almost seemed as if she wore a fitted patterned long-sleeve turtleneck underneath her shirt.

Cam looked up at Hunter expectantly.

"Hi, yes. I have an appointment with Leslie. My name is Hunter."

The petite woman smiled broadly and extended her hand in greeting. "That's me. You mentioned tattoos and scars over the phone. What do you need?"

Cam lifted his sleeve to reveal his scarring and ink. "Can you do something with this?"

Leslie reached out and grabbed Cam's arm. She turned and inspected his bicep to assess the extent of the damage and work needed. Cam wanted to cringe but patiently allowed the woman to touch the raised skin in some areas.

"Definitely," she said with a smile. "I'm sure we can work up a design that will make that unnoticeable. It all depends on what you want to do."

Cam listened to her as she explained the different requirements of tattooing over and around the scars. She explained how the ink would take more than one pass to show up properly on the scar tissue and how some of the scars, especially the keloids, might hurt more than the others. They discussed different concepts and designs. Within seconds, Cameron knew what he wanted—a simple piece that would take advantage of the scar tissue to look as if parts of the design were embossed on his skin. The design would expand on the existing prison black ink with the addition of a little color and extend past the one side of his arm into a partial wraparound tattoo with the use of curved lines that followed each shape of his scars.

Hunter quietly observed and listened intently to the exchange, never interrupting.

Leslie sketched a design, which she then transferred to Cam's arm. Using the faint brown lines as a guide to where the new art would be, they then discussed a few freehand additions should the scar tissue become more of an issue than expected.

Cam looked in the mirror and moved his bicep around to see the back of his arm. "I don't want to overdo it with the ink. I prefer to keep it as simple as possible but just enough to do something with…this," he said, lowering his shirt sleeve.

"We'll stick to a very basic palette of reds and yellows. We'll use the current black you have for the shadows and I'll work in a little more so it blends in with the other parts of the piece. Instead of making the lines straight, we'll use the jagged black ink you have and the scars to add curvature to the lines. Don't worry," Leslie finished with a smile.

Anything was better than the curved slashes that marred his arms, but still, he couldn't help worry they'd be too stubborn to incorporate into the simple piece. "How long will this take?"

"It's a relatively simple design. Depends on how long you can sit in my chair in one sitting."

He looked over to Hunter, hoping there were no other plans for the rest of the day.

"He's all yours today all day if you've got your schedule free," Hunter responded.

Cam hid his smile. He loved how Hunter knew what he was thinking without saying a word.

"I can try to get it done in two visits but it all depends on how stubborn your scars are and if they'll need a second pass." She guided him to her chair and prepped her station.

Cam settled back into the chair and took a deep breath. Hunter grabbed a nearby stool and slid it over to sit close to him when Leslie stepped away for a moment to speak with another staff member to block out her schedule.

"Nervous?" Hunter asked.

Cam nodded.

"Why a sunrise? You didn't even need to think about it."

"My mom. We used to start in the garden so early we'd always take a break to watch the sun rise. She believed it was one of God's masterpieces," he finished with a sad smile. He looked over to Hunter. "Sunrises give me hope. Regardless of what happens, the sun always rises above everything."

Leslie returned to her station, slid her stool and table of items close to Cam, then began.

Cam barely felt the initial outlines of the design. It felt no different than a mild scrape of a sharp nail across his skin. He winced when she filled in some sections, coloring around some of the mild scars.

Maybe this won't be so bad.

He had spoken too soon.

Cam didn't turn to see her work but instinctively knew exactly where she was on his arm and which scar she would hit next. He tried to level his breathing, inhaling deeply and clenching his jaw when she colored over the two worst scars.

This. Fucking. Hurts.

He screwed his eyes shut and tried to bite back the pain. The scars that he hated for so many years would now be critical to the design. They would become the rays of light emitted from the sun and the raised skin would make it appear as if the rays were embossed on his arm.

The pain was too familiar.

His mind drifted to that day in the laundry room when his arm was first pierced.

"Cam?"

He opened his eyes as Hunter's voice jolted him back to the present. He hadn't realized his hand was shaking until the weight of Hunter's palm steadied him.

"Did I ever tell you about that one fishing trip to the Keys with my dad when we caught that sailfish that jumped into the boat?"

Cam shook his head, barely able to speak as he pushed through the pain of the billion hot needles poking his arm.

Hunter grabbed Cam's hand and began a rhythmic stroking of his fingers as he spoke.

He focused on the tone of Hunter's soothing voice and the gentle caress against his skin. His voice, always comforting, helped to shut out most of the pain. Hunter talked about driving trips with his family, endless fishing experiences, school growing up, Cole's obsession with his car, his addiction to Lucy's cookies, and even a few stories of his time in the Marines. Hunter talked about everything and nothing. Ramblings. He knew exactly what Hunter was doing, distracting him from the discomfort.

Cam smiled. Hunter had never spoken this much non-stop not even during their phone conversations at night.

After several hours of work, Leslie held up a mirror for Cam to view his arm. "It's a bit red right now but it'll look better once the ink settles. This is as much as I can do today but I think we can get this finished up with a second short visit. You can get a better look over there." She pointed to a large mirror at the side wall.

Cam immediately rose from the chair and walked over, stretching as he made his way to the mirror. He looked at his arm and was amazed to see the old ink was barely visible. The scars that once looked as if an animal had fiercely clawed the flesh of his arm now appeared as rays of sunlight.

Hope.

He bit his lower lip. It was the first time he looked at his marred arm and didn't see the scars or its ugliness. He shifted his arm to see it from every possible angle.

Hunter walked up from behind and placed his hand on Cam's waist. Cam stilled, looking at their reflection in the mirror.

"We look good together," Hunter whispered in his ear. Hunter's eyes sparkled with mirth, passion, and unmistakable love.

Cam had to look away.

Leslie walked over and applied cream on his arm and wrapped a plastic sheet to cover her work. She told Cam how to care for the design for the next few days then scheduled the follow up appointment in three weeks.

Hunter immediately withdrew his wallet but Cam stopped him.

"I want to, it was my idea to come here," Hunter said.

"And it was a great idea, but I got my first paycheck, and this is something I need to do." He looked at Hunter intently, pleading with him not to argue. He hadn't made much at the diner and after the percentage to the halfway house, and stashing a little for expenses, there wasn't much left. He needed some sort of independence. Even if he could only pay for a portion of the tattoo, it was still more than what he had been able to do for himself in the last ten years. "I know it's going to be expensive, at least let me pay for part of it."

Hunter looked at him and nodded.

Outside the shop, in broad daylight, he ignored the slight ache in his freshly tattooed arm and pulled Hunter in for the tightest embrace he had ever given. He screwed his eyes shut, trying to contain the emotions bubbling within. No one had ever taken the time to do something like this to make him feel good about himself.

Hunter's arms tightened around him, tugging him closer.

He pressed a kiss to Hunter's cheek and held him close. "Thank you."

Chapter TWENTY-TWO

More than a week after their weekend together, Hunter could still feel the pressure of Cam's body against his, the way they fit so perfectly together, the sounds he made, the lazy smile so early in the morning—the one that radiated like the sunrise Cam loved so much. Hunter smiled wistfully as he remembered Cam's shock Saturday evening after spending the day at the tattoo shop.

"Where are we going?" Cam asked as they drove away from the shop in the direction opposite from Hunter's house.

"I'm taking you out?"

"We're already out, smart-ass."

"Out on a date." Hunter looked over and glared. "Smart-ass."

"What do you mean?" Cam asked, scrunching his brows. "Like a dinner and walks on the beach type of thing?"

"Yeah, dinner, a movie, and I'm going to hold your hand the whole time. So don't argue with me," he responded, holding back a grin.

Cam mumbled something inaudible as he crossed his arms and looked out the passenger side window.

"What was that?"

"I said I'm not dressing up or anything like that."

"Okay," Hunter responded.

"I want steak."

"Steak?" Hunter asked with raised eyebrows, surprised Cam was actually continuing the conversation.

"Yeah, no pasta stuff. Julian overdoses on Italian and Matt has too many salads and vegetable dishes. I haven't had a steak since I went in."

Hunter smiled. "Okay. Anything else?"

Cam looked over. "Pick a short movie."

Hunter laughed. "Average movie is about two hours. Is that short enough?"

Cam didn't respond to the question.

When Hunter looked over, Cam had turned in the seat to face him. "Is two hours not short enough?"

Cam looked at him intently. "I can do a lot to you in two hours."

"Fuck," Hunter groaned. It was too easy to give in to Cam but Hunter knew he needed to stick to his guns. "Dinner, then a movie...a short one. Afterward, we go back to my place and hibernate the rest of the night and most of Sunday if you want."

"All of Sunday."

"Most, not all. And that's not up for negotiation. I want to take you to Bayside for a while."

"What the fuck for?" Cam asked, exasperated. "You know I'll put out. You don't need to wine and dine me."

Hunter elevated his tone. "I'll spend time at the diner while you're on breaks during the week, but on *our* weekends, you're mine, and I'm showing you off, taking you out, and holding your hand the whole fucking time. Got it?"

Cam scowled and exhaled heavily. "I'm paying for something," he grumbled, finishing the conversation.

Hunter smiled as he remembered their date. The sounds Cam made while enjoying his steak were torturous. Cam was no doubt teasing him, trying to cut their date short, but Hunter was not giving in. He wanted Cam to know how much he enjoyed every moment he had with him, regardless of whether they were in bed. After finally realizing it was a losing battle, Cam eased into conversation over dinner and nuzzled Hunter while they sat in the theater watching a movie featuring The Rock.

"He's hot," Cam said casually.

"Not funny."

"You're hotter," Cam said before licking up Hunter's neck in the dark theater.

Hunter groaned. "Nice try. Watch the movie. There'll be a test afterward."

"You're impossible. I can't win with you."

"Nope, so stop trying."

"All of Sunday."

"Nope," Hunter said, trying to hide his smile.

"Okay," Cam said and settled back in his seat, still leaning on Hunter's shoulder.

Hunter knew Cam well enough to know there was something else spinning in his thoughts. "Okay?"

"Yup. You'll get Sunday but you're not sleeping a wink tonight. That way, we both win," he said nonchalantly as he watched the movie.

Hunter chuckled. There was no argument there. They'd both win with that arrangement. He slung his arm over Cam's shoulder and pulled him closer. "Okay," he said, smiling.

They watched the film for some time in silence. "Hunter?" Cam asked quietly after a while, before the movie was about to end.

"Yeah?"

"I like date night," he finished in a whisper before nuzzling closer in Hunter's embrace.

Hunter touched his lips and closed his eyes as he remembered Cam's mouth pressed against his—soft and gentle yet strong and demanding. The way they held hands walking in Bayside completely disregarding the crowd of people, the laughs they shared at the street shop items with the snarky sayings, and how they sat together closely as they listened to the Sunday band play a set by the water. He wanted more kisses, more smiles, and more than just weekends.

The knock on the door brought Hunter out of his daydream.

"Hey, boss?"

"Come in," Hunter said, and he waved in Jessie. "What's up?"

"The mayor's office called, he wants to meet with you today."

"We have our meeting for the end of the week. Did he say what this was about?"

"No, just that he would like to bump the meeting up to this afternoon. I told him you were in court this morning so he's leaving his afternoon open to speak with you."

"Have we received any more files?"

"Nope."

"What about Mel?"

Before Jessie had a chance to answer, Mel appeared in the doorway.

"What about Mel?" she asked casually.

Hunter looked over Jessie's shoulder as his assistant turned. "Have you gotten any more red files in the last three weeks?"

"Nope."

Hunter frowned. "Why would they have stopped all of a sudden?"

"Hey, honestly, we've got so many of them, I'm still working the files we have. I could use the breather," she said, taking the seat on the side couch.

Jessie took that as his cue to leave and looked back at Hunter.

"Thanks, Jess. I'll stop by later on. Here's the file from this morning's case and my notes at the end with the ruling."

With a nod, Jessie exited his office and shut the door on his way out.

"Mayor finally called for his meeting?"

"Yeah, today. Do you know what that's about?"

"Don't have a clue. He wants to meet with me next week as well."

"Why not just meet with the both of us here?"

"I don't know what's going on, but I can't meet this week. I've got to be in court in an hour and I'll be there all damn week on this case. I just stopped by to find out if you wanted to grab something quick for lunch before I have to head back to the courthouse?"

"I can't." Hunter sighed then looked at his watch. "I want to wrap things up here first then I'll grab something before heading off to see him. I don't know how long it's going to take."

Mel stood and glanced at her watch. "Frank can get pretty long-winded when he gets on his high horse." She stopped in the doorway before walking out and looked at Hunter.

"What?" Hunter asked after a few moments of staring.

"You look good. You look happy," she said with a teasing grin.

Hunter smiled. "I won another case this morning. That always makes me happy."

Mel shook her head and huffed a laugh. "Smart-ass. This is a different kind of happy, it's oozing out of every one of your pores. You're smiling too much. People are going to think you're a softy."

Hunter laughed and tossed the pad of sticky notes at the door before she ran out to avoid getting hit.

After some time, his phone vibrated across the desk. "Hey, what's up?" he said after seeing the phone display.

"Still nothing," Aidan responded in his usual direct manner. "I've got the day off tomorrow so I'm going to switch it up. Are you up for an all-nighter?"

Hunter looked at his morning schedule. "Yeah, I can swing it. I don't have court in the morning. What are you thinking?"

"Since our meet, every other day after work, I'm usually there seven to nine or ten at the latest…and nothing. I noticed a few changes between my last two visits so I know something's going on. I figured I'd call you and find out if you could go on a stakeout with me. Nothing's official so I can't get one of the guys in on this."

They coordinated the time and place to meet then disconnected.

Hunter's mind wandered, thinking of Cam, hoping they were closer to wrapping this up. He absently spun the woven blue bracelet on his wrist Cam had given him during their first weekend. They had walked past a shop at Bayside housing handmade items. Cam grabbed the dark blue braided bracelet with small silver beads. Cam inspected it as if he were some expert on the material and asked the shop owner if it was waterproof.

"Yes. All bracelets are wax coated."

Cam nodded, paid the person, then turned to Hunter and yanked his wrist. Cam remained quiet while he tied the material, securing the bracelet.

"It's the dark color your eyes get when you tease me," Hunter commented with a smirk.

Cam looked up after the double knot was complete and still said nothing. He pulled Hunter down for a demanding, branding kiss in the middle of the aisle of shops. He then grabbed Hunter's hand and continued walking down past the kiosks, as if nothing had happened.

Hunter rubbed his face in frustration, trying to return his focus. The stress was getting to Cam and it was only a matter of time before the man's anxiety kicked in again. He was putting up a great front for Hunter, but every now and then, Hunter could see the cracks in the façade when the fear would make its way to the surface.

He gathered a few files and his briefcase then headed out of his office. "I'm off. Lunch then meeting with the mayor," he told Jessie as he passed his desk.

Jessie nodded.

"I might be a little late coming in tomorrow so if something comes up, just give me a call, okay?"

"Yes, boss," his assistant finished with a smile.

Finally, he was out of the office and smiling as he made his way to the diner for a little piece of heaven.

* * * *

Hunter stood in line and watched Cam tend to the few lingering post-lunchtime customers. Cam's smile came a little easier and his stance less guarded.

His body, although still lean, was tighter and a little broader from the yard work at the halfway house. A slight tan colored his skin now, the faint golden tone further accentuating the blue in his eyes and the white of his smile. His hair had a sprinkling of highlights as if the sun had kissed his head. Sunrises gave him hope, but they also seemed to awaken a natural physical beauty that had been hidden for far too long.

"How can I help you? Sir," Cam said when it was finally Hunter's turn at the register.

Hunter leaned over the counter. "You know that drives me nuts."

Cam smiled and grabbed Hunter's tie to pull him closer. "I know." After a quick peck, Cam released him.

Hunter reached over and rubbed Cam's stubble. "Are you letting this grow out?"

Cam shrugged. He looked away and scratched his growing scruff. "It makes me look older."

"Since when do you want to look older?"

Cam shrugged again and fidgeted with the receipts.

Realization finally hit Hunter. He grabbed Cam's chin and forced him to make eye contact. "Are you doing that for me?"

Cam's mouth narrowed and his brows lowered. "There's not much I *can* do for you. So if growing some hair on my face will make you feel a little less self-conscious, then I'll grow a full fucking beard if I have to."

Hunter stroked his thumb on Cam's cheek. "You do a lot for me whether you realize it or not." He leaned over the counter and whispered in Cam's ear, "I do love it when your stubble scrapes across my skin."

Cam closed his eyes and exhaled heavily. He opened his eyes and looked over to the other customers in the diner.

"Have you had lunch yet?"

"Not yet. I was waiting to see if you'd stop by. Let me go get Bill so I can take my break," Cam said before walking to the back.

Bill emerged within moments and waved at Hunter. "Why don't you boys take a break and have lunch in the back room. I think Julian is starting to go stir crazy here. He could use a few minutes."

"You sure it's okay, Bill? I don't want to—"

Hunter stopped when Bill placed a hand on his shoulder. "I've never seen Lucy happier or healthier than in these last few weeks since Cam's arrival. And that, to me, is worth any drama anyone brings into this diner. I hate that you guys are going through this, but I know that as long as you guys are here, we're fine. She feels as if she's got a house full of kids and that's something we couldn't have. Now, go relieve Julian then suck face for a bit with Cam so you both can go back to work with a smile."

Hunter rubbed his face to hide his embarrassment. "Bill, you're worse than my dad," he grumbled.

Bill beamed and, for the first time, pulled Hunter into an embrace. "You've just made my day, now go."

"Thanks," Hunter said before retreating to the back room.

After Julian left and Hunter was alone with Cam, they sat at the table and prepared to have lunch.

Cam sat up and reached for Hunter's tie.

"What are you doing?" Hunter asked.

"You look uncomfortable," Cam said as he loosened the knot. "I don't want you feeling that way around me."

Hunter watched him and tried to stop the smile from forming on his face. It was the little things Cam did that spoke volumes about his feelings, whether he realized it or not.

Cameron looked over to Hunter and reached for his soda. He grabbed the straw in his mouth and a smile escaped. Hunter couldn't resist and gave him a quick peck on the cheek. A chill traveled his body when he rubbed his face against Cam's stubble.

Cam snorted a laugh. "You're like a big cat."

"Hopefully you're a cat person." Hunter nuzzled him and kissed the sensitive skin below his ear.

Cam inhaled sharply. "I like cats and dogs. So feel free to rub, growl, bite…"

Hunter kissed a trail along Cam's throat. He bit across Cam's jawline and peppered kisses along the side of his neck.

"You need to stop," Cam said breathlessly.

Hunter withdrew. The want in Cam's eyes was mesmerizing. Hunter pressed his forehead to Cam's and stroked the back of his neck. "You're addictive."

"You're not helping."

Hunter straightened in his seat and clasped Cam's hand. He could forgo the nuzzling as long as he had some form of contact.

Julian poked his head in the back room when he returned from his sanity break then retreated to the front dining area.

They finished their lunch and cleaned up the back room table.

"I'm going with Aidan to check out the house for an all-nighter to see if anything comes up," Hunter said.

Cam nodded, his mood sobered. "I'm sorry," he said quietly.

"Don't be."

"I can't help it. Everyone's adjusting everything because of me...you, Julian, Lucy and Bill. I don't want to be a bother."

"You're not a bother. We care. That's why we're doing this."

Cam nodded again and didn't say another word.

Hunter looked at the wall clock. "I've got to go." He rose from his seat and pulled Cam to stand. "I've got a meeting with the mayor and I'm not sure how long it will run."

"Okay."

"I'll call you when I get out of there."

Cam nodded again and reached for Hunter. He rested his head on Hunter's shoulder and took a deep, shaky breath.

"It'll be over soon, okay. Just hang in there," he said, rubbing Cam's back, hoping to soothe him.

"Please be careful," Cam said.

Hunter separated from the embrace and stroked Cam's cheek. He hated seeing the distress in Cam's eyes. "You, too. And remember, don't go anywhere without Julian by your side, okay? I don't want anyone to have an opportunity to get to you."

He kissed Cam good-bye and left the diner, hoping tonight's stakeout would be productive so Cam could finally move on from his nightmare.

* * * *

Hunter arrived at Mayor Frank Weston's office in the middle of the afternoon.

"Hi, Lydia, I'm here to see Frank," he said with a smile.

"He's in a meeting now but I believe he's wrapping it up." She picked up the phone to notify the mayor then hung up after a few seconds. "He'll be with you in a moment."

"Thanks."

He took a nostalgic walk around, looking at the various photos in the waiting area. Decades of history were framed on the walls, political figures shaking hands, front page news clippings of apprehended media-worthy criminals, building grand openings, and more. Hunter's chest swelled as he recalled some of the events and how proud he was to make a difference in his city. He circled the perimeter of the reception area as he waited, reliving the current history markers on the walls before ending up back by Lydia's desk. She diligently worked on the computer and answered the phones. Her inbox neatly stacked with documents, the stapler, sharpener, and pencil holder organized in a linear manner, the books sorted on the shelf, all of equal height in what seemed to be a progression—with the shorter books on the far right-hand side of the shelf, and the tallest on the far left.

He smiled as he thought of how organized she was—probably with a touch of OCD.

The smile slid from his face when he noticed the stack of red files neatly tucked upright against the tall books on the bottom shelf. His heart began to race, and he immediately looked up to Lydia with a questioning glare.

She looked at him at that very instant and gave him a knowing look. "Yes, Mr. Styles, I'll make sure to relay the message," she said, finishing the phone call.

He said nothing while he continued to look at the mayor's assistant.

"Things aren't always as they seem," she spoke quietly in a steady tone.

"I can see that. So it's you," he stated rather than asked.

She bowed her head subtly in agreement.

"Why?"

"Let's just say I don't always agree with everything I see and hear and this is my way of trying to change things."

"Why not just go to someone with everything you know?"

"It's a lot more complex. I don't know everyone who's involved, and I'm just one person with too much knowledge of things I've heard. Besides, I have an aversion to the thought of mysteriously disappearing and having everything swept under the rug."

He glared at her, firmly, and continued in the low tone to avoid anyone listening to their conversation. "The red files. Scapegoats?"

"Yes."

"Why?"

"Easy targets who wouldn't turn and seem to know tiny bits of information which, together, can add up," she responded quietly and quickly as she casually looked around to ensure their exchange remained private.

Hunter spotted a stack of the white envelopes with the blue stripe on the return address area on her desk, the same used to deliver Cam's file that day to his office. "Why not the red for that one? Why this?" he asked as he touched the envelope to clarify his question.

"That was for you. I didn't want to risk someone seeing the red and being alerted. If anyone is going to be able to do something with that particular one, it's you. I don't know much more than what was in there, but I do know that whatever it is he knows makes them very nervous. It's been quite a frenzy since they discovered his release."

"Why?"

"They didn't know he was out, and getting information on a current residence has not been easy through their regular channels. It was all very sudden to them and they don't like surprises. Seems it wasn't part of the plan to let him out."

"Out early?"

"At all."

Hunter's breath hitched. "They tried to…eliminate him while inside?"

"Eliminating him would have shown some level of mercy. They tried to break him, hoping he would do it himself, but he's apparently much more resilient than they had anticipated. From what I've gathered, it seems they have a team inside and throughout the system. So all the red files go back in and they will slowly begin to fade away."

"Why me? Why am I the one you knew would do something?" he asked hurriedly. The mayor would conclude his meeting at any moment.

"Because they talked about whether *you* needed to be watched as well so I knew you weren't part of this."

That raised Hunter's hackles more than they already were. "Are they watching?"

"Not closely," she responded. "They are listening to your office line. They've partially disregarded you as an overworked county employee."

"Good."

They feigned a conversation regarding one of the pictures on the wall when Frank emerged with another person from his office. "Hunter," Frank greeted loudly. "I'm so glad you're here."

Hunter shook his hand and plastered on his best fake smile. "Hello, Mayor Weston. I was told you wanted to meet with me."

"Yes, yes. Come on in. Lydia, please hold all my calls."

"Yes, sir," she responded as the door closed.

"Congratulations, I heard you had another win this morning in court." The mayor took his seat behind the desk and signaled Hunter to sit in one of the opposite chairs.

"Thank you, sir," he said as he sat. "So what brings me here today?"

"A man straight to the point, I like that," he responded with a boisterous laugh. "We need more straight shooters."

Hunter smiled at the irony. "I agree."

"Please, call me Frank."

"Very well, Frank," he emphasized the name.

"I wanted to talk to you about your future plans."

"Plans?"

"Yes, what are they? Do you wish to move up in the ranks or do you wish to transition over into a political role?"

"I've been a bit up to my eyeballs lately with work and haven't really thought much about it."

"Yes, we've noticed you've been putting in a lot of hours."

"We?"

"Of course. I've noticed because you've helped me bring down the crime numbers tremendously since the last election, Melanie raves about you all the time, and the judges"—he laughed—"man, they're happy when you walk into a courtroom because they know they've got a short case—quick and simple without all the courtroom smoke and mirrors. You go straight for the jugular and you end the cases quickly. They love the fact that they don't need to put in the extra hours to listen to the excess bullshit."

"Thank you."

"So, let's talk about your future."

"I'm assuming this has been on your mind more than mine at this point."

The mayor laughed. "See, straight for the jugular."

Hunter played along and laughed, sitting back in his chair and crossing his legs.

"Which would you prefer, state attorney or a councilman position?" he inquired.

So this is his way of buying me. Shit. "What about Melanie?"

Frank stood and walked over to his minibar to pour himself a drink. "Would you like one?" He pointed to the whiskey glass.

"No, thank you. I'm still on the clock."

The mayor laughed and shook his head. "Mel is a bulldog in the courtroom, and I don't want to lose that. But I'd like to have you in a more relevant position."

"I thought I helped you with the crime stats, that's not relevant?" he couldn't resist challenging.

The mayor laughed louder. "My goodness, it's no wonder you win cases. What I meant was, in a position where you could reap the rewards of your hard work. Just tell me which position appeals to you most, and I'll take care of the rest. It would be great to promote you as part of my team with the upcoming reelection."

"Can I think about it?" he asked. He didn't want either role, especially not with everything going on, but there was no way he was going to admit to that now and risk revealing himself.

"Sure! The sooner the better of course."

"Of course. Was that all, Frank?"

The mayor laughed again. "Anxious to get back to work, I see."

"Always. Gotta work on keeping those crime stats down for you." He laughed, sick to his stomach at this point, but trying his best to maintain the façade of bullshit.

"Don't let me keep you. Let me know once you've made your decision. I'd love to have you move up in the ranks."

Hunter stood from his seat, ready to race out of the mayor's office. He extended his hand to Frank with a half smile. "Thank you."

The mayor gave his political picture smile and firmly shook his hand. "No, thank *you* for your hard work."

Hunter walked out of the mayor's office and closed the door. He took a deep breath and steeled himself before taking a step. He looked over at Lydia as he passed her desk.

"Be careful." She glanced at him, stacking the files in her inbox.

He casually nodded, acknowledging he had heard her concern, and then walked out to the hallway, avoiding contact with others.

Finally finding the men's room, he pushed inside and splashed some water on his face to try and cool the boiling heat from the anger slowly working its way to the surface. He dried his face then took a deep breath to steady himself. One of the reasons he had opted to branch into the field of law was to make a difference in his city, reduce crime, and hopefully make his town a safer place to live in. He couldn't believe he was now getting pulled into a circle dirtier than the streets that he tried so hard to clean up. He was disgusted and pissed at not having seen the bullshit that surrounded him and enraged that Cam was a target. There was no way he was going to wait and let this all play out anymore on their time table.

A straight shooter who went for the jugular? They had no fucking idea just how right they were.

Chapter
TWENTY-THREE

"So, you and Cameron are a thing?" Aidan asked as they sat in his dark truck watching the house. After staring at the empty house for a few hours, it seemed inevitable the conversation would steer in this direction.

Hunter lowered his binoculars and looked at his friend. "Yeah," he responded with a smile.

"I'm assuming it's serious or headed in that direction."

Hunter nodded. "I'd like to think so."

"He looks like a good kid—"

Hunter cringed. "He's older than he looks."

Aidan huffed one of his rare laughs. "I think you've developed a complex since your birthday. He's obviously crazy about you."

Hunter eased back into the seat and smiled. "He's a great guy who's been dealt a shitty hand."

"I did some poking around. You do realize some of this shitty hand he's been dealt is going to rub off on you, right?"

Hunter rested his head back and sighed. His friend knew him well enough to know he'd do anything for Cam if the situation called for it. "Yeah, I know. I accepted the consequences the moment I set foot in the halfway house to see him. At the end of all this, I really can't see myself doing this anymore anyway."

"Have you thought about what you want to do?"

"That seems to be the question of the day." He laughed sardonically then told Aidan about his meeting with the mayor earlier that day. "So I'm thinking when all this is over, I'll take the money I've been stashing for years, retire, and go fishing or something."

"That's what old people do."

"Fuck you."

Aidan chuckled as he looked over to the house.

"Let's take turns, one of us naps while the other is on watch then we switch off. No sense in both of us missing out on some sleep," Hunter suggested.

"I call dibs on the first sleep shift." Aidan adjusted his seat back and closed his eyes.

"Damn, man, at least give me a chance to respond," Hunter grumbled.

"You're too slow at your age," Aidan said with a hint of a smile.

"Fuck you."

* * * *

"Heads up!" Hunter nudged Aidan's shoulder to wake him.

"What is it?" Aidan asked, immediately alert.

"A car just pulled up over there," Hunter said as he pointed to the back of the house.

Aidan looked at his watch. "It's two in the morning." He grabbed the camera with the telephoto lens from his bag as another car pulled up the side of the house.

"The mayor just drove up." Aidan clicked shots of the man who exited the third vehicle.

Hunter shifted his view and confirmed the man who had arrived was Frank. "What the fuck is going on here?"

"It looks like a meeting, it's too perfectly timed. Can you make out any of the other three people?" Aidan asked.

"Not with this shit," he said, handing over the binoculars. "Is this police issued? We should have brought our service ones. Give me the camera."

Aidan handed over the camera and took the binoculars. "Anything you see, you click a shot, we can figure things out later when we see it on the monitor."

One of the people took out a paper and waved it to the others. The larger figure then corralled everyone into the house.

"Shit."

"What?" Aidan said.

Hunter clicked a series of images as the other three people entered the house.

"What is it?"

"Hold on, I need a second look to be sure," he said, patiently waiting for the people to become visible again.

After a few moments, the four individuals emerged from the house. Hunter continued to click off more photos.

"That was quick and it looks like they're pissed," Hunter said, observing the stabbing hand gestures of one of the smaller shadows toward one of the bulkier figures. He waited anxiously for them to enter the cars. "C'mon, c'mon, c'mon."

"Mayor's gone," Aidan announced as one of the vehicles drove away.

"Bingo." Hunter clicked off the images he needed when the remaining three people were exposed by the interior car lights. He sighed, returned the camera to Aidan, then leaned back in his seat. The beginnings of one hell of a headache formed behind his eyes.

"Talk to me. I know that *we're fucked* look. What did you see?"

Hunter turned his head and saw Aidan reviewing the images in the camera's LCD display. He took the camera from him and fast forwarded to select the image where the faces were visible.

"The large guy, that's Anthony Sprinter, he's one of the attorneys who defended Carlos Ortega in that case that got thrown out by Mackler. He's also one of the guys who was at the diner looking for Cam that morning."

Aidan's jaw muscles clenched. "You sure?"

"Yeah."

"Do you know the other two?"

"Yeah," Hunter confirmed.

"I think the pissed off guy poking Sprinter was probably one of the bosses—if not *the* boss," Aidan assessed.

"That's what I'm afraid of."

"Why?" Aidan asked, still scanning the images.

"If that's the case, then his name is Rick."

"How do you know him?"

"Because the person next to him, holding his hand, is Mel."

Chapter
TWENTY-FOUR

Cameron was having breakfast in the kitchen with Matt and Julian before heading into the diner. Luke's girlfriend had picked him up early at the halfway house to take him to work and Cole was on another job interview.

He heard a knock at the rear door that startled a jump in response.

"Stay here," Julian instructed as he walked to the back of the house.

Moments later, Hunter joined them in the kitchen. Hunter immediately pulled him into an embrace, his shaky breath warming Cam's ear.

Cam tightened his hold on him. "You look tired, you okay?"

Hunter shook his head as he released Cam. "We've got a problem."

"What's going on?" Julian asked.

"The shit is a bit deeper than I think any of us had guessed."

"Who's involved?" Matt asked.

"Everyone."

"Hunter?" Julian asked, prompting him to continue.

Cam wrapped his arm around Hunter's waist to offer the same support he'd received from this man on several occasions.

Hunter looked to Cam and cupped his face as he delivered a gentle kiss. "I need you to sit down for this."

After grabbing one of the chairs and taking a seat next to Cam, Hunter let out a long sigh then told them about the meeting with the mayor and the career bribe. After another pause, he finally revealed who he and Aidan had seen last night at the house.

Cameron reached out and placed his hand behind Hunter's neck. "I'm sorry."

"Don't be, I just need you to hang in there. Julian, I need you to be extra vigilant the next few days."

"What else is going on outside of this clusterfuck?" Julian asked.

Hunter looked over to Cam and grabbed his hand. Cam entwined his fingers into Hunter's and squeezed tighter, the worry in Hunter's eyes triggering his pulse to speed.

"Seems they're not happy about Cam's early release."

"I figured they didn't want me getting out early," Cam said, perplexed.

Hunter held Cam's gaze steadily. "The plan was for you to not get out at all."

Cam tried to put up a strong front but he was slipping. "What do you mean?" he asked quietly.

Hunter squeezed his hand tighter. "They're scared of what you know. They haven't been able to find where you're staying, but I'm guessing that's just a matter of time at this point since they know where you work."

"Everything is running a little slow," Matt clarified. "Cam's record was just updated with employment information, but *this* house is still not showing. I'm guessing it's because it's so new we're still not coming up in the search results in the BOP housing system. Sam had a hell of a time getting the guys scheduled to come here."

"Let's work on the assumption that they know since he got the job the day after getting here. Matt, you don't accept any deliveries from anyone. Have them leave that shit outside. No government staff unless there's an appointment. I don't care who it is, no one."

Matt instantly nodded at Julian's instructions.

Cam wasn't sure when or if any additional discussions happened after that point. The voices around him began to fade into a hum. All he remembered was Matt and Julian leaving the kitchen.

He was still in a daze when Hunter pulled him up from the chair. "Hey, you're going to be fine."

Cam's head was spinning, still trying to process all the information. His arms instinctively found their way around Hunter's shoulders for support.

Hunter whispered in his ear. "I'm not giving up on you. I just need you to hang in there. Besides, we've got another weekend coming up," he finished in a more playful tone.

Cam rested his head on Hunter's shoulder and sighed. "That's what's gotten me through most of this week," he finished with a smile as he withdrew.

Hunter held him closely and gently placed a kiss on his lips. He searched Cameron's face, the worry still etched in his expression.

"It feels as if I've been fighting for so long, I just get tired of it, you know?" He smiled weakly. "I'll be okay."

Hunter rubbed Cam's cheek with his thumb. "I know you will. You're tougher than you know and a lot tougher than they expected you to be. Just a little while longer and this will be all over."

"You think so?" he asked hopefully.

Hunter chuckled. "It better. I think I've gotten a gray hair or two in the last few weeks so we've got to wrap this up before you start to think I'm getting too old for you."

"I don't think you're old," Cam smiled. "Sir."

As expected, the color began to creep into Hunter's face.

Cam's smile grew and he pulled Hunter in for a quick kiss. Hunter's hands spread around his waist to the small of his back.

Cam brushed his cheek against the side of Hunter's neck and inhaled the scent he had come to associate with peace and safety. He let Hunter's heat and strength envelop him in a protective shell. He leaned into Hunter and closed his eyes, enjoying the last few moments before Hunter left.

* * * *

Cam heard a faint noise. He sprang from the bed and neared the doorway to listen more closely. He quietly opened the door to find a barefoot Julian in the hallway wearing his sleep pants with a bat in hand. He looked over to Cam and signaled him to go to Cole's room. Cam shook his head with determination, willing to stay and fight if needed. Julian gave him a piercing stare, pointed the bat at him, and then pointed the bat at Cole's room, not leaving any room for discussion.

Cam knew this look in Julian. It was pointless to argue. He made his way quietly to Cole's room.

"I want to help Julian," Cole complained in a hushed tone as Matt spoke to the police on the phone.

"Shut the hell up," Luke said.

Cam shushed them both and listened for any noises in the hallway. One thing he'd learned about fights was the value of the element of surprise. With a stampede of guys, it was too easy to reveal where they were. He peered out of Cole's room into the hallway. He saw Julian slowly take a few steps forward and look between the balusters of the stairwell. Then, within seconds, Julian jumped over the railing and a fight broke out. Cam immediately sprinted out of the room with the others following closely behind.

He was able to make it downstairs within seconds to find Julian lifting a screaming, large man by the throat with the bat. Even though the man was both tall and wide, Julian held him up off the floor where the man was practically on his tippy toes to avoid choking.

A small trickle of blood stained Julian's temple.

Cam looked over and saw the gun thrown on the floor.

Julian looked at him and followed his line of sight. "Don't touch that," he said firmly.

Cam nodded then ran to the back closet and grabbed the sledgehammer he'd used to break the concrete out back. When he reappeared, sledgehammer in hand, Julian arched an eyebrow.

Julian looked back at the man he was holding against the wall and sneered in his face. "You know, if you think you can get through me, you're still going to have to get through him. And he's not too happy right now that you guys keep fucking with him."

The big guy looked over to Cam and smiled. His face reddened and strained. "Hi, Ken. You're prettier than I remember."

A wave of rage surged in Cam. Everything dimmed except the pounding in his ears and the son of a bitch who had just spoken. A veil of red blinded him and launched him forward with the sledgehammer in hand.

A force pulled him by the waist and threw him to the ground. His limbs were stretched and held. His vision still blurred from the anger.

Just like before...when the guards held me down to beat me.

"Get off me!" Cam struggled to break free. His neck corded with the yell. His veins were ready to burst. He writhed, pushed, pulled. It was useless. He yelled again and grunted, forcing his weight against the hold on him.

"Cameron!" Julian yelled. "Snap out of it!"

His face was slapped. His chin gripped tightly. "Dude, snap out of it."

Cameron's chest heaved with each breath. His vision focused on mismatched eyes staring at him. "Get off me," Cam yelled at Cole who straddled his chest. His face heated and the thumping in his head needed release. He pushed his head back to see Luke pinning his hands. "Let go of me, right fuckin' now!"

"You want to go back inside for this piece of shit? I don't think so. Chill, man. Julian's got this," Luke said, tightening his hold on Cam's wrists.

"Aidan's on his way." Matt knelt by Cam. "Cam, J has this guy and he's not going to let him go until Aidan gets here."

Cam's gaze shifted from Matt to Cole. "Get the hell off me, now," he yelled again as he fought the tight wrestle-like hold Cole had on his body and legs.

"Dude, I'm an Italian who was raised with big brothers. Stop fighting."

The big guy managed to chuckle.

Julian's muscles flexed as he pushed the bat deeper into the man's throat. "You're begging for me to break your other knee cap. Shut the fuck up," he warned through gritted teeth.

Matt gently placed his hand on Cam's forearm drawing his attention. "Cam, please…you're safe here. I need you to try to calm down. I know you're angry, but don't let this guy screw up all the progress you've made."

Cam looked up at Matt and saw the concern. He closed his eyes and tried to calm his breathing. His mind drifted to Hunter, his touch, the sound of his voice. He imagined Hunter's fingers at the base of his spine, caressing him with his fingertips. His breathing began to level and his pulse began to slow to a normal rate. He took a deep breath then opened his eyes to look over at Julian. *Yeah, he's got it under control.*

"Guys, please let me go." He looked up at Luke.

Luke peered at him for a second, nodded, and then freed Cam's wrists.

Cole looked at him. After assessing him, he finally released his grip and slowly stood then reached out a hand to help Cam stand.

Cam took the offered hand and stood. He rubbed his wrists and flexed his fingers, trying to get some feeling back into them. Damn Luke was a brute bear. He looked over to the man who was reddening under Julian's bat-lock hold. The same man he had seen at the house that night. The same man who had reported back about seeing Brad's boyfriend and ultimately affected almost a third of his life. He closed his eyes, bent over, and rested his hands on his knees. He took a few deep breaths and tried to control the anger that threatened to take over again.

His thoughts returned to Hunter, and how this could potentially be another step closer to ending all this bullshit. Being together with Hunter, alone, without all this drama…*that* was enough to bring him to the point of serenity. He opened his eyes and found himself more relaxed. He straightened and took a deep breath.

"You think this is all—"

"Shut the fuck up, asshole," Cole said, stuffing the sock he had just removed from his foot into the goon's mouth. "I've got another one ready if you think you can talk through that."

Cam gave Cole a wry grin. Cole grabbed the sledgehammer off the floor and stood quietly next to Julian's left side while Luke stood on his right holding a PVC pipe. They guarded him like watch dogs, waiting for their command to attack.

These guys were there for him and had the situation under control. Cam did what he had never felt comfortable doing...he turned his back and walked away.

Matt followed him into the kitchen and silently started a fresh pot of coffee. Cam pulled out a chair and took a seat. He crossed his arms on the table then hunched over to rest his chin on them.

He didn't move from this position until Aidan arrived at the scene about five minutes later.

"You okay?" Aidan asked, taking a seat next to him.

Cam nodded, still resting his chin on his crossed arms.

"I called Hunter on the way here. He should be arriving any minute."

Cam nodded again, not saying a word.

Aidan patted him on the shoulder then returned to the living room to rejoin the police officers who had arrived.

Moments later, Hunter raced into the kitchen. "Cam?" he asked with the worry crease evident between his brows.

Cam slowly stood. "I'm okay."

Hunter took the few steps to reach him and scooped him up, almost lifting him off his feet into one of the tightest embraces Cam had ever felt. He wrapped his arms around Hunter's shoulders and simply held on. Cam didn't panic, he wasn't freaking out, he wasn't dazed. Clearer than he had been for some time, he realized that, finally, he had a few people around him who cared. For the first time, he thought maybe there would be a life for him after all this was over.

Hunter's body shook in his arms. He tightened his hold on Hunter. He couldn't remember what life was like when he didn't have to look over his shoulder every moment. But somehow, hope had bloomed within him that it was a possibility, and it was simply because of this man who held him so tightly.

Hunter loosened his hold on Cam and searched his face.

Cam smiled and stroked Hunter's cheek. "I'm okay and I'm hanging in there. How about you do the same?"

Hunter exhaled and chuckled. "You never cease to amaze me."

Cam's smile grew even more as he reached for Hunter again. He tightened his hold on this man, never wanting to let him go.

* * * *

"You're good for him, you know," Matt casually said, walking up to Hunter.

"He's good for me, too," Hunter responded, intently watching Cam as he spoke with the police about the break-in. "I just want to see him happy and at peace."

Matt looked at Hunter appraisingly. "As long as you're a part of that, I think he can be." He patted Hunter on the shoulder then walked off to sit with Julian who was still being interviewed by another officer.

Hunter stayed with Cam until the police finished their questioning. He'd occasionally observe him as he answered each question, checking his tone of voice, body language, gestures. Hunter didn't detect any panic or worry. Cam was composed and responded to each question as thoroughly as possible without letting his emotions take control.

Hunter was a strong man, but didn't know if he could live life completely isolated from friends and family and always on guard. It was the kind of thing that totally screwed with a person's head. He remembered one of the many times he went on a mission with a skeleton crew, isolated for twelve weeks in a foreign country with no contact outside of his small team—always on guard, watching over his shoulder, their shoulders. Adrenaline would pump in his body at will, endlessly, keeping him focused, in charge. His leadership never wavered, his steadiness never in question. He did what he had to do to protect his crew, but the undercurrent of fear and panic wore away at him. When he returned home, the slightest sound or quick movement would set him off balance, push him into a tailspin of anxiety and dread. He hated the loss of control, which ultimately drove him to leave the service after eight years.

He didn't know how Cam was able to maintain his sanity and handle this for almost a decade.

He reached out and grabbed Cam's hand. Fingers entwined, he didn't care about the looks of the remaining police officers in the room. He needed the contact. To know Cam was still with him and to let Cam know he was there for him.

Cam responded to the questions without chancing a look at Hunter. He squeezed Hunter's hand in acknowledgement.

Hunter sat quietly for the remaining ten minutes of questioning until the last officer left.

"Thanks," Cam said.

"I didn't do anything." Hunter raised their clasped hands and kissed Cam's knuckles.

Cam smiled. "For that. For knowing exactly when I needed you." He leaned into Hunter and pressed his nose against the crook of Hunter's neck.

Hunter chuckled and wrapped his arm around Cam's shoulder. "I just wanted to hold your hand. I'm not psychic or anything like that."

"Just take a damn compliment. You're my hero so you're just going to have to deal with it."

Hunter smiled, kissed Cam's forehead then tugged him closer.

"That's it, everyone's gone," Matt said after closing the back door behind the last of the investigators.

"Well, that's my cue to leave." Hunter looked at his watch before standing. He'd be lucky to get a few hours' sleep before heading into the office in the morning.

"Do I go to work tomorrow as if nothing happened?" Cam looked at Hunter expectantly.

"Yeah, don't raise any additional red flags. I'll pick you up at five from here after work."

"Is that still okay?" Cam asked Matt.

"I've got you guys already set up with the weekend pass before all this happened. Besides, you're still local so this shouldn't be an issue," Matt said.

Cam sighed and smiled at Hunter.

"C'mon, kid. Get your ass upstairs," Luke said as he herded Cole up the stairs.

"Hunter, I want a ride in that baby one of these days," Cole yelled before disappearing.

"I swear that guy is obsessed with my car," Hunter said before wrapping his arms around Cam from behind.

"You have no idea," Cam said with a chuckle.

"We're heading off to bed. Cam, lock up, okay?" Matt asked with a yawn as Julian guided him up the stairs.

"No problem, and hey, Julian?"

Julian stopped midway and looked over to Cam.

"Thanks."

Julian half smiled in response before nudging Matt up the remaining steps.

Cam rubbed Hunter's arms and pulled on the blue bracelet.

"Don't pick at it," Hunter said, kissing Cam's cheek.

Cam looked up and over his shoulder. "I can't believe you never take it off."

"I like it. It reminds me of you."

"Cheap, ragged, and twisted."

Hunter turned Cam in his arms. "Unique and thoughtful."

"You're reading too much into it." Cam wrapped his arms around Hunter's neck and rested his head on Hunter's shoulder.

"Bullshit. You're an undercover romantic, admit it."

"Shh. I'm trying to have a moment here before you leave. Don't ruin it," Cam said. Hunter could swear he heard the words said through a smile.

Hunter loved to tease Cam but secretly craved the day when Cam would just open up and voice his emotions. He lost his train of thought as Cam alternated between kisses and bites along Hunter's jaw.

"Mmm. I might not want to leave if you keep doing that," Hunter said.

"Might? Shit, we're out of the honeymoon phase already?"

Cam's throaty laugh, the soft kisses, the gentle bites, and...*oh fuck*...the lick up the side of his neck, were wreaking havoc on Hunter's control.

"Promise me something," Cam said.

"Anything."

"We'll do some wall slamming tomorrow night," Cam said as he continued his torture.

"You keep this up I won't make it to a wall."

Cam placed a last kiss on Hunter's lips before retreating. "Then I guess I'll stop...for now," he finished with a wicked grin.

"Evil man."

Hunter didn't see the usual tells and quick shifts in expressions to indicate Cam was freaking out. He couldn't imagine Cam had been unscathed after what had happened. "You sure you're okay?"

Cam shrugged and quieted for a few moments. He bit his lower lip and shuffled his feet. "I lost it earlier."

"Panic attack?"

Cam ducked his head.

Hunter cupped Cam's face and gave him a gentle kiss. "Are you okay now?"

Cam nodded. "I thought of you. That kinda grounded me."

Hunter's chest tightened and his breath caught in his throat. "You thought of me?" he said with a grin.

Cam shook his finger at him. "Don't get sappy on me. You need to go and get some sleep before work so you're well-rested for our weekend." He waggled his eyebrows.

Hunter laughed. "You too, lock the door behind me."

"Yes, sir."

The heat spread across Hunter's face. He looked at Cam from the corner of his eye, knowing he'd see a smiling Cam waiting for his reaction.

"I'll see you later."

Yup. Wall slamming weekend was definitely in order just to prove he wasn't an old fart after all.

Chapter TWENTY-FIVE

This was pure bliss. Cam would forgo the sunrise in the morning for a repeat of this. Waking in Hunter's bed, encased in his protective embrace with their legs tangled. Cam took a deep breath and closed his eyes as he gently rubbed the arms that held him. He exhaled and nestled a little closer to the warm, hard chest against his back, wrapping his arms around Hunter's hold. He had never felt freer in his life.

He had eagerly waited for Hunter to pick him up at exactly five in the afternoon the day before. They drove to his house for their weekend getaway, but after only one quick romp on the couch immediately after entering the home, they crashed. He was exhausted, they both were. The stress and anxiety of it all coupled with the lack of sleep finally wore him down. Cam couldn't even remember making it to the bedroom.

"Good morning," Hunter mumbled, in a still sleepy voice.

"Hi."

"Hungry?"

"Not yet," Cam answered, turning in the embrace then resting his head on Hunter's chest. He softly stroked the sprinkle of hair. "Can we just stay like this for a bit?"

Hunter tightened his hold on Cam and grunted an approval before drifting off again.

They woke mid-afternoon and decided to stay in for the weekend. They ordered pizza and managed to squeeze themselves on the couch together for hours as they watched movies Cam had missed during his time inside—a movie marathon with plenty of exploratory intermissions. Cam loved the quiet time with Hunter. He could stay nestled between those strong legs with his head resting against the muscled chest all weekend. He was safe in Hunter's arms and with an inner peace he hadn't experienced before.

Cam had lost count of how many movies they watched but knew he was too tired to watch another. They retreated to the bedroom and Cam eyed Hunter's desk area in the corner.

"What are you thinking?" Hunter asked with a raised eyebrow.

Cam bent his finger in a 'come here' motion.

Hunter obviously didn't need to be asked twice. He immediately pulled off his sleep pants and placed them at the foot of the bed. Cam quickly removed his pants and threw them to the side.

Hunter walked up to him and slowly snaked his arms around Cam's waist. "What's on your mind, Mr. Pierce?" Hunter said as he kissed Cam's jaw.

That seductive way Hunter huskily whispered and slowed certain words always seemed to make him shiver. He couldn't think between the nibbles, licks, and kisses. Each brush against his skin left him craving more.

They'd christened most areas of the house during their weekends, but Hunter's work area—desk, chair, and small sofa—had been almost sacred. He lured Hunter to the couch in the corner of the bedroom and pushed him down.

Hunter landed on the couch with a bounce, looked up at him, smiled, and played along. Cam walked over to the dresser and grabbed the lube and condoms. He returned to Hunter and straddled him, resting his weight on Hunter's lap.

"What are you up to, Mr. Pierce?"

A shiver traveled Cam's body at the sound of Hunter's tone.

A slow smile spread across Hunter's face.

Fucking tease.

"We haven't done it like this yet."

"Did you want to switch it up?" Hunter asked.

Cam dipped his head and traced Hunter's lips with the tip of his tongue. He retreated slowly then placed a few unhurried open-mouth kisses along Hunter's jawline, working his way up to Hunter's ear. "I like the way you feel inside me."

Hunter moaned and turned his head to capture Cam's mouth. Cam gasped when the whisper graze of Hunter's fingers traveled his body, down his spine. He closed his eyes and arched into Hunter's touch. He wanted to extend this, enjoy every second of pleasure Hunter always gave him, but the need to have Hunter overpowered him. He dove down for a frenzied kiss when Hunter's slick fingers began to prepare him. The slight burn, the stretch, it was exactly what he needed yet not enough. He pushed back and dug his fingers into Hunter's hard-muscled shoulders and pulled him closer, demanding more.

He ran his fingers up Hunter's neck into his hair and gripped tightly as he tried to steady the ravenous wave of desperation. He heard the rip of the packet and his pulse quickened with anticipation. Cam leaned forward and rested his forehead against Hunter's, trying to level his breathing.

He heard the snap of the cap. A slight whimper escaped and his grip in Hunter's hair tightened. Hunter lifted him and pulled him forward.

His heart beat madly.

He couldn't wait anymore.

He needed...wanted...

He threw his head back and moaned, relishing the sensation when Hunter finally entered him.

Hunter reached for him. Cam immediately grabbed Hunter's hands to stop him. He pushed the held hands above Hunter's head against the back of the couch. Cam watched Hunter's chest heave with each breath. He stared at Hunter and tried to telepath his desire, want, and need for him. Hunter closed his eyes and let out a moan as Cam sank deeper onto him. Hunter's head lolled to the side, his eyes lazily opened in a drunken stare.

Cam entwined his fingers with Hunter's and reached down for another kiss as he slowed the pace, pushing back, binding them closer, inch by inch. The muscles of his thighs burned from the forced tension as he moved slowly, sinuously, enjoying the rise and fall and fullness of Hunter filling him.

Hunter gasped and arched his body as he squeezed their hands tighter. He bit his lower lip and pushed his head back farther into the couch.

Cameron latched onto Hunter's neck and licked, kissed, and sucked, renewing one of his marks that dared to fade this past week. He continued to tug and pull at the sensitive skin until Hunter hissed under the pressure.

"I'm close," Hunter said, spellbound, his pupils dilated and his eyes colored in that shade of molten silver Cam loved so much.

"Wait for me," Cam commanded. He slowed the pace, wanting to extend their lovemaking as much as possible.

Hunter groaned with each slow grind. He could see the tension in Hunter, obvious restraint in every inch of his body. He heard a low rumble escape Hunter like the growl of a predator, the sound further igniting Cam's desire.

He released their hands and sat up. He grabbed Hunter's thighs as sparks of white light invaded his now blurred vision. Shocks of electricity began to travel up his spine and spread through his body—every muscle hypersensitive to the slightest movement, to the barest touch.

He wouldn't last long.

"Finish us off," he said weakly, unable to control the shudders that began to ripple within.

Hunter straightened and took control. He grabbed Cam's hips and bucked up repeatedly, unleashing the desire he had kept restrained. Cam was numb to everything but the feeling of Hunter inside him, the friction of his skin, the pressure of the grip on his hips. The spring that had coiled in his body finally snapped with one last powerful thrust and pushed him off the ledge. He gave in to each shudder and every pulse until he finally heard Hunter reach his peak.

Strong arms pulled Cam down moments later. He fell onto Hunter, still straddling him. He rested his head on Hunter's shoulder. Their shaky breaths mingled, their bodies quivered. Hunter held him tight until their breathing settled to their usual rhythm.

Cam smiled when Hunter's fingers trailed along the curve of his back until they reached the dip. The soothing circular patterns he traced on his skin always felt like an intimate caress. He sighed, his body melting onto Hunter's.

"I like this couch," Cam mumbled against Hunter's neck.

Hunter chuckled. "I think you like being in control."

"Sometimes," he said absently. "Does that bother you?"

"Not in the least. I like everything you do to me."

Cam stroked a single finger along Hunter's neck, smiling as he circled the mark he had renewed on him. "So if I wanted to blindfold you, make you beg, and have you at my mercy while I bend you over your desk—"

"I trust you. If I'm going to let anyone top me, it's you. No one's ever dared manhandle me the way you do and I fucking love it." Hunter nuzzled Cam's cheek and kissed him below the ear.

A chill traveled Cam's body. "Even though I've got you all bruised and marked," Cam said. He looked at Hunter and stroked a teasing finger along Hunter's full lips.

Hunter grabbed his exploratory finger and gave Cam a fierce glare. "I'm game for anything as long as it's you and only you. I don't fucking share."

Cam groaned as he delivered a lazy kiss. He was possessive of Hunter and tried not to linger on the reasons why but was happy to hear the territorial streak ran both ways. He sighed with contentment, glad to stay exactly where he was, brushing his lips against Hunter's and tracing each slope and curve, enjoying each twitch of Hunter's muscles under his touch.

Hunter wrapped his arms around Cam tightly and rose from the couch, taking Cam with him. He encircled his arms around Hunter's neck, never wanting to let go. He rested his head on Hunter's shoulder as he was hauled to the bed. The exhaustion overtook his body when he pressed against the soft mattress.

"I'll be right back," he heard Hunter say in a hushed tone.

A cool towel gently pressed against his skin before he drifted off to sleep with a smile on his face.

"Where are you going?" Hunter mumbled as he reached for Cam.

"I'm going to get something to drink, I'm thirsty as hell. Go back to sleep," he said, finally freeing himself from Hunter's hold. He loved how Hunter always seemed to have either an arm or a leg wrapped around him to keep him close in bed.

"I'll be right back." He grabbed the sleep pants at the foot of the bed.

Hunter groaned then shifted before settling back to sleep.

Cameron quietly shut the door when he walked out of the room. He knew his way around Hunter's place and exactly how many steps were needed in between rooms to avoid stubbing a toe. He walked into the kitchen and opened the refrigerator. He scanned the contents then decided on the juice at the back of the shelf. He closed the door and saw the looming shadow of a man waiting in the darkness.

He grabbed Cam by the throat with one hand and the bottle of juice in the other. The large man casually placed the bottle on the counter as he effortlessly held Cam by the throat. With his other hand now free, the man grabbed Cam's throat with twice the force. Cam reached for the grip around his neck and desperately clawed at the hands and fingers. His face burned and his vision began to blur. He kicked viciously when he was lifted off the ground, held only by the suffocating hold.

Save Hunter.

His heart raced, and he kicked, punched, and thrashed, trying to break free. The grip on his neck tightened and the heat and pressure in his face intensified. He had to fight, he had to break free.

Something.

Anything.

Save Hunter.

He gasped. He couldn't breathe. He could barely see.

His hands were roughly tied behind his back while another shadow taped his mouth. The tape would have stopped any screams if the suffocating pressure at his throat hadn't.

The breath-stealing grip around his neck stopped. The hold on his arms held him up as his body slumped.

"You're a little fucking troublemaker," the large man in front of him growled once he released Cam.

"Be quiet, Joe," the man behind him whispered with commanding authority. "Grab his feet."

Additional figures emerged from darkness like an army of ants. They came from the dining area off to the side and around back. They hid well in the shadows in their dark clothing and moved around silently with practiced barely-there shifts in movement.

Save Hunter.

His heart raced as panic surged throughout his body, awakening his limbs. He fought the hold on his arms. He didn't care what happened to him. *Hunter.* Warn him, get to him, protect him, and make sure nothing happened to Hunter were the only things that mattered.

Cam was on auto-pilot, thrashing, needing to break free.

Save Hunter.

A kick landed on one of the large shadows in front of him knocking them to the floor. Another came at him.

"Grab his fucking feet," the man behind him said in a hushed tone.

"He's kicking too damn much," the other shadow said. Even though it was a whisper, Cam could swear he heard a woman's tone in that voice. "Where the hell are the other knuckleheads?"

"They went to get the other guy," the large man, the one called Joe, responded.

Desperation began to build—he needed to get to Hunter. *Now.* The thought of something happening to him was too much to bear. Cam kicked with more force, pushing his body off the man in the back who held him tightly. He managed to land a second kick and the woman hit the edge of the pantry before she fell to the ground.

"You son of a bitch!" she hissed.

Cam yelled as much as he could, hoping some sound would escape his taped mouth and resonate throughout the silent house as a warning. His heart beat fiercely, echoing in his chest, head, and ears. His face was hot, ready to explode. The tension in his neck painfully building from his muffled yells as his head pounded. The trickle of sweat fell into his eyes, stinging, forcing them shut. He kicked with greater force and fought the hold on his arms, trying to free himself.

God, please.

Save Hunter.

The large man delivered a blow to Cam's stomach that instantly stopped him, followed by a second punch even harder than the first and another to his face. He doubled over in pain, an unbearable pressure in his stomach and a taste of blood in his mouth numbed him.

"Stay still, you little shit," Joe said through gritted teeth as he grabbed Cam's jaw and dug his fingers into Cam's pained cheek.

Cam couldn't focus on anything past the pain in his gut. He met the man's gaze—dark and filled with nothing but cruelty. His nostrils flared with each intake of breath. He could barely breathe past the sharp pain.

He released Cam's face and reached a hand over to help the woman off the ground. She stood and walked over to Cam to deliver a punch to his cheekbone. His head swung to the right and his vision blurred from the impact—compounding the pain in his face.

"That's enough, baby, you don't want to risk messing up your hand." The man behind him held Cam's arms painfully tighter. "It'll all be over soon," he whispered in Cam's ear.

Cam had a hard time focusing. His head throbbed and his vision was still blurred. He barely made out the other shadow that appeared in the room, shorter than the man who held him but just as muscular as the larger man standing before him. "So you're Brad's pretty boy?"

"Enough. Get the other guy," the man who held him ordered.

The other large shadow rose from the ground after recovering from the kick to the groin. "Hey, boss, where do you need me?"

"Go find out what's taking the guys so long."

Cameron heard a gunshot coming from the bedroom.

Oh God.

His vision snapped to the hallway leading to Hunter's bedroom.

He looked over and saw the man race to the hallway with a gun in hand.

Oh God. Please.

Cameron looked back at Joe and lost control as rage overtook his body. He threw his head back and made contact with the man holding his arms then launched forward into the large man with the mocking grin just as another gunshot echoed throughout the house.

* * * *

Hunter sat up in the bed with a start. His heart raced. Something wasn't right. He stilled and listened. He grabbed his cell phone off the night stand and quickly got out of bed to look for his sleep pants.

Gone. *Cam must have worn them when he went to the kitchen.*

He grabbed his discarded jeans from the side of the bed and quickly dressed. Barefoot and light on his feet, he stealthily walked to the door and listened while he absently redialed the last number on his cell.

"Hunter?" Aidan's alert voice came though the line.

Without saying a word, Hunter slipped the phone into his back pocket.

He straightened and backed up against the wall as he heard the faint click of the turn of the door knob. The door slowly opened and a man walked through followed closely by a second man.

"Where the fuck is he?" one man asked the other in hushed tones.

Hunter slowly came out from behind the door and jumped the man closest to him in a neck lock. The second man lunged toward them, gun in hand, while the man in his grip gasped for air. He jerked his arms snapping the man's neck in his hold then threw him onto the second man to slow his approach. The guy caught his limp companion and Hunter took advantage to downward kick the man in the knee.

The man howled in pain. Hunter sweep-kicked his good leg, knocking him off his feet, disarming him during the fall. Adrenaline raced through Hunter's body, recharging his muscles. He reached for the gun and was pulled back by the hair by yet another man entering the room. He elbowed backward at an upward angle and connected with the man's face, breaking his nose.

"What the fuck!" another man said when he entered the room.

Cam. I need to get to Cam.

Hunter's heart pounded furiously. He dove to the floor for the gun, quickly turned and took aim. He pulled the trigger and shot the new guy in the middle of the forehead. The man dropped to his knees then fell forward, slumping on to the floor. Blood seeped from his face and pooled by his head.

Another man ran into the room with a ready pistol. Hunter instinctively shot off another round, hitting the second man in the chest. The man clasped his shirt, fell to the ground, and coughed a spray of blood before his movements stilled.

Hunter was grabbed from behind by the man with the broken nose. They struggled and the gun slipped out of Hunter's hold. They fought to reach the weapon, grabbing and pulling, searching for purchase using each other's limbs as they slipped in the pool of blood. Finally, Hunter back kicked the man and leapt to reach the gun, turned, and discharged the weapon into an already bloodstained face to finish him off.

"Don't you fucking move!" came another voice from the doorway, behind Hunter.

Hunter stilled as much as his heaving chest allowed.

I can't help Cam if I'm dead.

"Drop the gun, now!" the man demanded.

Hunter dropped the gun, raised his hands, and slowly turned.

"What in the hell is going on in here?" asked another man he recognized as Rick from the stakeout. He looked around and surveyed the room. "What. The. Hell."

"Get up," the large man said.

Hunter slowly rose from the floor, his jeans and torso stained with blood.

"Move." The man stepped aside and signaled Hunter to walk through the doorway out into the hall.

Rick disappeared from the room and returned within moments with a roll of duct tape in his hand.

"Wait a minute, Joe," Rick ordered. He looked over to Hunter. "Hands together. There's no way you're getting out of this room with your hands free."

Hunter did as he was told and Rick wrapped duct tape around his wrists.

"You did all this by yourself?" he asked with a devilish grin. "I knew you had some skills based on our background check but my girl swore you were a paper pusher."

Hunter glared. He tried to control his heart rate, level his breathing. Too much adrenaline had pumped too fast. His lungs painfully burned with each intake of breath. He needed to calm himself, get to Cam, ensure his safety, but all he could think about were a thousand different ways he wanted to rip this man apart.

"You should come work for me. You've already killed off four of my best men, and it looks like Vinnie's going to have a little bit of trouble walking. I've got a few openings, what do you say?"

A steady glare was his only response.

"Suit yourself."

"What about Vinnie?" Joe asked.

Rick assessed the man on the ground still grabbing his knee. "Leave him here for now."

They walked out into the hallway, Rick in front, Hunter in the middle, and Joe followed with his gun pressed against the center of Hunter's back.

"So here we are," Rick announced. He entered the living room and flipped the light switch on, flooding the room with brightness.

Hunter immediately flinched as his eyes adjusted.

Cam sat on a chair, mouth taped, hands behind his back and his legs bound together. His eyes half closed, unfazed by the sudden brightness. His face showed the color of bruising on the left side, a patch of blood on the left side of his head, and a trail of blood along his right temple. He looked tired, drained, his hair drenched in sweat and stuck to his forehead.

"Cam," Hunter snapped in a forceful tone through the tightness in his throat. He needed to control the simmering panic as he watched Cam withdraw into his protective shell.

Cam swayed in the seat. His vision pegged to the floor, barely blinking, dazed in a trance, staring at nothing.

Oh, God. I'm losing him.

"Cam!" Hunter yelled past the unbearable tightness in his chest.

Cam blinked and looked up, a blank expression on his face. He made eye contact with Hunter and blinked repeatedly. His eyes rounded, his nostril flared, he forced a muffled yell and tried to stand only to be stopped by his bound feet and the knife Mel held at his throat.

"Sit still, you little shit," she said with a sneer.

Cam had a crazed look on his face. Hunter breathed a sigh of relief, even if only for this little ray of hope that Cam was still with him. Cam stared at him, his wild eyes roamed Hunter's body from head to toe, pleading.

"It's not my blood," Hunter said in a steady tone.

Cam closed his eyes and sighed heavily.

"Mel," Hunter said with a sneer.

"Hunter."

"Why?"

"Do you seriously think I want to sit in that fucking office every day for the rest of my life just barely making a living for all those ungrateful assholes? Please. We've talked about it a hundred times.

How there's something better out there. The difference is...I actually did something about it."

Hunter clenched his jaw. He tried to stave off the anger that boiled under the surface—at the helplessness and for not having seen through the façade sooner.

"Thing is, I know you like that shit...helping people and all that other crap. I was pushing to get you promoted. But noooo," she chastised in a sarcastic tone while wagging her finger. "You had to go after this one." She smacked the back of Cam's head. "I couldn't believe it when our friends told us you were with him last night, holding his hand while he was being interviewed."

Friends...dirty cops.

"We figured he'd probably be with you. So thank you. Now we finally have him."

Cam cringed when Mel flicked the knife in his hair.

Hunter's chest tightened. "If you hurt him—"

"What are you going to do? Sic Jessie on me or something?" she said with a laugh.

"Hun, don't tease. You didn't see the other room."

"How about we get this wrapped up already?" Mel said.

"Let's go," Rick said as Joe pushed Hunter toward the back porch. Rick walked over to Mel, gave her a gun and a peck on the cheek. "Use it if he acts up."

Before Hunter turned to move, he looked at Cam. "I'm coming back for you."

Cam closed his eyes and took a deep breath. When he opened them, he looked at Hunter with a softer expression in his eyes. Hunter could swear on everything that was sacred to him that Cam was telling him those three words he had been denied.

Hunter's heart raced and his breath caught in his throat. There was no way in hell he was letting this end in any way other than the two of them getting out of there alive and together.

He was pushed again. He turned to walk out to the back with Joe and Rick.

He was coming back for Cam, now he just needed to figure out how.

* * * *

He's coming back.

Cam closed his eyes and tried to calm his breathing. Hunter had never broken his word, and given the look in the man's eyes, Hunter would do everything he could to try to come back to him.

Hunter had revived thoughts, dreams, and wishes Cam had taken a decade to bury. The thought of losing him and returning to a life *pre-Hunter* was unbearable. His brain had switched off after the gunshot. He was in survival mode, disconnected from everything around him, all the sounds, scents, every sensation. Nothing mattered if Hunter wasn't with him.

Then he heard Hunter's voice in the midst of the darkness, one word, firm and strong. His name called—*commanded*—to return to this world. When he saw Hunter, he thought his eyes were playing tricks on him. Was it possible? There he was, alive and strong to renew his faith that maybe there was a chance they could come out of this together.

"What the hell are you thinking about?" Mel asked, with her arms crossed, holding the gun in one hand and the knife in the other.

Cam looked at her with a glare that would rival Hunter's. His nostrils flared with each intake of breath.

She bent over to look him in the eye. "What? Did I piss you off?"

Cam leaned back slightly, clenched his teeth then lunged forward and head-butted Mel's face.

"You. Son. Of. A. Bitch!" She dropped both the knife and gun to the floor to grasp her face as blood seeped out between her fingers.

Cam took advantage of her disorientation and kicked her with his bound legs. Mel fell back against the sofa table then to the ground, unconscious.

Cam threw himself onto the floor and tried to grab the knife with his bound hands. He felt the knife, gripped the thicker base, and tried to angle the serrated edge to cut the tape. He flinched when the knife cut his skin. *Shit.* He tried to look over his shoulder, in the reflection of the stainless steel appliances, anything to try to see what he was doing. Finally, he freed his hands with minimal damage, ripped the tape off his mouth and immediately began to cut through the tape binding his legs.

Mel stirred.

His heart hammered against his chest as he steadied his hands and focused on cutting the tape as fast as he could. Finally free, he reached for the gun and knife moments before Mel stood from the floor, ready to attack.

Keeping his distance from her, he held up the gun and pointed it at her.

A decade ago, he had killed a man by accident. Now, almost ten years later, he was staring down the line of sight of a gun consciously aimed at a woman.

Life was a bitch with a cruel sense of humor.

* * * *

It seemed like an eternity since Hunter had woken to what sounded like a muffled scream, when in reality, only a few minutes had passed. He stood on his back porch, his hands bound in front of him with Joe's gun pointed at point blank range.

"Since you plan on killing me anyway, why don't you tell me why?" he asked Rick.

"I thought that was obvious. You're a pain in my ass."

Hunter sighed heavily. "I'm not an idiot, I figured that one out. Why Cam? Why all this for him?"

Rick held Hunter's gaze. "Kid was in the wrong place at the wrong time. Fucked with the wrong guy…literally."

Hunter tried to contain his anger. "You wanted to keep him quiet, so you put him in prison."

"Wasn't my doing. I take care of my own shit. Although I'm pissed the fucker tried to give me a nose bleed," Rick said, casually pressing the bridge of his nose.

Hunter thought of the man's words, he immediately recalled a prior case. "I noticed you're a lefty. Was Preston something you had to take care of?"

Rick laughed. "Do you seriously think I'm going to start copping to shit? I know better than to say anything that's going to get my ass in the sling. Preston was an ass with a big mouth. But everyone knew that," he finished with a cynical shrug.

Joe looked off to the side of the house and backed away.

"What?"

"Sorry, boss. I thought I heard something."

When Joe neared again, Hunter reached out and grabbed Joe's head with his bound hands then thrust his knee into his face. Joe dropped the gun to grab his broken nose and lost his balance on the porch steps, tripping backward onto the grass.

Rick instantly withdrew a gun from his back and fired a shot at Hunter, grazing his arm. The adrenaline rush pushed him past the burn as he elbowed Rick in the face just in time to misguide his second gunshot upward to hit the edge of the roof. Rick immediately took two steps back. "Son of a bitch!" he yelled as he trained his gun on Hunter again.

Hunter didn't give him a chance to release another round, he quickly stepped forward swung his arms in a defensive move and disarmed Rick.

Rick immediately recovered and threw a punch, which landed on Hunter's cheek. The fucker was not slowing down in spite of a broken nose and Hunter couldn't keep this up much longer. Joe pulled his way up the steps and reached for the gun.

"Police, don't move!" Two men dressed in black, wearing vests, guns aimed, appeared from the side of the house.

About fucking time.

His heart raced and his breathing was labored.

Hunter heard a gunshot from inside. His head whipped around, and he launched back into the house, leaving the officers to handle the two men.

He bolted inside then froze when he saw Mel on the ground, dead. Her face was covered in blood, but the blood spilling from the side of her temple seemed to have been what finished her off.

Aidan stood by Cam and reached for the gun he held, still aimed at where Mel would have been standing. He noticed Aidan grabbed the gun by the barrel. *It's not hot.* Hunter released a sigh of relief. Cam would have battled with himself if he had taken the shot, regardless of the circumstances.

"It's okay, Cam, just let it go," Aidan coaxed as he held the gun shaking in Cam's grip.

"Cam," Hunter said, in a soft tone.

Cam was dazed, non-responsive. His cut arms were held straight out, holding the gun to aim at a target that was no longer there.

"Cam," he said in a stronger tone. He neared Cam as panic began to set in. He looked at Aidan who still held his hand firmly on the gun's barrel.

Finally, Cameron looked over to him, and when their eyes made contact, Cam's body became limp. Aidan took the gun from his hands as Cam fell to his knees.

Hunter rushed over to him on the floor and raised his bound hands around Cam to hold him. He released a breath he hadn't realized had been stuck in his throat. "I told you I was coming back for you," he said softly, rocking Cam in an embrace.

Aidan came up behind Cam with a knife and freed Hunter of the tape bindings.

Cam slowly raised his arms up Hunter's back. He lifted his head until their eyes met. Cam's voice shook. "When I heard that shot again—"

"I'm fine," Hunter said with a smile. "We're fine."

"I couldn't do it. I couldn't shoot," he said weakly.

"'Cause you're not a murderer."

"But she—"

"She was unarmed."

Hunter released Cam of the embrace and cupped his face. He had a lost, distant look in his eyes. His face was bruised and blood oozed through his hair. The white of one of his eyes was red, either from a hit or from broken vessels from forced pressure, he didn't know and couldn't bring his mind to think of it.

"Why couldn't I do it? I did it before."

"What happened ten years ago was different. Accident or self-defense, at this point, it doesn't matter. If you were a murderer, you could have easily pulled the trigger without thinking about it."

Hunter watched the play of emotions cross Cam's face. Finally, their gazes met. A youthful innocence made its way to the surface of those brilliant blue eyes.

"Say it," Hunter said.

Cam immediately threw his arms over Hunter's shoulders and held him tightly.

"You need to say it, Cam." Hunter winced when his shoulder throbbed.

"I'm not a murderer," he whispered.

Hunter smiled, released Cam, and placed a gentle kiss on his lips. "No, you're not."

Cam looked at Hunter's shoulder and his eyes darted back to Hunter's. "You were shot."

"Grazed, big difference. It just burns a little bit. Are you okay?"

"I've got a headache," he said quietly, resting his head on Hunter's uninjured shoulder.

Hunter wasn't exactly sure what the hell had happened, but he didn't care right now as long as Cam was okay. Cam's voice was scratchy, and it cut in and out while talking. Exhaustion trickled into Hunter's body; he was just too damn tired to think right now and there was no way in hell he was going to admit he was getting too old for this shit.

Hunter wrapped his arms around Cam and helped him stand. He held him close, both for his own comfort and for Cam's support, while Aidan searched the house.

"If you ever argue about being my hero again, I'll kick your ass," Cam said, muffled against Hunter's chest.

Hunter chuckled. Every muscle in his body ached. "Right now, I don't think I'd argue about anything. I just want to soak for a bit, grab some painkillers, and sleep for a few days."

"Sign me up for that."

Hunter smiled and softly rubbed Cam's back.

"Is this over now?" Cam asked, looking up at him.

"I sure as hell hope so. I don't think I can handle a sequel."

Cam kissed him and rested his head on Hunter's shoulder again.

"Nice work in there, sir," Aidan said, pointing to the bedroom.

Hunter smiled.

Cam looked up at him, questioning. "Why is it okay for him to call *you* that?"

"Because I know he's not imaging me naked when he says it."

"Oh yeah." Cam smiled.

"I so didn't need to hear that," Aidan commented and shook his head as he continued to write notes on his pad.

Two scene investigators walked in through the front door with their gear in hand. Aidan briefed them on the crime scene and directed them to the other areas. Two medics arrived at the scene and were immediately dispersed, one stayed with them and the other went into the bedroom.

"I can get your statements tomorrow on what happened here tonight. This is going to take me a few hours, considering the mess in the room. You guys have somewhere else to go? This house is a crime scene now so you can't stay here this weekend."

"I'm not giving up my weekend with you," Cam firmly told Hunter as the medic checked the cuts on his arms.

Hunter smiled. "Yeah, I've got a place I can go. I'll call Matt and let him know to avoid any problems."

"Good. Do you need anything from the room?"

"Cam's bag, it's on the couch in there."

Aidan nodded and disappeared from the room.

"How do you feel about meeting my dad?" Hunter asked.

"Is he anything like you?"

"Worse."

Cam smiled. "Then I'd love to meet him."

* * * *

Cam patiently waited as Hunter used his key to unlock the door.

"Get in here," Hunter's father said, jumping up from the couch. He shuffled them inside his home. "What in the hell happened? Are you okay?"

"Hey, Dad. Yeah, we're fine."

"You look like shit."

Cameron chuckled.

"You must be Cameron, the young man who is driving my son to talk to his father about bunnies."

"What?" Cameron burst into laughter then immediately winced and wrapped his arms around himself as a jab of pain hit him. "Sorry. It's nice to meet you. Um, bunnies?"

Hunter waved him off. "Don't ask. This is my dad, Thomas Donovan. Dad, you're sure it's okay for us to stay here tonight?"

Hunter's father looked at him with a smirk. "I already told you over the phone. You know you've got a room set up for you here whenever you want. Besides, you guys already look like you've gotten the crap beat out of you so I figure any moaning will be out of sheer pain."

Cameron snickered as Hunter's face burned with embarrassment.

"Fuck," Hunter groaned.

"I seriously doubt that's going to happen in your condition."

"Dad!" Hunter snapped before storming out of the room with Cam's duffle bag.

Cameron and Thomas laughed in unison then looked over at each other.

"It's too much fun to mess with him. I can't resist," Thomas said.

"I usually get him worked up about his age," Cam said with a grin.

Thomas laughed. "He told me a while ago you called him sir."

"Still do."

Hunter's father shook his head. "I like you. I think you'll do just fine with him."

"Thanks," Cam said quietly. "I hope so."

Hunter reentered the room and glared at them.

"Don't give me that look," Thomas said and waved his hand in a shooing motion. "It won't work on me."

"It damn sure works on me," Cam said in a hoarse voice, which immediately caught Hunter's attention.

"That's my cue to go back to bed. You know where the sheets and towels are. Goodnight," Hunter's father said before leaving the room with a wave good-bye.

Hunter remained staring at Cam, never breaking eye contact, as he stalked toward him.

Cameron's skin tingled in anticipation of Hunter's touch. Hunter's gaze roamed Cam's face with unmistakable desire in their depths. Cam swallowed hard when the warmth of Hunter's body neared him. Cam closed his eyes as Hunter inched forward.

He placed a gentle peck on Cam's lips.

Cameron opened his eyes. "That's it? I know you've got more than that in you."

A slow, seductive grin spread across Hunter's face. "That's all you're getting while we're in my dad's house," he said on a whisper, brushing his lips against Cam's.

"Evil," Cam responded on a groan as he licked Hunter's lips, hoping to entice him.

Hunter gave him another quick peck then retreated. "C'mon, I've got a tub ready for us to soak in for a while." He tugged Cameron flush against his body.

He laughed as he wrapped his arms around Hunter. "I promise to behave as long as you stay this close to me."

Hunter smiled. "As if you had a choice this weekend."

Cameron buried his head at the side of Hunter's neck as he tightened his hold. It was a choice he was willing to forgo for more than just this weekend.

Chapter
TWENTY-SIX

Hunter reached for the source of the annoying buzzing.

"Morning," Hunter grumbled into the cell phone without reading the display.

"Rise and shine," Aidan said. "Is the old fart tired this morning?"

"I'm going to kick your ass," he mumbled into the phone, in far more pain than he had been in quite a long time. He felt every muscle in his body down to his toes. He refused to lift his head but extended his arm and found that he was alone in bed.

"When are you guys coming in to give your statements? I'd like to start trying to get this wrapped up sometime soon and actually get some sleep."

Hunter looked over to the clock on the table and saw it was almost eleven in the morning as he stretched his arms. "Shit, man. Sorry, I didn't realize the time."

"It's fine, I've been busy as hell."

Hunter sat up and heard laughter coming from the kitchen. He smiled, glad to hear Cam and his dad getting along.

"What have you got?"

"As expected, the guys aren't talking."

"I figured."

"I'm going to poke the bear here, get things moving along."

Hunter rubbed his face then winced when he hit a bruise. "Let me guess, Cam's father?"

"I don't have a choice, man. At least we'll get some direction on the link through him."

"Yeah, I know," Hunter said with a sigh. He knew this wouldn't sit well with Cam. "I'm assuming you're going to want to get his sister's statement as well?"

"Yup. I need the address."

"I'll text you the information when we hang up," Hunter said on a yawn. "We need to control what info's getting out there about last night. Once Mackler or the mayor hear about it—"

"I'm way ahead of you. The few guys I had last night were part of my team so I know we can cap some of the grapevine chatter. I'm channeling all communications and case work through a very tight network until we can figure out who's with them. I've already informed the chief that some of the cops from the halfway house break-in were dirty and he's looking into everyone who was there. He's fuming, man."

"I can imagine." Hunter sighed. "Harry was pissed at that meeting in our office."

"He's having a field day flexing his authority. He said some of the shit made sense now about searches getting thrown out and other screwy shit with evidence."

"Yeah, as they say, hindsight's 20/20," Hunter said as he rubbed his face again.

"Dude, stop beating yourself up. You didn't know about Mel. When are you coming in?"

"As soon as I get out of bed and eat something."

"Harry called the police commissioner in the middle of the night."

"That couldn't have gone well," Hunter said with a chuckle.

"No kidding. The commissioner was pissed about getting the call but even more so after being told he had some dirty cops. So they're working together on rearranging a few teams and getting the story straight for the media."

"Dude, how much caffeine have you had today? You're so damn wired you're tiring me out already," Hunter commented.

"We've also got—"

"Aidan," Hunter said calmly. He knew his friend well enough to know when he was in crisis mode and dealing with the fear of losing someone. He'd seen it firsthand.

"What?" Aidan said in an icy tone.

"I'm sorry."

Aidan remained quiet on the line. The only evidence of him still on the phone was his controlled intake and exhale. "You ever scare me like that again and I'm going to skin you alive. You got it?"

"We wouldn't have gotten out of there had you not shown up. Thank you."

"You would have figured out a way, you always do."

Hunter shook his head, even though he knew Aidan couldn't see him. "This was different. I'm not sure if I could stand it if—"

"I want you to have your gun with you. Why the fuck didn't you have it last night? You could have easily taken care of everything yourself."

Hunter sighed heavily. "I can't risk Cam getting screwed because I've got a gun in the house. Look what happened last night. He might have a problem now because he touched a fucking gun."

Aidan sighed. "Carry it anyways. I'll talk to Harry and the commissioner about it. As far as I'm concerned, there were extenuating circumstances. What if I hadn't answered the phone? What if—"

"Aidan, I'll carry the gun."

"Thank you."

"Anything else?"

"Yup. Something hasn't been sitting right with me for a while so I did some poking around on the house Cam pointed out in the boonies."

"What about it?"

"Well, I was able to tie the name on the deed to a partnership contact on one of Rick's shell companies. I already went to see Judge

Stanford. After last night and this little bit of info, I got a green light on the warrant. I'm here now."

"Did you find anything?"

"Tons. The drug dogs found a stash behind a false wall. They have a room with a small-scale lab setup. I'm totally guessing here, but I think this might be where there was some testing or some initial drug mixes done. No way is this the actual lab for production or distribution. We found documents with formulas on them and files, ledgers, and a stack of other shit we're taking to the station to review. I've got forensics here so I'm hoping we can pull prints for Mackler and the mayor since we know they've been here. That'll help cement things."

"That would be good."

"I had cadaver dogs here, too. It looked like a kennel."

Hunter rubbed his eyes. "Dude, don't tell me there were dead bodies in the backyard."

"No. But at this point, I just wanted to be sure."

"True."

"Go have your coffee and get your brain in gear and your asses into the station for your statements. I should be back there within the hour and we'll talk more," Aidan finished before disconnecting.

Hunter searched his bag and found the red file containing Jasmine's information and texted the address and phone number to Aidan. He changed the bandage on his shoulder then cursed every muscle in his body as he dressed. He dragged himself into the bathroom and splashed some water on his face, trying to look presentable past the obvious bruising.

Finally satisfied that he looked relatively decent, he slowly followed the chatter to the kitchen. He leaned on the doorway and watched his father show Cam how to prepare the ingredients for the pancakes. He smiled at Cameron's focused expression as he listened to his dad explain the dos and don'ts of making the perfect batter.

"Good morning," he finally said.

Both Cam and his father looked up and smiled.

"It's about time you woke up," his dad said.

Cam immediately walked over to Hunter, reached up, and gave him a quick kiss.

As much as Hunter's body hurt, it pained him more to see the bruises coloring Cam's face and neck. He gently grazed his fingers on Cam's cheek. He reached down and grabbed Cam's hand to inspect the cuts on his arms.

"You okay?" Hunter asked. His stomach roiled when he focused on the red hemorrhage surrounding Cam's bright blue iris.

Cam nodded and smiled. "Yeah, I've had worse. Are you okay?"

Hunter closed his eyes with Cam's touch to his face. His bruised cheeks didn't hurt as much as his entire body, but Cam's hand on his skin was comforting. He didn't want to let his mind wander regarding Cam's comment of prior 'worse' experiences.

"I'll survive," he finally said.

"I'll give you a massage later," Cam whispered in his ear.

Hunter groaned and raised his hands slightly to grasp Cam by the waist. "That would be nice."

"Son, go grab a seat before you fall over. Cam and I are almost finished here."

Hunter worked his way to the table and had never been happier to settle in his seat. Within moments, his father and Cam filled the table with food and pushed him to take some pills for the pain.

"Cam filled me in on what's going on. What now?" his father asked, cutting into his pancakes.

"Cam and I have to go give our statements. Aidan's going to be at the station within the hour. Then I guess we'll go from there."

"Do they have any information? Did the guys say anything?" Cam asked expectantly.

Hunter shook his head. "They're not talking but Aidan's at the house you told us about and searching there. He's also out looking for other leads."

"What other leads?" Cam asked.

Hunter hesitated.

"Hunter?"

He deliberately chewed slowly, trying to think of how best to break the news to Cam. Hunter took a sip of juice and paused.

"They're tracking your father and they're going to have your sister come in to give her statement since there isn't one on record."

"Why are you trying to track him?" Cam asked quietly.

He could see the concern in Cam's expression. "We need to know what role he played in all this. We're thinking he can give us more info on the link to Mackler."

"Oh," Cam said quietly. He grabbed his fork again and poked at his breakfast.

"Cam?"

"I know you want me to talk to my sister, and I'll do that for you. But I won't talk to him."

Hunter reached out and placed his hand behind Cam's neck. "You don't have to talk to your sister if you don't want to and you don't have to talk to your dad either."

"Don't call him that," Cam said fiercely.

"Cam—"

Cam looked at him with fire in his eyes. "I don't have a choice in him being my father, but he was never a dad to me. Excuse me." Cam pushed his chair back from the table and walked away.

"Hunter, what's going on?" his father asked when Cam exited the dining room.

He went to stand but his father's hand on his arm halted him. Hunter ran his fingers through his hair. He just wanted all this crap over with already. He hated the tension that pushed beneath the surface when he looked at Cam. Hunter glanced over his shoulder to his bedroom where Cam had disappeared to.

"Hunter?"

He sighed. "I think Cam's father made a deal and sold out his son."

Hunter's father stood from the table. "You stay here, I'll go."

"Dad, please don't push him."

"I did learn a thing or two from your mom. You sit and eat," his father said, pointing at the plate full of food.

Hunter pushed the breakfast around on his plate. He wanted to go to Cam, be with him, and let him know he was there to support him.

He'd give his dad five minutes before he broke into the room. He owed his dad the respect of staying put, but he was not about to leave Cam when he needed support.

* * * *

Cam stood by the window and looked out into the yard.

"Cameron?" he heard Hunter's father say as he knocked on the slightly open door.

Cam looked over his shoulder and half smiled. Hunter's dad was so different from his own father. "Sorry. I didn't mean to disrespect you by leaving the table."

"You didn't, Son, don't worry about that." He walked over to Cam and stood next to him.

Cam would cringe at the sound of his father calling him son, but coming from Thomas, it sounded so natural.

Thomas placed a gentle hand on Cam's shoulder. "Hunter won't force you to talk to your sperm donor if you don't want to."

Cam chuckled and looked over to him. "I've never called him that, but it fits."

Thomas shrugged. "Some men can be pretty stupid. Luckily that part isn't hereditary."

"I'm glad. Hunter does seem to take a lot after you."

"Well then, I'll take that as one hell of a compliment considering how much you love him."

Cam stilled. Speaking openly about his feelings with his boyfriend's father was definitely new to him.

"Um, we haven't talked about that." He looked away, not really sure what the hell else he was supposed to say.

"Well, it's obvious to anyone who's in the room with you guys for a few seconds. If he's too much of a wuss to tell you then I'm going to have to smack him. He knows we're not on this earth long enough and should enjoy every chance we have with the one we love."

Cam winced. "He's not the wuss, I am."

Thomas slid his arm over Cam's shoulder. He mirrored Cam's stance, staring out the window. "Something tells me you haven't had much luck with people who care about you."

Cam shook his head. He looked down and shoved his hands in his pockets. "Everything changed after my mom died when I was ten. My father hated raising two kids on his own. He worked two jobs and drank every chance he had in between. I was the one who took care of things at home. I was too young to work but I made damn sure he didn't drink away the money he made. We fought a lot. He told me being gay wasn't natural and I needed to work on changing my mind."

"Well, he was an idiot. You took care of him and your sister whether he wants to believe that or not." Thomas shook his head. "You know what the best part of having a gay son is?"

Cam looked over to Thomas and cocked his head. "What's that?"

"I inherit a second son," he said earnestly.

Cam inhaled a shaky breath as emotions tightened his chest. Thomas pulled him into an embrace. "If that asshole father of yours didn't appreciate you, then he doesn't deserve to see you."

"Thank you," Cam whispered. He raised his arms and embraced Thomas's frail body. "Hunter was right."

"That's a shocker. What was he right about?" Thomas asked, releasing Cam.

"He said you were worse than him."

Thomas smacked Cam behind his head. "And you're just as stubborn as he is. You guys are perfect for each other."

They both laughed as Hunter entered the room.

"You good?" Hunter asked cautiously, the worry evident in his expression.

Cam nodded with a half smile hoping to calm the concern in Hunter's voice. He looked over to Thomas then back to Hunter. "More than good."

Hunter sighed with obvious relief. "We need to go to the station to give our statements."

Cam nodded and walked toward the door to follow Hunter out of the room. He looked back at Thomas who shook his head and grinned.

"Few seconds, that's all it takes," Thomas said before finally walking over and joining Cam at the door before exiting.

Chapter TWENTY-SEVEN

Hunter reached over and rubbed the back of Cam's neck, hoping to ease some of the tension in the muscles.

"That wasn't too bad," Cam commented after Aidan left the room.

Cameron's father had been detained and was due to arrive at the station at any moment. Hunter didn't have a clue how Cam would react but knew his fidgeting and constant biting of his lower lip were a telltale sign of his nerves.

"That feels so fucking good." Cam groaned and lowered his head, encouraging Hunter's touch. "What happens now?"

Hunter continued to stroke Cam's neck. "Aidan's getting our statements typed up, then he'll be back and we'll sign off on them. Once that's done, we're free to leave."

Cam looked up, his face more relaxed. "We still have some weekend time left," he teased with that half smile that shot a bolt of lust through Hunter's body every time.

"Would be a shame to let it go to waste."

Cam sucked in his lower lip and nodded.

Hunter groaned and pulled Cam in for a kiss. Cam tugged him closer, wanting more.

"You guys should get a room," Aidan said when he returned.

"We did have one. Go away." Cam laughed.

Aidan just shook his head. "I need the room. You want to sit in?" he asked Hunter.

Hunter exhaled and looked over at Cam.

The smile slid off Cam's face. "He's here already?" he said weakly.

"I've got him a few doors down in holding. Hunter said you didn't want to talk to him so I figured I'd give you a heads up."

"You want to sit in while they question him?" Cam asked Hunter.

Hunter reached over and grabbed Cam's hand. "Aidan will be doing most of the questioning, but yes, I want to sit in."

"Okay."

"We can put you in the observation room. He won't know you're there," Aidan offered.

Cam nodded and worried his lower lip again.

When they stood, ready to exit, Cam slid his hand into Hunter's.

Hunter immediately looked over and saw Cameron looking down. Hunter squeezed his hand and gave him a quick peck. "You're stronger than you know," he whispered in his ear.

"I'm not as strong as you think I am." Hunter's chest tightened at the crack in Cam's voice.

"You've already surprised me a time or two. Just take it one day at a time, okay?"

Cameron finally looked up and made eye contact. A rare innocence that twisted Hunter's gut made an appearance in his expression.

He inched closer to Hunter. "Please...just don't...don't give up on me."

Hunter smiled and brushed the hair out of Cam's worried face. "Never." He gave Cam a chaste kiss before they exited the room.

"Cameron, is that you?" Jasmine's voice carried across the room. She sat in a chair, talking to an officer a few desks down. She finally stood and approached them with a smile.

Cam's grip tightened so hard Hunter thought his bones were going to snap. He could see the muscles flexing in Cam's jaw and his nostrils flare with each breath.

"You look really good." She stood in front of Cam, looking up at her big brother. She was petite next to him, thin and barely reached his chin. "You got taller."

Cam forced a smile but didn't say a word.

"Hello again," she said, extending her hand to Hunter. "I didn't catch your name the first time we met."

"Hunter," he said as he extended his hand, his other still holding Cam's in a vise grip. "Are they taking your statement?"

Jasmine nodded. "I came over as soon as they called." She looked over to Cam again. "Did he give you my message?"

Cam nodded.

Before Cam had a chance to react, Jasmine threw her arms around his neck. "I'm so sorry I wasn't there and for the things I said."

Cam refused to release the grip on Hunter's hand or wrap his arms around his sister to reciprocate the embrace. He stood there, arms down at this side and his face void of any emotion while his sister hung on.

Jasmine slowly retreated and looked at Cam. Tears began to fill her eyes. "You can't find it in your heart to forgive me?" she asked, her voice shaky.

Cam visibly swallowed. "I'll forgive you, because that's what brothers are supposed to do," he said in a level tone.

"Thank you," she said then deeply exhaled. The tears vanished from her eyes before a single drop fell.

Cam began to shift his weight from one foot to the other.

"Well, I need to finish answering a few questions before I head back home. It was good seeing you again, Cam," she said. She brushed something off her dress, then turned and walked back to the cubicle of the waiting officer.

Hunter felt a sudden coldness to his core. He had hoped, for Cam's sake, that she would at least push harder, try to make amends.

Instead, she had managed to turn and depart just as quickly as she had greeted him once she got the forgiveness she sought. She didn't even bother to ask Cam if he was okay considering the bruising on his face and the bandage on the side of his temple.

"Over here," Aidan said, guiding them to the neighboring room.

The space was small, dark, and narrow enough for a few standing people but nowhere near the size of the interrogation room now viewable through the glass.

"He won't be able to see me?" Cam asked.

"No. But you'll be able to see him."

As if on cue, the door opened in the other room and a thin, tall, older man was escorted by another detective. Cam inhaled sharply and stilled.

"I need to get in there. Come on in when you're ready," Aidan said before exiting.

Hunter cupped Cam's face and forced eye contact. "Just hang in there. We're almost out of here."

"Try to be quick," was all Cam managed to force out.

Hunter's chest tightened when he saw the pain in Cameron's expression. He nodded, gave Cam a quick kiss then exited the room to join Aidan. He entered the interrogation room and stood silently in the corner as Aidan began to fire off questions.

John Pierce sat in his chair and glanced everywhere but at Aidan or Hunter. He straightened his shirt and exhaled heavily with each question Aidan asked.

"Answer my question, Mr. Pierce," Aidan said.

"You still haven't told me why the hell you brought me back to this godforsaken place."

"You are being questioned about what happened ten years ago and your relationship with Mr. Mackler," Aidan clarified.

John slowly turned to Aidan with a grin. "I don't have a relationship with Mackler. I'm not a queer like my boy."

Hunter pushed off from his place in the corner and stood planted, his feet wide and arms crossed. His jaw muscle ticked and the vein at his temple pulsed. "I swear, if you don't start talking, I'm going to rip that smirk off your face."

John looked over to Hunter and sneered.

In a flash, Hunter pushed forward, grabbed Cameron's father and pressed him up against the wall. John's eyes filled with horror. His face began to darken from the pressure grip of Hunter's arm across his neck. He could feel the old man begin to shake before deciding to release him.

John leaned on the back of the chair and rubbed his throat. He looked at Aidan, his eyes bulging. "He can't do that to me," John said on a gasp. "That's like harassment or something. He can't threaten me."

Aidan pulled his pen out of his jacket and thumbed through the sheets in the folder. "I haven't seen or heard anything. So I don't know what you're talking about."

Hunter smiled wickedly. "Start talking."

"Back off and I'll talk."

Hunter stepped away. Aidan looked over to Hunter with a scowl. Hunter didn't care. He could barely control the rage thrumming through his body at the thought of this man starting the chain of events in Cam's life for the last decade.

Aidan turned to John again. "Talk."

John straightened his clothes and returned to his seat, cautiously watching Hunter who retreated to his spot in the corner. "Is this how you guys do things over here? He's obviously not a cop by the look of all that bruising on his face. What is he, your muscle?"

"He's the guy who can put your ass away for the rest of your miserable life so I suggest you shut up about everything other than what happened ten years ago."

Cameron's father straightened in his chair. "Mackler told me my boy and his were together. Since my boy shot his, he thought it was fair for Cammy to do some time."

"And you thought that was his decision to make?" Aidan said.

John shrugged. "When I resisted, he offered up some money. I realized really quick that the quieter I was, the higher the offer got. I was quiet for a long time," he finished with a laugh, which he immediately stifled once Hunter straightened.

"So you got some money. What was the deal?" Aidan asked.

"If I talk, what do I get?"

Hunter inched forward.

John rose from his seat and stepped back against the wall. "Keep him the hell away from me," John yelled and pointed toward Hunter. "I don't mind dishing the dirt on Mackler. He's a son of a bitch who screwed me over."

"What were the terms of your arrangement?" Aidan asked again. He glared at Hunter and signaled him to return to his corner spot.

"I was supposed to sign off on the papers, take the money, and disappear. So I did."

"Were you aware of the charges?" Aidan asked after jotting down a few notes.

"What the hell did I care? That son of a bitch fucked me over and he owes me."

"How so?" Hunter asked.

John remained quiet. Hunter wasn't sure if he opted for silence simply because Hunter was asking the question. He had had enough of this bullshit. He pushed off the wall and neared John.

"Get away from me," the old man said, cautiously watching Hunter as he took a step closer. "Keep him away and I'll talk."

"Hunter, down boy," Aidan said then raised his hand to Hunter before he could protest the reprimand.

John chuckled and sat.

Aidan leaned over the table. "If you don't start talking, I'm going to let him loose and walk away. Believe me, you do not want to give him free rein. So if you want to get out of this room, you will start fucking talking now," he finished with an uncharacteristic yell.

John was visibly shaken, his focus ping-ponged between Aidan and Hunter. "I don't know what the charges were and I didn't care. He was supposed to go to juvie for a few months and that was it. I found out he served ten years so Mackler owes me at least ten times more money for keeping him inside so long."

"You son of a bitch," Hunter said with disgust. He couldn't stand being in the same room any longer with this man. He walked out and, with quick strides, was at the neighboring observation room within seconds. He hesitated for a moment, holding the door handle. He needed to compose himself before joining Cam.

He took another deep breath and finally opened the door.

The light shone through the two-way glass and cast a faint glow against Cam's features, enough to see his stern expression. Even in profile, Hunter could easily see he was making every effort to maintain his composure.

"He fucking owes me more money," John's tinny voice echoed through the speaker.

Hunter immediately reached for the switch to turn off the audio.

Cam had heard everything.

Hunter closed his eyes and exhaled as he replayed the prior exchange in his head.

He looked over to Cam again. He remained motionless and took slow deep breaths as he focused on the exchange in the room. Aidan was now standing, hovering over Cameron's father and talking with a sneer.

"Cam?"

He watched as Cam stood, stock-still, fixated on his father through the glass.

"Do you want me to stay or give you some time alone?" he asked, hoping for some cue to keep the worry at bay.

Cam continued to stare without saying a word.

It was unbearable to stand on the sideline but he needed to let Cam process everything that had happened at his own pace. Otherwise, he'd simply lock it away until a panic attack surfaced.

His instincts told him to wait.

Hunter leaned back against the door and grabbed the door handle behind him. He needed something to ground him to the opposite side of the room when all he wanted to do was race over to Cam.

He can handle this. He's stronger than he thinks he is. He chanted, hoping to convince his stubborn mind that if Cam needed him, he would call for him—even though Cam had never asked for anything.

So he waited.

* * * *

Cam was terrified to move. He was in a tailspin and the slightest movement would result in his crash and burn. His protective iron wall wobbled. Everyone had decided to appear from his past, all at once, to remind him of how worthless he was to those who were supposed to love him. His father had abandoned him long ago and simply confirmed it with his words today. His sister felt guilty—a prison of her own doing. She was in search of forgiveness, nothing more.

He fought to gather the little bit of dignity he'd barely managed to hold on to.

Flashbacks of his mother and their special times held him together all these years but his memories grew fainter with each passing year. He didn't even have a photograph to remind him of the lines that shaped her face. How could he expect anyone to love him if he had difficultly remembering the face of the one person who did?

He inhaled a slow, shaky breath and closed his eyes, trying to keep himself together. A tingle in his head waited to take over.

Cam opened his eyes and looked at the frail figure through the glass. His father's life of drinking had obviously caught up with him. He had aged, quite ungracefully. The hands, which had landed too often on him in anger during a drunken state, were now deformed. Karma was a bitch and she had shown no mercy on the man.

He swallowed hard, trying to rebuild his defenses as he replayed everything he had heard. Every word echoed in his mind and the underlying disgust in his father's tone.

Cam took another slow deep breath, hoping to control the panic attack he knew would come crashing in if he allowed it to take over.

He watched as Aidan cuffed his father then exited the room. He swallowed, trying to fight the tightness in his throat and the pain in his chest.

He closed his eyes and lowered his head. He took another deep breath and fought the prickling sensation starting to take over.

He could feel Hunter's gaze on him, caressing every inch of his skin.

Hunter was an anomaly. Cam had not been able to decipher why this man was still standing by his side through all this. Why Hunter wanted him when his own family had discarded him so easily.

"Why?" he finally managed to voice past the huge lump that had managed to take over his throat. He reached for the wall to steady himself as he waited for Hunter's response, fearing he would abandon him as well.

"I don't know why your father would have done what he did. He's an asshole. I'm not going to attempt to come up with an excuse or reason for his stupidity."

"No, not him."

Hunter took a step closer. His step was different—usually more determined, certain of its destination. These steps were lighter, hesitant. Insecure. *Odd*. Hunter didn't *do* insecure.

Cam turned his head to make eye contact. The pained look in those piercing silver eyes shot a stab of remorse throughout Cam's body. His eyes stung and his throat constricted even more. He rubbed his chest, trying to ease the sudden, sharp pain.

"Why are *you* still here?" He swallowed again, that fucking lump in his throat made it too difficult to speak.

"You didn't tell me to leave."

He turned to face Hunter.

Hunter hadn't moved. He stood vigilant, watching him, waiting.

Cam closed his eyes and took a calming breath. He shoved his hands in his jean pockets to hide the tremble. He was at the brink of falling apart. He exhaled heavily. The lump finally leaving him long enough to allow for more than just a few choice words.

"Why are *you* still here…with me? You heard what he said, what he did. You were there when Jas walked away. Why are you still sticking around?"

"You asked me to not give up on you."

"Everyone leaves, Hunter," he said, exhaling heavily as he looked upward.

"You are stubborn. I've told you a billion times already, I'm not going anywhere," Hunter said. He moved closer, his steps more certain, closer to his usual gait.

"Everyone wants something from me then they leave when they get it. What do you want?" he said in a more elevated tone.

Hunter took the final steps and stood in front of Cam. He reached up and cupped Cam's face. "I want you."

"You've already had me…a few times actually."

"I'm being serious."

Cam pleaded with his eyes. "I don't understand." He stepped away, unable to handle the emotion screaming through Hunter's eyes. He wanted—needed—to believe, but everything that had happened in his life had caused him to become jaded.

Hunter grabbed Cam's waist and prevented his escape. He cupped Cam's face again and forced eye contact. "Listen to me very carefully, Mr. Pierce, and get this through your thick, stubborn skull. Stop thinking I'm going to leave, because I'm not. Stop thinking I'm going to abandon you, because I won't."

Cam stared at him blankly.

"Do you really want to know what I want or not?"

"Yes," Cam grumbled. "And something tells me you're going to get sappy on me."

Hunter tightened his hold on Cam's face and smiled. "You're right. And you know why?"

"You're predictable."

"You're the only one who thinks so. And that's because you know me. So you shouldn't be surprised I'm still by your side."

Cam's stomach twisted. "You can have anyone you want. Someone who doesn't have a ton of—"

"I want you, no one else. It's your choice to look at me the way you do, touch me the way you do, kiss me the way you do. I can't just take these things from you or force you to feel something you don't. You don't seem to realize you're the one with the power in this relationship, not me."

Cam closed his eyes and exhaled a shaky breath. He gripped Hunter's arms to anchor himself. He opened his eyes and looked at Hunter, his silver gaze intense with desire and promise.

"I want to wake up with *you* in my arms every morning. I crave the way *you* look at me as if I'm a fucking superhero. I love the way *you* touch me, the way your fingers dig into my skin. I love it when you get all territorial and feel the need to mark me."

Cam shook. He tightened his hold on Hunter's arms and looked away. "I know you can walk away at any moment. I don't want anyone taking you away from me a moment sooner," he said in a small voice.

"As long as you want me, I'm not leaving. I promise," Hunter said with fierce determination in his tone.

"I...need...you," Cam said weakly, unable to finish voicing his thoughts. He moved his hands from Hunter's arms down to his waist. He clutched the edge of Hunter's jeans in a white-knuckle grip. "I...can't..."

I can't do this alone.

Hunter tightened his hold on Cam's face. "I'm here," he said and placed a gentle kiss on Cam's lips.

Cam blinked repeatedly and tried to process Hunter's words. He looked away. His breath hitched. He couldn't imagine having any sort of power over a man like Hunter.

He's not abandoning me.

He tightened his grip on Hunter's waist.

Hunter stroked Cam's cheek. "I'm with you and we're going to get through this. And when this is all over, we're getting a house together and making it a home. We're even getting a dog if you want. Got it?"

"A cat," Cam said absently, looking off to the side.

"What?"

"I want a cat, too," he said, looking at Hunter.

"Then we're getting a dog and cat. Hell, we'll have a farm if you want. I don't care. But we're doing this together. Understand?"

Cam tried to nod in Hunter's grip. He exhaled heavily and closed his eyes, reveling in the heat of Hunter's hands on him.

"I'll be patient with you until you're ready, but don't you dare try to deny this thing between us. Life is too fucking short and I want you in my life every day, all day. Got it?"

Cam nodded again slowly.

"Good," Hunter said before pulling Cam in for a passionate kiss.

When they separated, Cam felt light-headed with Hunter's gaze on him. It was desire mixed with unmistakable devotion. Hunter could claim to never say those words but he spoke them in his actions and through those piercing silver eyes Cam loved so much.

He's really mine.

Cam's body began to shake, and he instinctively threw both arms around Hunter's neck in a powerful grip and held him close, needing to feel the heat of Hunter's body against his. Hunter grabbed him around the waist and worked one hand under his shirt, seeking skin to trace those soothing circular patterns that always seemed to calm him. He knew he should loosen his grip on Hunter, but he needed him closer, needed his unrelenting strength to ground him.

Cam sighed when the shakes subsided. "I give you a hard time about the sweet shit but that doesn't mean I want you to stop," he said quietly against Hunter's ear, still holding tightly.

"And here I thought you were trying to strangle it out of me."

"I could let go if you want," Cam responded. He tightened his hold on Hunter and pushed his body subtly against him to close the inch of space between them.

"Not in a million years." Hunter pulled him closer and buried his face at the side of Cam's neck.

Cameron relished the offered safety of the strong arms encasing him. He sighed and buried his face deeper into the heat of Hunter's body.

"I'm scared."

"What scares you the most?" Hunter asked gently, tracing his fingers along Cam's back as he pressed soft kisses along Cam's temple and face.

"Aside from losing you—"

"We've covered this already."

"I know, I know. As long as I keep giving you the pervy hero worship puppy eyes and manhandle you, you'll stay," Cam said, hiding his half smile against Hunter's shoulder, hoping to goad him.

"I'm going to pretend you didn't say that."

"I was trying to answer before you cut me off."

"What scares you the most?" Hunter said in a growly voice, forcing the focus back to the question.

Hunter's fingers circled Cam's lower back, soothing his nerves.

Cam remained silent, still embracing Hunter tightly as he tried to string the right set of words together.

"I'm scared I can't give you what you need. I know you want me to just let my guard down and open up about everything but I can't. I'm used to being guarded, keeping stuff inside. It's what's held me together all these years. I know you said you were staying, I get that. Really I do. But you've promised to stay with the guy I am *now*. Not the guy who's going to be mumbling in the corner freaking out because he's broken and doesn't know how to put the pieces back."

Hunter separated from the embrace and gently held Cam's face in his hands again. The intense gaze he loved so much stared back at him with fierce determination. "I need you to trust me."

"I do."

"Then trust me when I say you can totally let go with me and you won't scare me off. I'll be there with you to put the pieces back together."

"I'm doing the best I can," Cam said, his voice broken with desperation. He didn't know how else to explain things. He *was* trying.

"Stop fighting by yourself. I'm here if you want me," Hunter said, gently stroking Cam's cheek.

"I do want you."

Cam ran his hands through his hair then clasped them behind his own neck. He looked up and exhaled heavily. "I'm not good at this, Hunter."

"You're getting better."

He dropped his hands to his sides and looked at Hunter. "I'm trying. I swear I am, but I'm not ready."

"I know."

"You're really okay with that?"

"I know that when you *are* ready to say it, it'll be forever." Hunter pulled Cam into another embrace.

Cam exhaled deeply, letting Hunter's heat filter through his system and settle the shudders that traveled his body. He prayed this man would not give up on him. Cam held him tightly for a little longer, hoping to absorb some of the strength Hunter offered.

"This is the part where you tell me I'm a sap," Hunter said.

Cam buried his nose at the crook of Hunter's neck without responding, reveling in the protectiveness of Hunter's embrace.

"Are you ever going to get tired of saving me?"

"Never."

With the heat and scent surrounding him, his heartbeat began to calm. He nestled more snuggly when Hunter's arms tightened around him. He could stay like this forever.

"Let's get out of here," Cam whispered.

"Sounds like a plan."

Chapter
TWENTY-EIGHT

Hunter exited the elevators and tried to ignore the stares and ceased conversations that surrounded him. He had wrapped up the morning trial without any case issue but desperately needed to avoid any more snarky remarks about him taking a beating from anyone because of his face. He was pissed and had been brutal in court that morning. He half smiled as he recalled just how badly he had beaten the defendant's council. *Bet that bastard will think twice before being a smart-ass with me the next time.*

He was sure the news had traveled like wildfire through the grapevine regarding Mel. The problem was, he didn't know the details the rumor mill had churned or his involvement in what had happened. He'd left it up to Aidan and his trusted handful of staff to report about Mel's death and the circumstances surrounding it until they could get a better handle on the associated parties. He'd been in court all morning and hadn't had access to any information other than a text from Aidan informing him that a statement had been made that both he and Mel had been attacked out of retaliation.

"Here's the case summary from this morning's trial," Hunter said as he dropped the folder onto his assistant's desk Monday afternoon before making his way to his office.

"Thanks. I didn't think…" Jessie lost his train of thought when he looked up and saw Hunter's face. "Are you okay?"

"I'll live," he said, retreating to his office, trying to avoid the stares from the staff.

Jessie quickly followed before he had a chance to shut the door.

"Everyone is a bit freaked out," Jessie said, closing the door behind him.

"About what exactly?"

Jessie arched an eyebrow. "I've worked with you long enough to know you wouldn't let a mugger sneak up on you and do that to you," he said, pointing to Hunter's face.

"A mugger?" Hunter commented, roughly putting away some files in his drawer then slamming it shut. He was going to have to beat the shit out of Aidan when he saw him. He could have at least said it was a mob of muggers, a street gang of a dozen, something a bit more ballsy than a lone street thug.

"Hunter?" Jessie asked with concern. "I know something's not right, and I just want to make sure you're okay. If you need something, all you have to do is say the word."

Hunter looked up at his assistant of four years. After getting blindsided with Mel's involvement, he wasn't sure who he trusted anymore. He rested his elbows on the desk and crossed his arms. If Jessie was part of this whole network, Cam would have been caught immediately after that white envelope had been delivered to his office.

"What else did you hear?" he asked.

Jessie took a seat opposite Hunter. "Just people talking. I've heard you were jumped by a mugger on your way home and Mel was out on a date and was attacked and killed. That's about the only consistency in what I'm hearing."

"What are the variations?"

Jessie raised his eyebrows. "Um, about the only thing I'm not hearing is an alien abduction. I didn't know what to believe until you came in and I saw your face."

Hunter didn't have the luxury of time to find what he needed on his own and no one was better at research than Jessie. He sighed and ran his fingers through his hair. "Jess, I need to know if I can trust you. Look me in the eye and tell me."

Jessie's shoulders slumped. "Have I ever given you a reason not to?"

Hunter rubbed his eyes in frustration. He hated this, his gut was telling him he could trust Jessie but he needed to hear him say the words. Jessie had a horrible poker face and a gentle nature, both of which were reasons why he wasn't a lawyer. "Jess, please, just humor me. I need to hear you say it."

Jessie straightened, inched over the desk and looked at Hunter. "Hunter, I've never lied to you even when I knew you'd get mad. I love working with you and actually care what the hell happens to you. So put a little trust in me and know that I would never, ever, do anything to make you regret that."

Hunter assessed him. Jessie was going for fierce lion but what came across was territorial kitten. Regardless of his level of intensity, Jessie was being indisputably honest. "Did you trust Mel as much as you trust me?"

Jessie shook his head. "There's a reason I accepted the assistant position with you and not her. I didn't trust her any farther than I could throw her and you know I'm not athletic enough to do that."

Hunter couldn't help the smile that spread across his face. "Okay. I'm going to need your help with something but it's only going to be you and me on this. I can't run the risk of anyone else getting involved right now or my life could be at stake."

Jessie inhaled sharply. "Okay. Just tell me what you need me to do."

"I need you to be hyperaware right now. Don't disregard any detail or comment."

Jessie nodded. "Did this have anything to do with those red files?" he asked hesitantly.

Hunter gave him one of his piercing glares. "Yes. Why?"

"Too many easy cases and things are never that simple. I'm worried there might be someone else in this office."

"Why?"

"That last file wasn't a messenger, Hunter, it was left on my desk so it's someone who was in the office."

"I know who it was."

Jessie sighed. "Good."

"I've got to make a few phone calls and get some things in order. Then we'll regroup and plan what we're going to do."

Jessie nodded and rose from the seat. "Okay."

"I need you to gather all the red files that came in to Mel so I can get them to the police. But I need you to be low key about it please. I don't know about Mel's assistant so—"

"Be careful. Got it," he said as he exited the room.

Hunter dialed the mayor's office from his cell.

"Mr. Weston's office, how may I help you?" the familiar voice said.

"Lydia, is it safe to talk?"

"Yes, but he's contacting everyone he can think of to gather information. Are you okay? I heard you were hurt," she said in a hushed tone.

"Yes, I'm fine. I need your help."

"What do you need?"

"Information. What have you got?"

"Tons, but I'm not sure what you need," Lydia said quickly in a hushed tone.

"Quick question. Are the police commissioner and captain clean?"

"Yes, as far as I know. They don't discuss anything with them."

Hunter breathed a sigh of relief. "Can you give me access to anything you have so I can comb through it and see what helps?"

"Yes, but it's a lot."

"That's fine. Where do you have it?"

"I'll send the information. Don't come here."

"Okay."

"I'll send—" She stopped, then continued. "I'm sorry, Mr. Weston is busy this week and unable to meet with you."

"I'm assuming you can't talk further?"

"That is correct, sir."

"Send it to my assistant like you did the last one so it doesn't come directly to me. He'll make sure I get it."

"Yes, sir. Thank you for your time," she finished before disconnecting the call.

Hunter hung up the phone and exhaled deeply. He unlocked the bottom drawer of his desk and withdrew the gun safe he began storing in his office since his weekends with Cam. He unlocked the box, inserted the full clip and holstered the pistol. He leaned back in his chair and closed his eyes. He didn't know if Lydia was in danger or if any of the information she had would help. His hands were shaking and his leg was bouncing obsessively. He couldn't stand this useless state of being at the mercy of these unknown bastards who would attack him or Cam. His protectiveness was in overdrive. He just wanted to find each one of these assholes and slowly rip their limbs off, until they screamed from the excruciating pain.

And that still would not satisfy his need for justice.

He was in his, as Aidan had coined during the service, *itchy and twitchy* mode. His senses were heightened and he was jittery. The faint creaking of his chair echoed loudly like an opening door in a horror movie, the hum of the chatter outside his office sounded as if he were in the middle of a screaming crowd, and the honking horns of the outside traffic were trumpets blowing in his ear. He opened his eyes and took a deep breath. This was how he had been after quitting the service. In the field, acute senses made the difference between life and death, but in everyday life, it could drive someone to madness.

His phone chirped, and he nearly fell out of his chair from the reflexive jump. "Fuck," he said, aggravated with himself. God help the poor bastard who attempted to attack him in this state. He was more than capable of snapping someone's head off with the level of energy charging through his body. What the fuck was he thinking when he had promised to carry his gun on him. He was dangerous in this state of mind and with an itchy trigger finger. He blew out a frustrated breath and ran his fingers through his hair.

He looked at the display and smiled.

Hoping you're OK. – C

He immediately responded…

Need 2 see u

For some reason, the keys were especially tiny today and he couldn't seem to settle his fingers enough to type more.

Hunter quickly launched from his chair when he received Cam's response...

Come on over.

"Jess, I'll be back in a few minutes," he said in passing as he raced by his assistant's desk.

He arrived at the diner in record time and stood in line behind several customers. He shifted his weight from foot to foot, waiting to catch a glimpse of Cameron. Lucy saw him, whispered something to Bill then walked around the counter to where Hunter stood.

"We were worried about you." She reached up and placed her hands on his face and gently rubbed his cheeks with her thumbs.

Hunter nearly broken down from that simple gesture, the same his mother always seemed to do when he'd come home from a tour of duty.

"Sweetie, come to the back room. Cam is sorting a supply delivery."

He didn't need to be told twice. He didn't trust himself to speak, so he nodded and headed to the back room. Arriving within seconds, he saw Cam reaching over, placing one of the boxes in the storage closet. Cam immediately turned and barely had a chance to react before Hunter reached him and lifted him off the ground in a bone-crushing embrace.

Hunter released a shaky breath and held Cam even tighter. He rested his head in the crook of Cam's neck and inhaled deeply the soothing scent of the man he desperately needed. Cam wrapped his legs around Hunter's waist and tightened his arms around his neck.

"You're shaking," Cam said, muffled against Hunter's neck.

Hunter shifted a hand below Cam's ass to hold him in the carrying embrace. He didn't want to say anything, he just needed to hold Cam and know he was safe and near him.

Cam stroked the back of Hunter's head. "I'm okay."

After a few moments of silence, Cam inched back and cupped Hunter's face to make eye contact. He gently stroked Hunter's bruised cheeks. "I'm okay," Cam repeated.

Hunter rested his forehead against Cam's. His body began to settle. His skin no longer itched like a drug addict looking for a fix. The exterior sounds of the cash register opening and closing no longer sounded like crashing cymbals in his ear.

"You know, you can put me down anytime you want," Cam said with a teasing smile.

"Not yet," Hunter said in a gravelly voice. He didn't want to let Cam go, ever, but at least needed to wait until his body was semi normal again. He held him tighter and returned to the crook of Cam's neck to deliver a ghost of a kiss.

"I needed this," Hunter said quietly.

Cam's arms tightened around him in response. They held each other for a few more moments until Hunter reluctantly set Cam down on the floor.

"Sorry about that," Hunter mumbled.

Cam reached up and firmly gripped Hunter's jaw. "Don't you *ever* apologize for that," he said with fire in his eyes. "Are we clear?"

Hunter nodded and inhaled a shaky breath. *He's fine. He's safe here.*

"Have you eaten anything? I'd offer you a coffee but I don't want you to spontaneously combust."

Hunter chuckled. "I'm okay now. I grabbed something to eat when I left the courthouse."

Cam searched his face, worry clearly evident in his lowered brow and tightened lips. "How about a cookie?" he asked slowly.

Hunter couldn't control the burst of laughter.

"What?" Cam said, laughing, his features relaxing.

"For some reason, the way you said that sounded so twisted," he said with a smile, finally starting to return to his usual self.

"'Cause you're a perv and I'm a cookie tease, I can't help myself," Cam said as he grabbed Hunter by the waist and pulled him closer.

Hunter pushed the hair out of Cam's eyes. Cam reached up and placed a soft kiss on Hunter's lips.

"I hate being away from you," Hunter said, running his hand along Cam's face then down his neck.

"'Cause you're a helpless romantic underneath that growly strong-armed exterior."

The heat rushed to Hunter's cheeks.

"You're humble, too," Cam whispered as he leaned up to bite Hunter's ear. "And you're mine."

Hunter closed his eyes and enjoyed the warm puffs of breath against his ear as Cam spoke. He couldn't control the groan that escaped as Cam continued to bite and kiss along his jaw. "Fuck, I can't wait for the weekend," he said on a moan.

Cam chuckled.

"You're a fucking cock tease."

Cam smiled wickedly. "Oh, I can guarantee you I have no intention of teasing. I'll have my way with you this weekend."

Hunter cupped Cam's face and gave him a chaste kiss.

"Who's the tease now?" Cam retorted.

Hunter smiled at the mischief in Cam's eyes, diverting his focus for a moment from the bruises coloring Cam's skin and the cuts still bandaged on his arms.

"We're still on for the weekend right?" Cam asked.

"Yup. I'm going to be busy this week so I might not be able to come around as much." Hunter pulled Cam into another embrace.

"Is it anything I can help with? I get the feeling it has to do with me," Cam said, nuzzling closer to Hunter's neck.

"I'm not sure yet. I've already asked my assistant, Jessie, for help. I don't even know what we're getting so I'm not sure if I can go through it at the office but I'm guessing it would be safer to do it at my house."

"You do realize it's taking every ounce of energy right now to not freak out about this Jessie person, right? The woman you worked with mentioned him."

"You have nothing to worry about. I'm yours."

"It's not you I'm worried about. It's that Jessie dude," Cam said as he separated from the embrace to make eye contact with Hunter.

"He's not my type. So don't worry. You're not going to have to pee in a circle around me," Hunter said with a grin.

"Why is he not your type?" Cam said, firmly pulling Hunter by the waist until their bodies were flush against each other.

Hunter groaned. "Because he can't do that," he said before delivering a heated kiss.

Cam chuckled. "I think you're a glutton for punishment."

"Only for you."

Cam laughed and pushed Hunter out of the back room. "Text me in a little bit so I know you're okay."

Hunter exited with a huge silly grin on his face. Lucy was wiping down a table and turned toward him, a look of relief washed over her features. Hunter walked over to her and engulfed her in a hug.

"What was that for?" she asked, patting his back. When she withdrew, she had tears in her eyes and a huge smile.

"Just for being you," Hunter said before giving her a peck on the cheek. "Thank you."

He walked out of the diner still wearing the ridiculous grin on his face. The city sounds were now a tolerable hum, making him acutely aware of his surroundings but not enough to drive him to wear a white jacket.

Those few minutes with Cam would hold him over for now.

Hunter returned to the office a little calmer. When he arrived, he was greeted by a stack of red files on his desk. He turned and saw his assistant standing in the doorway.

"That was fast," Hunter commented.

Jessie shrugged casually with a smile. "I can be a charmer when I need to be."

Hunter chuckled. "She just gave them to you?"

"She's a bit distraught with everything going on. I, being the wonderfully supportive and humble public servant," he said in an overly dramatic tone with his hand on his chest, "offered to help and suggested I'd take care of any pending case files she had. She let me into Mel's office and I grabbed all the red files I saw plus a stack of regular ones so it wasn't too obvious. Easy peasy."

Hunter smiled. "I would have just charged right in there."

"Like a bull, I know. That's the phone, I'll be right back," he said before darting out of the office.

Hunter looked at the stack of folders, easily totaling over fifty files in addition to the red files he had received over the course of eight months.

He reached for his ringing office phone. "Yeah?"

"It's the mayor's office on the line. Mr. Weston would like to speak with you," Jessie responded.

The color drained from his face and his blood ran cold. "Put him through."

"Mr. Donovan, how are you?" the mayor asked.

"I'm fine, Frank," he said hesitantly, unsure of what the mayor actually knew.

"I heard the report that you were attacked. I've been trying to get more information but everything is tighter than a frog's ass. Do you know who it was? Why they attacked you?" the mayor said with both urgency and desperation in his voice.

"I don't have a clue. I was taken by surprise and the guy managed to get away. Mel wasn't so lucky."

"Yes, I heard. It is truly a shame, such a young life. How are you holding up at the office?"

"Trying to get caught up with the case work and seeing what else Mel had pending that needs attention."

"Well, you shouldn't have to worry about that stuff. I'm sure most things can get rescheduled without much of a fight considering what you went through. You focus on getting better and taking it easy. It might be best to take a few days off and recover. It's not every day someone gets attacked and makes it out alive."

"Thanks for your concern. You're right, it might be best if I took some time off," Hunter said. He could use the time to go through Lydia's information without worrying about the office.

"It's more than concern, Hunter. You're next in line for a promotion. You just need to tell me which position you'd like. Mel's no longer with us, so your options just expanded a bit more."

Bastard.

Hunter cringed. He hated being a hypocrite and dishing out so much bullshit. "Thanks, Frank. I'll let you know. I'm still trying to wrap my brain around Mel not being here, so I'll need some time."

"Of course, of course. Anything you need, just give my office a call," he said before disconnecting the call.

Hunter turned to his computer and entered his password to access his desktop. He logged in to the county court site to check the docket. Jessie entered his office just as Hunter had confirmed that Mackler was still scheduled for trial all week. Good, he hadn't fled.

"This just arrived. It has my name on the delivery slip but it's got a file with your name on it," his assistant said as he handed over the envelope.

"Hold on a sec," Hunter said as he opened the envelope to discover a single sheet of paper and a key. He read the few lines printed on the letter informing him of the basic organization used to sort the information, the address for the storage facility, and passcodes for entry.

He looked up at his assistant who patiently waited.

"Are you up for a field trip?"

Chapter
TWENTY-NINE

Hunter anxiously turned the corner only blocks away from the diner.

"We really don't need a break," Jessie said from the passenger seat as he tried to stifle a yawn.

They had spent hours going through paperwork and audio for the past three days. Jessie had nodded off at the table or had crashed in the guest room for short bursts but continued to work through the evening hours alongside Hunter. Aidan had helped bring the two stacks of boxes with documented telephone conversations, office memos, emails, and more from Lydia's storage room to Hunter's house and had helped in the evening hours each night, sneaking a few hours' sleep on Hunter's bedroom couch before going in to the station.

"We're taking a break while Aidan supervises the crime scene cleanup crew at the house. Besides, I want you to meet someone."

"Cameron?" Jessie asked with a smile.

"Yup," Hunter said as they drove into the parking lot.

They entered the diner and stood by the sandwich area. Hunter anxiously looked around, hoping to get a glimpse of Cam. Phone calls and texts just weren't enough.

Hunter's phone chirped and he looked at the display to get an update from Aidan on the cleanup progress. The cleanup service he hired was working on getting the blood stains out of the living and bedroom flooring that wouldn't budge.

"Is that him?" Jessie asked quietly with a gentle touch to Hunter's arm to get his attention.

Hunter looked up and saw Cam exiting the back room and smiled. When Cam looked over and saw him, his eyebrows arched downward. He yanked off his apron and threw it on the table before stalking over to Hunter.

Jessie visibly cringed and took a few steps back until he stood behind Hunter.

The fire in Cam's eyes shot a jolt of lust through Hunter's body. He'd missed Cam, that fire, that territorial streak. His body itched for Cam's touch as he approached. He imagined this was what a helpless animal was like at the mercy of a lion, and he was damn ready for that type of attack.

* * * *

Cam tried to not think about the billion different ways he wanted to rip apart that smaller man who felt the need to touch Hunter. He was obviously terrified.

Good.

And what the hell was Hunter thinking, bringing some guy into the diner and getting chummy with him. His blood ran so fucking hot he just wanted to grab Hunter, throw him over the counter, and completely, totally, absolutely claim him so it was unmistakable who Hunter belonged to.

Hunter had this silly grin on his face as Cam approached.

Cam reached Hunter, grabbed the back of his neck forcefully, and pulled him down for a branding kiss. Hunter moaned and reached for Cam's waist, pulling him flush against his body. Hunter broke the kiss, gasping for air.

"Who the fuck is this?" Cam snarled at the small shaking man.

Hunter worked his hand under Cam's shirt to his lower back and touched his skin in that rhythmic way he always did to soothe him. He didn't need soothing, he wanted to know who the fuck this guy was standing so damn close to *his* Hunter.

"This is Jessie, my assistant." He then looked over his shoulder. "Jess, *this* is Cam," Hunter said with a smile.

The color drained from Cam's face. He looked up at Hunter who still wore this silly grin.

"I totally hate you right now. You could have warned me," Cam mumbled, trying to hide his face at the side of Hunter's neck.

Hunter chuckled. "And miss this? No way."

"Hi, Jessie," Cam finally said with a wave, his face still buried at the side of Hunter's neck.

"Hi," Jessie said quietly, still standing behind Hunter.

"I'm so sorry. Shit. I just wasn't thinking when I saw you walk in here with Hunter."

Jessie's eyes rounded. "You thought me and Hunter—"

"Sorry," Cam responded. He looked up to Hunter who wore an even wider smile. "I swear, if you don't wipe that grin off your face—"

Hunter chuckled and kissed Cam's neck, cutting off his train of thought.

Cam looked over to Bill. "Sorry," he mouthed to the older man. Bill simply waved him off and laughed.

He was so going to rip into Hunter about this later. "Have you guys eaten yet?" Cam asked.

"Not yet. They're cleaning up the house so we figured we'd get a break and pick things up later on today," Hunter said with his arm still wrapped around Cam's waist.

Cam nodded and looked over at Bill.

"Son, I'm already on top of it," Bill responded then asked Jessie about his sandwich preferences. "Do you want some coffee to go with this?"

"Or a latte," Hunter added. "Cam makes an awesome latte." He circled his fingers on Cam's lower back. Cameron leaned into the touch, enjoying the contact he had missed for the past few days.

Jessie hesitantly looked over to Cam.

Great, the guy probably thinks I'm going to poison him.

"Um, okay," Jessie responded quietly.

Cam nodded in response, gave Hunter a quick peck, then walked behind the counter area.

As he heated the milk, he was still kicking himself in the ass about the way he had reacted. He seriously needed to get a grip on himself. Hunter wasn't going anywhere. He'd made that crystal clear, he just needed to let it sink in. He took a deep breath and tried to calm his shaking hands. There was no way in hell he would be able to make one of his designs if he wasn't a bit more steady.

"Go ahead and take your break, hun," Lucy said.

What the heck was he supposed to do? Sit with them and torture the poor man further? It was obvious the guy wasn't comfortable around him. "Nah, that's okay."

Lucy placed a hand on his shoulder. "Sweetie, take your break. Hunter's obviously here to see you, and regardless of what happened, I'm sure he'd like to spend a little time with you while he's here. Besides, I think he rather enjoyed your protectiveness," she said with a shy smile.

"Protectiveness?" Cam shook his head. "Lucy, I wouldn't call it that. It was embarrassing," he mumbled.

Lucy rubbed a circle on his back. "It was an instinct to protect what the two of you have. I've known him for years, and never, ever, have I seen him this happy. Even with everything going on."

"That's what he tells me," Cam said on a sigh.

Lucy squeezed his shoulders in a half hug. "You haven't had it easy, sweetie. So I'm sure he understands why you get territorial. Besides," she inched a little closer and whispered, "I think he enjoys being the center of such devotion."

Lucy, all grandmotherly with her hair picked up and apron tied around her waist, giggled like a teenager. Cam couldn't contain a chuckle that escaped.

"You're not helping," he said as he finished the second latte.

"Go, take your break and spend some time with them so that scared young man can see why Hunter loves you so much."

Cam knew Jessie was working his ass off this week to help Hunter, which meant he was helping Cam. He counted to ten to try and calm his nerves. He took the two lattes he had prepared and walked over to Hunter's corner where they sat.

"Is that a bear?" Jessie asked with a huge smile.

Cam sighed with relief. "Yeah."

"Cam keeps learning new designs each week and practices until he gets them perfect," Hunter said with a proud tone.

Cam's cheeks heated. He wasn't much of a bragger, but he couldn't deny how much he enjoyed hearing Hunter compliment him to someone else.

"It's called latte art. I figured it'd be nice to do something different with that big coffee mug."

"Just make sure you drink it, Jess. Cam's territorial about people drinking his coffee," Hunter finished with a smile as he bit his bottom lip.

"You're beggin' for it," Cam said under his breath as he plopped himself in the chair.

Hunter leaned over and kissed the side of his neck.

Cam playfully pushed away Hunter. "Stop it. I'm supposed to be mad at you."

Hunter laughed and leaned in again.

Cam couldn't help but laugh. He looked over to Jessie, hoping their playful display hadn't freaked out the poor man into having a heart attack. Instead, Jessie had a wistful look on his face and grinned as he took a sip of his coffee.

"Sorry about that," Cam said.

Jessie quickly shook his head and waved his hand. "Don't be."

"Thanks for all the work you're doing to help me this week. Hunter tells me you've been spending hours up to your eyeballs in papers and other stuff. I really appreciate it," he finished quietly, the knot in his throat preventing any more words from being spoken.

"You're welcome," Jessie said, hiding behind the big mug to take another sip.

Hunter reached over and pressed the back of Cam's neck. Cam leaned into the touch, enjoying Hunter's hands on him. The goose pimples rose on his skin as Hunter's thumb stroked the side of his neck. He glanced at Hunter and saw the same need for closeness staring back at him through the silver gaze. He leaned over and rested his head on Hunter's shoulder, hoping to convey how much he had missed seeing him these past few days.

They finished their lunch while recapping new developments in the case. Jessie caved and told Cam some office stories about working with Hunter. Cam genuinely laughed and eased into a comfortable discussion with Jessie, no longer threatened by his proximity to Hunter.

"Don't you get bored out of your mind going through all that paperwork?" Cam asked.

"Not at all, I actually enjoy it. And with Hunter and Aidan there," Jessie began then trailed off.

"Aidan's a nice guy," Cam said and cocked his head to the side when Jessie nodded.

"Yes, he is. He's very easy to be around which surprises me," Jessie added casually. "Do you think he'd like us to bring him a coffee?"

Hunter squeezed Cam's knee. He wasn't sure if that was his way of encouraging the line of questions or his way of telling Cam to back off. "Aidan's a great guy and easy to talk to. What part of him surprised you?" he asked in the most nonchalant tone he could fake.

Jessie shrugged. "Big guys usually aren't like that."

"I'm like that," Hunter said defensively.

This time, it was Cam's turn to squeeze his knee. It was obvious, even to Cam who lacked social interaction for a decade that something was up with Jessie. Now he felt really horrible about earlier when the man had arrived at the diner.

"You're not the norm," Jessie barely whispered.

"No, he's not and I'm thankful for that," Cam said then grabbed Hunter's face and gave him a loud kiss on the cheek. "I'll get that coffee ready for Aidan. You behave," he said to Hunter then turned to Jessie. "Thanks again for all your help. Sorry about earlier."

Jessie smiled and shook his hand. Cam instinctively knew to avoid the firm double pump handshake he usually did.

After a few moments, Hunter answered a call on his cell then they stood to leave. Jessie took Aidan's coffee to-go and headed out. Hunter immediately followed with a wave good-bye over his shoulder and a smile that promised much mischief. If Hunter was getting his house cleaned, then there was a chance they could have their weekend alone. He smiled when he returned to the coffee machine to fill a few new orders and think of creative ways he could pay back Hunter.

Chapter
THIRTY

Hunter stared intently through the two-way glass, his teeth were starting to hurt from the pressure of his clenched jaw. He had spent endless hours with Jessie, reviewing boxes of information last week, breaking only for his weekend with Cam. They had found a wealth of evidence on Frank, nothing solid on Mackler.

He had taken Cam for his follow-up tattoo appointment on Saturday, then they spent a few hours at a music festival in South Beach after having dinner with Hunter's dad. Cam got his wish for Sunday and they spent the entire day in bed. Apparently Cam seemed to think tying him down while he had his way with him suitable punishment for Hunter goading his territorial streak. *Sucker.*

Hunter inhaled sharply, his laser focus still pegged on the man in the next room arguing with Aidan.

He knew time was not on their side. After dropping Cameron off at the halfway house, Hunter changed his strategy and tried to think outside the box for evidence. He set a personal goal of seventy-two hours to find whatever he could get to nail Mackler's ass to the wall.

He found it in twenty-four.

"Do you honestly think I'm going to sit here like a moron and talk about anything? That's for the idiots that end up in my courtroom. I've exercised my right to an attorney," Mackler said. "He should be here any minute and we'll continue after he arrives."

"Very well," Aidan said as he closed the file then exited the room. So far, everything had played out the way they had hoped. The warrant had been served for Mackler's home and office and nothing had been found. They had arrested Mackler and provided a small bit of information, which led to Mackler immediately contacting his attorney.

"So far so good," Aidan said as he entered the observation room. "He probably thinks we have nothing or he thinks we'll get nowhere now that he's lawyered up."

"Good," Hunter said as he continued to stare with his arms crossed. "I want that cocky son of bitch to fucking piss in his pants when he realizes just how fucked he is."

"Are you sure we can use it?"

"In this case, yes," Hunter said confidently.

"Lydia's not going to get burned here is she?"

"Nope. The most incriminating documents didn't come from her. I've got to play the other stuff right for it to hit its mark."

"Are you sure we can't just use Cam's father's statement? That bastard said enough about Mackler to do some damage."

"His credibility is shit. Any lawyer can rip him apart in two seconds flat. We need something from a credible source that sticks."

"I hope you know what you're doing because, otherwise, we can't nail that Rick guy. That arrogant son of a bitch is in custody right now on breaking and entering and attempted murder of you and Cam. That's not enough. I want that fucker to rot in prison and pray for a quick death every time he wakes up in his roach-infested cot. I need the drug and conspiracy charge to stick. I know it's part of your plan, but I hate that this fucker's lawyered up."

Hunter's jaw muscles flexed. "I know. He's full of himself and his ego won't let his attorney take control. He's bluffing. I'm just going to call his bluff. Don't worry, I'll set it up all nice and pretty and make you look like a king."

"Aw, you're so thoughtful."

"I try," he said, playing along with Aidan but still focused on the man on the opposite side of the glass. His mind raced through the various arguments the judge would present and how he would handle his responses. His brain had shifted into courtroom gear and he was ready to slam Mackler and any excuse he would present in his defense. Mackler was a challenge, but the thought of getting this guy to turn and possibly free Cam's name in the process sharpened his focus. "Just make sure you get what you need to nail these fuckers and clear Cam's name. I also want to make sure Peter can come back with his career intact."

"You set it up and I'll go in for the kill."

Hunter nodded. His jaw twitched wildly as he clenched his teeth to try and bite down the anger waiting to be unleashed. He needed to keep his temper at bay and put on his best poker face, now more than ever. He wanted this son of a bitch to suffer, to know firsthand what Cameron had dealt with during his sentence. All through their weekend together, all Hunter could think about was spending each waking day of the rest of his life with Cam just as they had done during those precious few weekend hours. It didn't matter what they did, their time together had become a basic need to his existence. He craved waking with Cam pressed against him, the sound of his voice, his laughter, the twitch of the muscles under his touch, the quiet and subtle requests for closeness.

The nightmare had begun with *this* man. The smug bastard on the other side of this glass had managed to create a barrier between him and Cam that he still had not been able to break through. He wanted to say the words, *needed* to say them, but he could see the plea in Cam's eyes to not push. The fear that something would happen to Hunter haunted Cam. That same fear Hunter had seen in Cameron's eyes the day of the attack when he thought the gunshot had hit its mark.

Hunter swore he would do everything in his power to wipe away that memory for Cam. His mission was to finally break that iron wall Cam had taken a decade to build—to convince Cam to let him in and allow himself to be loved, completely, without fear.

This son of a bitch behind the glass had stolen Cam's sense of security and had taken Hunter's freedom to completely and totally enjoy the love he had been blessed with. He wanted to nail the bastard to the wall.

Mackler's attorney entered the interrogation room.

"It's showtime," Hunter said through gritted teeth as he exited the observation room with Aidan.

"I have a recorded conversation—"

"Which obviously is inadmissible in court. Quite frankly Mr. Donovan, I'm rather surprised you'd attempt that with me. That's illegal as you know." Mackler huffed a laugh then looked pointedly at Aidan then back to Hunter. "You two should know better."

"Mackler—"

"Show a little respect, Mr. Donovan," the judge said.

"I'm not in your courtroom, and I am using your name rather than a more appropriate term to address you in this instance in order to present *myself* in a professional manner. So, I suggest you listen very carefully before you attempt to interrupt me again."

Mackler looked at Hunter hesitantly as if trying to decipher his next move. Hunter imagined Mackler knew him well enough to know when, and if, to call his bluff. Mackler cocked his head to the side as a sign to proceed.

"I have a recording," Hunter repeated, pausing to wait for another interruption, then continued when none came, "of you and the mayor having a discussion."

"And that was a private conversation," Mackler responded.

"My client is not admitting to having said conversation," Saul Miles, Mackler's attorney, immediately interjected. "What was discussed during this alleged communication?"

Hunter leaned back in his chair to establish a casual air to the exchange. "Mackler chatted with the mayor about a party and who would be attending. Big wig party for an upcoming political candidate. The mayor offered up a county vehicle to escort the political candidate, his staff, and family to the event."

Mackler burst into laughter. "Sounds like you've got Frank's ass in the sling for misappropriation of funds, not mine. Listen, Mr. Donovan, I don't have time to waste—"

"I wasn't finished," Hunter said, crossing his arms, maintaining the casualness of his demeanor.

Mackler sat back in his chair and waited.

"So it got me thinking about possibly getting *you* doing something casual, something most people wouldn't figure you'd do or might overlook."

Mackler's composure subtly shifted.

"See, I know certain government officials are granted credit cards for official use only and any sort of deviation of this is subject to disciplinary action."

"I don't have a government issued credit card, Mr. Donovan. You're reaching," Mackler responded confidently.

"No, *you* don't," Hunter confirmed. "But your wife did for many years."

Mackler paled and his attorney immediately looked in his direction. "Don't say a word." Mr. Miles then turned his focus to Hunter. "Whatever the ex-Mrs. Mackler did with her credit card was her decision."

Hunter laughed. "I already have a sworn statement from her where she provides extensive details regarding *Mr.* Mackler's purchases, and I even have signatures on receipts to confirm they were made by *Mr.* Mackler."

"The card was in her name," Mackler said before he quieted under the glare of his attorney.

"Excellent point, the problem is, your forgery of her signature doesn't match her actual signature but it's a perfect match for your writing according to the handwriting specialist who I've had review the numerous receipts we found archived in the system."

"That's one opinion," Mackler's attorney responded.

"Three actually, I wanted to be sure," Hunter responded in the same tone. "It's rather interesting the things you've bought when you think no one's looking at you."

"Mr. Donovan, Mr. Mackler and his ex-wife have been divorced for some time. Regardless of whatever misappropriation of funds may have occurred, there are statutes of limitations involved which

I'm sure have exceeded their timetable since they've been divorced now for many years."

Hunter leaned forward. "That's the funny thing. Most of the charges would fall into that category except one thing."

"What's that?" the attorney asked while Mackler remained silent.

"The gun that was used ten years ago at Mr. Mackler's home, which resulted in a death."

Hunter waited for a reaction from Mackler, but he remained seated, unresponsive.

"Here's what I find interesting," Hunter said sardonically. "You buy a gun, illegally, using your wife's federal job credit card with a forged signature. You then put that gun in *your* name. You somehow manage to convince a judge to charge your son's boyfriend with manslaughter even though that same weapon in *your* name was used in *your* house. To add insult to injury, you further get him accused of a ridiculous list of crimes including a drug violation. Now, that little cocktail of charges throws your statute of limitations out the window. So you're looking at several years for that alone and I'm sure I can find a few more things to throw in there that would give you a good feel for what you did to Cameron Pierce's life."

"What do you want, Mr. Donovan?" Mackler asked in an icy tone.

Hunter leaned in and rested his forearms on the table. "I didn't say I was finished."

The attorney straightened. "What else is there?"

"As I said before, I have a recorded conversation."

Mackler rolled his eyes. "Which you already said was Frank talking about—"

"Oh, not that one. That was just another interesting call that led into the discussion about the misappropriation of funds and what got me to look into that where you were concerned."

"What recording, Mr. Donovan?" Mackler asked.

"The one where you are having a discussion with the mayor about making sure Cameron doesn't get out of prison," Hunter finished with a sneer.

"Any such conversation would require all-party consent in order for it to be admissible in a Florida court. As an attorney, Mr. Donovan, you should know that," Mackler said with a half smile.

"The statute only covers confidential and private conversations."

"Any conversation I've had with the mayor is private, and I can assure you I did not consent to the recording of any said conversation."

"Your discussion was held during a lunch break in the outside patio of a restaurant in Coconut Grove, paid with the mayor's credit card I'd like to add. The privacy analysis fails for the statute in this case so it no longer applies since anyone out in that patio could have heard your conversation."

"No one was there!" Mackler yelled as he rose from his seat, knocking his chair back on the floor.

"Be quiet and sit down," Mackler's attorney said.

"It doesn't matter if anyone was there or not, the location and circumstance are the relevant factors in the assessment. I would expect a judge of your stature to know such technicalities in the law."

"What the fuck do you want, Hunter?" Mackler asked, picking up the chair from the floor and taking his seat again.

"You need to keep quiet," Mr. Miles said as he placed his hand on Mackler's forearm.

Mackler raised his arm abruptly, pushing his attorney's hand off. "And you need to just shut the hell up like you've been doing all this time. Get the hell out of here."

"Are you waiving your right—"

Mackler pressed his index fingers to his temples. "If someone else throws the law in my face again, I'm going to plead temporary insanity and won't be responsible for my actions."

"I think your services are no longer needed here, Mr. Miles," Hunter said with a pointed look to the attorney.

Mackler exhaled once he was left in the room alone with Aidan and Hunter. "What do you want and what will I get in return?"

"You need to make a choice."

Mackler laughed mournfully. "Something tells me my options are going to be varying degrees of misery."

Hunter gave him a wry smile. "You can choose to be charged with misappropriation of government funds, embezzlement—"

"Or?" Mackler interrupted.

"Or," Hunter said casually, "you provide us with information to take down the drug network. Not some bullshit hearsay or generalizations. I want names, addresses, dates, times, everything. You are not the kind of man to work with someone on something like this unless you've got some security. So don't attempt to feed us a line of crap about how you don't know what's going on and aren't sure who is doing what."

Mackler laughed. "Seems you know me relatively well, Mr. Donovan."

"I'm sure you know I've got enough to put you away for the rest of your life. The minimum I'm willing to do is ten years and that's not up for discussion."

"Tit for tat. I'm assuming this is why you mentioned Cameron's name earlier," Mackler said sarcastically.

"Exactly. I should add more but I'm willing to negotiate if, and only if, you provide enough information that Aidan deems relevant and useful to his case. If not, the deal is off the table and you are on the hook for every fucking thing I can possible nail you on. I don't give a shit how small a detail it is. Understand?"

Mackler sighed then nodded. "You're ruining me, you know that? Do you have any idea how long it took me to build this nest egg of mine? For us to build the network of contacts? I was working carefully on planning my retirement and making sure I didn't have to worry about living on a judge's salary. And now, one little son of a bitch has torn it all to shreds," he finished, rubbing his face in obvious frustration.

"I'm heartbroken," Hunter deadpanned.

"I was careful as hell. I knew he would get out and screw with everything. I fucking knew it," Mackler continued, clearly missing Hunter's disinterest in his misery.

"Pretend Aidan is a priest and you're in a confessional. Go ahead, keep talking," he said before rising from his seat.

"Did Amy really give me up about all the charges?" Mackler looked up and asked with a pained expression.

Hunter nodded. "She was very thorough in her statements. Guess the marriage wasn't as pleasant for her as it may have been for you. She knew this stuff would come back to haunt her even though she had made every effort to replace all the money you spent in her name. She kept supporting documents for everything just in case she needed it in her defense. You did a real number on her."

Mackler shrugged. "A lot of years and too much history."

Hunter walked to the door and paused. "Why Cam?" He could leave Aidan to ask whatever questions were needed, but he had to know why.

"You can blame my idiot son for that. He made the mistake of taking that boy to the one place that was completely off limits. He would have been better off just fucking him in the backseat of his car like the slut that he is."

"Careful, Mackler."

Mackler huffed a laugh. "My son was so dense he thought he could somehow prove to me that he wasn't gay. So what does he do? He decides to date a female mirror image of that boy in hopes of trying to convince me. Idiot. He actually thought I would change my mind about the will if he convinced me he had switched teams."

"So, it wasn't supposed to turn out like that but it ended up working out for you anyway."

Mackler looked at Hunter and was lost in thought for a moment. Hunter glared, waiting for the connection to be made.

"Sound familiar?"

Finally, Mackler shook his head slowly and laughed. "How the hell did you hook up with that little shit?"

Hunter shifted his weight and paused to control his temper. He had Mackler exactly where he needed him to be for Aidan and didn't want to risk screwing that up. "That little comment just added another two years to your reduced term."

"You can't—"

"I just did," Hunter snarled. He then turned to Aidan and took a deep breath before speaking. "Aidan, if Mackler chooses to mention anything derogatory about Cameron's character during his statement, I'm adding an additional year to his term for each instance. Got it?"

Aidan nodded.

"Have a nice life," he said to Mackler before finally exiting the room.

* * * *

Hunter answered his phone on the first ring.

"How did it go?" Hunter asked. "Did you get what you needed?"

"Yup, and then some," Aidan said, laughing. "I swear that man wanted a few Hail Marys after he spilled."

"So you've got enough to clear Cam of all the charges?"

"Yup. It'll take some time, but yeah, we've got enough to get that going."

"What about Peter? I want to make sure we've got enough to clear him so he can get his ass back here."

"Yeah, he's good too. Go ahead and get a hold of him. We're going to need a few judges we can trust to get moving on this. I've got enough to get the ball rolling on the mayor and our favorite drug superstar as well. We're bringing in the mayor based on some of the stuff in Mackler's statement and we'll use the stuff you've got from Lydia as leverage to get him to talk."

"Great. Anything else come up?"

"Yeah, but you're not going to like it. According to Mackler, he was doing business with Rick one day and somehow the conversation veered toward one of Rick's goons mentioning seeing Cam at the house with the judge's son. That's when Rick reached out to his contacts about keeping Cam inside. Mackler put him in, but it was Rick's idea to keep him there."

Hunter sighed. "I fucking hate these bastards. I want that son of a bitch to pay for this."

"Don't even go there. I know where your mind is headed. I need you to trust that I'll take care of this."

Hunter took a deep breath and tried to calm his boiling anger. He knew this tone in his best friend. It was pointless to continue arguing. Aidan said he'd take care of it and nothing Hunter could say would change that. He wanted to aim a bullet at Mackler and gut shot that bastard so he'd know what a painful slow death felt like. But Aidan would not allow that. Not to keep Mackler safe, but to protect Hunter. Besides, Aidan was also a man of justice—but his brand of justice was a little more creative at times and with greater control.

"Okay, okay. Anything with the files I sent over?" Hunter finally asked, trying to move on.

"I've been interviewing each one of the guys in the red files to collect some more info from them so I've got a well-rounded case ready. But man, there are so many of them, why didn't you say anything sooner?"

Hunter rubbed his eyes. "I wasn't sure where they were coming from and the level of detail in each file seemed suspicious. I didn't know who I could trust with them."

"I'll kick your ass later for saying that. At least they give us a checklist of names to question. Unfortunately, some of the red file subjects can't be questioned so—"

"Why?"

"They either died in prison or are mysteriously lost in the system. It's fucked up, man. We've still got a healthy list of people, but so far, we're looking at about a loss of twenty-five percent of these guys who went back in the last few months."

"Shit." Hunter rubbed his eyes harder. *Cam could have been one of those statistics.* "How the hell did no one notice that?"

"That's been weighing on me. There's no connection with these files other than a drug charge and a parole violation. Personally, I think they've got people in their pocket scattered throughout the system covering this shit up. It's like a cancer that's spreading all over and killing everything. I don't want to think about all the people involved right now. It'll take some time because it seems the judge and that Rick guy had a greater reach than we thought, but we've got enough to take them down. I'm just trying to tackle it one asshole at a time."

"I'm assuming the red file people are getting re-evaluated for parole?"

"Yup, already on that. I've got the entire department working on this thing."

"Yeah, I know. What about the other stuff?" Hunter asked.

"I'm working on that. I didn't want to wait until today so I've been trying to cover all the bases. I've got your list of requests, and I found a place that meets our requirements as well."

"Have you gone to check it out?"

"Not yet. I was planning on leaving that for tomorrow just to step away from this mess for a day or two."

"I want to come along, if I can."

"I'll make sure that's fine."

"Thanks, Aidan. I really appreciate you busting your ass on all this."

Aidan laughed. "Dude, I'm sitting here looking like a fucking king right now with the entire department at my beck and call. Thank you."

Hunter chuckled. "I'm glad to hear it. Text me the information, and I'll meet you at the airport."

"You got it, see you tomorrow."

Hunter hung up the phone and smiled.

Soon, it'll be over soon.

Finally, maybe Cam could get some peace.

He picked up the phone again and called his childhood friend so she could relay the good news to her *tio*.

Chapter
THIRTY-ONE

Cam stared at the ceiling, waiting for sleep to come. He had been anxious all week for those few precious weekend days with Hunter. Hunter was doing everything possible with Aidan to clear his name and had been able to finally get enough evidence against Mackler to turn him on the others.

He was thankful, but he wasn't kidding himself, it had cut into their weekend and he was pissed. It was selfish, but he didn't care.

It was Saturday night and he was alone. He missed Hunter, hated that he was in bed alone rather than pressed against him. The extra sheets to cover up and muggy Miami heat didn't seem enough to keep him warm.

He sighed as he kicked the sheets to the foot of the bed. It was pointless to keep fighting with them knowing they were no substitute. He pushed his head farther into the pillow, trying to find a comfortable spot. Nothing worked. Times like these, he'd pick up the phone and dial Hunter's number just to hear him laugh or say his name in that soothing voice. He scowled, remembering that one night where he actually fell asleep with the phone still pressed to his ear. He had a hell of a time dealing with the Julian jokes about the phone mark on his face.

He'd deal with whatever jokes came his way if he could hear Hunter's laugh tonight.

Hunter had mentioned a short trip and that he would be unreachable. He hadn't spoken to Hunter in two days. No calls, no texts. He was going stir crazy.

He punched the pillow under his head and repositioned them. He pushed his head back, fighting for a position that would ease him into a few hours' sleep.

He'd give anything to hear Hunter's voice right now or feel his arms wrapped around him.

Cam's mind raced with what-if thoughts about where things would lead with his case, his life, and with Hunter. They were on a path that seemed to be going their way, but they were also clear that it would take time to get everything sorted. He was tired of fighting and always being on guard. He wasn't sure how much longer he could sustain the façade.

He finally gave in to his fatigue and fell into a fitful sleep as thoughts continued to race through his mind.

* * * *

Hunter arrived at Halfway House directly from the airport. It was late but he couldn't stand being away for another moment. Cam had been at the forefront of his mind with every detail of his trip. He hoped Matt or Julian would show a little mercy on him and let him see Cam, even if only for a moment. Cam had gotten some leeway since his record was under review for expulsion, but Hunter didn't want to push his luck.

He walked up to the back door and gently knocked.

Julian answered after a few moments.

"Hey, I thought you were out of town?"

"Yeah, I just got in and wanted to see Cam…if that's okay?" He was raw. He could no longer stand being away from Cam for extended periods of time. He hadn't seen him in days and with a *no contact* restriction, he hadn't been able to talk to him at night like they often did.

"You look like you're going to pass out, man. You shouldn't be driving," Julian said with a lowered brow.

As if on cue, he tried to hide a yawn. Hunter ran his fingers through his hair. "I haven't slept well for the past few days," he said.

"Everything's fine on this end. No drama. Did you get everything squared away?" Julian asked, moving aside so Hunter could enter.

Hunter nodded. "Yeah, Aidan's going to get things in order this week and hopefully that'll be it. Any chance I can see him?" He knew he was pushing his luck. Residents were only permitted guests in the common areas, not the bedrooms during their stay.

Julian assessed him in his usual way then rubbed his shaved head. "Well, technically, you've got all the forms approved for this weekend, which means you're not really standing in front of me and we're not having this conversation." Julian returned to his seat on the couch and seemed to resume writing in the notebook he had apparently abandoned to answer the door. "His room is upstairs, last one on the right. No locks on the doors so keep it G rated please. I don't want Matt to wake up in the morning and freak out," Julian said with a pointed look and a raised eyebrow then resumed writing his notes.

He could only imagine how desperate he must have looked if Julian was willing to bend the rules.

"Breakfast is at nine if you guys are up by then," Julian added as a half smile escaped his control.

"Thanks," Hunter said before going upstairs, taking two steps at a time. His pulse raced when he reached Cam's door, anxious to see him, hold him. He listened carefully but didn't hear a sound. He slowly turned the knob and looked inside.

The streetlights cast a hint of light through the window in a spectrum of colors, enough for Hunter to see the strain in Cam's expression. He was asleep, but it was obvious it wasn't a peaceful slumber. Hunter exhaled a shaky breath, thankful to see Cam was safe but wondered if the tension he saw etched in his face was due to

Hunter's absence or something else. He entered the room quietly, careful to not make a sound.

During their weekends together, he'd wake in the middle of the night sometimes just to watch Cameron as he slept. He'd be peaceful, as if the stress of everything surrounding him no longer existed. He'd usually have a hint of a smile or just a serene expression. Looking at him now, both were absent. He had a crease between his brows and his lips were a tight, thin line. He was curled in the bed in a fetal position, the sheets partially off him, with his hands fisted between his legs. He was tense, guarded.

Hunter toed off his shoes and removed his jacket, gently placing them on the dresser.

"Are you just going to stand there and stare or join me?"

Hunter closed his eyes as the smooth tone of Cam's voice flowed through his body and filled his heart. He snuck into bed and inched himself as close to Cam as possible. He pressed his chest to Cam's back and snaked an arm around his waist.

Cameron's hands instantly caressed his arms and pulled him closer.

"I missed you," Cam mumbled before turning his face slightly toward Hunter.

Hunter's breath hitched at Cam's rare declaration. He wedged his leg between Cam's and gently placed a kiss on the soft lips he craved.

"Sorry my trip cut into our weekend."

"You're here now, that's what matters," Cam said as he straightened and pushed back to eliminate the inch of space between them. "Stay with me tonight," Cam said quietly before his voice trailed off.

Hunter raised his head slightly to look at Cam after he had been silent for a few minutes. He had fallen asleep again, the edges of his mouth were upturned slightly and a serene expression finally made its appearance.

He pressed his cheek to the back of Cam's head and deeply inhaled the scent he had craved for days as he effortlessly eased into sleep.

* * * *

"Wake up, lover boy."

Something wasn't right. The warm arm wrapped around him, the strong leg wedged between his and the hard chest against his back, all perfect...but the voice was wrong.

He heard a growl from behind and the arm tightened around him. He smiled. Yeah, that he knew.

"Guys, it's almost nine, and Matt's finishing up breakfast. If you get out of bed, you can make it in time before Julian and Luke eat all the food."

"Cole, we're going to sleep in. Go away," Cam said.

"You've got to get up. Please."

"Why?" Cam said in a raspy voice.

"Because I've got an interview thing at ten and I need to leave soon."

Cam narrowed his eyes. "And?" Cam said, inching back a little to get closer to Hunter's warm chest.

Cole leaned in closer to Cam and whispered, "Hunter's here."

"I *can* hear you, Cole," Hunter said with a growl.

"Good, you're awake so you can get out of bed," Cole said with a bounce on the mattress before standing to lean against the wall.

"Dude, you know how Julian's always telling you when something isn't the right time or place?" Cam said.

"Yeah?" Cole said, cocking his head.

"This is a perfect example," Hunter mumbled.

Cole looked down and shuffled his feet. "Please?"

Cam sat up and shifted his weight on his elbow. "What's up, Cole?"

Cole tugged on his beanie and fidgeted.

"If you get out now and save us some breakfast, I'll take you for a ride in the car before you leave," Hunter said in a still sleepy voice.

Cam laughed as Cole raced out of the room.

Cam turned to look at Hunter who still rested his head on the pillow beside him with his eyes closed. "Can you read *everyone's* mind?"

Hunter chuckled in that low rumbly way that always seemed to spike the need in Cam. He leaned into Hunter as he whispered, "You know, if we get out of bed, we can still have most of Sunday."

Cam laughed when Hunter bolted out of bed and started getting dressed.

After having breakfast and taking Cole out for a joyride, they finally left the halfway house to take advantage of what was left of their Sunday.

"This car is fast right?" Cam said.

"Yeah, why?"

"Then drive faster," Cam said, reaching over to grip Hunter's leg. He held back a laugh when he heard the engine rev. He inched his hand higher, casually stroking his fingers as he moved.

"You go any higher and we're going to have a problem."

"Why is that?" Cam said, his breath came faster as he shifted his fingers higher. He leaned closer toward Hunter, thankful he had finally figured out how to control the seat belt.

"I'm serious," Hunter said in a low rumble.

"You're really growly today," he mumbled in Hunter's ear as his fingers grazed Hunter's arousal.

"Fuck," Hunter groaned, pushing up into Cam's touch. He turned his head slightly and captured Cam's lips as he kept his eyes steady on the road.

"You should focus on driving," he said, rubbing Hunter's arousal with more pressure.

Hunter reached over and slid his hand inside the front of Cam's jeans. Cam moaned and lifted himself off the seat, pushing himself into Hunter's hold until his hand wrapped around Cam's rock hard shaft. He licked Hunter's earlobe as he applied more pressure to his grip on Hunter while pushing his own body upward into Hunter's touch.

"We better get to your place fast," Cam said with another moan, enjoying the firm slide of Hunter's grip.

"Who's the growly one now?"

"I'm so fucking hot, I'm about to blow you in the car if you don't hurry," he said with a firm squeeze to Hunter's hardened arousal.

Hunter hissed, then removed his hand from Cam's jeans.

"What the fuck, man?" Cam said, removing *his* hand from Hunter in protest.

"Grab my bag in the back."

"This better be good." Cam turned in his seat and reached for Hunter's overnight bag. "What am I looking for?"

"Side pocket."

Cam unzipped the compartment and a wicked grin spread across his face when he pulled out a small tube of lube. "Should I be worried about what you were doing with this while you were away?"

Hunter responded with a momentary glare in his direction before returning his focus to the road.

"So what do you want to do?" Cam said, biting his lower lip as he swung the tube like a pendulum between his fingers. Oh how he loved to tease Hunter.

Hunter grabbed the bottle of lube while maintaining a hold of the steering wheel. He spread some slick on his fingers, keeping his focus firmly on the road.

"You're a road hazard right now," Cam said with a chuckle.

"It's your fucking fault. Come here."

Cam reached over and bit along Hunter's jaw, working his way to Hunter's neck then back to the sensitive skin below his ear. He inhaled sharply when Hunter's fingers slid into the back of his jeans. He bit back a moan as Hunter entered him with a finger. He tugged on Hunter's earlobe as he arched into the touch.

"How long before we get to your place?" Cam asked breathlessly when a second finger joined the first.

"Just enough time," Hunter said, his intense concentration still on the road ahead.

Cam looked over Hunter's shoulder and was thankful for the light Sunday morning traffic. The car's windows were tinted, but not enough to hide everything. He lowered his head onto Hunter's shoulder when a third finger stretched him.

"Fuck, please tell me we're almost there."

"Just around the corner," Hunter said quietly.

He looked up when he heard Hunter's voice. The tone was steady, his focus unwavering. Cam hesitated, not sure if the look of concentration was partly anger.

"Are you mad?" Cam asked, trying to stay in control enough to stroke Hunter's chest.

Hunter shook his head slowly.

Cam arched his body as Hunter's fingers continued to move inside him.

"Say something."

Hunter shook his head again in a controlled, measured movement.

Cam rested his forehead onto Hunter's shoulder. He reached up and gripped the back of Hunter's neck. "Sorry," he mumbled between gasps, reveling in the burn and stretch of each shift of Hunter's fingers. "Shit, that feels so fucking good."

Hunter responded with a twist of his fingers. Cam closed his eyes and groaned. He shivered when a current traveled up his spine. His chest heaved with each breath when Hunter's fingers shifted and pressed. "I'm going to come."

"No, you're not. Not until we get to the house and I'm inside you."

Cam gripped the back of Hunter's neck with one hand and the front of his shirt with the other. "I'm not going to make it," he said, barely audible as he brushed his lips by Hunter's jaw.

"I've been holding off since the second you touched me. You. Better. Not. Come."

Cam brokenly moaned as he pressed his nose against the crook of Hunter's neck. He tried to focus on baseball, football, knitting, anything other than the glide of Hunter's fingers inside him and the pain of his angry hard-on begging to be released from the now tight jeans. He counted sheep in his head, but knew it was hopeless when the sheep started humping each other as they jumped the fence in his mind.

"We're here," Hunter said, withdrawing his fingers.

Cam was dazed. He exited the car and walked toward the house with a drunken sway, each step taking extreme effort to stay steady. He reached the door and barely made it past the threshold when Hunter grabbed him from behind and pushed him up against the wall.

Through the desire clouding his mind, he heard Hunter unzip his pants and the rip of a pack. His zipper was undone and his jeans pulled down. He kept his cheek pressed against the cold wall, hoping to last long enough to enjoy the hard-driving torture he knew was coming. He loved to tease Hunter, push him to the edge where he lost control and drove into him without inhibition.

He held a gasp when Hunter pushed himself inside in one swift move. He bit down on his lip, refusing to let the groan escape him with the sharp burn—the silence would drive Hunter to push harder, stronger.

Hunter pistoned into Cam with unforgiving force. His body slapped desperately against Cam's, pressing him against the wall, holding him up. Cam arched his backside, needing a little space between the hard wall and his equally hard arousal. His entire body screamed to life with the primal pounding. He tightened his mouth to quiet the moan when Hunter's fingers wrapped around his hard shaft. He screwed his eyes shut and bit the inside of his cheek. No way was he giving Hunter a single sound of pleasure that would end this delicious torture. His legs weakened and he began to slip slightly, held only by Hunter's constant push inside him.

"I know you're trying to torture me," he heard Hunter's strangled whisper in his ear. "I know you're close. Admit it."

No way in hell was Cam admitting to anything that would stop this. His chest tightened with emotion, knowing he caused Hunter to shed his façade of control and desperately take what he needed. He leaned his head back onto Hunter's shoulder as the shudders traveled his body with each push of Hunter inside him and the glide of his hand taking him closer to the peak he desperately wanted to delay.

"You know it's you, and only you, who can do this to me. I'm yours," Hunter said as he licked the edge of Cam's ear.

Cam couldn't hold the groan that escaped. Hunter knew exactly how to break him. If he was coming, Hunter was going with him. He reached behind and gripped Hunter's thigh. His fingers brutally dug into the hard muscles just as the bolt of electricity shocked his entire body and blinded him with a white light.

After a few quick thrusts, Hunter immediately followed him. He wrapped both arms around Cam and held him tightly against his chest.

Hunter embraced Cam until their breathing settled, one arm around his waist, the other wrapped around his shoulders.

"I love it when you touch me like that," Hunter said, his breath warming Cam's ear.

A chill traveled Cam's body with the scrape of stubble against his nape. "I know," Cam responded, craning his neck in search of Hunter's mouth.

After a slow brush of lips, Hunter broke the kiss and looked at him intently, his voice low and thick. "You also know it drives me nuts when you tease me like that."

Cam nodded before looking away. He knew how Hunter felt without hearing the words, and he loved when Hunter took his time to slowly torture and worship every inch of him. But there was something primal that shifted when Hunter lost control, when he didn't hold back for the sake of being the nice guy.

That was when Cam would know how much Hunter truly wanted him.

Hunter pulled Cam's chin to turn his head. "You don't have to tease me. Just tell me what you need," he said, firmly holding Cam's face, not allowing him to turn away.

Cam's heart hammered against his chest. He closed his eyes.

I can do this.

Cam opened his eyes but avoided eye contact. "I want nice and slow later. I…I missed you so much…" he said and tried to swallow the lump in his throat. He closed his eyes again and took a deep breath. "I…I need to know you missed me too."

I can be completely honest. I can tell him what I need and he won't run away.

He opened his eyes and looked at Hunter firmly. "Right now, I want you to fuck me stupid until I can't remember my damn name."

Hunter released Cam and stepped back slowly.

Cam's pulse raced as he carefully watched Hunter, his expression closed, serious, and his movements slow and measured.

In a flash, Hunter grabbed Cam, turned him, and roughly threw him on the living room couch. Cam looked up and his breath hitched at the desire staring back at him.

Hunter reached over into the drawer of the entryway chest for another condom. He withdrew his hand and threw a few packets on the side table then reached for the lube. Cam's chest heaved with each breath, watching every slow, deliberate movement Hunter made.

Hunter lowered himself on his knees between Cam's legs and slid on a new condom before methodically spreading more lube against his covered, already erect hard-on.

Cam's heart slammed against his chest in anticipation. He gripped the cushions and tried to maintain control of his body as he watched Hunter.

Hunter looked up from his task and focused his intense, darkened glare on Cam.

Cam closed his eyes as a moan escaped. That look alone screamed how much Hunter wanted him.

Hunter neared and rubbed himself against Cam.

"Fuck," Cam said, throwing his head back into the couch and tightening his grip on the cushions. They hadn't started yet and he already felt as if he was ready to explode.

Hunter roughly pulled Cam's legs open and entered him again in one quick move.

Cam arched his body and gripped Hunter's powerful thighs. Hunter jackhammered into Cam with brutal force, taking him, owning him. Cam dug his fingers into the hard muscles and moaned loudly with each fierce glide, reveling in the carnal possession he knew could only happen because Hunter needed him just as much. Hunter pulled Cam's legs up, straight against his shoulder and pushed harder, faster, with relentless force, taking Cam higher than any peak he thought was ever possible to reach.

Cam's vision blurred and his skin was slick with sweat. In his daze, gasping for breath, Hunter captured his mouth and fiercely kissed him with a possessive growl. He returned the kiss with equal brutality, one hand digging deeper into Hunter's thigh, the other pulling at his hair. He broke the kiss, gasping for breath.

He didn't have the energy to fight the tremors rippling through his body or hold back the incoherent mumblings each time Hunter hit his gland perfectly.

He willingly dove off that cliff in a blinding white haze as electricity coursed through his body.

Moments later, he finally opened his eyes. Everything was a spinning blur. Warm puffs of air tickled his ear. He felt the full weight of a body on him he instinctively knew was supposed to be with him. He reached up and gripped the hard-muscled, broad back, trying to ground himself.

"What's your name?" he heard in that seductive tone of voice he loved so much.

"Huh?" he mumbled.

"Good."

Chapter
THIRTY-TWO

Hunter sighed as he reviewed the last of the depositions for his case file. It was only eleven in the morning and he was already starting to get cross-eyed after having reviewed so many transcripts. He put his pen down and rubbed his face.

The office was incredibly quiet and the crime stats were dramatically down. He was finally able to get up to date on both his and Mel's lingering cases. Aidan had made great strides with the case and many involved were apprehended or hiding. It seemed as if the local crime world had decided to lay low until the surge of adrenaline coursing through the legal system died out a bit. The news headlines, normally riddled with reports of robberies and shootings, showcased community news usually reserved for the back end of a newspaper. The breaking news last night: a kangaroo had escaped the local zoo and was spotted hopping along the side of the road.

It had never been this peaceful on the streets.

He reached for the next folder on his desk and sighed.

Off the streets was a completely different story. Judges, lawyers, policemen, elected officials, and an endless list of business owners had been arrested. All had clean records and were respected members of the community. They would have gone completely undetected. The network of contacts that had been cultivated for more than a decade, took only a few weeks to break apart. Hunter was disgusted with everything they had uncovered. He had spent years serving his city. Now, he just wanted to walk away.

His cell phone chirped with a new call.

"Hey, what's up?"

"I've got an update," Aidan said.

"Yeah?" Hunter prompted as he rested the phone on his shoulder while he finished handling the files on his desk before his meeting.

"Mackler."

"What about the son of a bitch?"

"Well, the police commissioner and I had a rather lengthy conversation."

"And?"

"We're both in agreement that it's just not fair to give special treatment to some inmates when our prison systems are so overpopulated. Sadly, we've had to put Mackler in with the general population," Aidan said.

An evil grin spread across Hunter's face. Times like these, he was thankful for Aidan's sometimes twisted form of justice. "You do know he won't survive genpop. If Rick's people won't get him, I'm sure one of his prior convictions will."

"Not my problem. He doesn't deserve any favors."

"Agreed." Hunter sighed as a sickening sense of relief filter through his body. He'd taken an entirely different position on justice lately.

"Seems the commissioner has no sympathy for the man. Mackler's managed to tarnish all branches of the judicial system, including his police force. He hasn't taken too kindly to that at all."

"He won't last long once the word gets out. Do you have everything you need and will it stick?"

"Yup. We've got depositions and subsequent depos from others as well confirming everything he's stated. We're good."

"I give it twenty-four to forty-eight hours, tops."

"I'm leaning more toward twenty-four or less."

"That's too quick."

"I may have hinted to Rick during one of my recent interrogations that Mackler was going in, can't remember."

"You never were one for patience," Hunter said, snorting a laugh.

"Nope, that's your department."

"I've got to go, I've got a meeting with the governor in an hour," Hunter finished with a sigh. The governor, police commissioner, and police captain of the local precinct were some of the few who remained committed to ridding the streets of any lingering contacts. He had done things in the past few weeks that didn't follow protocol. He guessed his meeting with the governor in the afternoon would seal his fate.

"He's going to ask you to run for mayor now that Frank's out," Aidan said.

"What?" Hunter asked.

"Yeah, seems the governor and the commissioner are friends. We chatted about it."

"Why the hell didn't you talk him out of it? You know I'm not built for politics. Shit man, I thought he was going to reprimand me or something."

"You know how the commissioner is when he's set on something, and you know how I hate wasting my time. He thinks you'll get a strong public endorsement taking down these guys, and with his support, he seems to think you're a sure thing."

"Well, I won't do it. You should recommend Peter for the job now that he's back. How are the other things coming along?" Hunter said as he finished the last pending file he was working on.

"I got the green light so I'm getting the paperwork finalized. I'm hoping to have everything ready so you and Cam can come by the office this afternoon, tomorrow at the latest."

"That would be great."

"Talk to you later," Aidan said then disconnected the call.

Two hours later, while sitting in the governor's office, arguing his position as to why he would not run for mayor, Hunter's phone chirped.

He stopped the conversation to read the text message from Aidan.

Mackler found beaten and hung in cell.

He paused for a moment then cleared the display and resumed his argument with the governor.

* * * *

Cameron rolled his shoulders as he looked at the wall clock for the hundredth time.

"Why are we here again?" he asked Hunter.

"Aidan wants to talk to you."

"Why here?" Cam looked around the room, shifting again in the chair. The room was immaculately clean and bare. He knew he was in a federal building because of the sign outside, but couldn't see anything beyond the four walls to get any additional information. "What's wrong?"

"Nothing's wrong. Stop worrying."

Cam straightened in his seat when Aidan arrived.

"Sorry, I saw something on one of the forms that needed updating."

Cam stared at Aidan, willing him to get to the point.

"I'm going to cut to the chase. You've got two options," Aidan began.

Cameron's heart slammed against his chest. He clasped his hands and rested them in his lap.

Hunter reached for him under the table and squeezed his hand.

"Options?" Cam said.

"Option A. Stay here. We're working on getting your record expunged, considering the charges were bullshit. With your sister's statement and your father's confession along with all the info Judge Mackler provided and the supporting testimony coming in on a daily basis from all the red file cases, it shouldn't be a problem. We don't know how extensive the connection is yet regarding the network of contacts. We know it's large, but we're slowly cracking down on them a little bit at a time with each person we interview. The network spreads both in and around the system so we're moving along carefully. We don't know how long you'd be looking over your shoulder, but we figure it's going to be a while until the mess is all cleared up."

"What's the other option?" Cameron asked.

"Option B. Leave. Witness Security Protection."

"Witness protection?"

Aidan nodded. "Clean slate, new identity, new life. No one would know your WITSEC location other than the FBI agent assigned to your case, his boss who leads the protection assignment department, and me. Hunter knows both the FBI agent assigned, Connor Ellis, and his boss, but I've already checked them both out just to be safe. We've got a house ready for you, with big windows on the east side for a great view of the sunrise each morning and a big yard in dire need of landscaping. It was an old estate home so it's got tons of space. You will have one neighbor and he's far enough away to ignore. It's a very private house, sitting on three acres in the country. The only catch is, when you leave, you're gone. No further contact with anyone. Friends, family, no one. We won't run the risk of anyone finding out where you're located."

Cam didn't really know what to say. He heard a hum in his head that seemed to get louder. Only a few select people would know his location. To everyone else, he'd vanish. Hunter wouldn't know his location. He wrapped his arms around his midsection to fight off the sudden chill in his body.

"Cam?" Aidan prompted before his phone chirped. "Think about your answer. I'll be right back," he said before exiting.

"Cam?"

The way Hunter said his name was loaded with tons of emotions. He looked over to him and saw confusion in his piercing silver eyes.

"This is a no brainer," Hunter said, leaning forward.

Cam shrugged. He did want to escape this nightmare and option B held much more promise except for one huge factor...Hunter. He didn't care what he had to go through as long as he had Hunter by his side.

"Cam? I can't imagine you'd want to stay here," Hunter said, frowning.

Cam stood and began pacing the room with his arms crossed, trying to hide how his fingers drummed while his mind raced. He wanted to go but he needed to stay. He finally stopped pacing and turned to Hunter. "I want to stay with you. Looking over my shoulder, *pfft*, I've been doing that for so many years I'm kinda used to it by now."

Hunter crossed his arms and leaned back in his chair. "Doing that for the rest of your life is going to wear you out." He paused for a moment and just stared at Cam. A smile slowly spread across his face. "Besides, I told you, I wasn't going away."

Cam slowly uncrossed his arms and shoved his hands into his back pockets. "You'd come with me?"

Hunter simply nodded.

"But your job—"

"My heart's not in it anymore."

"What if you change your mind? Once you leave, you're gone."

"I'm too stubborn to change my mind. I already had the governor talk to me about running for mayor in the upcoming election and I turned him down. After everything that's happened, I just can't do this anymore."

Cam resumed his pacing. His mind raced with what-if scenarios. "Your dad—"

"I've already spoken to him about it."

Cam thought about Hunter's last minute trip this past weekend and stopped pacing again. "Is this where you went to when you were gone this weekend? To see the house?"

Hunter nodded. "I hated not being with you but I wanted to make sure the house had the sunrise views and the land for your gardening before getting Aidan to push the offer through."

Cam smiled warmly. He'd love to escape and finally have a home with Hunter but his thoughts drifted to Thomas. He deflated at the thought of Hunter's father being alone. "I can't let you abandon your father. I know what that feels like and I can't do it to him," he said sadly as his mind drifted to the morning after the attack when they were at Thomas's house making breakfast.

Hunter stood and reached for Cam's hand, snapping him out of his thoughts. "He already gave me a lecture about life being too short and how I'm a wuss. He finally stopped when I told him I had every intention of going with you."

Cam shook his head. "You're all he's got. I can't hurt him like that."

"Cam, I've already told you. I go where you go. You're not getting rid of me that easily," he said, placing a hand on the side of Cam's neck, pulling him closer. His thumb gently stroked Cam's cheek as he delivered one of those wicked half smiles of his. Hunter's other hand reached under Cam's shirt to his lower back.

Cam closed his eyes, relaxing under the gentle ministrations.

Hunter's warm breath tickled his ear. "Besides, where we're going, you get to see snow."

Cam immediately opened his eyes. "Snow? I've never seen snow."

"I know. Where we're going, you get snow, hot summers, changing leaves, sunrises, and a whole lotta me," he finished with a low rumble chuckle that sent sparks throughout Cam's body.

Cam shook his head and laughed. "I'll go with option B on one condition."

"What's that?"

"Your dad comes with us. Aidan said the house was an old estate home so it should be big enough for us and then some. Right?"

"It's got plenty of bedrooms and part of the house is actually separate so it would work. I'm just not sure I can handle the two of you ganging up on me," Hunter teased.

"Well, that's the deal. Take it or leave it." Cam backed off and crossed his arms in a very poor attempt to appear as if he had the upper hand in this negotiation.

"Deal," Hunter said before pulling Cam in for a quick kiss. "But you're the one who's going to break the news to him."

"Why?"

Hunter chuckled and placed his hands on his hips. "You think I'm sappy? Get ready for the waterworks when you ask if he'll come along."

Cam shuffled his feet and bit his lower lip. "I don't want to upset him. He was more of a dad to me in that one weekend than my father ever was. I'd love to have him around all the time."

Hunter looked at him with a smirk and arched an eyebrow.

"What?" Cam yelled, raising his arms.

"Are you gonna tell him that when you ask him to come with us?"

"Yeah. Why?"

Hunter chuckled. "Take a box of tissues with you when you do."

When Aidan returned, Cam informed him of his decision and condition. Aidan assured him there would be no problem as long as Thomas agreed. They spoke further regarding the arrangements, finances, what could be taken, and what had to stay.

"It's going to take me a few days to get everything in order," Aidan asked.

"Saturday."

"You want to leave this Saturday?"

Cam nodded. "Is that enough time?"

"I'll make it happen," Aidan confirmed in his typical matter-of-fact nature as he made a notation in his file.

That evening, Hunter and Cam stopped by to invite Hunter's father to join them when they left. Cam told Thomas the best part of having a boyfriend with a father like him was that he could finally have a dad who gave a shit.

Thomas willingly accepted the invitation.

One box of tissues wasn't enough.

Chapter
THIRTY-THREE

Hunter hurriedly left the office and headed to the halfway house late Friday afternoon. When he arrived, he saw Aidan's SUV parked in the back area, waiting for him.

"What took you so long?" Aidan asked.

"Sorry, man. I had to make sure Jessie was up to date on all the cases should something come up. He's on his own now."

"He'll be fine." Aidan approached the back porch and knocked on the door.

"Hey," Matt said, opening the door. "Come on in."

Hunter was immediately greeted by an armful of Cam. "Hi," he said with a grin as he gave Cam a chaste peck. "You all packed?"

Cam quickly nodded. "Bag's already by the door. Hi, Aidan."

Aidan smiled in response.

Hunter tightened his hold on Cam's waist. "This shouldn't take long." He herded Matt, Julian, and Cole into the kitchen with them. "You guys know we're leaving," Hunter said.

"A clean start is good," Matt said. "I think it's exactly what Cam needs to finally get his life back."

Hunter placed a file on the table. "Well, we've got everything squared away except for one thing."

Matt cocked his head. "If I need to get something done, you don't have to worry. I'll take care of it."

Hunter shook his head. "Aidan's keeping my house but that leaves one other thing. I can't take my car with me so I've got a proposition."

"Proposition?" Julian asked.

Hunter looked over to Cole. "Cam mentioned how you've been there to listen to him when he needed to talk, especially before I found out about what had happened."

"Part of talking so much is listening," Cole said with a devilish grin.

"So I'm willing to make you a deal." Hunter propped his elbows on the table and clasped his hands. "I'll give you my car if you stay out of trouble."

Cole blanched. "What?"

Hunter reached into his suit jacket pocket and withdrew his key fob. "You heard me. She's yours if you get your act together. That means, no more boosting cars, no more back-talking Julian, and you need to keep a job for the rest of your six-month term here. If you get fired, no car. If you get in trouble, no car. Do anything to land you back in prison, no car. Got it?"

Cole was uncharacteristically speechless. He was hypnotized, staring at the small rectangle that served as the key for the car.

Cole looked up. "Luke's working and even got another offer. I've had three jobs but they've sent me home at the end of the day." He shrugged and looked away. "No one wants me."

"What about the diner? I'm leaving, so they could use someone," Cam offered.

Julian looked at Cam with a deathly serious expression. "You've had a chance to get to know Bill. How do you think that would work?"

Cam chuckled and slapped Cole on his back. "Sorry, Boost Boy. I think you'd turn Bill homicidal."

"We need to work on that brain-mouth filter of yours," Julian said with a half smile.

"I've already talked to my brother. He'll take you," Aidan said.

Cole crossed his arms and pursed his lips. "I'm not a joint you can just pass around." He frowned and fidgeted in his seat, uncrossing then crossing his arms again. "I don't even know what the hell he would expect—"

"He works with exotics and collectibles."

Cole stilled. The frown disappeared from his face and his eyes widened. "Oh."

"I figured you could learn to work on them rather than boost them," Aidan said.

Cole inched forward in his seat and leaned over the table. "I know how to work on them, it's just that boosting them is more fun," he said with a hint of mischief that was quickly erased from his face when he looked over to Hunter. He straightened and sat still in his seat, placing both hands in his lap.

"Do you understand my proposition?" Hunter asked.

Cole tugged on his beanie. "But you're leaving, how will you know?"

"Aidan's going to watch the car and he'll keep her safe until your term is up here."

"Aidan? Hell no!" Cole stood and paced the room.

"Why?" Aidan asked.

Cole stopped and put his hands on his waist. "Dude, I've seen you drive. You'll wreck her in an hour and I'll never get her."

Aidan laughed. "My brother's going to keep her stowed away at his shop. She'll be safe there and you can drool over her whenever you want as long as it doesn't interfere with your work."

Cole scratched his head through his beanie. After a few moments, he took his seat again. "Sorry," he said to Aidan.

"But if you screw up, I won't hesitate to put you back inside, and he will keep her instead," Aidan finished with a wicked grin. "He'd love to have her."

Cole looked at Hunter pleadingly. "He works with cars all the time. He wouldn't want her, she's a sleeper. She's mine, right?"

Hunter gave Cole one of his courtroom glares. "Only if you stay out of trouble. Period. You won't get her until you're finished here and with a spotless record. And after you're out of here, if you get in trouble, you lose her. I've put her title in a trust, and I've got a contract if you agree to these terms."

Cole looked as if he had sucked a lemon. "Dude, a contract? Seriously?"

Cam laughed. "Cole, he's a lawyer. You didn't think he'd walk in here with an offer like this without one, did you?"

Cole grumbled. "If I get her, I'll be good."

"If you're good, *then* you'll get her," Julian corrected with a quirked eyebrow.

"I'll be good. Where do I sign," he grumbled.

After letting Cole take a gleeful drive in the car, they finally said their good-byes. Hunter watched as Cam hugged each of the guys and thanked them for *putting up with his shit* while he was there.

They finally left Halfway House and swung by the diner. Cam refused to leave without a proper good-bye to Lucy and Bill even if that broke the standard rules of witness protection. After a tearful departure with tons of hugs and a box of cookies for the trip, they left the car at Aidan's brother's shop. Aidan then dropped them off at Hunter's house with a promise to pick them up early in the morning for their flight.

"I can't believe we're leaving tomorrow," Cam said quietly.

"Yup," Hunter said, snaking an arm around Cam's waist. "I already called my dad and he's all packed and ready to go."

Cam nodded.

"You okay?" Hunter asked, dipping his head.

Cam looked up and smiled. "More than okay," he said before wrapping his arms around Hunter's neck and resting his head on his shoulder.

"Any regrets?"

"Nope," Cam said.

"Good," he said, wrapping his other arm around Cam's waist.

He looked forward to his new life with Cam and couldn't wait to get away. He pulled Cam closer and rested his cheek against the side of Cam's head.

"You in the mood for a shower," he asked in that tempting tone he knew always seemed to set Cam off.

Cam groaned. "Always."

Hunter guided Cam to the bedroom and neither wasted a single moment before stripping down. They'd leave tomorrow, but their time together started a blessed day early.

Chapter
THIRTY-FOUR

"Wake up," Cam heard whispered in his ear. He didn't want to open his eyes. He was surrounded in heated bliss, a hard-muscled chest pressed against his back, a leg wedged between his, and an arm slung across his waist. Goose bumps spread over his flesh as puffs of warm breath danced across his skin. "It's midnight, wake up." He heard the soothing voice as a kiss was placed at the side of his head.

Cameron groaned. "I don't want to," he finally said.

"I'll make it worth your while." Hunter squeezed his arms tighter around Cam's waist.

"You always do, but I've got a really comfortable spot. I don't wanna move." He didn't care if his voice bordered on whiney.

Hunter pulled his leg from between Cam's and withdrew his arm from around his waist.

Cam turned, his back now flat on the bed as he glared at Hunter. "That was cruel, Mr. Donovan."

"Happy birthday," Hunter said with a huge smile.

"My birthday's not today."

"It's after midnight. Technically, it is."

Cam sighed. "How did you know?"

Hunter sat up and rested his weight on his elbow and looked at Cam in disbelief. "Did you seriously think I wouldn't know?"

"I never told you."

"You do realize it's in your file?"

Cam exhaled heavily and pushed his head back farther into the pillow. He wasn't sure what upset him more, that most of his life had been exposed to everyone who looked at his file, or that Hunter had not let on at all that he knew today was his birthday.

"Don't you think I know that's why you picked today to leave and start over?"

Cam looked at Hunter with a glare. "Tomorrow."

"Today." Hunter reiterated with an equally firm scowl.

"Tomorrow," he repeated stubbornly.

"Okay, then you'll wait until *tomorrow* to get your gift. Good night." Hunter turned and pulled the sheets over his shoulder.

Cam sat up like a rocket. "Wait, you got me a gift?" He hadn't received a birthday or Christmas gift in so many years the thought of unwrapping anything was exciting. "Really?"

"Uh huh, but it can wait until tomorrow. Night!" Hunter pulled the sheets higher and tugged the pillow more comfortably under his head.

Cam pushed Hunter's body. "Fine, I'm up. Don't be a dick. I'll give you a blow job if you give me my present."

Hunter turned with a grin. "You'd give me one anyway."

"Yeah, I would," Cam grumbled and rubbed his face. "My brain is still asleep. I can't come up with anything witty right now so cut me some slack."

Hunter chuckled and gave him a quick peck on the cheek. He reached over the side of the bed to retrieve a flat, wrapped box.

Cam took the present and tried to ignore the tightness in his chest. The gift was beautifully decorated in blue paper with a large silver bow. Hunter probably picked the paper to match Cam's eyes and wouldn't put it past him to have picked the ribbon color because of his own. He couldn't resist teasing. "Is the bow silver for the same reason the paper is blue?"

Hunter's face heated. "Just open it."

"Yes, sir," he said then smiled when Hunter's cheeks reddened further. His heart raced as he ripped the paper open to reveal a plain white box. "You didn't get me a tie, did you?"

Hunter arched an eyebrow. "That would be one hell of a big tie."

"Maybe you got matching socks, underwear, or something," he said, wanting to enjoy the mystery of the gift for a few moments more. "Maybe you want to play dress up."

Hunter chuckled. "Just open it."

Cam pulled off the top and separated the tissue paper to reveal the gift. The smile slid off his face. His heart beat furiously, and he found it difficult to swallow or voice words with the lump in his throat. He couldn't focus on anything but the face staring back at him in the picture of the one person from his past who had loved him, standing alongside a younger, smaller version of himself holding a ribbon.

His eyes burned as he turned to Hunter with a questioning look.

Hunter leaned over and placed a tender kiss on Cam's lips. "You said you didn't have any pictures of your mom. I remember you told me you entered that contest with her and got fifth place. I know local papers sometimes publish stuff like that so I did some poking around and found a newspaper that had published an article on it. They didn't have the negatives in archive anymore but they did have the actual photograph from that day so I was able to get it. We can probably get it scanned and enlarged—"

"It's perfect," Cam interrupted, his voice thick with emotion. "Just perfect." He ghosted his fingers over the glass. A flood of memories invaded his mind, his mother's face now sharply focused in each of them. Every line of detail, every hair, even the sound of her voice, the laughter, outfits she wore, and the smell of her soft perfume. All triggered by a simple reminder of her face in this picture and the smile full of joy. He closed his eyes and inhaled a shaky breath as he tried to steady himself.

Hunter reached over and took the picture frame from the box. "I didn't want to go with a fancy frame until we were at the new place and knew what would go better with the room, so we can change this."

Cam nodded. He didn't care if the frame matched or not, it was going on display, front and center, in their new home. He took the frame Hunter offered and held it close to his chest as Hunter pulled out a laminated newspaper clipping.

"The reporter actually had a few copies of the newspaper because it was her first published article. We can't take this with us since it has your name on it, but I wanted you to be able to read it before we left."

Cam nodded again and took the newspaper cutout. Still clutching the framed photo to his chest, he read the short article reporting on the contest and smiled when he saw his mom's name listed with his at the close of the clipping. He gently placed the picture frame back in the box and returned the article to Hunter. He didn't trust his shaky hands to move the box anywhere, so he handed that to Hunter as well.

Hunter took the box and set it on the nightstand. He turned and delivered a soft kiss on Cam's lips. "Happy birthday," he whispered.

Cam's vision blurred, he couldn't contain his emotions anymore. He wrapped his arms around Hunter and hid his face in the crook of Hunter's neck. His body uncontrollably shook with a tidal wave of emotion swirling within. Hunter's arms tightened around him, pulling him closer as he placed his hand on Cam's lower back. Hunter shifted to lay flat on the bed, pulling Cam on top of him. He threw the sheets over them and wrapped his arms protectively around Cam, holding him closer.

After some time, Cam finally settled himself and pulled back to look at Hunter. He ran his fingers through Hunter's hair and gazed into the pool of silver staring back at him. "So, how about that blow job?"

With a quick shift of arms and legs, Hunter flipped Cam on the bed so he was flat on his back. He stared at Cam intently. It didn't seem as if he was doing so to ponder his next move, rather, it was as if he was drilling into Cam's soul, breaking through that iron barrier before letting his words reach the protected core.

"I want more than that."

It took every ounce of energy Cam had to keep his guard up. The gift had taken a sledgehammer to his shield and left him vulnerable.

He knew what Hunter wanted, but he had been guarded for so long, he wasn't sure how it felt to allow himself to just...be.

"My mom always told me, don't settle, be with the person you can't live without. For me, that's you," Hunter said with conviction.

"You're going in for the kill, aren't you?" Cam tried to tease, knowing Hunter had him right where he wanted him.

"When I'm away from you for too long, I can't stand it. It's as if I can't breathe."

His chest tightened and his breath quickened. His now fragile shield wavered. He had spent years building it, and this man had managed to chip away at it, little by little. Hunter continued to stare at him, more determined than usual, mentally pounding at that cracked iron door, seeking entrance.

"Do you know I still have that first voice mail you left me? I listen to it when I need to hear your voice just to function." Hunter bent and kissed Cameron's lips, his cheek, then his neck. "Please let me in," he said on a broken whisper.

When he pulled back, the declaration of love and need screaming from Hunter's gaze was the final blow that broke Cam's protective shield.

Cam reached up to touch Hunter's face with a trembling hand. He ghosted his fingers over Hunter's features, afraid to allow his fingertips to make contact. He hesitated, worried the slightest touch would make Hunter disappear in a puff of smoke and leave him alone, unprotected, and lost.

Hunter slowly wrapped his fingers around Cam's wrist and pulled his hand toward his face. He kissed Cam's fingers then his palm. Hunter closed his eyes when he pressed Cam's hand to his cheek.

He released a shaky breath when his fingers touched Hunter's heated skin. He would usually push Hunter away with humor or sarcasm when his protective armor chipped. This time, he ran his hand behind Hunter's neck and tugged him forward for a deep, all-consuming kiss. Cam kissed him with desperation and little grace—aggressive, messy, demanding and frantic—as he tried to draw strength from Hunter. He grabbed and pulled Hunter closer, his nails scraped across Hunter's scalp, his neck. Cam ignored the groan from

Hunter and continued to pull, suck, bite, and devour until he could no longer breathe.

They separated, gasping for air. Cam's body began to shake uncontrollably on the brink of losing control. He fought it, trying to keep himself together just as he had for so many years.

"Let go," Hunter whispered in his ear, peppering kisses along his neck as he wrapped his arms around Cam. "I'm here. You're safe."

Cam wasn't sure which set of words unlatched the dam before a flood of emotions unexpectedly surged through his body. His breath sped uncontrollably and his body stiffened as anger burst to the surface. He had been robbed of so many years—his life, his family, and innocence. His blood boiled and heated his skin. He began to wildly twitch, his arms, his legs, all jerked as he tried to contain the untamed fury that coursed through his body. He threw his head back farther into the pillow, screwed his eyes shut, and gritted his teeth to hold back the yell as he fought the urge to give in to the series of still shots flickering through his mind, mocking him with so much he had missed in life.

He slammed the mental door shut on the anger only to have fear throw another door open.

He gasped as a chill rose in his body and tightened his throat. He tried to fight the ghosts that haunted him, the insecurity of whether he could handle a normal life after so much time, but worst of all, of losing this treasure that held him so closely. His body shuddered violently. His arms pushed against the hold encasing him, his legs kicked aggressively, and his heart slammed against his chest wanting to break free.

Hunter held him tighter as the tremors rippled throughout his limbs. Cam's body was no longer his own, it became a vessel that unleashed a decade of dormant pain. A scream tore from his lips as the rage ripped through him. The cage of hard muscles and flesh surrounding him tightened, comforting him while his own body continued to resist and fight. His body began to spasm. His skin heated and the pressure in his neck threatened to rupture the corded veins as he continued to scream. Sweat burst from every pore, trickling into his eyes, stinging and blurring his vision.

A single tear tracked down his cheek when his voice abandoned him, no longer able to yell at the fear that threatened to break him apart.

The iron grip around him tightened further, the legs of steel wrapped around his own held him closer, and the gentle kisses on his skin continued between whispers of comfort.

He heard the words again.

Let go, I'm here, you're safe—among the phrases he needed to hear most—*I'm yours, I'm not going anywhere*.

He knew the words, had heard them endless times before.

Hunter slowly released his hold on Cam as he continued to mumble words of affection.

Cam gritted his teeth as he fought his flight instinct—the need to run, shut down, and close himself off from everything and everyone. He gripped Hunter closer, losing the will to control himself when the tears surfaced and finally broke free.

Oh, God. Please.

He frantically wrapped his legs around Hunter in a panic to keep him close and prevent his escape. He dug his fingers in Hunter's back as he sobbed, needing him—his body begging for this man's shelter, love, safety, and unwavering strength.

He held on tightly as everything faded to black.

Cam lay weakly in bed, exhaustion weighing down every inch of his body. His arms and legs still wrapped around Hunter. He buried his face at the side of Hunter's neck as shame flooded through him.

Hunter pulled back to look at him but Cam turned away.

"Look at me." Hunter gripped his chin when Cam refused.

Through the burn in his eyes from the flood of tears he had shed, he could see Hunter staring down at him with nothing but love and support. His breath hitched and his throat tightened. He had to look away, for fear of breaking down again.

"I know that was hard for you," Hunter whispered as he brushed a kiss along Cam's jaw.

"It's a weakness," Cam said in a raspy, broken, barely there voice.

"Sometimes being strong means knowing when you need to let go. It scares the hell of out me to think what can happen if you keep all that bottled up inside," he finished with a slight tremble in his voice, inhaling Cam's scent at the crook of his neck. "It's taken me too long to find you. I can't lose you, Cam…please."

Cam reached up and rested his shaky hands on Hunter's arms just as Hunter pulled back to look at him again.

Hunter brushed the hair away from Cam's face and smiled. "I've already told you. You can let go and do what you need to do with me. You're not going to scare me away. If you need to scream, hit, anything, you do that with me. Okay?"

"I'm not hitting you," Cam said, outraged, his voice still cutting in and out.

Hunter brushed his cheek with his thumb. "We'll figure out an outlet that works. Maybe we'll setup a punching bag at the new place. Or maybe we'll wrestle." A playful grin spread across Hunter's face as he waggled his eyebrows.

Cam huffed a laugh. How this man managed to always bring him out of an emotional downward spiral was beyond him. "We could try some angry sex."

Hunter chuckled. "I'm pretty much marked all over in some way. I don't think I can handle angry war wounds from you."

"Wuss," he said, looking away.

"Whenever you need to let go, don't be embarrassed to do that with me. It lets me know you trust me. I can handle it, good and bad, okay?"

"Makes me sound needy…I hate that," he finished quietly.

"I like the idea of you needing me," Hunter said as he turned Cam's face to deliver a tender kiss. "It's a two-way street."

Cam ran his fingertips along Hunter's features and down his neck. He couldn't remember ever allowing himself to be so exposed and vulnerable. Without question or hesitation, he loved this man and knew he was blessed Hunter wanted to start a new life with *him*. He wanted to say the words, but he was too raw to go there and didn't want Hunter to think he was saying them out of some post-weakness meltdown. He had never said *I love you* to another man and wanted to make sure that when he said those words to Hunter, they were as strong as the love in his soul for him.

"Make love to me."

"Always," Hunter said breathlessly as he dove in for another brush of lips and sheltered Cam's body with the protective heat of his own.

Their bodies danced against each other in a slow sway, each movement familiar, yielding and unrestrained. Cameron's body sang with the knowing friction of Hunter's touch, the glide of skin, the slow thrust of uncontrolled desire, and each tender kiss. When he finally let himself shatter into a thousand sated pieces, Hunter was there with him, in sync.

He rested his head on Hunter's shoulder as they both tried to settle their breathing. He pulled Hunter flush against his body, needing to feel Hunter's heat against his skin and the hard body as his surrogate shield. Hunter pulled the sheets over them and wrapped his arms protectively around Cam, gifting him with the safety he desperately needed.

He finally eased into the hard-muscled cocoon and let the exhaustion of the night take him into the darkness of sleep.

* * * *

Cam opened his eyes and saw the faint hint of a new day filter into the bedroom. *A new life and a fresh start.* He looked over to the man still resting on the pillow facing him and couldn't resist making contact. He smiled as Hunter leaned into the touch and slowly opened his eyes.

"Since it's officially *tomorrow*, I can say happy birthday," Hunter said, sleep still thick in his voice. He reached out and brushed the hair out of Cameron's eyes. "Good morning."

"Yes, it is," Cam replied matter-of-factly, his voice still a little gravelly from a few hours ago. He ran his fingers down Hunter's neck, finally stopping at his chest, feeling Hunter's heart beat strong against his palm.

"If you don't get out of bed, you're going to miss the sunrise," Hunter said, nestling deeper into the pillow.

"I'm looking right at it." Cam stared at Hunter with a serious expression. He didn't know what he had done in this world to deserve someone who offered him such unconditional love, but he no longer questioned it. With Hunter by his side, he was safe enough to dream of tomorrow and strong enough to face it.

Curiosity colored Hunter's expression as a smile filled with mischief began to spread across his face. "I think my sappiness is rubbing off on you," he said playfully.

The three words he had denied Hunter were unmistakably screaming back at him through the silver stare.

"You remember our deal?" Cam asked, returning his wandering fingers to Hunter's face.

Hunter nodded against the pillow and turned his head to kiss Cam's palm. "Don't worry, I haven't forgotten. I can wait however long until you're ready."

He watched Hunter scan his face. Within seconds, Hunter's eyes widened and his chest heaved with each breath. Just as he had known so many times before, he understood what Cam was thinking at that moment and what he would say next.

Cameron stroked Hunter's cheek just as Hunter had done to him endless times before to calm him. He slowly smiled and firmly said two simple words Hunter had been waiting to hear.

"I'm ready."

Epilogue

Hunter grabbed his bag and shut the car door. He smiled when he saw Cam's truck and business trailer at the side entrance. Cam usually didn't make it home before him, especially not on Fridays when he tried to squeeze in as much work on a landscaping project for a client before the weekend. In a matter of months, word had spread like wildfire about the new landscaper with the creative flare. Cam had managed to nail a few lucrative contracts which then led to steady opportunities at the local country clubs and golf courses. His work ethic had garnered such a strong word of mouth recommendation that he now had his pick of local and neighboring county contracts.

"Hey, Dad," Hunter said when he entered the house. He followed the scent of a meal to the kitchen. "How was your day?"

"Good," Thomas said.

Hunter raised his nose and sniffed past the seasonings in the air. He smiled. "Am I smelling cookies?"

"He made some as soon as he got home. So you're too late, he already hid the recipe."

Hunter pursed his lips and frowned. "Damn it. He's taking Lucy's promise too damn seriously."

"He's a man of his word. Sounds like someone I know," Thomas said in that proud paternal way.

"What are you making?" Hunter couldn't resist lifting the cover of each of the pots to peek inside. "It smells great."

"I thought I'd make you guys a quick dinner before you went out on your date night. Your movie is at eight, right?"

Hunter nodded and craned his neck to look for Cam in the backyard. "Yeah. I'm surprised he's here already."

"He's been working on my garden for over an hour now. I think he's almost finished."

"Thanks, Dad," he said before exiting the back door to see Cam.

Cam turned when the screen door opened then closed. "Hello, Professor. How was class today?" he asked, turning to finish planting the new flowers in the soil.

"Good. The students are still teasing me about my hot fiancé bringing my lunch in yesterday." He bent to greet Cam with a quick kiss.

Cam returned the kiss then pressed the soil around the last flower before gathering his tools into the box. "You shouldn't have left home without it. I wasn't going to let you starve."

"I'm at the university. How the hell am I going to starve on campus," Hunter said with a chuckle.

Cam stood and took off his work gloves. He laughed in that low rumble way that drove Hunter crazy. "Unless you have the bag in front of you, you'll lose track of time and forget to eat."

Hunter wrapped his arms around Cam's waist and pulled him close. "I love how you worry about me."

"I'm all sweaty, you're going to get dirty." Cam discarded his work gloves then wrapped his arms around Hunter.

"I don't care." Hunter delivered a peck between words. He deepened the kiss when he heard Cam's sharp intake of breath. Hunter pulled Cam closer when he felt the tug behind his neck. They separated, but remained close enough for their breaths to mingle.

"How's your ass?" Cam asked with a devilish smile.

Hunter snorted a laugh. "I had to do most of my classes standing up."

"Sorry. I kinda lost control yesterday."

"Don't ever apologize for taking what you need from me," he said, kiss-biting Cam's jaw.

"You didn't tell me you had so many hot guys in your class," Cam grumbled, looking away.

"You're the only guy I think about."

Cam glanced back at Hunter with a wry grin. "Sap."

"Smart-ass. You know, when the students started teasing me about you, I mentioned that class you were thinking about teaching. Apparently they knew about the mystery artist who did coffee designs at the local shop. I think you'll get most of those guys to sign up. Probably even some of the girls who were mentally undressing you," he said with a grunt.

Cam loosened Hunter's tie and undid the top button of the shirt, a casual habit he had acquired whenever he saw Hunter still wearing his tie at the end of the day.

"I'm not sure if I want to take the vocational school up on their offer. It's only a couple of hours a week but, seriously, a latte art class? It's a nice change, but who the fuck would want to attend? It has no academic bearing whatsoever," he said with a shrug then looked away again.

Hunter stroked Cam's cheek with his thumb. Cam had become stronger than ever and more confident, but he still had random moments where he questioned himself and the interest of others. "Sometimes people take classes just to learn something new without a need to have it be career-based. Besides, do you know some of these high end coffee shops send their baristas to schools where they teach classes on latte art?"

Cam's vision snapped back to Hunter. "Really?"

Hunter nodded. "I know you say it's not a big deal but I see you smile every time someone gets excited about a design."

He brushed the hair out of Cam's eyes, carefully watching a mix of emotions flicker across his expression. They had visited the local café soon after their arrival to the new town. Cam fidgeted when he saw the barista fighting the machine—the same model he had used at the diner. Hunter asked the distressed cashier, who was also the owner, if she'd mind if Cam showed her barista how to work the machine. She immediately agreed and Cam raced behind the counter to rescue the poor teenager before she burned herself. Within minutes, the teenager had brewed her first cup without a burn.

"That's the first time she's made a cup without cursing up a storm," the owner confided. "Thank you."

Cam handed the owner a cup with a heart design, sealing the deal for a job offer. Cam respectfully declined but asked if he could swing by the coffee shop and help if he had an itching to do more art. The owner enthusiastically agreed and Cam had made random appearances every month when he needed to do something creative, outside of the landscaping.

Small town with people so open and nice. A quick invitation like that would have never happened in Miami. They were still getting accustomed to the slower pace and new life.

"People spend their hard-earned money on those coffees, they should get something nice," Cam said, jolting Hunter back to the present. "I'll think about it. They gave me until the end of the month to give them an answer on the class for the next semester."

Hunter looked over to the newly planted flowers along the perimeter of his father's area of the house. "This looks really good. I can't believe you finished it so quickly." He lifted Cam's shirt and stroked his lower back.

"I wanted to make sure Pop had his garden nice before Father's Day."

Hunter smiled at Cam's endearment. Cam had refused to call Thomas by his new name and said it was too weird to call him Dad.

"Pop's making dinner. Do we have time for a quick shower before then?"

Hunter smiled wickedly. "Our showers are never quick."

Cameron laughed. "C'mon, perv," he said, dragging Hunter by the hand to their room. "We've got about thirty minutes before it's time."

After a quick shower with mutual blowjobs and a promise for more post-date, they returned to the backyard again for their daily ritual.

The sunrises, Cam said, he had shared with his mom.

The sunsets, Cam declared, belonged to Hunter.

Hunter lay in their hammock with Cam resting against him as they waited for the sun to begin its descent. He pulled Cam closer, enjoying the body heat and the smell of fresh soap mingled with the scent he had fallen in love with instantly almost a year ago. Cam inched closer and rested his head on Hunter's shoulder, pressing his nose against Hunter's neck.

Cam reached under Hunter's shirt and splayed his hand on Hunter's chest, running his fingers through the sprinkling of hair.

Hunter closed his eyes as his chest tightened with each puff of warm breath that skated across his skin. "How did your meeting go?"

"They hate me," Cam mumbled.

Hunter slid his hand under Cam's shirt and ghosted his fingers along Cam's lower back. "You have a bunch of contract options. Not getting this one—"

"I did get it."

Hunter stopped stroking Cam's back and tried to sit up. "I thought you said—"

"I have to wear a polo shirt uniform while I'm on the golf course. Me, in a fucking polo shirt. Even though I'm a contractor, they're making me stick to the damn staff dress code. Fuckers hate me."

Hunter tightened his lips as he held back a smile. Cam had become accustomed to rebelling against imposed structure and requirements. It was what drove him to want to start his own landscaping company.

"Polos aren't bad," Hunter said, sitting back in the hammock.

"They're yellow and black."

"Those colors work well together," he said, resuming the circular patterns on Cam's lower back.

"The polos are striped. I'm going to look like a fucking bumblebee."

Hunter bit the inside of his cheek and screwed his eyes shut, holding back a laugh.

"You're my bumblebee."

"You'll pay for that later." Cameron laughed.

"Mmm, I'm looking forward to it," he said, kissing Cam's temple. Hunter sighed, enjoying the rumble of Cam's laugh. That beautiful sound came more easily than it had so many months ago. He would never tire of hearing the melody of Cam's laughter, especially when it echoed throughout the walls of their home.

"You could always decline the contract if you really hate it."

Cam shifted, lifting his weight on his forearms to lean over Hunter. "Hell no. I've been itching to do something with all that green space they have. I'll have everything finished there in a few months. After that, I want to take you on vacation somewhere."

Hunter smiled. "Where do you want to take me?"

Cam shrugged. "I don't know yet. But I want to do something for you."

"You always do something for me," Hunter said, staring into Cam's fierce gaze. He reached up and rested his hand against the side of Cam's face.

The corner of Cam's lips curved upward in that teasing way that always seemed to make Hunter's breath hitch. "I always do something *to* you, not *for* you."

Hunter pulled him down for a slow kiss, the ones that still drew the sounds from Cam that drove Hunter crazy with need.

Cam withdrew and laughed. "Later. I promise," he said, returning to his spot pressed against Hunter.

Cam stroked Hunter's chest while Hunter grazed his fingers along Cam's lower back. Hunter would never get tired of the way Cam's body contoured perfectly against his. They patiently waited in their hammock for another ten minutes until the sun decided to make its descent. The bright orange rays cast their light on the bottom of the clouds, leaving a hint of darkness to border the moon's new home for the night. The sun fought through the clouds, trying to paint its colors wide before it disappeared leaving a wash of deep blues, purples, and pale pinks to illuminate the sky against the dark silhouette of the mountain edge.

Hunter heard Cam sigh. He held him closer and rested his cheek against Cam's hair.

"I love you," Cam said quietly, nuzzling into the crook of Hunter's neck.

Hunter closed his eyes and let the words fill the silence between them. Since the day they left their other lives behind, Cam had made every effort to open up to him—yell when he was angry, talk about the nightmares that still haunted him, and share a memory, however difficult they were to relive. Not a day had passed without the three words spoken. It seemed Cam needed to hear them just as much as Hunter craved saying them.

"I love you, too."

~The End~

About the Author

Jaime Reese is the alter ego of an artist who loves the creative process of writing, just not about herself. Fiction is far more interesting. She has a weakness for broken, misunderstood heroes and feels everyone deserves a chance at love and life. An avid fan of a happy ending, she believes those endings acquired with a little difficulty are more cherished.

Email:
jr@jaimereese.com

Website:
http://www.jaimereese.com/

Facebook:
https://www.facebook.com/author.jaime.reese

Twitter:
@Jaime_Reese

THE MEN OF
HALFWAY HOUSE
Series

A Better Man
A Hunted Man

…More to come…

CPSIA information can be obtained
at www.ICGtesting.com
Printed in the USA
LVHW082249131121
703278LV00027B/778